A DAY AT THE THEME PARK

PART 1: FALL SEMESTER

RYAN WAGNER

Ryan in 2012

Cover design by Ryan Wagner and Chorfia Meliantha
Cover artwork by Chorfia Meliantha

Paperback ISBN 9798999005502
Ebook ISBN 9798999005526

First edition: September 2025

For Steve Dora, who showed me how much more
fun life can be when you don't take it too seriously.
So it goes.

A DAY AT THE THEME PARK has a soundtrack!

(Movies and games have one, so why can't a book?)

The first playlist is a compilation of all the songs the story mentions by name that are meant to go along with that particular scene, while the other five playlists are simply meant to set the vibe for certain stretches of the story. Keep an eye out for the headers as you read! (Not that anybody's telling you what to do.)

Search 'ryan_the_wagner' on Apple Music or Spotify!

▶ 1. POV: You're reading "A Day at the Theme Park" and don't wanna look up the songs

▶ 2. POV: College isn't as scary as you thought so now you're just vibin'

▶ 3. POV: It's cold and it's dark at 6 p.m. but it's just you and baby blue

▶ 4. POV: You're turning up at 370 Rock and you just connected to the speakers

▶ 5. POV: You're at 'some loser concert' and it might be your favorite one ever

▶ 6. POV: It's summer break and you're trying to enjoy it but you don't know what to do with your life

I. POV: You're reading "A Day at the Theme Park" and don't wanna look up the songs

August 25

A.S. (antescript, because P.S. is overused)—"Placeholder" by The Story So Far

Dear Trevor,

The meaning of life is this: everybody just needs to get the stick out of their ass already.

I think Dr. Valentino was onto something when she suggested that I give journaling a try. Let's be real, my first journal was half depressive and angsty and half erotica, but I think having an outlet for my thoughts helps keep me a little bit sane, so here we are again. I'm going to try to lay off the semicolons this time though, because Kurt Vonnegut said not to use them unless you want to sound like a pretentious prick.

I can't believe that it was just the other day that I was cruising down the boardwalk, feeling the ocean breeze break against me, hoping to catch the eye of some snack, and thinking about how different things were the last time we were at the beach. Ryder was still around, COVID wasn't a thing yet, I was still in the closet— and I wasn't days away from heading off to college. *Big yikes.*

I'm still fucked up over that thing I saw on Twitter about how "*life begins at the end of your comfort zone*" because it made me realize just how much of my life I've spent inside of my comfort zone. I've accepted that my teenage years are almost over and that I didn't spend them as well as I could have, though lockdown certainly didn't help—but then again, neither did the people who I thought were my friends hanging

1

out without me and leaving me awake at 3 a.m. to wonder what's wrong with me. God, do I miss what it was like to spend most of my nights actually asleep.

I may not *believe* that everything happens for a reason, but we're products of our pasts for better or worse. My teenage years would've been a hell of a lot easier if I'd just known from the start that I was gay rather than fight *that* whole battle with myself. But even if I had, would I *actually* have been brave enough to be myself? *Pfft.* Look who you're talking to. Either way though, I've had all kinds of shit happen to me and here I am, more Trevor than ever.

More Trevor Than Ever: An Autobiography.

I could've saved money and stayed local, but going away to college almost feels like a chance to redeem myself. That, and I read somewhere that if something scares the hell out of you and excites you at the same time, then it's a sure sign that you should do it. I'm not saying I'm going to join all kinds of clubs and stuff, but the thought of having my world blown open—meeting new people, discovering new things, the possibility of being told that everything I know is wrong? I'm kind of stoked for it. And if nothing else, it'll be an exercise in vulnerability and character growth. But it's going to take more than just physically *going* to school to make that all happen. Like The Lorax said, *"Unless."* There's another life out there for me, and as scary as it is, I don't want to be afraid of it—'want to' being the key phrase.

Principal Yoakum told us that while it's easy to think of graduation as the end of a chapter, our lives aren't divided into set chapters. "Change is the only constant," she said, explaining how everything is always changing gradually at different times, instead of all at once. It sounds nice when you're sitting in an auditorium and your boyfriend hasn't broken up with you yet, but it hits different when you're spending your last night at home with one of your best friends since childhood, listening to *American Football* and reminiscing about your lives and all the times you've had together. It's going to be weird not having Logan or Madi around all the time, but I have to keep reminding myself that 'weird' doesn't always equal 'bad.'

"You're going to be okay," was Logan's parting advice to me. "Even when it doesn't feel like it, you're going to be okay." I mean, if the past couple years didn't teach me *that*, then what did it teach me?

I'm trying to remember that this isn't just an ending for me, but also a beginning. Like death and like heartbreak, we fear endings because they're the end of what we know and what we're familiar with. But if we knew what the beginnings were really the beginning of, then maybe we wouldn't be so afraid of the endings.

Am I just rambling because I'm alone in my new dorm room and I'm trying to distract myself from how fucking nervous I am? It's likely.

Love,

Trevor

A Day at the Theme Park

Trying to be confident
Reads a lot
Everything is art
Very self-conscious
Observant
Ravenclaw

Bad at making conversation
Easily gets caught up in thoughts
Nerdy, sometimes high-key
Take me to Southern California
Longboarder
Extrovert? I wish
Yearns to fit in while staying true to myself

Hates making phone calls
Unworthy, apparently
Fractured
Frequent insomniac
Music is how I numb myself
Alliteration calms me down
New situations make me anxious

An hours-long drive sure doesn't feel like an hours-long drive when you're lost in thought about what your life away from home might look like—the people I'll meet, lectures, college parties, golden showers, orgies, professors offering me blunts. *What will the other kids on my floor be like? What if my roommate doesn't like me? What if nobody likes me? What if I don't make any friends? What if my teachers are all assholes? What if people stop being nice to me when they find out I'm gay? Maybe I should have just gone to school back home. Life begins at the end of your comfort zone, life begins at the end of your comfort zone.* If I had the stick farther up my ass I'd say something like how I'm Henry David Thoreau and NHU is my Walden Pond. A big 'JESUS HAS YOUR ANSWERS' sign on the side of the road had me rolling my eyes, but the campus clock tower that came into view, jutting above the trees like a hard-on, made my throat go dry. The road gracelessly gave way to the town of New Halle and the beehive of activity that was Main Street. Blue-and-white banners with New Halle University's seal hung from every lamppost like we forgot where we were. 'Welcome Freshmen!' signs and overenthusiastic welcome volunteers directed the traffic to their respective dorms. A girl with a smile like a sadistic doctor told me how to get to my building practically in song.

Mom and Dad had insisted on making the trip down with me, even though all my stuff could fit in my car, and the drive down and back is a good five hours out of their day. But can I really blame them when their only child is finally leaving home? I gave the guy who was helping unload my car an apologetic look when Mom told him for the second time to make sure my stuff doesn't get sent to the wrong room. With my backpack strapped on and my student ID in hand, I led the way into the lobby of Swafford Hall, where more welcome volunteers directed me to the east side, second floor. I remember the calm I felt when I learned my room number was my Everywhere Number, like it was a sign that it was all just *right* somehow. *Doesn't mean I'm any less nervous about it though.* The hallways weren't the highways of loud capital-S Straight guys like I expected them to be—which made me feel a little more at ease—but the voices and laughter told me that the others weren't as nervous as I was. Two construction-paper leaves had the names 'Trevor' and 'Tylor' written in dots and lines like constellations on room number 222, the last door on the right. Tylor seems chill from the few emails we sent to each other over the Summer, but it sucks that he's a sophomore. As much as I hate the idea of living with a stranger, I was actually looking forward to rooming with another freshman. I imagined us stressing over assignments and papers together, telling each other stuff we learned about campus or something one of our professors said, sharing in the anticipation of going to our first college party together, being there for each other as we navigated the freshman experience together. I couldn't find him on Instagram, but with a last name like 'Hayashi,' I get the feeling that he *won't* be bearing a striking resemblance to Timothée Chalamet. He doesn't move in until Sunday, so I'll have plenty of time to myself at night, if you sniff what I'm smelling.

I swiped my card and punched in my four-digit code—the year Constantinople fell—and thought about how it felt like when we'd go on vacation and open the door to our hotel room for the first time. My room felt the opposite of welcoming though, with its plain white walls and tasteless furniture. Since Tylor might somehow be more introverted than me, I claimed the side of the room with a view of the hallway. Mom and Dad looked through all the cabinets for severed heads or whatever they expected to find and started unpacking my stuff without me saying they could. Mom made my bed in XL sheets that she insisted on washing beforehand, while Dad dumped all the Target-brand supplies from my 'freshman dorm checklist' into whichever desk drawer he felt like. They talked like they were getting paid to do it and hung around after everything was put away to try to hold onto me for as long as they could. I didn't want to go out to eat with them anywhere since 12,000 other people probably had the same idea, but I'm low-key regretting not going to the bookstore now because I'm worried they'll be out of the books I need, and I'm not trying to be that slacker kid who doesn't have the books the first day of class. I walked them out to their car to say goodbye, and to move my car off the street and into an actual parking spot. Mom was nothing but tears and wouldn't let me go.

"Call us," she told me. "Let us know how you're doing. Let us know if you need *anything*." Behind her, I saw some girl's mom telling her the same thing by the looks of it.

Dad wore a somber smile, having already given me the talk that wasn't as cringe as I expected it to be. "I was in college once too. I know what kind of stuff college kids do, so I'm not going to tell you not to do them," he lectured from across our coffees and toast the day before we left for vacation. "You're an adult now. You're smart, and I want you to enjoy yourself. But *please* just make good decisions and be safe. Your mother and I aren't going to be around for you." I'm sure it's hard to let your only son go off on his own without knowing what he'll be up to, what he'll be getting into, who he'll be hanging out with. But today, it was just, "You're going to do great. You're going to have such a good time."

After telling me that they love me 50 times, they finally got into their car and drove off. I waved after them until the street sucked their car away, and I gulped. *TFW you realize you're on your own now.*

I put on music while I fine-tuned all my things, but kept changing the artist every two songs because I was high-key anxious that my floormates would be judging my tastes. Just the thought of all my new neighbors petrified me, but I kept my door propped open because I'm going to have to meet them sooner or later. I made awkward eye contact with a girl in the room across the hall and gave her an uneasy smile. I'm just glad I don't have to share a bathroom with the entire floor like in the traditional dorms, because all I need is for all these people to hear me taking a shit.

A knock at my open door took me away from organizing my sock and underwear and condom drawer. "Hi! Trevor, right?" a girl a foot shorter than me smiled from just over my threshold. "I'm Sunita. I'm the resident assistant—RA for short—for this floor."

"Hi—yeah, Trevor. It's nice to meet you." *Smile back, you dork.*

"I'm happy to see you're getting all settled in," she said as she peered inside without stepping in, which is to say that she may or may not be a vampire.

"Yep," I awkwardly chuckled. *Physically settled in, anyway.*

"I just came by to say hi and to tell you that we're going to have a floor meeting down in the common area by the elevator, just to go over some stuff."

"Sounds good," I lied as I tried to not look too worried about having to meet the entire floor at once.

Sunita turned to give the same spiel to Girl Across the Hall. Instead of going around and introducing myself to people, I stayed put in my room and pretended to keep busy. I tried to finish my story about humans coming to Earth and driving the native civilizations to extinction as they colonized it, but I was too anxious to concentrate. Thankfully, getting caught up in the world map I taped above my desk and wondering which team would win the next world war if the countries were allied by color helped pass the time. The clarity of the early 2010s pop coming from next door made me wonder what other things I'll have to hear through the walls. I stood over the sink and paid a Trevor-amount of attention to myself in the mirror before heading down to the common area. I almost even changed clothes. *Shirt look okay? Check. Two-day-old fade look obviously fresh? Of course it does. Circles under my eyes look too dark? Absolutely.* After running my fingers through my hair and across my eyebrows, fidgeting with my studs, and wondering if I had too many freckles all of a sudden, I grabbed a notebook and a pen to take with me, I guess to let everybody know that I have a stick up my ass.

215 Swafford's door opened as I went past it, and the guy living there gave me an up-nod like we were already friends. "Hey, how's it going?" he greeted me with the rizz game of a content creator. "You headed to the floor meeting?"

"Uh huh, yep." *Introduce yourself, you turd.* "I'm Trevor, by the way."

"Calvin," he said with a confident handshake. Room 209 already had 'DON'T DRINK THE WATER!!' scrawled on the whiteboard on its door.

Sunita and a few other people were already in the floor's common seating area when we got there. Calvin and I sat together and made small talk about when we visited campus, but it turned into Calvin nodding and going "Yeah" as he watched the girls on the floor come in. I just ended up doom scrolling as I judged people by their shoes and thought about how the patterns on the couches look like the paper cups they have in waiting rooms. *Of course nobody else brought a notebook.* The more punctual of Swafford 2 East's residents made awkward eye contact with each other while we waited for everyone to show. One kid kept moving his mouth like he was about to start saying something. One kid looked like he had just shit himself and was pleased about it. One girl looked like she had just shit herself and *wasn't* pleased about it. Somebody else wouldn't stop blinking. A guy wearing flip flops kept saying "Oh girl, you *didn't!*" and "What's the *matter* with you?" to his phone.

Sunita spoke after the last resident—a shy-looking boy who's easily the cutest one on the floor—showed up. "Welcome everyone, to Swafford Hall 2 East." She introduced herself to us again and then had us go around and say our names and our majors, which is better than having to come up with a fun fact. There's Simone, Braddock, Anton, Emmie, Steph, Kevin, either Becca or Becky. Girl Across The Hall is Elisha. Cute Shy Boy is Dayton. Flip-Flop Gay is Rory. AJ's a total femboy, but his roommate Trent would be more my type if he didn't seem like an ass. "You don't have to be best friends with your roommate," Sunita told us. "You don't even have to *like* your roommate. But you're gonna *respect* your roommate. You will not act like children if you can't agree on something." Then she went over all the stuff like

6

laundry machines and quiet hours and signing guests into the building, and then she said that we were all going to head over to the football stadium together for a freshman welcome rally in like five minutes.

In terms of content, the rally was pretty dumb. Some upbeat song about this being the best time of our lives played over all the speakers, and we all had to make a 1,500-person human chain and ran around in a big zigzagging train. The President of the student something-or-another spoke, and then the President of the university spoke. It was all brochure-quality stuff, like "A standard in excellence," "Established in 1902," and "We bleed blue and white." And then they led us in singing the alma mater, which nobody else knew the words to. But in terms of making me loosen up a little, the rally wasn't totally useless. Calvin introduced me to his roommate, Theo, who's from Pittsburgh. Calvin's from Gettysburg, which he insists is actually pronounced 'Gettisburg.' We gave Elisha our condolences when she said she's from Kentucky, and laughed at Theo's impression of her snapping turtle senator. They all started talking about the shooting at the grocery store when I said I'm from Buffalo.

I didn't realize how hungry I was until Sunita mentioned that we were going to head over to get dinner at Patnick Dining Hall, where one swipe of your student ID gives you access to an all-you-can-eat smorgasbord of pretty mid food. Every other RA must've had the same idea, because the place was *packed*. The only table the four of us could get that was close to the rest of our floor was a high bar table. Elisha told us her roommate's a sophomore too, which makes me feel a little better about having to room with one.

"There's an ice cream bar over on the far wall in case you missed it," I told my friends-by-default when I went back to our table with a bowl of two scoops of cookie dough ice cream.

Calvin was on his feet in a second. "No *way*."

"Didn't you say you were lactose intolerant though?" Theo asked him.

"Listen," Calvin said seriously, "some things are just worth shitting yourself over." I wonder how many people throughout history were killed because they were suspected of being witches when they were just lactose intolerant or had a nut allergy?

I'm not sure if *I* became lactose intolerant or what all of a sudden, but I felt a *furious* shit coming on on the way back to Swafford. It was like one of the top ten times I've had to shit in my entire life. Like you know how you have to shit so bad sometimes that you don't even care what else happens? *That's* how bad it was. I almost didn't think I'd be able to punch in my code for my door. I danced out of my shorts like they were on fire and gave thanks that Tylor hadn't moved in yet as I made peace with the world.

And now I'm spending my first night alone in my new home in a town in western Pennsylvania. All the other doors were shut when I poked my head out into the hall. Is everyone out doing something else and I missed the memo? That wouldn't be anything new. For as thin as the walls are, it's almost eerie how quiet it gets when the air conditioner shuts off and the blind slats stop knocking against each other. Other than the occasional door swinging shut or something going *bump* or a toilet flushing somewhere above me, there's *nothing.*

I didn't feel like calling Madi or Logan, so I just dropped a message in the group chat letting them know I survived my first day away with some pics of my setup.

Pretty sure we have the same exact furniture lol

Looks good! 😊

Somebody is in *desperate* need of a mood board

Oh, the Places You'll Go! took itself from my fun-sized bookshelf and found itself being read for the twentieth time since I got it as a graduation gift. Dr. Seuss might be just a kid's author, but he's dropped some of the realest shit I've ever heard in my life. God, what the hell were we thinking when we couldn't wait to not be ten years old anymore?

August 26

It's wild to think how I was lying on the beach just five days ago, and now I'm spending the morning naked in my new bed, where I just bought my parking pass, blasted some rope, and reserved my textbooks—in that order. And Jesus Christ are textbooks *expensive*. Nine books came to like $460, and five of them were just novels for British Literature that were like 20 bucks total.

We headed to Bixby Student Center this morning for our first round of orientation 'classes,' the first of which was about safe sex and what constitutes consent. I guess once you have thousands of hornt-up teenagers in one place you have to go over it, kind of like how you can only have so many people in a room before it becomes a fire hazard. After taking pics in a big cutout Instagram frame with my two-day-old floormates like we were besties—*#instanhu #classof2026*— Sunita sent us on a campus-wide scavenger hunt that she and the other Swafford RAs concocted to keep us busy. I felt like the token male cheerleader when I tagged along with Elisha and a few of the other girls to familiarize ourselves with all the points of interest from here to Main Street. We probably looked freshman as hell with our paper maps and all the selfies we stopped to pose for. A few buildings—the clock tower, Kessler Hall, and a couple administrative buildings—on the older side of campus and the school's website and every freshman's Instagram have the typical 'collegiate' look that only exists in movies. I'm a fan of the Alumni Amphitheater too, which is just a big semicircle of stone blocks in the grass going down to a wide slab of a stage. The shade of its trees seems like it'd be a chill place to read or study or get high. Elisha and I were the only ones not going out of our way to kill whatever spotted lanternflies we came across. I mean, aren't humans invasive and destructive? Wouldn't *we* be upset if a higher species labeled us as undesirable and started indiscriminately killing us? Forreal though, I'm surprised there aren't people on street corners going on about plagues of locusts, just like how people used to preach the end of the world when everything was fine—but then an actual global fuck pandemic shows up and then they all disappear. Maybe they were all anti-vaxxers.

A handful of us went to a casino night event in the Field House after dinner, where we were each handed a stack of play money that you could trade in at the prize table for pencils and Cheez-Its and shit like that. We steered between card tables and roulette wheels before we settled at a blackjack table with oversized cards. "My bank account is like a game of reverse blackjack," Theo said with a *it's-funny-but-not-really* laugh. "I go as low as I can without going under." The dealer was a sweet older lady who would slide your bills back to you if you lost, and who paid you out extra if you won, which is to say that her grandkids have it made.

Perhaps because we'd just won more money than we'd ever seen in our collective lives *and* got snacks out of it, we were in too good of a mood to go back to our own rooms when we got back to Swafford. We ended up hanging out in Lizzy and Becky's room for a while, which smelled like patchouli thanks to an oil diffuser, and is decked out with so much Harry Potter merch that you think you're in a gift shop. We listened to Lizzy talk about anything and everything—what it's like to be colorblind, how her grandfather has a real estate license but doesn't use it, how her neighbor was almost gored by a deer ten years ago, how her family goes to the streetcar museum every December, and how her cousin's pigs have won ribbons in the county fair. I caught Theo's eye and we shared a sigh. I don't know how Becky's going to be able to listen to that all year.

Fortunately, a way out revealed itself. Unfortunately, it was in the form of the loudest fire alarm of all time. We can't even be here for two days without someone going and burning a bag of popcorn. It was the first room right when you enter our wing too, and it fucking *reeks*.

August 27

Last night's episode of 'Things Keeping Me From Falling Asleep' featured the way people perceive colors and how they might not all be the same—on top of the usual *I-wonder-if-Dillon-misses-me-at-all-or-if-he's-moved-on-to-somebody-else* black hole, of course. Like, what if what I think of as red is green to somebody else? Or if purple is polka dots to everybody else, or something else I can't even imagine?

I took my longboard out for a ride this morning and to visit the nearby PokéStops, though I'm sure people saw me going by and playing The Story So Far from my phone and probably thought I was trying to flex on them. I explored the parts of campus where yesterday's expedition didn't take us, drifting down lazy thoroughfares, meandering beneath a tunnel of trees, past grass manicured like a city park, under the building's receding shadows, over the bridge that spans the pond. I may just be a freshman, but I feel like the CEO when I'm on that thing.

We had the rest of our orientation classes today, so now I also know all about bullying, how to contact the campus police, and plagiarism. When I swung by the bookstore to pick up my books afterwards, the guy who handed them to me legit told me that since some books get new editions printed literally every year, they might not be able to buy them back at the end of the semester. "Well *fuck* me," I accidentally said out loud. The book for Physical Science came with some kind of remote, which helps explain—but sure as shit doesn't justify—its exclusory price. Maybe the class is like a game show or something.

"*Madison,*" Logan chastised Madi when she joined our FaceTime call later on, "you've been there for a week and you're *still* not unpacked?"

"*Most* of it is! I've been busy!" Madi said like she was tired of it.

Logan raised an eyebrow. "You have *that* many assignments your first week?"

"Not *just* assignments!" she rolled her eyes. "There's so much other stuff going on here. You'll see, Trev." *Wow, way to make Logan feel even more left out. It has* been a busy few days though, and classes haven't even started yet.

I walked them through my new home, showing them the mini fridge and microwave, the bathroom, the sink, my closet. My side of the room is studious with books and lively with pictures of us clipped to my memo board, while Tylor's side looks like a prison cell. "You really need to get some posters or something," Logan smirked.

"I have my map! And my *flag!*" I said as I gestured to my California Republic flag on the wall above my bed.

"Inadequate," was all he said.

"When does your roommate move in?" Madi asked.

"Tomorrow," I sighed. I've been getting more and more anxious about it. *Try not to think about it,'* Mom would say. *Okay, Mom. Done. Great advice. Thanks.*

"What do you two think about *my* dorm room?" Logan asked, spinning in his chair to show us his bedroom.

Madi squinted at it. "Why do I feel like I've been there before?"

"So is it just me, or are textbooks hella expensive?" I segued to something we could all relate to.

"Oh my god, don't *even* get me started," Madi groaned.

"It's *fucked*, dude," Logan spat.

Madi had to go so she could get ready for a party the sorority she's rushing was hosting. "They have parties at 6 in the evening?" Logan joked, earning himself a look from her. "Do *you* think you might join a frat?" he asked me after she hung up.

I snorted. "Pay to let a bunch of capital-S Straight guys bitch me around? No thanks."

"Maybe you could just let them use your body and you won't have to pay," he said casually, making me almost choke on the water that a whiteboard warned me not to drink. "So how've you been holding up so far?"

"So far? It *actually* hasn't been as bad as I was expecting it to be," I said slowly, afraid I might jinx myself.

"I guess that's one upside of being anxious about everything—you'll always be pleasantly surprised," he chuckled. "You make any friends yet?"

"My floormates are nice, but I wouldn't call them *friends* just yet." I thought about Elisha and Theo and Calvin, and about what Logan had said the other night about how I'll make new best friends. I haven't clicked with anybody I've met so far, but there are still a lot of people to be met, like Tylor. I'm as nervous as I am stoked about meeting him. What if he *does* become my new best friend? Maybe he's a low-key nerd, or likes alternative music, or loves to read, or likes to think about different ways the world could end. *Or* he could be a dumb, homophobic, capital-S Straight guy, and we'll end up loathing each other.

I distracted myself by swiping through the pics I took of campus for the most Instagrammable ones. As much as I don't like following the crowd, the most photogenic ones were of the most overdone parts of campus. I'm sure the clock tower was in every freshman's post, but I like to think that only the cooler kids had pics of the Amphitheater. *Take a seat, Trevor.*

wallowing_tbh I'm here, I'm queer, and I'm full of fear 😂 🎡 #tbh #nhu #basicbitch

August 28

I woke up this morning to the sound of Rory's voice. *What in hell?* I stumbled over to my peephole to see him sitting right in the middle of the hallway on his phone, typing away on his laptop. Like who are you even calling at 7 a.m.? And why right outside of *our* door? He wasn't even trying to be quiet about it or anything.

A knock at my open door later on pulled my eyes away from my Switch. "Hey, we're gonna go get some sheets," Calvin said with an up-nod. "You wanna come with?"

I furrowed my brow. "You didn't get your sheets yet?"

"No? We were gonna go take a walk over there now. I figured I'd see if you wanted to come too."

"I already got my sheets," I said, more confused than ever. *What the hell's he been sleeping on?*

"Oh, okay," he frowned, sounding unconvinced.

We stared at each other, waiting for the punchline.

"Are you talking about sheets for your bed?" I said louder than I meant to.

His mouth fell open and he cracked up. "Not *those* sheets, dude! Sheetz with a 'z!' Like the gas station?"

I'd never heard of Sheetz before, but I guess they're all over the place down here. I followed Calvin and Theo across campus and down Main Street, trying to speak more than only when spoken to, and soaking up the small town vibe—the trees and the ornate street lights springing up through the sidewalk, the little park and its war memorial, one or two Victorian-style houses with their large front porches, the 'S. Butts Agency' sign outside of an insurance office—all while avoiding the sewer grates in case my pocket decided to grow a hole and let my phone fall out. One house's yard has backpack-wearing, Halloween-decoration skeletons headed off to class, and another waving them off from the porch. It's the kind of town Grandma would say is 'just delightful'—if not for the bar, the three tattoo parlors, the psychic shop, and the smoke shop with products for 'tobacco use only.' And if I'm not in the mood to deal with the Patnick shits, there's Subway, McDonald's, Taco Bell, a Chinese place, and of course, Sheetz. I just ended up getting some snacks because the made-to-order food menu intimidated me, and the place was busy with people filling up their cars and themselves before their drives home. I sipped my raspberry tea and flung Poké Balls while I waited for the other two's food.

"Goddamn are these mac and cheese bites *dank*," Calvin practically moaned like he had a dick in his mouth.

"Mac and cheese bites?" I asked, instantly curious. "What are those?"

"*What are those!*" Theo yelled softly before taking a drink of his kombucha.

Calvin stared like I'd slapped him. "You've never had a mac and cheese bite before? Aw man, you gotta try them sometime!" I would've gone back in for some if I was worried about holding them up.

We took the scenic route back to campus through some of the residential streets. One house had a flagpole out front flying an American flag as big as America itself, and a sign zip-tied to the chain link gate saying 'WARNING: NO STUPID PEOPLE BEYOND THIS POINT.' *I wonder who the fuck they voted for,* I almost said out loud.

I pushed open the door to 222 Swafford when I got back and got startled by a laundry basket full of Nike and Adidas clothes that wasn't there when I left, wedged between the door and the wall. "Hello? Trevor?" a disembodied voice called out.

"Hi?" I answered as I took in the brass-and-glass steampunk-looking pitcher sitting by the microwave. *Will Queen Victoria come out of it like a genie if I rub it?*

"I'll be out in a minute! Don't mind the mess!"

I wouldn't call it a *mess* as much as I'd call it a little chaotic—but then again, my parents weren't there to put things away for Tylor. There was a collapsible-looking two-seater couch and a square side table on wheels. I tried to piece together a picture of the person I'd be living with from his belongings—the electric toothbrush that may or may not double as a vibrator, the PS5 and paper-thin TV, the Mac with a retro-pink Mt. Fuji sticker and another that said *"Earth without art is just eh."* I counted three pairs of running shoes, a pair of slides, and a pair of Hey Dudes tucked under his bed, which made my four pairs of Vans not feel so extra. *Those sleeveless shirts with the armholes cut all the way down the side still have me low-key scared though.*

The toilet flushing sent my pulse running like a gunshot. I stared out the window while he washed his hands, playing with my studs and contemplating self-defenestration. I listened for the towel, counted to two, and turned around. His messy hair and glasses gave him Harry Potter vibes but cooler—and yes, the nose ring has a lot to do with it. "It's good to finally meet you, Trevor," he said genuinely as he set down his three-camera iPhone. My eyes fell on his Apple watch as we shook hands.

"Glad to meet you too, Tylor," I said, immediately easing up a little.

"When'd you move in?"

"Thursday." I looked around at his still-boxed stuff sitting around his side of the room. "It didn't take you too long to get moved in."

"Yeah, my mom didn't hang around for too long. My sister wanted to get back home."

"I gotcha. Where's home for you?"

"Hudson, Ohio. It's between Cleveland and Akron—just a straight shot across 80. What about you?"

"Buffalo. New York."

He surprised me by asking, "Don't you guys get a shit-ton of snow up there?" instead of *'wasn't that where that shooting was?'*

"Yeah, we get a blizzard like every other day."

"Well, the weather down here's not *that* bad. It's more unpredictable than anything. Wait until Spring comes—we go through all four seasons in a week."

"At least it stays fresh?" I offered. "And nice PlayStation, by the way."

"Thanks," he said as he glanced at it. "Are you much of a gamer at all? I saw you have a Switch."

"I wouldn't really call myself a *gamer.*" *Gaymer?* "Or at least I didn't until I played *Breath of the Wild.*"

"*Excellent* game."

"But I mostly just play *Pokémon* or *Mario* anymore."

"Who doesn't like *Pokémon?*" *Okay, yeah, I'm definitely liking this guy already.*

Tylor finished rearranging his furniture, which left an empty space under part of the window where his dresser used to be. "Do you mind if I turn my bed sideways?" I asked him.

"Of course not. It's as much your space as it is mine."

"Okay." I looked from him to my bed and back again. "Do you mind helping me turn it?"

"Now you're pushing it," he joked. It's a little tight, but we got the couch between our beds and across from his TV. "Perfect for if we ever wanted to have movie night," he said, which is exactly the kind of thing I'd say to somebody if I ever wanted to make out with them.

We talked more while he unpacked and organized. He's going for a Journalism major with a minor in Photography, which explains his artillery weapon of a camera. "What's that, a cannon?" I joked.

"A Nikon, actually," he said as he turned it over in his hands. "I'd *love* to be a photographer for Nat Geo or something. Any kind of job where I can travel the world, really."

"Hashtag *goals*," I daydreamed. "What kind of music is this, by the way?" It was upbeat and jazzy, and made me think of a lazy late Summer afternoon in the urban sprawl of the inner city.

"Just a chillhop station on Spotify," he said to the Batman poster he'd taped above his bed. "Oh, I almost forgot—Sunita dropped this off earlier," he said, taking a stapled packet off his desk. "It's just the roommate agreement for us to read and sign. You know, in case one of us eats the other one's food and we can't act like adults about it," he rolled his eyes. "But you seem like you're pretty chill, so I doubt it'll come to that." I took it from him, bowled over by the fact that the person I'd been stressing out over this whole time just described me as being 'pretty chill.' *I bet he won't be saying that once I tell him how I like to read the endings of books first,* I laughed to myself. I kept glancing up from the packet as he gave more life to his room. He brought twice as many movies as I did books. His other posters are of a skull with a Latin phrase that Google translates to 'remember death,' and a neon bowl of ramen surfing *The Great Wave. I really do need to get some stuff on my wall.* I took in his signature at the end of the agreement, how his *H* in Hayashi looks like a blocky square *U.*

"Hey, I'm gonna go meet some friends for dinner," he said after reading a text. "But we can catch up some more later on, aight?"

"Sounds good," I smiled. *'Catch up,'* like we were already friends.

My favorite part of the roommate agreement is *"residents are not to set off fireworks inside of the residence halls."* I'd love to know the story behind that.

August 29

Survive the first day of classes? Check! Survive the first day of classes without embarrassing myself? Of course not!

I went over the route I'd have to take from building to building while we brewed our own coffees—my coffee-pot coffee seemed uncouth compared to Tylor's French press—and had America's favorite toaster pastry for breakfast. I joined the rest of the student body on the arteries of campus like blood cells, and was halfway to Devlin Hall of Physical Sciences when I realized I forgot my schedule in my room—because who needs *that?*—and had no clue where the fuck *in* Devlin I was supposed to go. I backtracked to my room to grab my schedule off my desk, and across the empty Quad to the lecture hall, where class was already ten minutes in. There were a couple open seats near the front, but I didn't want people thinking I'm that asshole douchebag who's late to the first day of class on purpose. I spent the period sitting at the top of the steps in the back, and I avoided meeting Dr. Eubanks' eye when I asked him for a copy of the syllabus afterwards. And then I expected Dr. Padar, my professor for Computer Concepts, to be a middle-aged Indian lady, but it turns out she's like the whitest woman ever. I guess she gets a lot of surprised looks because she explained that it's a Hungarian name. And then she told us about how she used to be a firebreather.

I had a couple of hours until Critical Writing—taught by Dr. Conrad, who has a mustache like he's either a general for the German Empire or like he's trying to sell you a bucket of chicken—so I had lunch at Patnick before heading back to 222 Swafford to shit my brains out. I was working on my latest idea for a story—vignettes of the spotted lanternfly apocalypse progressing in reverse, all the way back to somebody not killing the very first one—when Tylor came back to the room. "Don't tell me you have assignments *already*," he groaned sympathetically when he saw Google Docs pulled up on my Mac.

"Oh, no," I chuckled as I instinctively tilted my screen down. "I'm just journaling," I lied. As lame as it sounded saying it out loud, I wasn't in the mood to hear him ask if he could read my story.

"Oh, that's cool," he said as he slung his backpack off and onto his chair. *Huh?*

"You think so?"

"Do you not?" he laughed.

"I mean, yeah. I do it to help clear my head more than anything." I didn't tell him that I started doing it on the recommendation of my therapist.

"Hey, I'm not judging," he insisted as he flopped back onto his bed. "I like the perspective aspect of it."

I twisted myself in my chair. "What do you mean?"

"Like, you only journal about the things that are important to you, or that you find interesting. Everything else still goes on, but as far as you're concerned, it's like it never even happened. It's like the world according to you."

The World According to Trevor: A Historical Survey.

"So this might be TMI," I gingerly asked him when he came back out of the bathroom, "but does the food from Patnick make you have to use the bathroom? Like a lot?"

"It absolutely does," he chuckled. "I forgot how bad the Patnick Poops were."

I lit up. "So it's *not* just me?"

"It's not just you. It's an NHU tradition."

"Oh thank god," I laughed with relief. "I was starting to get worried."

"I always thought they put laxatives in the food or something, until my friend Jax got a job there last year and told me what *really* happens," Tylor said seriously.

My eyes widened. *Body parts. I don't know how or what, but body parts.*

He leaned in. "If you eat a lot and if you eat like shit, it's gonna mess up your stomach," he said behind his cupped hand. Which makes sense—not only do they give you pizza and pasta and cookies and ice cream for dinner, they also don't tell you not to have it all at the same time.

August 30

Tylor told me last night that his old roommate tried to make cheese in his dresser. "I never even knew there *was* such a thing as a smell complaint until we got three of them," he laughed over a game of rec room pool. "I had to switch rooms at the end of the semester."

"Your new roommate probably didn't have to try very hard to be a step up," I frowned.

Tylor shrugged. "He was okay. He couldn't hold a conversation about anything other than girls, football, and farting, but at least he was hygienic." *So are you saying I'm your favorite roommate since I can hold a conversation and I don't stink up the room?* But then later as he was getting into bed, Tylor joked for me to wait for him to "fall asleep before you start jacking off to me," which got me worrying all over again about what he'll think of me once he finds out that I actually *like* jacking off to guys.

Tuesday/Thursday History and English were the classes I was looking forward to the most. I took a liking to Dr. de Conto, my professor for Western Civilization III, right away when she had us go around and share one of our pet peeves instead of telling everyone a fun fact about ourselves. I was torn between 'when people move into the left lane only to drive slow as hell' and 'when books don't start on page 1' until I figured the book one would make me look like I have a big stick up my ass. And then instead of just going over the syllabus, she started spitting fire on day one.

"Think about everything you've been taught," she told us. "Think about everything you've been conditioned to believe, and leave them at the door. Entertain the possibility that everything you know might be wrong. *That* is how learning begins."

"*Hell yeah,*" a kid with purple tunnels in his gauged ears and a 'ONE HUMAN FAMILY' sticker on his own Mac whispered. He caught me glancing back at him and gave me a smirk.

"If you're unwilling to do that, then why come here in the first place?" Dr. de Conto went on. "College isn't the place for you to stay inside your comfort zone."

Every Tuesday and Thursday at 12:15 is Common Hour, a period-length break of no classes, which is when campus really comes alive. It's also the worst time to try to get food anywhere, because literally *everybody* has the same idea. Bixby gets even more crowded than Patnick, with fraternities and sororities taking up entire blocks of tables in the common dining area. And here I thought I was going to enjoy some wings from Percy's Grille, the place in Bixby named after the school mascot, for lunch.

I like seeing all the decor people put in their dorm windows—happy-to-be-here NHU flags, bold flags and pennants for their hometown sports teams, solemn Ukrainian flags, welcoming Progress flags and other different Pride flags. I already like the person in Gladby Hall who has a California Republic flag. Some windows have signs taped to them—'No Place for Hate' with a Star of David and some diamonds, 'Black Lives Matter,' 'Protect Trans Kids,' 'Love Is Love,' 'No Dumping.' One fourth-floor room has a big inflatable palm tree with pink lights on it. Another has a life-size cutout of the Pioneer Woman smiling down on all who pass by. I saw them all again an hour and a half later when I walked back to Shaver for British Literature, which might not be as enjoyable as I thought it would be. Dr. Gallagher, a stern woman who bears a striking resemblance to Rachel Maddow, had us move our desks into a big circle so we could all see each other—I got to check out the cute guy named Roman with glasses across from me—before dropping a heavy-as-hell, *Encyclopedia Britannica*-sized tome of poems and plays and short stories on our desks that she compiled, printed, and bound herself, and telling us we each owe her $20 for them.

"I accept checks and cash," she said matter-of-factly. "I am *not* giving out my Venmo account." And that's *on top of* five novels. What, does she think her class is the only one we have? She does this thing too where she says "please see myself," which makes me want to throw something. Like for fucking real? You're an *English* professor for god's sake. To her credit though, she *did* ask if there was anybody in the class who would prefer not being called on. I stupidly kept quiet, which will probably come back to bite me in the ass—like how not taking my umbrella with me bit me in the ass when it started *pouring* down rain on my way back to Swafford. I was *drenched.*

"I'm fucking *wet,*" I announced when I got back to 222 Swafford.

"Oh *are* you?" Tylor asked from around the corner.

August 31

I wonder if the university has a way to deter people from hitting one of the blue emergency buttons just for fun. Like, do you get sprayed with ink like when you open the bag of money from the bank you just robbed?

We had an actual fire drill yesterday, when they figured most of the residents were back in for the evening. Some people, like Lekan next door, somehow knew about it and made sure they were somewhere else when it happened. Other people, like me, ignored the rumors and had to evacuate the building. Other *other* people, like Steph, had no fucking clue at all and had to stand outside wrapped in a towel because she was in the shower.

My walls were making me feel self-conscious, so I swung by Bixby on the way back from class to check out the poster sale that was going on. I figured I wouldn't have any trouble finding a *Pokémon* one, but the wavy blue-and-white *Nothing Happens* poster sideswiped me. And of course I had to get 'Welcome to the Party,' with Karl Marx and Lenin and other big names in communism getting turnt. I was taping them up when the sudden thought of what Dillon decorated his dorm room walls with almost knocked the wind out of me. Luckily, a Waterparks song playing from Elisha's half-open door took my mind off the life my ex is living without me. "So I heard you like Waterparks," I said into the room from her doorway.

"What makes you say that?" a girl who wasn't Elisha smiled. "And also hi. Can I help you?"

"Oh," I said as I rubbed the back of my neck, "I'm sorry—I thought that was Elisha's music. I live across the hall." I jabbed my thumb over my shoulder.

"Compliment taken," she nodded. "I'm Nikole by the way." We talked for a couple minutes before she went back to whatever she was doing. She's an English major too, and I get the feeling she likes a lot of the same music as me.

When we're not fleeing a building that may or may not be on fire, my floormates and I have been hitting up the rec room or hanging out in each other's rooms, talking about lockdown and high school and trying to make each other laugh with our favorite TikToks and YouTube videos and Instagram reels. Marcel the Shell's newest fan felt kind of bad that nobody let Lizzy know that we were chilling in Shawn and Rory's room—Shawn has a *legit* gamer setup with two screens and everything, while Rory's wall is covered with Disney princesses—but it was nice not having any one person hijack the conversation. Nobody believed Elisha when she said she's a contortionist until she folded herself into shapes people aren't meant to be folded into. Between that and her telling us that she has a collection of knives back home, I'm not convinced she doesn't work for a traveling circus. Most of the floor are Music or Dance majors—which makes sense, since our floor is part of the Humanities LLC —but Theo and Nikole are the only other two English majors I've met. Anton, a Vocal Performance major who smells like sour cream and onion potato chips, had us cracking *up* when he told us his nickname in high school was 'The Nutman,' because he's *super* religious.

"What?" he asked, trying to figure out what was sending us. "It's because I used to eat a lot of nuts!"

September 1

September 1, 1939 was the day Poland awoke to find itself getting ass-fucked by the German scourge, not unlike the way college ass-fucks you with textbook prices. Yeah, I'm still salty about it. And *then* I discovered that the $30 'technology fee' in the admissions cost is just so we can use the printers, which silly me just assumed was an inalienable student right. At five cents a page, I'd have to literally waste paper if I want to get my money's worth. And you'd think that a technology fee would give us Wi-Fi that can handle the traffic of a university-worth of students, but nope. If it's after 9 p.m. when everybody's back in their rooms for the night, forget about it.

I'm actually not too upset about not having another freshman for a roommate because Tylor's sophomore *savoir faire* definitely has its perks, like knowing which drink machine in Patnick is the one with the orange pop. Plus, he has the stuff I would've never thought to bring, like a collapsible dishwashing tub and a little cordless vacuum. I think he's a low-key germaphobe though, because he washes his hands every time he touches even just the toilet handle or the outside of the trash can. But there are worse things he could be though, like someone who forgets to flush or says that the 2020 election was rigged.

We took our relationship to the next level by following each other on Instagram, and it turns out that hayashi_photography *is* him after all. "These are actually some pretty bomb-ass pics," I complimented them as I scrolled through them. "Like, this one is just leaves, but the *detail* in them."

"I like to try to show the beauty in everything, even in the things we take for granted," he said. "Ja feel?"

"I feel. Like, think about flowers. We're so used to seeing them, but look at all the planets out there that don't have flowers. Or strawberries. Strawberries are like the trippiest things, but nobody thinks twice about them."

"Exactly! Or the moon! How would you explain what it's like to look up and see the moon *right there* to somebody from a planet that doesn't have one?"

Taking the Moon for Granted: Life Before the Catastrophe, by Trevor Huffman.

"I wonder what kinds of things other worlds out there have and take for granted that don't exist here, things that our meager three-dimensional minds keep us from even *beginning* to imagine."

"Bruh." Tylor fell back in his chair. "Passes blunt to the left."

"Passes it back, because I don't smoke."

"Neither do I," he chuckled just as I got a follow request back from him. *"wallowing_tbh?"* he asked with a smile. "Why are you being honest about your wallowing?"

"My initials are TBH, and Wallows is a band. They're a little more on the obscure side," I said maybe a little smugly.

"Oh, I know Wallows! They have a few songs I like." *Woah, that's a first.* "I like the pics of campus you took."

"Thanks. I felt like a basic freshman bitch taking pics of the clock tower though," I chuckled.

He shot me a look over his glasses. "You can stop feeling like a basic freshman bitch by calling it Old Main, you ignorant little shit." He held it together for four good seconds before busting out laughing.

We met up for Common Hour lunch at Zukoff, the dining hall on the other side of campus. I hadn't been there yet since it costs real dollars instead of a meal swipe, but its rice bowls, gyros, sushi, stir-fries, smoothies, and burgers make it worth it, especially after having almost nothing but "beige food"—as Elisha likes to call it—from Patnick. "And it doesn't give you the shits like Patnick does," Tylor told me as we waited in a 30-minute line. As much as I wanted some General Tso's, I know I wouldn't be able to stomach it without seeing Dillon scarfing it down in my mind, saying how he could eat it every day for the rest of his life whenever we'd go get Chinese. Fuck you, Dillon. Didn't you ruin things for me enough when you broke up with me?

Tylor and I cut through the Quad on the way back, where the Club and Organization Fair was underway. Booths and tables lined the pentagram of sidewalks, equipped with poster boards and shit to give away to try to attract freshmen to clubs for anything and everything—Greek life, house councils, the Blue & White Society, the Student Government Board, academic clubs, language clubs, ethnic heritage clubs, Black Action Society, Autism Speaks, an organization against human trafficking, a ceramics club, a glass-blowing club, a ping-pong club, a disc golf club, Dumbledore's Army, a LARP club, a *Magic: the Gathering* club, an aquaponics project, a pollination club, club sports, dance clubs, a kickboxing club, a weightlifting club, a positive body image club, bassoon choir, a park ranger society, an equestrian club. If it exists, there's a club for it. There's even a food foraging club that had berries and mushrooms and wild onions laid out on their table, but I think they just don't want to pay for a meal plan. I wanted to join something to nudge myself out of my comfort zone, but I didn't know what. There's a longboarding club, which was intimidating since the people seemed *way* cooler than what I'm fit for. The Gamer's Guild people seem neglectful of their personal hygiene. *The Herald*, the NHU school newspaper, prefers Communications majors. The obnoxiously loud gays representing Proud as Halle, the university's equivalent of a GSA, gave off exactly the kind of vibe I'm not going for.

"What's your opinion on fraternities?" I asked Tylor as I read some big paper letters that I mentally pronounced as MAO.

He was silent for a good 10 seconds. "I wouldn't recommend."

"Why?"

"I was in one last year, and—"

"*Really?* You don't seem like the frat bro type."

"Oh trust me, I'm *not*," he said as we ducked under some Color Guard ribbons. "I saw shit happen that wasn't okay. So I quit."

"What kind of shit?"

"I'll tell you later," he said in a low tone. "But I think that if you do college right, you'll find your own fraternity." *What does 'doing college right' even mean? Being a straight-A student? Being involved with as many things as you can? Making as many friends as you can? But then what's doing college 'wrong?'* "Hey, what about that one?" Tylor pointed to a table that read 'Literature Club' in uneven block letters. "That sounds like the kind of club for an English major."

Hearing 'English major' was all it took for the guy behind the table to go into a stuttering spiel about it. But that's how you get us introverts to stay and listen—you just have to come off as at least as awkward as us. The Literature Club basically sounds like a Meetup for people who like to read, which seems pretty casual. Thinking about how pathetic I probably looked to the guys at the bear-wrestling table next door, I scrawled my name and email on the clipboard. Awkward Guy introduced himself as Ashton, and told me to be on the lookout for an email from him.

In the privacy of 222 Swafford, I asked Tylor again about his fraternity experience. "Well for starters, I had to wear a penis cage for a week."

"What?!" I exclaimed.

"Yeah, *that* was fucking fun," he scoffed. "Imagine not being allowed to get hard for a whole week. And I'd get piss all over the place."

"I can't imagine." Really, I can't—boners are how most of my days begin.

"They did everything they could to remind you that you were their sub. But the thing that *really* did it for me was..." He pressed his fingers to his eyes. "I don't even wanna say it."

"Well don't then. I get the idea though, it's a bunch of Straight"—*oh shitfuck*—"up *douche*bags making people their bitch."

So that's how I almost accidentally outed myself to my roommate.

September 2

So I came out to my roommate.

Tylor's alarm for Fridays is the song "Friday", which scared the shit out of me when it started playing all of a sudden. "I used to have a crush on Rebecca Black when I was younger," he smiled as he scooped heaps of coffee from an air-tight jar.

"Oh really?" I said in my pretending-to-care voice.

"Yeah, I used to get shit for it, but I thought she got kinda cute, don't you think?" *Just say yes.*

"Um...not really," I said, dreading the inevitable next question.

"Do you remember your first celebrity crush?" he asked in a way that suggested he never had to lie about it. *Lie, and you'll be upset with yourself. Don't lie, and...well, we'll see.*

I held my breath and squeezed my eyes shut, glad that my back was to him. "Josh Hutcherson?" I winced, bracing myself for giving the wrong answer.

"I haven't heard *that* name in a hot second," he said casually. "Yeah, I guess he's kind of a knockout." *Wait, what?*

My eyes snapped open. "That's it?"

"What do you mean?"

"You don't care that I like guys? That doesn't bother you?"

"No? Should it?"

"No! I mean—I'm just not used to..." *That's what I was stressing out over?* "People usually aren't that cool about it that fast. And even if they say they are...I can tell they think differently of me."

He abandoned his coffee to prop himself on an empty corner of my desk. "Trevor, I am more than cool with it, and I don't think *any* differently of you."

"Well that's...good to hear," was all I could say. *Why is it so hard for everybody to be like him? And also how does burned popcorn set off the fire alarm, but the steam from his electric kettle doesn't? Plot holes.*

"I already kinda knew," he added.

"Really? How?"

A smile crept across his face. "You aren't exactly discreet when it comes to checking out guys."

I smiled back. "Am I that obvious?"

"You're like a...I don't know what you're like. A gay dude on a campus full of guys." *Move over 'kid in a candy shop,' there's a new idiom on the block.* "Thanks for telling me though. I'm sure it's not always easy." *It's not, and any hetero who thinks coming out is a one-and-done deal should try being queer sometime.*

"And thanks for..." I started to say. *Thanks for not judging me. Thanks for not calling me a faggot to my face. Thanks for not telling me I'm going to hell. Thanks for just letting me be me.* "Just thanks," I said, smiling back into his accepting eyes. His beeping kettle brought our moment to an end, but it was a great way to start the day. But then the thoughts about how things would've been different if Ryder had had that kind of unconditional support in his life started flooding in, and I couldn't stop them.

September 3

> I think I knew, that those games between us
> Were just unrequited friendship all along that I
> Reluctantly relinquished, like pulling myself away from
> Pictures of crushes who treated me like a fortune cookie—
> Break it in half and

If you don't like what you see
Throw it away and pick another
There are always more—
And like the pictures of crushes who made a fortune cookie of me,
I can't put away the memories of us—
Letting them keep me awake, thinking about
If things had gone differently,
Wondering if tonight will be the night I finally figure out
What it is about me that always sends people running.

September 4

Three things I learned about college today: condom vending machines are a thing, you can absolutely make ramen in your coffee pot, and don't let your laundry sit in the machine for too long unless you want to come back and find it sitting in a damp heap because your inconsiderate ass decided to hog one of the two washers the whole floor has to share. Forreal though, who's doing laundry already? We've only been here for like a week and a half.

My weekends start on Friday at 10:50 a.m. since Critical Writing doesn't meet on Fridays, but I guess a lot of people's weekends started the night before on Thirsty Thursday. Is there also Wasted Wednesday and Tipsy Tuesday? A few freshmen must've sucked the right dicks though, because they already had places to go out to. But even if my floormates *were* going out to a party and invited me along, I probably wouldn't have, and then I would've spent the evening being upset with myself. College parties scare me.

I was kind of hoping that Tylor would've asked me if I wanted to come along with him when he told me he was going over to his friend's place, even if the idea of being in a new social setting where everybody already knows each other makes me anxious. I didn't have to spend my Friday night alone though, because Calvin came a-knocking to invite me over for a wholesome game of *Cards Against Humanity*. Elisha, Nikole, Simone, Amanda, Anton, and Trent were already sitting on the floor of 215 Swafford, while Theo shuffled the cards from his bean bag chair. They must've hit up the poster sale too, because their walls were decked with *Mario* and *Stranger Things* and *American Idiot* and *Spirited Away*.

"Should we ask Dayton if he wants to play?" I asked, hoping to see if he and I could hit it off.

Calvin shook his head. "Nobody answered when I knocked. I swear I heard someone moving in there though."

"He could just be shy," Simone said. "Maybe all this is too overwhelming for him."

"Maybe he's a serious gamer," Theo suggested as some cards spilled onto the floor.

"Or maybe he likes to goon," Trent laughed.

Unfortunately for him, Anton had never played *Cards Against Humanity* before. We were 20 minutes into it before I realized the last time I played was back when Dillon and I were still together, which made me have to force more than a few laughs. The game had us so weak that I for sure thought we were going to get written up for being so loud past Quiet Hour.

I awoke in the night to the sound of a girl's voice in my room. *Oh dear god please don't let me have to listen to them fucking.* I opened my eyes just enough to see my wall, dimly lit from the entryway light. Tylor, the girl, and another guy were talking in low voices. My ears perked up when my name came up, half-expecting them to put my hand in a bowl of water like a 3rd grade sleepover. I laid frozen like I wasn't allowed to wake up in my own room, getting up to pee only after they left and after I could tell Tylor was asleep.

I took my longboard around campus alongside the morning runs and walks of shame before grabbing breakfast. The aroma of freshly-brewed coffee hit me like a wall when I got back to 222 Swafford, where I finally got to have some French press, which is good as shit. Like, it quite possibly might be the best coffee I've ever had.

"It was a pretty low-key night, but we had fun," Tylor answered when I asked how his night was. "A few of us just went over to my friend's apartment and got a little saucy." Hearing that he didn't hop from house party to house party made my night feel not so lame, and I felt even better for some reason when he came along with a few of us later on to see *Ready Player One* in the theater up in Bixby. I guess CPB—the Campus Programming Board—has a movie showing every week, sometimes out in the Quad on a big screen like a drive-in if the weather's nice.

We migrated back to 215 Swafford, where we ordered Domino's and played *Cards* again until I saw Calvin's copy of *Mario Kart* and mentioned how I was just playing it earlier. With shouts that startled me, they made me fetch my own Switch and copy of the game so we could all take turns playing. If we'd made a drinking game out of it where you take a drink anytime somebody says 'fuck,' we would've been hammered. It was like a Lewis Black comedy sketch.

"Fuck me!"

"God *fucking* dammit!"

"Fuck you, Theodore!"

"Holy FUCK!"

_____

September 5

I came back from dinner to find a guy standing in Swafford's lobby dressed like he was on his way to a luau, which got even weirder when he asked me if I wanted to get laid. "You know, lei'd," he smiled as he held up an artificial flower lei. I guess he was with the Health Center doing some kind of safe sex campaign. So now I'm one fake lei and four condoms richer.

We had our first floor social yesterday evening, which was just cartons of different ice cream set up in the common area. I don't remember how it came up, but Sunita said that there's an Indian proverb that goes something like *don't curse god for creating the tiger, but thank him for not giving it wings*. Wouldn't *that* be a hell of an apocalypse movie?

Ashton emailed me and a bunch of other people to tell us that Literature Club will meet bimonthly in the old Student Union starting tomorrow. You'd think that somebody would've come up with another term to distinguish 'twice a month' from 'every other month' by now. Like, it's 2022 for god's sake. Quit trying to give guns more rights than people and start figuring this shit out.

Tylor asked me if I wanted to join him and his friends for disc golf, but since I'm ass at both Frisbee and golf, I'm spending our Labor Day off under a tree near the pond. There's baseball practice going on in one field and soccer practice in another, which means there's eye candy either way I look.

I came to college thinking I'd walk around with some existential novel under my arm, discussing philosophies with students in sunglasses and cardigans. I'd stumble upon some underground student magazine and go to *Animal House* parties. Everybody would be listening to Vampire Weekend. I'd click with somebody from class and we'd go get coffee. But not a single movie I watched prepared me for all the sidewalks graffitied with chalk, promoting events or meetings or just telling you that you look great today, or that you got this smiley face smiley face heart heart. There are times when I wish I was in a traditional dorm because it seems like it'd be a more authentic 'college' experience, but then I remember the whole sharing-a-bathroom-with-everyone thing. And I still can't get over how lax college classes are compared to high school classes. I'd like to know where my teachers went to school that made them think all professors have a stick up their ass like Gallagher does. I've seen people buying shit online and scrolling through Tumblr and the professors don't care. People eat and sleep in class, or just straight-up don't do the assignment and they haven't gotten expelled. I couldn't be a professor, because I'd take it all personally.

I think universities are just social experiments and campus is a big Petri dish. What do you get if you put thousands of kids into a new, somewhat-controlled environment with a newfound freedom and little supervision and leave them to their own devices? Food foraging clubs, apparently. Demonstrations on how to build a working computer in *Minecraft*. Slam poetry. Student-led lectures and classes just for fun. And it's uncanny how much somebody here reminds me of someone back home. I thought Logan was here when I saw a guy with the same wavy black hair and patchy facial hair. Amanda on my floor has the same personality and mannerisms as Kristin Palmer. Chloe from work either has a twin or a doppelgänger who goes here. There's a guy who has Clay Daniel's signature strut—the same way I imagine how the Planters peanut guy walks—down-pat. Maybe human biology ran out of ideas and just started making copies of other people.

I think my favorite thing about college is that it lets you be whatever you want without judging you for it. People old enough to go off to war will be chasing each other down with Nerf guns and nobody thinks twice about it. Some guys wear makeup and some girls have their heads shaved. AJ wears cat ears like half the time. I've gone to Patnick for lunch and there've been a group of people playing a game together on their own laptops or some deck-building card game, and they're *still* going at it when I go back for dinner. Unlike high school, nobody is above anybody else. College is the great equalizer, or at least a reset button. The downside of that though is there are just that many more people who make me feel like I'm not smart enough, not attractive enough, not gay enough, not outgoing enough, not confident enough, not cool enough, not mentally-stable enough—and I don't think any reset button will make me any of those.

September 6

It's technically still Summer for a few more weeks, but Fall starts the day Starbucks starts serving pumpkin spice lattes. You'd have thought the place was giving away shit for free. I don't know how people can afford to get coffee there every day, sometimes more than once a day. Like, aren't we all supposed to be broke? Unless some hot barista's jerking off into it, there's no way I'm paying $6 for a goddamn coffee.

I finally rode my board to class today, which I won't be doing all the time. If you think maneuvering between Boomers on a boardwalk is tough, then you should try the Quad in the 10-minute gap between classes. Besides, all I'd need would be for it to fall over in Gallagher's class while she's in the middle of speaking and have a whole cul-de-sac of people judging me.

I poked around on the student employment portal to see what jobs were available. Everything must've gotten picked over last week, but there was one for a page at Rosenberg Library I applied for. It's pretty lame, but libraries are my vibe—more so anyway than tending to the vertical farm somewhere in Vollmer Technical Sciences Hall. By the time I was done with class I already had an email from someone named Kelly at the library asking me when I could stop over to talk to her about it. A conversation with her—she has the exhausted look of somebody who oversees a staff of untrained student workers—was apparently all it took to get me the job. It's only ten hours a week and it pays minimum wage, but at least it'll help keep me out of my room. So if you're ever in the library on a Monday or Wednesday afternoon, come holla at ya boy.

By dinner I got another email from somebody at the Student Employment Office with forms I had to fill out and take to Rosenberg with me, and links to four different trainings I had to do about confronting workplace bias and accommodating to disabilities and recognizing harassment. I was so caught up in getting everything done so I could start tomorrow that I totally forgot about the Literature Club meeting until Tylor and I were three-quarters of the way to Sheetz. But it's okay though, because those mac and cheese bites? Downright *dank*. It's like cracking open geodes and finding a steaming, oozing cache of gold. And *yes*, Dr. Eubanks, I *know* you can't find gold inside of a geode—it's called a figure of speech, goddammit.

September 7

So hanging around the Alumni Amphitheater, a.k.a. Stonehenge, isn't as cool as I thought it would be. I found a spot in the shade to read *The Idiot*—Batuman, not Dostoevsky—between classes, and yeah, there are sunglasses scrawling and sketching in folded-back notebooks, but it just smells like cigarettes. What was *actually* cool though was some guy sliding down the entire length of the hand railing on the big set of stairs that goes from Rafferty Classroom Building to the main sidewalk like a fucking CEO.

When I was leaving Computers this morning I saw somebody waiting for the next class wearing a 'Black Lives Matter' shirt, which I thought was cool because you don't usually see redheaded white kids wearing shirts like that. I remember one time I said something about how I wish there were more people like me, and Dad joked that there probably are but we're too afraid to say hi to each other, and apparently that's still the case. I could've at least just said 'nice shirt.' It's funny—and by 'funny' I mean 'sad'—how I say I don't have many friends, but then I never really make a real effort to *make* any. But like, how are you supposed to *do* that?

I wasn't too sure what the job of a library page actually entails, but putting books back and manning an anachronistic oak desk at one end of the computer lab isn't too far off from what I pictured. I had plenty of time to work on assignments too, since nobody bothers you at the desk unless they jam a printer or need an envelope. And Devon, the guy with snakebites and a septum piercing who I shadowed, is actually kind of hot. It's an easy gig, even if it is lonely work. Seeing other people studying together or socializing makes me feel bad about myself for not finding my niche yet. Is it selfish of me to wish that more people felt as lonely as I do? Why isn't there a club for lonely people?

I asked Tylor what the story is with the toadstool of a woman who swipes you into Patnick. I say hi to her every time—wondering if the 'Paul' on her name tag is short for Pauline or Paula or if her name's literally just Paul—and all I ever get back is a grunt or a growl. Maybe she's a retired throat singer. "Like, does she ever speak actual words?" I asked him once she was out of earshot.

"I might've heard her speak once or twice," he said, looking back just as she slithered down off her chair to retrieve the ID she dropped. "She's an NHU legend though. *She* should be the school mascot."

"*That'd* be a vibe," I laughed. Why have Percy the Knight dance around the football field when you can have a gravelly old smoker? Put that on the school's homepage and watch admissions skyrocket.

"My friend Jax who worked here last year said everybody joked that she should get a throat stoma put in so she could smoke hands-free," Tylor went on.

I pressed two fingers to my Adam's apple. "*Stick it in my stoma, hun,*" I croaked.

 ## 2. POV: College isn't as scary as you thought so now you're just vibin'

September 8

Reading *The Poky Little Puppy* to a girl seems like the kind of thing you do if you want to sleep with her, so don't ask me how I found myself in Amanda and Simone's room doing just that. I like their room the best out of the ones I've seen so far—they both have loft beds with their desks or dressers underneath, and one wall is covered in fake ivy. I wish I knew that loft beds were a thing, because I'd be down to fuck with one. I wonder if you could get a race car bed for your room? I'd dick someone down in a race car bed.

Casually scanning the code on a flier for WXNU, NHU's radio station, might have been the best decision I've made here so far. I've been listening to it almost as much as my own music. It's a lot of dad rock, R&B, some stuff from that banjo phase ten years ago, a random old doo-wop song, and the occasional pop or country song, but sometimes it fucking *slaps*. I almost couldn't function when Neck Deep and Wavves played back-to-back. I didn't even *know* anybody else listened to Wavves. Songs you like hit different when you hear them on the radio, especially after being told your tastes are shitty. It makes my chest want to take off. It makes me feel like I *belong* here.

We finally made it to the 20th Century in History today. Despite the course being *about* the 20th Century, we spent the first few classes talking about the French Revolution, Napoleon, and the 19th Century, since their legacies set the stage for 1914, when the 20th Century really began—kind of like how Millennials say the 1990s didn't actually end until like 2004. After making a stink about how Britons are saying 'god save the king' for the first time in 70 years, Dr. de Conto asked what we thought the most important event of the last century was. The responses were more or less what you'd expect—I said World War I, which was really World War III if you know your shit—until the kid with the gauges hit her with "the invention of instant noodles."

de Conto gave him an unreadable look. "I probably would've agreed with you when I was in college too. Do you have a real answer for us?"

"That is my answer!" he insisted. "In 2000 they polled people in Tokyo about what they thought Japan's greatest invention of the century was, and instant noodles was the top response!"

I surprised myself by speaking up. "I actually heard that somewhere too."

"Yeah, they're right," somebody on their laptop said. "I just Googled it and there's an article that says *'Noodles Voted Japan's Best Invention.'*"

de Conto looked bemused. "Well then, I stand corrected."

As class let out, I turned to compliment Gauges on his noodles answer, only to find him inside my bubble and looking me dead in the eyes with a blank expression, pointing a finger gun into my gut. We stood like that until he snorted and cracked into a smile. "Thanks for covering me back there. I'm surprised anybody else knew that."

I shrugged. "I'm good at remembering useless things."

"You're in the right place then," he said. "I have a photogenic memory though, so I'm right there with you on the whole remembering-useless-things thing."

"Don't you mean you have a *photographic* memory?"

"*No*, I meant photogenic. It's called making a joke, dammit."

I kept the conversation going, not entirely put off by him. "So why are you taking a History class if you think it's useless?"

"Because it's an easy elective if you can remember useless things," he said as he adjusted his backpack straps. "People say we can learn from it, but I don't think we do. Like what could we have studied to prepare us for our current political climate, courtesy of the previous administration? We can read about how authoritarian regimes come to power all we want, but that doesn't do shit for us when we have to deal with one." *I sniff what he's smelling, and it smells good.* "I think our efforts would be better spent focusing on trying to fix the problems we have here and now, but that's just me."

"I gotcha," I nodded. "I thought about majoring in History, but ended up going with English because it can at least be inspiring. History just gets boring. Don't tell my dad that though—he's a history professor back home."

A pair of Ray-Ban Clubmasters unfolded themselves onto Gauges' face as we traded Shaver for sunlight. "That's pretty sweet. My dad's a curator at a museum, so I credit my interest in history to that. And *Axis & Allies*."

"No way!" I chuckled. "My dad taught me how to play that too! Are you into board games then?"

"I am *very much* into board games," he smiled. "My great aunt used to play games with me a lot when I was younger, but then she got Alzheimer's."

"I'm sorry. That sucks."

"Yeah. We kinda knew she wasn't doing well when we found her trying to power-wash her sidewalk with a water flosser."

I just bit my tongue, not sure if I was supposed to laugh or not.

"We would put a *Monopoly* board on a lazy Susan and she'd just sit there for hours, rolling dice and moving pieces around the board," Gauges went on. "And then towards the end, she'd watch game shows and just call out numbers." He shook his head. "The last thing she ever said was 42."

"I'm Trevor, by the way," was all I said after a moment.

"Kaden, but my friends call me Kade." *Kade it is then,* I thought as I bumped his fist. "I'm headed to Bixby," he said as he split for the Student Center. "I'll see you in class though!"

"Yeah, I'll see ya!" I caught sight of his urine-yellow t-shirt again before the building swallowed him, already looking forward to seeing him in class again.

September 9

Imagine the anguish when I discovered
That after all this time
I'm the monster I was taught to despise.

September 10

Pro tip: don't tell people which movies you haven't seen. I mentioned that I'd never seen *The Nightmare Before Christmas*, and Tylor and Elisha and Nikole and Steph and Rory—who I learned thinks Africa is a country—and like five other people sat me down to have an impromptu movie night with them, because *that's* how you get me to like something. Same goes for books. If I *have* to read something then I automatically don't want to.

I believe it was Confucius who said that waking up is the second-hardest thing in the morning. I attended to the first-hardest thing while thinking about being roommates with Dayton and one thing leading to another, until Tylor put a stop to it when he came back from a run with his face and clothes damp with sweat. I finished the job while he showered.

"We're probably gonna have to make a trip to the store soon," he said after he got out. "I'd say we go today, but the shuttle only runs at night on Saturdays."

"I can just drive us," I shrugged as I scrolled through Buzzfeed.

"You have a car here?"

I flicked my eyes over at him. "Yeah?"

"How did I not know you have a car?"

"I dunno, you never asked me if I had one?"

"Well in that case, would you be opposed to going to Walmart instead? It's a little farther, but we can get more stuff there."

"Nah, let's do it," I said, swinging myself out of bed to get dressed. Tylor looked like a total College Bro in his sweatshirt, shorts, Hey Dudes, and backwards hat.

"Why'd I picture you driving a Mini Cooper?" he asked as I unlocked the doors to my not-Mini Cooper.

"I don't know," I chuckled. "Why *did* you picture me driving one?"

"I dunno," he laughed. "They seem like the kind of car that a gay guy who's always in a hurry would drive—no offense."

"None taken," I half-lied as I connected my phone. *I guess I gotta start slowing down a little—I don't want people to think I'm that type of gay.*

The drive to Wally World reminded me how there's not enough money in the world you could pay me to live out in the sticks full-time. Tylor was amused to learn that I can be an angry driver when a truck with angry headlights and side mirrors as big as my forearms rode my ass before illegally passing me. At the store, we made sure we got a balanced selection from all the food groups essential for the college underclassmen—two cases of Dr. Pepper, a crate of PopTarts, microwave meals, a 48-pack of assorted bags of chips, a tray of mac and cheese cups so large it had to rest on top of the cart, and ramen noodles. "Did you know," I said like a know-it-all, "that instant noodles were voted the best Japanese invention of the last century?"

He raised an eyebrow. "Of course I knew that. My *ojiichan* said they were a game-changer."

I think the real reason why he wanted to go to the store was so he could get coffee beans, which he picks out like I pick out shoes. "I'm surprised you didn't go with the cheaper ones," I said to the packages he set in the cart.

"I always get fair trade beans when I can, even if they're more expensive."

"But aren't we supposed to be broke college students?"

"Yeah, but do you think that all the coffee that's produced in the world is harvested and packaged and everything by people who get *paid*? You don't think there's not any slave labor or child labor going into your coffee? Not necessarily *yours*, but coffee in general."

"That's valid," I said, feeling guilty for not being as socially-conscious as I like to think I am.

"Every dollar spent on fair trade is a dollar that doesn't go towards the violation of human rights." So that's how I got sold on buying only fair trade coffee from now on.

After checking out the office supplies and digging through the bargain bin for any good movies, we picked up some Christmas lights for the room. I wanted to get a lava lamp too but Tylor said it would get confiscated faster than "a virgin cock getting milked," so that didn't happen. "It's a good color for setting the mood," I smirked as I took three boxes of cerulean-blue lights.

Tylor leaned in. *"Oh dad."*

I snorted so loud that I embarrassed myself. "Did you just call me *dad?*"

"Shut up, mom," he said flatly.

We swung through the McDonald's drive-thru for breakfast to take back with us —I kept my *but what if they're out of what I want?* conversation to myself—which Tylor paid for since I drove. One burdensome trip to the room later, we opened the window to let in the breeze and let out the music. Tylor's already also introduced me to lo-fi, retrowave, city pop, vaporwave, and K-Pop that sounds way more hip-hop than K-Pop, but it was an easy chillhop morning.

"If this isn't nice, then what is?" I broke our silence with orange juice on my tongue and the sky on my eyes.

Tylor chewed on that while he chewed on his hash brown. "I like that."

"Kurt Vonnegut," I credited him. "He said that whenever you're feeling happy you should always acknowledge it." There aren't many things I live by, but that's one of them. There are people who are nothing but negative and then they wonder why it feels like life's always shitting on them.

September 11

September 11 was the day, well...

I actually forgot what day it was until we were walking back from breakfast and there was a row of people in front of Bixby taking turns reading names off their sheets of paper, and it hit me that they were the names of the victims. It hits different for me since I wasn't around for it, but people who were say it was the defining moment of the American spirit. People can't remember why they walked into a room or what day of the week it is, but ask them what they were doing that day, and they can tell you what they had for breakfast and what color shirt they had on. I couldn't imagine what it was like to be watching that unfold in real fucking time on TV. A New York icon impossibly being on fire, smoking cavities where smoking cavities have no right or reason to be? An airplane and its passengers ceasing to exist in an instant? Empty air that two skyscrapers used to occupy? I guess it was kind of the same as watching an attempted coup on the government of the United fucking States on January 6th—*this can't be happening*, and *nobody knows how this ends*.

People point to survivor stories as proof of god's existence, but I guess they forget about the fact that he let the whole fucking thing happen in the first place. Same goes for the Holocaust. I don't know how Christianity didn't die with the Third Reich once people found out what god had allowed to happen. Shit like that is why I'm done with any god that might be out there. Parents will pray that their kid's little league team will win their game—and what, the people trapped in those towers or being marched to their deaths weren't fucking praying? I'm not saying there for sure isn't a god out there—people who are adamant that there isn't a god are just as full of shit as the people who are adamant that there is—but if there is then he's a fucking prick, and I'm done with him.

September 12

I thought you and I were impossible,
Even though the stars taught me to never use that word.

September 13

POV:

The Quad. 12:37 p.m. Common Hour. It's 76 in the sun, but October in the shade. WXNU is playing in one ear while your other picks up the *clack-clack clack-clack* of skateboard wheels on the sidewalk, an olive-skinned girl who could be a model playing an acoustic guitar, the soft rhythmic *thud* of palms catching a football, a guy asking passersby why some animals are pets and others are food. People are traversing the space between trees not already claimed by a hammock on slacklines strung like tripwires. Others are performing a coordinated dance in front of a tripod to hip-hop music playing from a portable speaker with surprisingly good bass. Somebody is squinting into the sun, watching their drone zooming around overhead like a gnat. The grass collects people in pairs, trios, fours, their to-go lunches spread between them like open notebooks. A table outside is selling cake pops for a fundraiser, the pockmarked stick of one still clenched between your teeth.

Campus is abuzz with life, and you're just vibing in the middle of it all.

September 14

I was coming back from Zukoff with an orange chicken bowl served to me by a woman who looked like she'd seen an explosion and her face was stuck like that when I heard angry shouting coming from the Quad. A beet-red, heavy-set man wearing a shirt that said 'GOD HATES FAGS' was waving around a bible and spewing the most homophobic and transphobic shit I've ever heard in my life—and yes, that includes church and family gatherings and the people who I used to hang out with. A silent line of students, I guess from Proud As Halle, stood in the grass across the sidewalk from him, holding open different Pride flags like a wall to hold back the hate. One of the girls had tears streaming down her face. I don't know how people were able to just stand by and listen. I may not believe in god, but I sure wish there's a hell reserved for fucking pieces of shit like him. It's funny how people say their religion is a religion of love, but then they only ever preach hate and fear, and by 'find it funny' I mean 'it pisses me the fuck off.'

At least one person had had enough. Black Lives Matter Shirt Kid from the Computers class after mine was fucking *livid* as he shouted back at him. As much as I respect him now, I wish he wouldn't have engaged the fucker, because that's all that the piece of shit wanted. That's all that red hats and yard signs and flags on trucks are there for—to get you angry and then to hit you with 'fuck your feelings' when you try to say anything back. Refuse to indulge them and they lose their power. They think they're the silent majority? Fuck *off*. More like the loud minority—the indecent, loud minority. Like, where the fuck is the rapture when you need it? In my room, I ran with my emotions. I went on a diatribe with nobody. I inhaled my orange chicken without even tasting it. Then I was upset at myself because I fell right into his trap. One minute I'm saying 'don't indulge,' and then the next I was indulging.

"Did you see the guy in the Quad too?" Tylor asked when he got back. *Triggered.*

"Yes!" I yelled. "Who the fuck is he? Why the fuck is he here?"

"I don't know. He was here last year too."

"So what, he comes just to piss people off?" I yelled.

"I guess. I can't imagine what it feels like for you to have to hear that though," he said cautiously, making me soften up. "You shouldn't have to hear that kind of stuff and have to put up with people's hate."

My anger gave way to warmth. "People are just hateful sometimes," I said like hate hasn't ruined the world and the lives of real people in it. I'll never get why people willingly and eagerly choose hate again and again. Despite what some of my family says, hating hate is different from hating people for being themselves. Just because they're something different than you doesn't give you the right to tell them they're abominations and work to restrict their human rights. Hating *that* and trying to put a stop to *that* isn't just okay, it's necessary if we ever want to have equality with liberty and justice for all. No, it's not a double-standard. Go ahead and call me a freedom-hating libtard faggot or whatever you want. It's nothing I haven't heard before.

September 15

You know that meme of the guy sitting at a table with a sign that says 'something-something, change my mind?' I want to set up a table in the Quad that says 'getting a piece of popcorn out of your teeth feels better than orgasming, change my mind,' or 'the last song on an album hits different than the rest of them, change my mind,' just to meet other people who get it.

Dr. Gallagher really doesn't fuck around with the reading assignments she gives us—we're supposed to have *Heart of Darkness* read by next class. It's not a super long book, but still. I guess she thinks we don't have anything else to do.

I was today-years-old when I learned there's a student-run magazine on campus —*Crane*, which I found out about at work. Published in all black and white, and filled with artwork, poems, photography, reviews of foreign films and albums and books

I've never heard of, it was exactly the kind of thing I hoped to discover at school. But as I flipped through the pages, it just made me feel bad about myself because the writing is *way* better than anything I could ever do. And I gave the music in it a try, but I just couldn't get into it. Maybe my tastes *are* more mainstream than I thought? *This is for the* legit *artsy kids*, I thought as I left it on the table for somebody else to pick up.

I was also today-years-old when I learned what a walking taco is. I was leaving History with Kade—who now sits next to me, thanks to the kid who withdrew from the class—and there were some people selling them for a fundraiser. Another thing about college: there's *always* some kind of fundraiser going on. Just this past weekend there was some kind of all-night fundraiser for liver awareness or something. "Are you *shitting* me?" Kade said as he popped out his mouth guard to dig into one. "We used to have walking tacos all the time in school!"

"Well *excuse me*," I said as I thought about what other things I've been missing out on.

I stole glances at him while he gazed off across the Quad at something, admiring how snatched he looked with his sandy curls and the dark wooden plugs he replaced his other gauges with. "Can I pick your brain about something?" he asked me without looking at me. "And then after that can I pick your nose?"

I smirked. "Why not start with my nose and work your way up like the ancient Egyptians?"

He snorted into his Fritos bag. "I think I might like you, fam. But forreal though, why is it called 'the Quad' if it's not a quadrilateral and if there are more than four buildings?"

"Fuck if I know," I shrugged.

"See? That's exactly what I mean. Wake the fuck up, America."

I laughed through my nose as my eyes landed on his wrist. "So what's your tattoo? Is it an eleven?"

"It's an equals sign, you uncultured *swine*," he said as he showed it to me. *So is he really into math then?* "Like the equality symbol? Equal human rights?"

"Oh, okay!" I chuckled. "Yeah, I fuck with that." *I fuck with it hard.*

We finished our single-serve tacos and tossed our trash. "Do you play chess at all?" he asked.

"I have, but not in a while."

"Would you wanna play sometime?"

"Yeah, I guess I'd be down."

He unzipped his backpack and pulled out a flat wooden box with a polished chess board inlaid in the lid. "Would you be down *now*?" *Okay, so he just casually carries around a chess board with him.* So that's how we ended up sitting cross-legged with a chessboard between us on a shady bench by the gazebo, taking the carved stone pieces from the velvet-lined compartment inside the board. I wished he would've kept his sunglasses on so we'd look more like the kinds of avant-garde people I imagined I'd see at college—*oh yeah, because playing* chess *is so avant-garde*—but that just let me steal glimpses of his serpentine hazel eyes. Either he's really good at chess or I'm really bad at it or maybe both, but it wasn't a very long game. "*Šāh māt,*" he announced when his remaining rook put me in checkmate. "The king is dead."

I gathered up all four of his pieces I captured. "So what are you majoring in?"

"Art," he said, making more sense of his high-cuffed jeans and folded-down Converse tongues. "And in case you're wondering, yes, I plan on dying penniless in a gutter."

"Hey, I'm not judging!" I chuckled. "I'm an English major, remember? I'm used to hearing that I'm wasting my time too."

"True dat," he said as he laid down to stretch out in the grass. "So do you wanna teach it, or what?"

"I'm not sure what yet. I just like reading and writing stories and stuff."

"Oh forreal? That's cool. That's art."

"Like Oscar Wilde said, '*All art is quite useless.*'"

He looked up at me with a half-frown. "Explain."

My fingers found my stud. "Like, art isn't supposed to be functional. Isn't the point of it to inspire or provoke or rouse some kind of emotion?"

He let himself fall back to the ground. "*Sheesh* fam. Have I mentioned how I like you?" he said as he sat back up. *TFW you think you make friends with somebody, and not just because they live on your floor.*

"Like, I've read books without plots that have stuck with me after I finished with it."

"Same with movies or songs for me," he said. "There's so much art out there to experience."

"So what kind of music are you into?" I asked because I'm not a Film major.

He shrugged. "Different kinds of rock, mostly. I'll listen to most stuff unless it's country."

"Country sucks *ass*," I laughed.

"Country's fuckin' *titty*. But yeah, I'd say alternative and indie are my faves."

I leaned in and raised my eyebrows expectantly. "Oh? Such as?"

My enthusiasm tickled him. "I've been listening to this band called Hippo Campus a lot recently." *Art kid. Art kid 100%.*

"No fucking *way!* You like Hippo Campus?"

"Wait—you know Hippo Campus?"

I stood up on the bench. "I fucking *love* Hippo Campus! I didn't think anybody else liked them!"

38

He jumped up too. *"I didn't think anybody else liked them!"* he practically yelled. "Did we just become best friends?"

"I think so!"

"Do you have TikTok?" he asked.

"Nope."

"Twitter?"

"Not anymore."

His face fell. "Instagram?"

"Yeah!"

He held out his hand. "Gimme your phone." I opened the app and passed it to him. "Please don't tell me your handle is a reference to the alternative rock band Wallows."

I grinned. "It might be."

"I can't with you right now." He handed back my phone as he took out his own. I started scanning the profile on my screen when a notification popped up.

oakleydokey started following you.

September 16

They should make a survival reality show where they lock a bunch of people who don't know when to shut the fuck up in a room together and see how long it takes for one of them to crack. Not that *I'd* have the patience to watch it, but still. You could even make it into a sport and put bets on it.

Most of the stuff that WXNU plays is tasteless at best, and ass at worst. The only time it ever really slaps is during DJ Twinkle Toes' two-hour alternative/pop-punk/emo/indie mix on Monday, Wednesday, and Friday afternoons—which is to say that you'll probably see me bopping my head along while I'm at work. I don't know if he's a fan of *Anchorman* or not, but he ends every show with *"Thanks for stopping by, NHU."*

Football season is upon us, which means all the capital-S Straight guys will have hard-ons until that big football thing in February is over with. Even the skeletons in that house-on-Main-Street's front yard were stoked for it, gathering in black-and-yellow football jerseys on a beat-up couch in front of a TV right there in the grass. Maybe being gay has something to do with it, but I don't get how people can be such sports nerds. Why is it okay to be a nerd about sports but nothing else?

"Why is being able to name all the Presidents in order nerdy, but knowing all the stats of a football player isn't?" I asked at dinner when the conversation at the next table over got me just the right amount of annoyed.

Nikole stared at me until her mouth wasn't full. "Don't tell me you can name all the Presidents in order."

"Yeah? Didn't you ever take a U.S. History class?"

"I don't believe it. Prove it right now. Somebody pull up a list." The others crowded around Calvin's phone to check me. I was low-key worried somebody would cancel me when I got to number 45.

"...Clinton, Bush Jr., Obama, Fuckface, Biden." I held my breath. "I can also draw a map of the world from memory."

Tylor stared me down. "Fuckface has a name you know, and it's Shitbag."

"No," I smiled, "it's Fuckface."

Calvin startled everybody by jumping to his feet. "That's enough. I'm not gonna sit by and listen to you insult all the other shitbags out there by lumping them together with Asswipe."

"But what about all the asswipes you just insulted?" Tylor laughed.

"And that's the problem with this," Theo said, bringing order to the table. "You can't call him *anything* because it's insulting to those other things. That being said," he went on as he speared a hunk of roast beef with his fork, "I personally enjoy Fuckstick."

I choked on my Brisk. "Ooh, he's Fuckstick from now on!"

We dragged the former, disgraced, twice-impeached, twice-lost-the-popular-vote, scandal-ridden, insurrection-inducing, racist, xenophobic, homophobic, transphobic, misogynistic, lying, hate-appealing—did I forget anything?—demagogue rapist without caring who we upset. "God, I'm glad we were able to clear that up," Nikole grinned. "I don't think I'd be able to stay friends with any of you if you liked him."

"Yeah," Elisha chimed in, "I deadass thought I was gonna have to flip somebody off."

—————————————————

September 17

Living is like trying to catch running water—

40

September 18

I'm about to join the rest of the floor and start keeping our door shut too. All within a half hour of each other, a burly pair of guys asked if I was interested in joining the rugby team, and then Sunita asked if I was interested in getting involved with House Council, and *then* Kevin asked me in his deeper-than-the-Mariana-Trench voice if I had any condoms he could 'borrow.'

"Please don't give it back when you're done," I said as I handed him one.

"Can I actually get two?" he asked with a shit-eating grin when he saw that I had some to spare. *As long as I don't have to* hear *you using them.*

The rain from that hurricane is here and it's just been shitting all over everything. People were legit slipping and falling in the entrance of Patnick from the floor being so wet. I'm sure Paul would've been getting a kick out of watching them if she wasn't pissed over not being able to step outside for a cigarette every five minutes. I don't know how people down South can lose everything in a storm and rebuild their homes over and over. Like if I lost all my possessions even *once* I'd be out of there—not that I'd ever live in the South anyway. I love how people down there are all about small government until they get hit with a hurricane.

This weekend is Friends & Family Weekend, but I told Mom and Dad they didn't have to come down since I'll be back home in a few weeks for Fall Break. Tylor's mom isn't visiting either because it's just a freshman thing, but Kade's are. I brought myself to message him what his plans for the weekend were, and the eye-rolling emojis in his response told me that he didn't go away to college just to have his family come visit him. He and I have been sending bands and history memes—*"Axis powers HATE them, find out how these two countries switched to the winning side with one simple trick"*—and medieval art memes back and forth to each other. I haven't heard of most of the bands he likes, but they're actually pretty fucking fire. I have yet to send him one he hasn't heard of, though I did introduce him to chillhop. I had to stop myself from liking his Instagram post from two years ago of a yard sign for Fuckstick on fire because I didn't want him to know that I was creeping on his profile. The pic on his story of a peach captioned *"why this peach lookin dummy thicc??* 👀*"* was fair game though.

After a dinner of Chinese takeout from the place in town—which I won't be ordering from again unless I'm ever in the mood to pay $14 for five fried morsels of chicken and some rice to soak up my sauce-and-onion soup—Nikole broke out a game called *What Do You Meme?* that plays like *Cards Against Humanity* but is *way* funnier. We were laughing so hard that the RA on duty knocked to ask if everything was okay, and to nicely tell us to shut up or get written up. Put that on a t-shirt and sell it for a floor fundraiser.

September 19

It finally stopped raining after 36 literal hours and now it's just humid as all hell.

We have our first test in Physical Science on Wednesday, and Dr. Eubanks knocked at least three of us out of our seats when he told us it'll be open book and open note, which is how tests should be. Like, what architect is going to be designing a building and not reference anything?

The fliers plastered on windows and bulletin boards and sweaty foreheads all across campus advertising an Open Mic Night at a cafe in town persuaded me to go check it out. Tylor already had plans, but had nothing but good things to say about the coffee there. Calvin had to get some practice hours in, Nikole was working a shift at Gladby Hall's front desk, and I didn't know where Theo or Elisha were. I debated messaging Kade to see if he wanted to go, but didn't and ended up wishing that I had. So that's how I found myself making my way down Quincey Street—which I always pass on the way to Sheetz but have never explored—by myself, passing by an expensive-looking stationary store, an even more expensive-looking chocolate shop, and a wellness store advertising 'natural remedies' before coming upon Brew 22 and its cozy, Industrial, low-key hipster vibe. I got a cappuccino and wished that I hadn't just had Subway for dinner, because the pastries they had looked *divine*. I'll definitely be going back there to study though, because working on assignments in the local coffee shop is a vibe that I live for—or should I say 'attempt to study,' because of my ADHD. I let a group of girls take the other empty seats at my table, which just made me feel lonelier. Doesn't it suck how being in a room full of people can make you feel more isolated than being by yourself?

Spotlights replaced the overheads as somebody took the 'stage,' which was just a raised part of the floor with the tables and chairs pushed out of the way. She thanked us for coming out—the mic made that ear-splitting sound that mics make—and introduced the first act before letting a guy with an acoustic guitar pull a stool up to the mic. *If I wanted to hear somebody play Oasis then I would've gone to the Quad*, I thought just before he surprised me with a folk song. A girl with a biblical-sounding name read poetry that makes my few and feeble attempts at the craft laughable. Poets are like the jazz musicians of writers. Another guy sang and played a keyboard along to that one Niall Horan song that Madi likes that had the piano and vocals removed from it. I wasn't too crazy about the song, but the guy playing it was at *least* a nine. Some improv group did a skit that was pretty funny and made me jealous of people who have that kind of personality and talent. But the most memorable performance of the night was another guy with an acoustic guitar who had me tearing up when he started playing Neck Deep's "December." My breath caught in my throat, and all of a sudden it was June again, when no amount of music or alcohol or tears could stop the pain that Dillon caused me. *There had to have been somebody else. Why else would he end things so abruptly, and without even wanting to try? Was I really just that bad of a boyfriend?* It took everything in me to not break down right there in the coffee shop. It's funny how a single line from a song can destroy you, and by 'funny' I mean 'is it ever going to stop hurting?' The guy put so much emotion into it that I wonder if he'd just gone through a break-up himself. Because what better catalyst is there for passion than pain?

September 20

So I guess Shawn walked in on Rory having sex with one of his girl Dance major friends, and now I don't know what's real anymore.

I got an email telling me that I had a package waiting for me at the mail center—not the mail *room* right in Malik Hall, but the off-campus mail *center* across from Abernathy Classroom Building. Too curious to wait until Common Hour, I swung by before class to find a care package from Mom and Dad in lieu of them not coming for Friends & Family Weekend. It was mostly Christmas-stocking stuff—deodorant, gum —but also Kind granola bars, some boujee chocolate, and a package of Puerto Rican coffee that's so creamy it's like you're not even drinking coffee. Maybe I should start telling them there's a family thing every weekend.

"Come on, lemme see your package!" Kade said in a low voice after I swatted his hand away from it for the third time while we waited for class to start. *That's what the actress said to the bishop.*

"Oh, I'm *going* to. And then after that I'll show you what's inside the box."

"Ooohhh!" he fidgeted in his seat.

"It's just a care package from my parents," I said as I folded open the flaps. "Are you happy now?"

He fell back in his seat. "That's lame."

"Do you want a granola bar?"

He sat up. "Hell *yeah.*"

"Would you ever wanna go to the Open Mic Night they have at that coffee shop in town?" I asked as I passed him one. "I was gonna see if you wanted to go with me last night, but I didn't know if that was your vibe."

"Open Mic Nights are *absolutely* my vibe. And whaddaya mean *'last night?'* Isn't it tonight?"

"Nope," I shook my head. "Every third Monday."

"Goddammit, I was gonna ask you if *you* wanted to go!"

Brit Lit was so dry that there was nothing to keep me from daydreaming about Roman. *He asks me if I want to come over to his room to study together. We start making out instead. I lift his shirt off. I press myself against him while I nibble on his neck, my hands on his shoulders as I—oh fuck, Gallagher's looking right at me.*

I sat up straighter. "Could you repeat that please?"

She looked around the circle instead. "Sundar, could *you* please tell us what you think Kurtz means by *'the horror, the horror?'*"

September 21

So open book tests are actually *way* harder than you'd think. You spend so much time flipping through pages to find the right answer that all of a sudden the period's over and you only have like half of your bubbles filled in.

I had to cancel Anton because he said how being trans is a mental illness. And then when I tried to explain in nice words that he's a dumb fuck, he kept trying to tell me how *I* was wrong. I don't get why people who think differently than me are always trying to convince me that I'm wrong. Just do what I do—accept that somebody's views are horrible and steer clear of the subject. Just because we don't agree on things doesn't mean we have to make each other's journeys through this thing called life any harder for each other.

I made it to Lit Club last night since I didn't have any forms or trainings to do to distract me. I took my laptop, my poetry book, *Call Me By Your Name*, and the same still-blank notebook I took to our first floor meeting since I didn't know what to expect. *Will somebody be reciting Shakespeare? Will people be debating over the Oxford comma? Will it be poets smoking pot?* I'd never been in the old Student Union before, let alone the bowels of it, but I know a lot of groups use the rooms to meet. Seeing another human dispelled my worry that somebody forgot to lock a door and I wasn't supposed to be there. I followed the trail of room numbers to the one in Ashton's email, which had a sheet of lined paper with 'LITERATURE CLUB' Sharpied on it taped to the door. *But what if it's the wrong Lit Club?* I thought as I walked into a mix of everything I was expecting it to be: a few people sat together with copies of *Catch-22*, a girl passionately read something to her friend, and others were writing in notebooks or typing on their laptops.

Ashton came over to greet me like he'd been waiting for me to show up. "Hey, welcome!"

"Hi. Sorry I missed the last one," I felt the need to apologize.

"No worries! We don't have an agenda or anything, so grab a muffin and some coffee and get comfortable!" he gestured into the room.

"Will do," I smiled. "Thanks Ashton."

"I'm sorry, what's your name again?" he winced like I was about to hit him.

"Trevor."

A girl facing away from me on the couch turned at the mention of my name, and my face split into a grin when I saw it was Nikole. I figured something like Lit Club would be below her, even if she is an English major. I took a muffin with nuts in it—*insert joke about nuts in my mouth here*—over to the space Nikole made for me. "Excuse me, but is this seat taken?"

"It is now," she smiled.

I set my backpack on the floor and nodded at the guy who broke my scale in a nearby armchair with his own Mac. He's so hot that he's like a statue that the ancient Greeks or Nazis built in celebration of the Caucasian male figure that came to life and decided to join a Literature Club. "I didn't think I'd know anybody here," I said as I took a crumbly bite. "Were you here last week?"

She shook her head with a flat smile. "Nah, I was on desk duty."

"Oh okay. I wonder if Theo—"

"Hold that thought," she shushed me as the room fell silent. "Stool," she nodded. A girl with half of her head buzzed right down the middle stood on top of a low, plastic step stool, commanding everyone's attention as she read a poem from a small paperback book with perfect inflection. Everybody clapped when she finished. "Whenever somebody gets on The Stool, you stop what you're doing and give them your attention," Nikole explained.

"What if everybody takes turns getting up on The Stool? Does nothing else happen then?"

She shrugged. "I guess not. Also, is that a bible?" She nodded to my book of poems I took out of my bag.

"What? Oh *hell* no." I *guess* I can see how somebody can mistake a plain black journal for the most damaging book in human history.

"I was gonna say," Nikole breathed.

"No, it's my book of poems," I chuckled as I opened it to show her. "I collect them. It's actually kinda embarrassing."

"I've never heard of anybody *collecting* poems."

"Yeah, I'd print out ones I liked, or tear them out of any books my school or library was getting rid of," I lied as I handed it to her. "Back when I used to have a stick up my ass."

Greek Statue Guy laughed through his nose.

"Do you write your own poems?" she asked as she leafed through the pages.

"No. Well yeah, but not in there. I'm not any good at it."

"I'm sure you are! You're a Vonnegut fan, right? Didn't he say something about how rewarding it is to create something even if it's not any good? And Mr. Rogers too?"

"Probably," I said, knowing full-well that he did.

"I'm going to the bathroom," she said, gathering her trash as she got up. "Start writing me a poem while I'm gone. A haiku. Make it about frogs."

I tried to concentrate on the task at hand, but got distracted by a nearby conversation about how *Scooby-Doo* is a more believable detective story than *Sherlock Holmes*, and then again by somebody talking to a guy who I assumed was a professor from the way he dressed how I expected professors to dress before I encountered them out in the wild. "You're looking very dapper today, Marvin," they complimented him.

Marvin, in his matching gray vest and pants, folded his hands behind his head. "Formal attire used to be a part of higher academia, and I feel like that's gotten lost over the years." *Talk about having a fucking stick up your ass.*

"I like your pins."

I looked around to see Greek Statue Guy looking up at me with a half-smile. "Your pins on your bag. I like them." I glanced down at them. *Which ones? "You Will Be Found?" Michelangelo's David blowing bubblegum? "Normality is a paved road where no flowers grow?" "I Don't Want to Talk?"*

"Oh, thanks," I said awkwardly. "I'm Trevor, by the way."

"I'm Miles. It's nice to meet you."

"Yeah, you too." The sleeves of his paisley t-shirt were full of his arms. "So, do you come here often?" *Way to not be cringe, Trevor.*

"This is my second time here this year, so I'd say two times out of two is often, wouldn't you?"

I didn't know what to say without sounding like I was flirting, so I was glad to hear Nikole clear her throat. "Do I need to leave you two alone?" *Oh please do.* "You haven't written anything yet!" she said to my blank page.

I fought to not blush. "I was talking to Miles!"

Five minutes later, I had not one, but two haikus about frogs. I was two words into the first when Nikole interrupted me to tell me to get up and read them from The Stool. "Nuh uh!" I protested. I wasn't about to read some amateur poetry in front of a room of people, regardless of what Kurt Vonnegut or Mr. Rogers said. "These are just for you!"

Miles raised an eyebrow. "I don't get to hear them?"

"No—I mean, yeah."

46

"Get up on The Stool," Nikole insisted.

"I am *not* getting up there," I growled.

"*Fine,*" she relented. "As you were."

I read my hastily-written poems for an audience of two.

"See?" Nikole said. "Those were good!"

"*I* liked them," Miles agreed.

The three of us sat around and talked until the group wrapped up. Nikole's a fan of Sylvia Plath and some other names I didn't recognize. Miles is all about feminist writers. They were both surprised to hear that Amanda Gorman is my favorite poet at the moment. "Really? I would've pegged you for a capital-R Romantic," Nikole said as her eyes landed on my poetry book.

"I mean, I think poetry that's pertinent to people's struggles today is more important." I enjoy Romantic poetry as much as the next English nerd, but white guys from 200 years ago talking about heterosexual love gets pretty boring.

By the time I was climbing the steps back up to the old Union's ground floor, I was already looking forward to the next meeting, which Miles had more than a little to do with. I pulled up Ashton's email to the group to see if I could find his last name, scouring all the M's on Instagram until I found Miles Barrington's strawberry-blond hair. I was upset that his account is private, but his bio perked me up. *'NHU '24. HOMO sapien just enjoying life* 🏞️📚🎭🎵'. My eyes widened. *Gay. HE'S GAY.* I swallowed. *Did he like what he saw? I wonder if he's seeing anybody? Did he think the poetry book was too dorky?* I'm going to wait to request to follow him after the next meeting, once I've gotten to know him a little better. *I don't wanna look like a creep,* I thought as I contemplated logging back on to my old social media accounts so I could stalk him.

September 22

So I guess Steven didn't know we were having room checks and left his weed grinder sitting out. Long story short, Krish has the room to himself for now.

I have yet to see if what Tylor said about going through all four seasons in one day here is true, but they sure are punctual. The first day of Fall saw a high of 63 and sorrowful clouds that swirled as they rode the breeze.

Kade wanted to hit up Zukoff after class for a gyro, which I'd never had before, but *had* to try after he said they're like tacos but better. "Are you doing anything until your next class?" he asked me after we paid. "We can go back to my room to eat and hang out if you want." I swallowed. *Is he hoping this goes where I hope it's going?* My chest ballooned with possibilities as I raced up Axworthy Hall's stairwell after him.

"Victor should be back by now too," he said as he swiped his ID at 239's door. *So that wasn't what he had in mind, unless his thoughts are even dirtier than mine.*

I just nodded. "Why'd you take your names down off your door?" Theirs was the only one that didn't have any construction-paper jungle animal silhouettes on them—but to be fair, the door that was totally covered in Post-It notes might not have had any on it either.

"Because I don't want my enemies to know where to find me," he said like it was obvious.

I know that all the suite rooms aren't the same, but I was still surprised to step into a wide, windowless antechamber of sorts—like they made the little entryway I have here in 222 Swafford into its own room. The sink and kitchenette took up a whole wall, and a table with two chairs sat off to the side. One open door led to the bathroom, and music spilled out of another. "Victor, we have company!" Kade called as he kicked off his shoes.

It's funny—just yesterday I was thinking about how I hadn't seen Black Lives Matter Shirt Kid waiting outside of Computers for a few days, the one who had a shouting match with the homophobe in the Quad. Fucking take a guess who Kade's roommate is.

"You're bringing another boy back to the room already?" his roommate smiled from his doorway with crossed arms in a 'DON'T SAY PRAY' shirt. *Boy? Another?*

"It was just *Will!*" Kade said with a flushed face as he pulled out a chair. "I asked one of our floormates if they wanted to play Switch since it was Saturday night and he didn't have anything to do," he explained himself to me.

"Is that what you kids call it these days?" his roommate asked as he bounced his eyebrows behind the frames of his square black glasses.

"You have Computers on Monday, Wednesday, and Friday right?" I asked him. "I think I'm in the class right before you."

"With Padar? Sure am."

"That class is kind of a waste of time," I chuckled. "Like, I'm in college now, I *know* how to use Word and Excel."

"*Kind* of? It's a fucking *joke.* She must think so too, because she fell asleep while I was giving my presentation."

"*Forreal?*"

"No cap. I still got an A on it though. Did you have to give yours yet?"

"Not yet. I'm Trevor, by the way."

He threw up his chin at me. "Victor. He/him." *Every time I see this kid I'm respecting him more and more.*

"Oh yeah, he/him for me too."

Victor turned to our food. "What'd you guys get? And why didn't you bring me any?" he asked Kade.

Kade held a hand up in front of his mouth. "Gyros, and because you didn't text me back."

"I did too!"

"Yeah, when we were back in the building!"

"Whatevs. I'll leave you two to go at it. Can I get you something to drink, Trevor? Since Kade's being a shitty host."

"Go eat a shit," Kade said as he gave him the finger. "Trevor, my dear companion and guest in our home, I'm going to make myself some tea. Would you care for some?"

"Yeah, sure."

I eroded my gyro—which was good, but not I'd-pick-one-over-a-taco good—while Kade dug around in a cabinet. They have an electric kettle too, but I didn't see a French press. A mess of Vans and Crocs and Converses and Nikes and New Balances sat either on a rack or on the floor by the door. "How about this?" Kade asked me as he held out an open tin. "Moroccan mint."

"It smells good. But doesn't tea come in bags?"

He laughed through his nose. "You have *a lot* to learn, sis."

He opened the door to his bedroom, which he doesn't keep locked. "It must be nice to have your own space," I said to Kade as I followed him in.

"Yeah. I like having my privacy if I need it."

"He means masturbating," Victor's voice called over. They're tight on a level that makes Tylor and I look like just acquaintances. As much as I like what he and I have going on, I'm envious of being able to, as Victor put it, "bring boys back to the room" whenever I want. *If that ever even happens.*

I expected there to be paints and sketchbooks strewn all over Kade's room, but he keeps it pretty tidy. He set down his bag before going back to prepare the tea. He has his bookcase on the floor under the window with some succulents potted in the cut-off bottoms of plastic bottles. The only books he has other than textbooks are about calmness and mindfulness and a couple adult coloring books. He has a few board games too that I've only ever seen in Barnes & Noble, aside from *Monopoly*. "No way—I have that same poster too," I chuckled at his 'Welcome to the Party' poster tacked up next to a print of something that could only be by Dalí. "Except I didn't give my leftist leaders googly eyes."

"*Everything* is better with googly eyes," he grinned.

He put on *Schitt's Creek* while we sipped our tea, which was a perfect complement to the rainy day. I wish I could've stayed since the show was sending me, but I had to run back to my room to get my stuff for Brit Lit. *I hope he isn't busy with plans this weekend,* I thought as I left their building, *because I'm totally asking him if he wants to hang.*

September 23

I snuck glances at you, my forbidden fruit,
And your eyes catching me in the act made
Me panic, but oh, did it thrill me
To find them smiling back at me.
If only you could've felt my heart throbbing,
You would've known that even then
You were always the best part of my day.
I had no reason to bump into you, but
I found reasons, I made up reasons, just to
Confirm over and over that I was undeniably smitten.
To everyone else at that party our quick kiss
Was nothing more than a drunken dare,
But a fireworks show was going off in my chest.
We left together, running down the street—
Laughing, tripping over ourselves—
Our hands resting on each other's shoulders a little too long
To be just friends anymore.

September 24

I've gotta say, I am *high-key* fucking with all the specials Patnick's been having for Hispanic Heritage Month. I was skeptical at first because I figured it would just be lettuce-and-cheese tacos, but even the tacos exceeded my expectations. Like did they bring in *real* chefs or what? And if so, can we keep them?

Yesterday after/between classes, Theo, Nikole, and I hit up Main Street to check out the Oktoberfest thing the town was having, which was as exciting as you'd expect any Fall festival in a small town to be. Since we weren't able to drink, and weren't interested in joining the German Club or whatever other local white supremacist groups had a booth set up in the parking lot, there wasn't a whole hell of a lot to check out otherwise—though there *was* a fundraiser that some organization was having where you could pay $2 to take a swing at an old, beat-up car with a sledgehammer, which was actually pretty cathartic. And I was hella thrilled when we stumbled across Kade and Victor and a bumpy pumpkin sitting on a megalith of a rock in the grass on the very corner of campus, dipping torn-off hunks of a pretzel into cups of cheese and mustard.

"What it do!" Victor greeted me with a grin.

"What it do," I smiled back. "This is a little lamer than I thought it'd be, not gonna lie."

"Yeah, it's pretty mid," Victor shrugged. "The plant bratwursts actually *aren't* too bad though."

"No?" Theo asked. "I was thinking about getting one. Are they a decent size?"

"They're like...bratwurst size?"

"Like, how are they in terms of girth?" Theo asked, making Nikole and me snicker.

Victor raised an eyebrow. "The same as the regular bratwursts I guess? I dunno."

"German sausage jokes are the wurst," Nikole said, making the rest of us groan.

"I didn't see you outside of Computers today," I said to Victor to distract myself from the thought of dicks and girths.

"*Oh,*" he chuckled. "Yeah, I broke my streak I had going for the number of times I showed up to it."

"How long was your streak?"

"Three times. I'm Victor, by the way," he said to Theo and Nikole. "He/him."

"Kade," Kade said. "Or Kaden, if you must."

Nikole and Theo told them their names and their preferred pronouns. "I like your gourd," Nikole said to Victor. "Oh god, that's not what I meant!" she said, trying not to giggle. "I like your *pumpkin!*"

Victor went red, looking like it was taking everything for him not to bust out laughing. "Thanks, it's for the room."

"You didn't want one for your room?" I managed to say to Kade.

"They didn't have any more of the curvy ones," he shrugged.

"*He just wanted to get one to stick up his butt,*" Victor said from behind his hand.

Kade gestured at the pumpkin with a pretzel nub. "You can't hit the P-spot with one like *that!*"

"Anything can be a dildo if you're brave enough," Victor simply said.

Instead of asking what other kinky shit they do, I just asked "I wonder why they don't have the Oktoberfest thing *in* October?" instead.

"*Because,*" Kade answered, "Oktoberfest is the two weeks leading *up* to October, you ignorant swine."

"Yeah, do you even know anything?" Theo razzed me.

"Apparently *not,*" I laughed. "What are you guys doing after this?"

"I'm gonna go back and roll some blunts," Kade said without skipping a beat. "That was a joke. Why, you tryna smash?" *Would you be offended if I said yeah?*

"Nah, we're probably gonna play *Cards Against Humanity* or *What Do You Meme?* or something later on, if you're into that kind of stuff." I looked around at Nikole and Theo, who nodded noncommittally.

Kade stared at me like he was trying to read my mind. "Are you inviting us to play?"

"Yeah?"

"Does the pope shit on little boys?"

Nikole and Theo and I traded looks.

"Yes," Victor translated. "The answer is yes we wanna play."

"Oh, okay," I chuckled. "I'll let you know what's up later."

"*Perf.*" Kade stretched out his legs. "Can I bring my better half?"

"Yeah, go for it," I said, a little bummed. "You're welcome to bring your better half too, if you have one," I said to Victor.

"Oh, I do," he grinned. "And just to be clear, we didn't mean the current pope—he's pretty chill as far as popes go. We just meant the pope in general. What's it called?" he asked Kade, who just squinted at him.

"The *papacy?*"

"Yeah, that!"

So that's how I got to spend a Friday night with Kade—and no, not like that.

Their better halves had me curious since I just assumed Kade was single, but I was disappointed and confused to see only Victor with him when he got to Swafford. "Are your better halves coming over later?" I asked as I signed them in.

"Oh, I just meant Victor," Kade said.

I turned to his better half. "What about you?"

"I meant Kade," Victor said as he walked on the balls of his feet. "Although he *wishes* I was his better—now who the fuck did that?" He took a step back to flip the light switch off in the empty laundry room.

"You basically *are* my better half," Kade said. *I am* all *kinds of confused right now.*

The romantically-ambiguous roommates followed me into 215 Swafford, which is basically just Theo's room at this point, thanks to Calvin's classes, his practice hours, frat stuff, and randomly saying he's 'going for a walk' without any explanation. Theo said sometimes Calvin will be gone before he wakes up and won't get back until like 8 at night. I guess the joke among Music majors is that the school should just put beds in Richter Music Hall and turn it into a dorm. "Ah, Green Day," Victor said to the *American Idiot* poster on the wall after he kicked off his checkered slip-on Vans and told everyone his pronouns. "Would the contemporary alternative music scene even exist without them? Good looks, Trevor."

"Oh, this isn't my room."

He spun on me. "What? Why aren't we in your room?"

"Because Theo's the one with the cards. And we're already here."

"And here I was preparing compliments for nothing—no offense, to whoever's room this is." Theo put his hand up.

"Do you mind if I use your bathroom?" Kade asked the room's resident.

"I actually *do* mind," Theo smirked. "You have to go piss out in the hallway."

"Oh," Kade chuckled, "it ain't piss."

The two of them managed to make the game even funnier than it already is. Victor read the cards like an announcer and Kade—who actually has kind of an ugly laugh when he really gets going—read them like questions, like "Did Michael Jackson, in his final moments, think about a gassy antelope?" or "Did Michael Jackson, in his final moments, think about Michael Jackson?"

"We don't have any plans for tomorrow," Kade said when I walked them out hours later. "Just throwing that out there." He looked to Victor, who nodded. *Wow, they might actually like me,* I thought as I felt myself smile.

September 25

I got to enjoy creamy Puerto Rican coffee in the nude this morning while Tylor was out with his new running buddy—until he came back earlier than I expected and caught a glimpse of my bare ass in 4K before I could jump into my closet. It's gray and rainy, which is the perfect weather for tea and reheated pizza.

"How late did *you* stay up?" Victor asked me when the three of us met up for breakfast yesterday morning.

"Like 12:30-ish," I answered. "Why?"

"You look tired. Did you not sleep well?"

"I *always* don't sleep well," I said, self-conscious of the dark spots under my eyes all over again. "It's been that way for as long as I can remember. I guess I always just have stuff on my mind."

"Right there with you, fam," Kade said.

"I can give you some tips for things I do to help myself relax when I'm in bed, if you want," Victor offered.

Kade laughed through his nose. "I'm sure he already knows how to masturbate."

Victor shot him a look. "I meant for when I practice lucid dreaming!"

"That could be fun," I said genuinely.

"Yeah. My goal is to eventually astral project, but that might take some work."

"And I have some herbal tea you can try out too to see if it helps," Kade offered. "That and the sound of a nice trombone puts baby *right* to sleep."

I stared at him.

"Jazz. I put on jazz to help me relax."

"Oh, I gotcha," I laughed. "Yeah, I think I'll take you up on all of the above. Thanks."

I learned that for as dubious as Patnick food is, they can serve up some pretty clutch omelets. I've had one before that was pretty mid, but the weekend chefs are the ones who know what's up. I sat down with my waffle—that I made *myself*—only to have Victor grab my arm and literally pull me out of my seat, which I didn't appreciate. Kade was already power walking towards the omelet station, where students of all walks of life were rapidly forming a line even though the station wouldn't start serving for another 10 minutes. "Last week I waited for like 40 minutes for one," Victor told me as we stood in line. "But *goddammit* are they worth it."

My waffle sat cold and forgotten by the time I returned to it with my ham and mushroom omelet. "Trevor Bentley Huffman, this is the *fluffiest* omelet I've ever had in my life, no contest."

"Did you just talk to yourself in the third person?" Kade asked leerily with a mouthful of his own omelet.

"Do you have multiple personalities?" Victor asked.

My hand found the back of my neck. "Oh, no, I say that instead of saying 'to be honest.'"

It was their turn to stare.

"My initials are TBH, so I like to say my name instead of 'to be honest,'" I said, realizing how stupid it sounds when I have to explain it. "It's just a thing I do sometimes. It's dumb."

"I like it," Kade said. "It's cool. It's original." *Dear diary, today Kade said that something I do is cool.*

"Yeah, ditto," Victor added. "You shouldn't worry about other people thinking what you do is uncool. You do you. We all have our weird things."

"Sometimes, when I'm home alone—" Kade started to say.

"Oh Jesus *Christ*," Victor laughed.

"—I like to get naked, roll around in cheese powder, and pretend I'm a Cheeto."

Since it was a sunny day, we made our way around campus to walk off our breakfast. "You up for a walk to the top of the hill?" he asked me, pointing ahead to the tent in the pants of the Earth behind Bamberger Stadium. "It's kind of a hike, but the view's pretty killer."

I marched onwards. "Well then, *allons-y.*"

Victor lit up. *"Ah, je ne savais pas que tu parlais français!"* he exclaimed, startling me. *"Combien d'années as-tu étudié?"*

"Uh…"

His smile faltered. *"Pas beaucoup?"*

"Yeah—I mean, *oui, pas beaucoup.*"

"That's still cool. Did you take it in school?"

"Ask me how many other languages I know," Kade said before I could answer.

"How many other languages do you know?"

"Fuck *none.*"

Victor wasn't kidding about it being a hike, but he wasn't kidding about the view either—you could see almost all of campus from the top. I picked out my open window among the jutting dorms, imagining whatever music Tylor had on cascading out and down the side of the building. Campus lay sprawled out like a geometry problem—students traveled like ants along line segments from point to point, veering off into green planes. The marching band sidestepped patterns across their field, barely audible. Down on the football field, members of the Color Guard moved in sync. Old Main stood higher than the trees, though it was dwarfed by the radio tower and the water tower on their own hills. I traced the stream between parking lots and under the bridge to the pond, which flashed the sun in our eyes. The woods stretched on and on, dipping down into the valley before undulating back up in a seemingly endless expanse.

We went back to 239 Axworthy—their whiteboard had *"Geology rocks but geography's where it's at"* scrawled on it in Kade's messy handwriting—where I got to see Victor's room. His window is the one with the Progress flag in it that I pass by every day. My eyes traveled from the framed pictures of Ruth Bader Ginsberg and Marsha P. Johnson—rest their souls—to the ubiquitous Ramones poster, to a stuffed animal shark on his bed, to the pumpkin he'd gotten the day before with black lines and triangles painted on it, to a collection of hats hanging on his closet door, to an electronic drum set that took up most of the rest of his space like some kind of gravity-defying mobile.

"You play the drums?" I asked.

He crossed his arms. "Yeah, but not with a band anymore." *I guess that explains why he's always tapping on things.* "I just play along to songs or jam with Kade sometimes."

I spun on Kade. "What do *you* play?"

"Bass," he said like it's nothing.

"*Shit,*" I muttered.

"You wanna play around on them?" Victor smirked, reading my thoughts.

I awkwardly sat on his stool and took the chipped pair of sticks he handed me. "What do I do?"

"Try doing this..." He stood beside me and held my wrists, guiding them as he gave me a crash course in toms and hi-hats and *1-and-2-and-3-and-4-and,* letting me go once he got me going.

"I'm doing it!" I said. I couldn't believe what my own limbs were doing—it was like he'd turned a key in my back and I couldn't stop. "That was fun!" I said once the gears inside me eventually petered out.

"That was actually really good for your first time," he almost frowned.

We switched spots so he could show off. He took the beat I played, but added more and more to it until it was something else entirely, moving faster with erratic precision until he was downright assaulting them. I gave up on trying to follow his movements. *This guy's a fucking machine.* He came to a rest with a fizzling *tsssssssss.* I didn't even realize my mouth was open. "Holy *shit.*"

"Thanks," he said.

"You said you were in a band?"

"Yeah, just a garage band," he said as he spun a stick like a propeller. "With Kade and our other friend from school."

"Hold up—you and Kade knew each other before coming here?"

"Yeah?"

"That's cool!" *They make a hell of a lot more sense now.* "Did you guys play your own songs?"

"Oh god no, we just played covers." He opened his Mac with a Biden-Harris sticker and an NPR sticker and a 'FUCK WAR' sticker on it to show me their YouTube channel. I scrolled past stills of the two or three of them—sometimes masked on opposite sides of a garage—playing Led Zeppelin, Red Hot Chili Peppers, The Who, Rage Against the Machine, Weezer, old Fall Out Boy, Neck Deep. He told me their band name was Rimjob Fairytales but they had to change it if they wanted to play in their school's Battle of the Bands, so they renamed themselves Soviet Onion. I tapped on a cover of *Dookie*-era Green Day, low-key surprised to hear that Kade can actually sing pretty well.

My eyes kept flicking from his Mac screen to the half-hidden tattoo just above his right knee. "What's your tattoo of, if I may?"

"You may." He pulled back the leg of his shorts so I could see the whole thing—lightning splitting apart a rook of a tower in flames. "It's The Tower."

"Oh, like from *Harry Potter?*" I perked up. "You know, the lightning-struck tower from *The Half-Blood Prince?*"

"This is the *OG* lightning-struck tower," he chuckled.

I waited for him to go on.

"The Major Arcana?"

I just kept on staring.

"Tarot cards?"

"Oh, okay," I said like I knew exactly what he was talking about.

"Here, lemme show you," he said as he reached over to take a small box from his shelf. He slid the cards—twice the size of regular playing cards—into his hand and fanned through them. "The Tower," he said as he produced it. *Much ominous.* "Symbolizing disruption and upheaval that are often seen as traumatic, it also represents change, fresh starts, and moving forward. I think everybody has some sort of Tower moment in their lives." *You don't even fucking know,* I almost said out loud.

"Do you know what all the cards mean?" I asked instead.

"Pretty much. Want me to do a reading for you?"

"As long as Death doesn't come up," I chuckled uneasily.

"No promises, although it's all in how you see it," he said as he gave them a shuffle. "Okay, try to think of something that's on your mind about the upcoming week. You don't need to say it out loud."

Like a birthday wish, I thought as I racked my brain. *It's not Fall Break just yet. There's Homecoming, but I don't care about that. Why do I feel like September 26th is —oh, that's right.* "Okay, I have something."

Death didn't come up, but according to the cards he flipped, I've reached a plateau and should reevaluate my current circumstances to find the way forward. "So kind of like The Tower a little?" I asked. "Like a fresh start?"

"Kinda, but without the calamity."

"Good." *Because I don't know if I could handle another Tower moment.*

I brought the two of them back to hang in 222 Swafford, which sure felt like a suite after being in their monk's cells, even with their antechamber. "Sheesh fam, peep that PS5!" Victor said to it like it was the Rosetta Stone.

"That would be Tylor's," I said. "Do you guys wanna go play pool or air hockey or something until he gets back?"

"I'll fuck up a pool table," Kade answered for them.

I opened my closet to trade my shoes for my slides. "Is that a *longboard?*" Victor asked as he caught a glimpse of it.

"Sure is."

"That's cool as shit. I used to have a mini one, but one of the trucks snapped off."

"That sucks. Do you ride, Kade?"

"Did you just ask me if I ride Kade?" Victor asked slowly while Kade cracked up. *Well* there's *an image.*

"No, I meant if you longboard!" I blushed.

"No *way,*" Kade chuckled. "Self-preservation, fam. I tried it *one* time and tore up my knee real bad. And I think I'm gonna need to take a shit before we go play."

I traded my ID for a pair of cues and a tray of balls with the desk attendant—DA for short—before leading them to the rec room. A game show called *Catch It Or Wear It* was playing on the TV, in which contestants get foam plates of food—saucy spaghetti, globby jelly sandwiches, mashed potatoes, you name it—thrown at them. If they don't catch it, then they end up wearing it. I couldn't make this shit up if I wanted to. And Kade wasn't kidding about fucking up the pool table, because he won every game he played. I Shazammed like every other song that played from Victor's phone, fucking particularly hard with The Wonder Years and Brand New.

Tylor was back in 222 Swafford by the time we returned. "So you're the Kade I've heard so much about," he said as he bumped fists with him.

My fingers played with my stud. "I might've mentioned you once or twice."

"*Only* once or twice?" Kade frowned.

"Do you go on runs?" Victor asked Tylor with a furrow of his brow after telling him his pronouns.

"Yeah. Why, do I look like a runner?"

"I feel like I've seen you before when I've gone on runs."

Tylor squinted at him. "You know what? I *have* seen you before a few times."

"Are you gonna go out tomorrow? I'd be up for going together."

"Let's do *iiiiit*," Tylor said. *Wow, I wish I could make friends that fucking fast.*

I caved and finally created a Domino's account, because I'm already over entering my info over and over and over. "Woah, pineapple?" Kade said when he saw what I was getting on my pizza.

"Yeah. What's wrong with pineapple?"

"Nothing! I just feel like pineapple on pizza gets extra shit, so I like it when I see it happen. It's like, the appeal of pizza is that it's a blank canvas. People can put whatever the fuck toppings they want on it." *I like my boys the way I like my pizzas —topped.* "That being said, I *will* judge you if you get anchovies on yours. Silently, of course."

Victor helped me carry the food and the pop up once it got delivered, where we walked in on Tylor and Kade bonding over their parents' lukewarm enthusiasm about them going into the arts instead of something more lucrative. "Do you remember that old meme of the overly-expectant Asian father?" Tylor asked him. "That was *literally* my dad. He always said that I should study finance."

"What'd he say when you said you were majoring in Photography?" Kade asked as he picked some fuzz off his sock.

"Photography's actually just my minor—I'm majoring in Journalism. And he left us years ago, so I couldn't tell you."

"Oh *shit.*"

"Yeah, it was hard for us for a while, especially with my sister having special needs. But my mom did it though, god bless her." He steepled his hands together. "She wasn't a fan about me going to a liberal arts school at first, but then she said one day it hit her that anybody can learn finance but not everybody is artistically inclined. The joke's on both my parents though—I'm secretly an accountant for the yakuza on the side." So that's how Tylor became The Yakuza's Accountant in my phone.

Nobody had a problem with throwing on *Anchorman*, even if Tylor and I had just watched it last week. "Quite possibly one of the best movies of all time," Kade said, "even with its misogynistic overtones."

"Yeah, but then it shits all over them," Victor pointed out.

The two of them must've seen it a hundred times. They were like those people who go see *The Rocky Horror Picture Show* in some dollar theater and get real into it —they knew *every* line, sang along to "Afternoon Delight," and jumped in the air with the team when they went to get new suits. I kept the door open so anybody going by would see that I had friends. Theo even popped in and watched it with us for a while.

Kade and Victor hung around for a while after the movie before leaving with their share of the pies. "We gotta start hanging out more," Victor said. "All four of us. Can somebody scissor me?"

Tylor and I each bit back a laugh. "Wait, *what* did you say?"

"He wants a pair of scissors," Kade explained.

"For what?"

"I like to cut the ring off of the necks of plastic bottles so some animal doesn't get stuck in it once it inevitably ends up in the ocean or wherever," Victor said.

"That's...admirable," I said as I slid open my desk drawer.

Victor's fiery red hair made him easy to find on Instagram. His first post is of him and Kade and somebody's parents all masked up at a protest after George Floyd's murder. I created a group chat between me, hayashi_photography, oakleydokey, and morozov_cocktail, thinking *is this how squads start?*

———————————————————

September 26

A.S. (antescript, because P.S. is overdone)—"Blink" by The Nicholas

Dear Dillon,

I'm not sure if it's only been a year or if it's already been a year since we spent the entire day texting back and forth the day after our first kiss the night before. Either way, I came *this* close to creeping on your Instagram, but I was too afraid of what I'd see to type out your name.

When does it ever stop? *Does* it ever stop? You moved on from me months ago, and yet here I still am, wishing—*wishing*—that it could be as easy for me. Or is it possible that you regret what you did, and all the 'what could have beens' keep you up at night too? I remember when I used to not be able to fall asleep because I couldn't stop thinking about you, and now you still keep me from falling asleep, except now there's just emptiness instead of butterflies.

How long did you know? Did you go to prom with me knowing that we had so few days left? How long were you just putting on a good face for me and going through the motions? If I had known how fragile hearts were, then maybe I wouldn't have been so willing to hand mine over to you. Why do they call it 'heartbreak' when the rest of you gets broken along with it?

Anyway, I'm going to try to get some sleep because I have to be in class in five hours.

Trevor

September 27

Today I went over to Rite Aid to pick up my prescription and there was a Two Door Cinema Club song playing inside, and I almost freaked out because I *never* hear anything I like playing out in the wild.

The recently-elected Swafford Hall House Council gave the building its first event—Condom Bingo, which is the only place where you can play bingo while learning a superfluous amount of sex trivia. Did you know that about 25% of women over 80 are still sexually active? I bet you wish you didn't. Whenever they called out O-69 everybody would cheer, and the people literally *threw* handfuls of condoms into the room. So now I have more condoms than I know what to do with. Actually, I know *exactly* what to do with them, but at the rate I'm using them—zero, for those of us keeping track—they'll last me until I graduate. The Health Center people brought bananas too in case anybody didn't know how to roll on a condom. I heard somebody ask the one guy—the same one who asked me if I wanted to get laid/lei'd—why they use bananas instead of cucumbers or some other phallic-shaped food.

"Because if somebody has a latex allergy then they can still eat them!" he answered a little too enthusiastically.

September 28

Tylor told me in his World Religions class that his professor introduced them to the idea of prayer as a form of meditation, which makes sense when you think about it—it's just you bringing peace to yourself. Even when I used to pray I always thought it was kind of pretentious. Like, god has his perfect divine plan and you think you know better than him? *Please god, just make this one little adjustment for me.* And then if it happens it was always part of the plan anyway, right? So why waste your time praying then? And if you *do* pray all the time but then still act like a piece of shit towards other people anyway, then what does it even matter?

Theo and I have been doing this thing where we whisper *"bitch"* to each other whenever we pass each other around campus. Neither he nor I nor Nikole nor Tylor are part of the Dance or Music or Hetero cliques that our floor has split into, so if I hang out with any of my floormates anymore, it's almost always with them. We still went over to Brubaker Auditorium to watch a dance performance that Amanda and Simone and Rory were in to support them though. I don't know if I was expecting ballet or what, but between the lights and the music that sounded like a computer having an exorcism, it was like a video exhibit you'd see in a contemporary art museum. But isn't the world just a big art museum anyway?

I gave my presentation for Computers today that Dr. Padar managed to stay awake for. Like always, I was nervous as hell at first, but was fine once I got going. I definitely did better than the guy who went after me. He kept saying *um* and *uh* so many times that I couldn't even tell you what he was talking about because all I could hear was *um* and *uh*. I counted 37 *ums* and 19 *uhs* after I started keeping a tally.

I was disappointed to find out that Devon from Rosenberg got a new job at the Health Center, but can I really blame someone for wanting a job that's literally in the same building that they live in? I'll just have to keep an eye out for any other eye candy who comes in to study or who jams a printer.

The Heteros down the hall started playing a new game called 'mattress jousting,' where two people take their mattresses and charge down the hall at each other holding them up like big shields, so I had to take the long way out to meet Kade to go bowling since I didn't want to die in a freak mattress accident. *Residents are not to use their furniture for martial games*, the future roommate agreements will read.

Kade surprised me when he stepped out of the glass smoke hut outside of Axworthy to meet me. "I didn't know you smoked," I said as he dropped his cigarette into the receptacle.

"Trevor Bentley Huffman I really *don't*," he said, earning a smirk from me.

"Did Paul make you try one and now you're hooked?"

"Dude," he laughed, "wouldn't *that* be a vibe? Nah, I've had the same pack for months. I only have one if I'm feeling extra stressed." He stuffed his hands into his pockets with a sigh. "I know there are better ways to ground myself, but sometimes they just do the trick. Do cigarettes expire?"

"I don't think an expired cigarette is gonna be any worse for you. Are assignments stressing you out?"

"Yeah. That, and I skipped my meds." *Oh.*

"You probably shouldn't do that," I said, trying not to sound patronizing.

"I just wanted to see if I would be okay without them. Clearly *not*," he scoffed.

"It's nothing to be ashamed of. I take antidepressants, and stuff for my anxiety, so yeah, I know what it's like to have to take pills just to feel normal. And it fucking *sucks.*"

"I used to not be able to sleep," he went on. "And then I'd stay in bed for as long as I could. I wouldn't go to school, and if I did it was like I wasn't even there." He fidgeted with his gauge. "I hate it when my thoughts take over and I can't do anything to stop them. The worst is when I just don't care about anything at all." Feeling sad is one thing, but complete apathy—reading a book without reading the words, putting on a song only to turn it off again, not having the motivation for anything, feeling like there's nothing that could ever make you happy again, feeling like everything is just so pointless—is a whole different demon.

"Have you ever thought about how easy it would be to kill yourself?" I heard myself say. "Like, what's really stopping me from finding a box cutter and dragging it along the inside of my forearm? Or just closing my eyes for a few seconds while I'm on the highway?"

He nodded with his eyes on the sidewalk as we passed the Quad, where *The Adam Project* was projected on a big screen rolled down the side of Kaminsky. "I've scared myself thinking about it. I almost have to make a conscious effort to stop myself from doing it sometimes. I think what's kept me from doing it is what it would do to my family and my friends, especially Victor. But not everybody who feels the way we do has people in their lives who care about them, and that's just not fucking fair."

Maybe it was the fact that he legit knows what it's like, but I managed to keep myself together, to not make up an apology and go back to my room to get away from there—though it wouldn't matter because the 'there' is inside of my own head. *Feel the sidewalk meeting your shoes. Feel the teeth inside your mouth. Feel your bones, your muscles. Feel the sensation of air filling your lungs, blood pumping in your veins. Think about everything working to make the miracle of you possible.* "There's a book by F. Scott Fitzgerald that I've never read," I almost stuttered, "but there's a line from it that goes something like, 'you can never understand how much of other people's lives they let you take up.'"

"I like that," Kade said, perhaps appreciating that he had somebody else with a mind that isn't always kind to them that he could open up to.

I spoke slowly, unsure of how to say what I wanted to say. "I know it's not always an easy thing to talk about, but if you ever wanna talk about it with somebody who's been there before, hit a boy up," I chuckled uneasily. But why can't it be an easy thing to talk about? Why can't we normalize talking about mental health, or pronouns?

"Thanks, and same for you too." He turned to face me. "Would it be weird if I said I kinda wanna give you a hug right now?"

"It's only weird if you make it weird," I smiled before we embraced. "So why didn't Victor wanna come bowling?"

"He hung back because he said it's too messy and he's not any good at it."

"I mean," I laughed, "*I'm* bad at it too, but it's still fun. Where do they have it anyway?"

"In the ceramics building in Arrowood," he furrowed his brow. "Where else would they have it?"

I thought it was weird that there'd be a bowling alley in the Arts complex, but if I'm learning one thing about college, it's that I know nothing. Like, it wasn't until we walked into a room of people spinning pottery that I realized he didn't mean sore-thumbs and gutter-balls bowling. "*That's* what you thought we were doing?" Kade laughed. "I'm *ass* at that."

It still trips me out to see people who aren't students doing things on campus, like walking laps around the Field House, or a family going out to dinner at Patnick—which, don't ask me *why* anybody would eat the fuck there if they didn't have to. Kade walked me through what to do as I got a feel for it—how fast to go, how to position my hands. Thank god there were aprons there for us because I would've been pissed if my shirt got flecked with all the wet clay I ended up wearing. It was even in my *hair*. I wouldn't say I had a blast doing it, but I didn't *hate* it. "I think I was better at the drums," I muttered as I took in the piece of shit I created. But isn't creating a piece of shit still better than not creating anything?

"It's not bad for your first try!" Kade encouraged/lied to me. My second attempt was marginally better, but I was content with just watching him work. His wet, shapeless mass took on contours and a smooth profile, transforming right before my eyes. I didn't think mine was worth drying and firing, but he talked me into keeping it, and even offered to pick it up for me when he grabs his.

On the way back, we found ourselves passing by the bottom of the big set of stairs in front of Rafferty, where The Railing that I've seen more than one person slide down called my name. "Wait a sec—I wanna try something," I told Kade, leaving him on the sidewalk as I bounded up the steps two at a time. At the top, I ran my hand along the smooth metal rail before hopping up onto it.

"You're gonna actually *try* that?" he called from the bottom.

"Yep!" I gave myself a nudge and slid about three feet before falling off backwards into the weedy, uncut hillside.

"Yikes!" I heard Kade shout. "You gucc fam?"

I shot him a thumbs up, too busy laughing at myself to be too embarrassed.

September 29

> Our first time was like going into French class—
> Nervous, modest, insecure—
> But astonished to discover our bodies so
> Fluently speaking an unfamiliar language.

October 1

I have a new favorite longboarding band, and they're called Standard Fare.

The fact that my tongue had yet to taste even a drop of alcohol after being at college for four whole weekends was starting to embarrass me, and I was determined to change that—somehow. Kade must've had the same idea too because he texted me **Do you know anywhere we can get some booze lol.** I asked The Yakuza's Accountant if he knew anyone who could get their hands on some stuff for us, wondering if Kade's "we" even included me or if he just meant him and Victor and their own friends.

"My friend who usually hooks me up went home for the weekend," Tylor said as a hairnet-clad Patrick employee dropped a scoop of ashtray-yellow mashed potatoes on his plate with a wet *pwlowp.* "But I'm going out with my friend Jaxon later on though. You're welcome to tag along with us if you want."

"Can Kade come too?" I asked, since being left out sucks, and since he's the one who asked about it in the first place. "But then he'll wanna bring Victor too."

"Yeah, that's cool. Tell them to bring some cash with them though since I'm guessing we'll have to pay a few bucks at the door."

> **Yes, but it would unfortunately involve going out with me and Tylor**

(͡° ͜ʖ ͡°)

I put entirely too much thought into what to wear for the night before Kade and Victor came over. We forwent—if that's even a word—the Homecoming pep rally and watching somebody get crucified to Old Main to just hang out until we headed out for the night. I fussed with my hair and gave myself an extra spritz of cologne before checking myself out in the mirror. *Would I make out with me? Absolutely.* Forreal though, can you imagine how much it would suck to get publicly executed? Like, getting killed is bad enough, but have other people *watching?*

Leaving the dorms behind with my friends and $1.25 in quarters—one for each drink I planned on having, to moderate myself—made going to a college party not feel as scary as I built it up to be. "Where's this party?" I asked Tylor. *Watch it be in the ceramics building.* "Are we meeting your friend there?"

"Southway. It's a few streets behind Subway. And nope, he's right there," he said as he nodded ahead to the person by the ATM notched into the side of Bixby. They pulled each other into a one-armed hug. "Whattup broski?" Tylor grinned. "Jax, this is my roommate Trevor, and my friends Kade and Victor. Guys, this is Jaxon. We were on the same floor last year."

"You got the best roommate, Trev," Jax told me as he slapped my hand.

"Aww, thanks mom," Tylor said.

"You're mom too?" I asked Jaxon.

He rolled his eyes. "All he says is 'shut up dad' or 'I hate you mom.'"

"Can I be mom too?" Kade asked eagerly.

"Goddammit dad, you're dad, remember?" Tylor said as he and Jaxon led the way. "Did Amina say if she's coming too?" he asked Jaxon.

"Nah, she's going out with Nikki and them."

I slowed down to keep pace with the other two. "Have either of you gone out to any parties yet?"

"Unh uh," Kade shook his head. "This'll be our first one."

We didn't see a single person walking by themselves as we trekked across campus to the three rows of single-story buildings that make up Southway Apartments. Pockets of people stood around with their drinks or cigarettes outside of doors with muffled bass that throbbed louder and clearer every time one opened. We tried not to laugh as we passed by a girl sitting on the curb who looked like she was .2 seconds away from puking while her friend loudly asked her if she needed any water. I expected the guy playing bouncer to be someone on the football team but he looked like a Math major. "What is *up*," he said to Jaxon as he gave him some dap. "Two for you guys, five for them," he said as he gestured at us newbie freshmen with his cup. We each handed him a five or five crumpled ones.

The smell of weed slapped us as soon as we stepped inside. It was *infinitely* more crowded than I thought it would be. We had to squeeze shoulder-against-back and back-against-chest between people—my apologies went unheard under the head-throbbing music—to get over to the kitchen, where empty liquor bottles lined the tops of the cabinets. I made sure I still had my phone and wallet on me before taking a wine cooler from a big tub of ice and transferring a quarter from one pocket to the other. Lights atop cabinets and shelves blended the room into a single, pulsating, color-changing organism. People's children pressed against each other, gyrating, making out, arms slung around necks. Sin hovered in the air like a haze. The whole place had a kind of wet smell to it, like a swimming pool locker room. I dropped my empty bottle into its graveyard with a glass-on-glass *clink* and paid another quarter for another bottle before watching a game of water pong on a folding table that somehow withstood the crowd. I was on my way to grab another drink when a girl who was so gone that her eyes were practically crossed grabbed my wrist and I asked if I wanted to take a shot with them. So that's how I found myself holding a colorful plastic shot glass with a random group of girls. *Please don't be vodka*, I prayed as we threw them back. My throat tightened from the cool scorch that made me shudder and gag. *Yep, that's vodka*. I grabbed a seltzer and noped the fuck out of there.

Kade and Victor somehow found themselves at one end of the pong table, where they faced off against a pair of absolute Heteros. I had a feeling that Kade's a lightweight, which had everything to do with the fact that most of his throws soared clear over the side of the table. I tried to catch one that flew my way but ended up swatting it into the back of someone's head. After Victor single-handedly racked up a win for them, they called me over to play face off against them. I didn't see Tylor or Jaxon anywhere, so I teamed up with a nearby girl who took all of her shots leaning over the table as far as she could, despite Victor calling out "Elbows!" over and over again. We showed the two of them to the door before a different pair of absolute Heteros handed us our asses.

Kade led us through the backdoor to the concrete slab of a patio so he could smoke, which I chalked up to him just being drunk and wanting to satisfy his oral fixation. Cool, fresh air never tasted so good. "*There* you guys are!" Tylor said when he and Jaxon found us, throwing an arm around me and another around Victor. "I was looking for you guys earlier!"

"I was looking for *you!*" I said. "I was gonna see if you wanted to play pong."

"You should've seen the girl we were playing against!" Victor basically shouted. "She kept leaning halfway across the table! And you know what this chick did when I called her out on it? Not a damn thing!"

"Somebody still has a bug up their ass about it," I smirked.

Kade dropped his cigarette butt into his can with a quiet, angry *hsssss*. "*Ha*. He said 'up the ass.'"

"Speaking of chicks," Tylor said to Jaxon, "did you see where that chick I was talking to went? Bookmark, or whatever her name was?"

Jaxon doubled over with laughter. "Bro, you mean *Paige*?" he howled, making the rest of us crack right the fuck up. Kade was legit rolling around on the ground.

"*Bookmark?*" he shrieked as he held his stomach.

"Goddammit mom," I laughed as I wiped my eye, "I thought I told you to stop kissing that bottle."

"You know what I meant," Tylor said as he went to go back in. "Imma go see if I can find her."

"Why, you tryna tap that?" Kade called after him. Tylor threw him a smirk.

"You sound like a fucking Hetero," I said to Kade. I held my bottle up to eye level and swirled it around before downing it. "Well that's all folks. I'm all out of quarters."

Victor froze like he sharted himself. "Did we have to pay for those?"

"Yeah?" I said with a straight face. "Don't tell me you've just been taking them?"

Victor gulped. "Please tell me you're joking."

"Can I lie?"

"No, you can't lie!"

"No, you didn't have to pay for them."

He raised an eyebrow. "How do I know you're not lying right now?"

"*Guys,*" Kade said urgently. "I kinda wanna go get Sheetz right now."

I gasped. "Oh my *god* do mac and cheese bites sound good right now."

Kade drained the last of his hard iced tea as we tramped across the parking lot towards Main Street. "You guys wanna do some punk shit?" he asked.

"What kind of punk shit?" I asked cautiously. Kade checked to see if anybody was looking before yeeting the bottle at a dumpster. It missed its mark and shattered on the pavement. *"Kade!"* I hissed/giggled as we fled.

"*That* kind of punk shit," he laughed as we slowed to walking pace again.

Jaxon had tried to warn us that hitting up Sheetz at 1 a.m. on Homecoming Saturday would be a nightmare, but that didn't stop us. The place was only marginally less crowded than the party, but no less drunk. There were even people lined up outside, waiting for a campus police officer to let them in as other people left. I felt bad for the employees working, because dealing with the public is a fucking pain when they're *sober.* "Number 677!" a worker called out. I looked down at the 716 on my receipt. *Fuck* me. It was almost 2 in the morning by the time we were out of there, but *goddammit* was it worth it.

"These mac and cheese bites are like the *best* orgasm I've ever had in my mouth," I said as I stuffed my face with the golden ooey gooey, making Kade choke.

"How many orgasms have you had in your mouth?" Victor laughed.

I swallowed. "No comment." I totally forgot about trying to slide down The Railing until we'd passed Bixby.

We hugged goodnight before we split for our own buildings, as much as I didn't want to part ways with them. "So I leaved," Victor mumbled as they walked off. I listened at the door to 222 Swafford for a full minute before going in in case Tylor and Bookmark were showing each other a good time. I was so tired that I could've fallen asleep in the hallway. I couldn't tell if the shape in Tylor's bed was just him or not, but he was the only other one in the room when I got up. I felt out of it enough to just have coffee and PopTarts for breakfast instead of dragging myself to Patnick, and I tried not to laugh as Hungover Tylor stumbled to the bathroom to take his morning piss with the door open.

"I hope you guys had a good time last night," he said as his bed caught him again.

"We did," I smiled. "What about you? Did you get a lot of reading done?"

"No?" he squinted. *Reading? The fuck are you talking about?*"

"You know, *reading*. With your bookmark?" It took him a second, but then he started laughing so hard that he almost fell out of bed, so hard that I was laughing at him laughing.

"I *can't* right now!" he said into his pillow. "I still can't believe I said that!"

After his own breakfast in bed, he asked me if I wanted to go to the Homecoming game with him. Sports are so far down on the list of things I care about that Jules Verne could write a story about taking a journey to it, but it feels like one of those college things you just *have* to do. Kade surprised me by tagging along with us too. "Victor said he's gonna hang back," he said. "He says that sports are an appeal to fascist misogynists by showcasing the male figure."

"*You* don't strike me as somebody who's into sports," I said.

"I'm a skinny art kid. What the fuck would make you think I like sports?" he spat.

"Weren't you wearing some black-and-yellow jersey in one of Victor's Instagram posts?"

"That was a gift that I wore *one* time at Thanksgiving to show my appreciation."

"Wouldn't that just positively reinforce people to get you more sports jerseys?" I pointed out.

He almost looked upset with himself. "They better fucking *not.*"

Between the booths, the stage that some band played on, the tailgaters, and the cow plop—sometimes I forget how rural of an area we're in, but then people betting on which spray-painted square in the grass a cow will shit in is there to remind me —it really felt like a festival. Campus is dry, but I guess the school makes an exception if you're in the parking lot of Bamberger Stadium on Homecoming. We trundled into the stadium with our thunder sticks and beaded necklaces alongside people who looked like they had a way wilder night than we did. I tried to pick out Calvin when the marching band did their hoo-hah, but I couldn't tell any of them apart. Percy the Knight and the Color Guard got the crowd pumped up/aroused for the football team before they stampeded onto the field. All the thunder sticks sounded like an artillery bombardment, and I wasn't even that hungover.

"Who are we playing again?" somebody with thinning hair in the row in front of us asked.

"Slimy Pebble," his friend said with a hearty burp.

"Don't you mean Slippery Cock?" his other friend said, making them all laugh the way you expect people who are piss-ass drunk at 2 in the afternoon to laugh.

The more the game went on, the more I found myself wishing I was doing something else. "Is it just me, or is this fuckin' lame?" Kade asked us after maybe 15 minutes.

"Yeah, this is ass. You wanna go do something else?"

Since we'd slept through the parade, didn't give two shits about Homecoming court or the antique car show, or weren't yet alumni, Homecoming weekend had nothing else to offer us. We took advantage of half the school being at the game to go to Percy's since we hadn't had any real food yet. Tylor bounced after we ate to go to the outlets with a friend of his, leaving me with Kade and an order of cauliflower wings to take back to Victor.

"So how was *that?*" Victor called from his room as 239 Axworthy's door shut behind us.

"Fucking *dumb*," Kade said as he dropped his low tops on the rack. "I brought you some foodles that you'll have to pay me back for, and some kid named Trevor."

Victor materialized in his doorway in a yellow-sleeved baseball tee. "What it do, Trev?"

"Oh, you know. It do."

Victor set down his Switch to eat, but froze when he opened the bag. He shot Kade a glare that sent Kade running to his room and howling into his pillow.

"Um, what's happening?" I asked.

Victor shook his head with a smile. "God *fucking* dammit." He pulled an envelope out of the bag. "Kade likes to do this thing where he gives me envelopes with garbage in them—dust bunnies, dead flies, crumbs, you know." He opened it to show me some hair and what looked like ice cream sprinkles stuck to a wad of tape. "And here his mom thought he was just being nice for cleaning under the couch cushions." He balled it up and threw it into Kade's room.

"The trick's to do it when he least expects it," Kade said when he reappeared with the thing I'd made at the pottery-spinning-bowling workshop. "So what are you guys feeling?"

"What kind of games do you have?" I asked.

So that's how we ended up on Kade's floor, separating *Settlers of Catan* pieces and drinking tea to a playlist of relaxing Nintendo music. The more they explained the rules, the more overwhelmed I felt. It was more fun than I thought it would be though, even if I lost spectacularly. And for as much as you'd expect him to be, Kade isn't a sore winner. "You'll have to give me some tips, because I'm *clearly* doing something wrong," I smiled after the second game.

Kade gasped. "You mean you're *not* gonna try to change the rules so they favor you instead of trying to get better at it, like the Reprehensibles are notorious for doing?"

"The Reprehensibles? Is that a band?"

"*Maybe*. But no, that's what I call the fanaticals with a fetish for red hats and restricting human rights."

"You know, the ones with the ideals that get less popular as America gets more colorful and diverse," Victor added.

"Oh, yeah!" I laughed. *Thank fucking god we have the same politics.* "I like to call them Repubes, but Reprehensibles works too."

"Repubes?" Victor frowned. "Oh, like pubic hair!" he laughed.

October 3

You told me distance wasn't an obstacle,
But empty words played from you like the
Songs stuck in my head playing from my phone.

October 4

Last night I accidentally spent an hour and a half torturing myself with happy-looking gay boys and couples on Instagram again—there's a young couple in Seattle I basically stalked the shit out of—which is to say that Kade and Victor's suggestions for falling asleep *didn't* work. The tea's still good though even if it doesn't help me sleep, and I've taken a bit of a liking to Dave Brubeck's music—"Pixar jazz," as Tylor calls it.

Kade headed for Arrowood to work on an assignment instead of joining me to get Zukoff after de Conto let class out early, but Victor said he'd go with me if I waited up for him once his World Art class let out. I hoisted myself up onto the wall out front and peered down at my phone at Miles Barrington twinkling up at me from his Instagram porthole. *HOMO sapien.* My thumb hovered over 'Follow' like it had half-a-dozen times already. I wanted to tap it—quickly, before I could think about it—but told myself I could wait until after I'd see him at Lit Club later on. *But what if he's not there?* Thankfully, Victor and his mint-chocolate-chip-ice-cream-green shirt that read 'DESTROY THE PATRIARCHY NOT THE PLANET' rescued me from having to think about it anymore.

I'd never actually eaten *in* Zukoff before since it's always packed, but we got there early enough that there were plenty of open tables for us to choose from. "Isn't tofu kinda gross?" I asked the tofu in his ramen as I dug into my gyro.

"It can be," Victor said, "but this isn't bad. Have you ever had tofu before?"

"Unh uh." I eyed the little white cubes. "Do you *actually* like it, or do you choke it down to do your good deed for the day?"

He slurped up a noodle. "Both—I don't eat meat. I'd love to go totally vegan one day, but that's kind of hard to do here."

"I'm sure it is," I muttered, thinking about how the students who try to convert people to veganism would probably have better luck if they projected a video of animals getting slaughtered onto the side of one of the buildings in the Quad instead of just handing out tracts like a Baptist family on Halloween. "What about eggs though?" I glanced at the egg half that was floating in the broth. "Aren't eggs meat?"

"Depends who you ask. I try not to get into it because it usually turns into an abortion debate, and *I* don't have time for that."

"Do *any* of us?" I chuckled. "Does it upset you when you see other people eating meat?" I asked, worried that he was judging me.

"I mean, a little. But I'm not about to tell anyone how to live their lives." *Take some notes, Repubes.*

We were halfway to the dorms—I would've tried sliding down The Railing if there weren't so many people around—when Victor said he wanted to make a pit stop at Starbucks. "Really? Starbs? I figured Kade would've turned you into a coffee snob."

"He's not really a coffee snob, but he *does not* fuck around when it comes to tea," he said as he drummed out a beat on his thighs.

The initial Common Hour rush had died down by the time we got there, but the tables were still crowded with textbooks and laptops. I didn't want anything so I just scrolled on my phone until one of the workers called out, "I have a caramel macchiato for Trevor!" I looked up to see who my doppelgänger was, but I was *way* more interested in the cute barista handing out drinks. *Where the hell have I seen him before?*

"Maybe I will get something," I murmured as I wondered why he looked familiar. *Open Mic Night,* it hit me as we made awkward eye contact. *He played the keyboard at Open Mic Night.* I ordered the same thing as Victor, and fought the urge to steal any more glances at the guy as I waited.

"Latte for Victor!" Cute Barista called. My chest throbbed. Go fucking figure though that he had to go into the back for something when my own latte was ready. I looked back as I held the door open for Victor on the way out, but there wasn't a cute barista in sight.

"Did you happen to see what that worker's name was?" I asked Victor as I sipped my own latte.

"I think it was Destinee?"

"Not the one who took our orders, the guy handing them out. The blond one."

"Oh, I don't know. I wasn't paying attention." He turned to me with a smirk. "Why, are you interested?"

"No," I lied. "I thought I might've known him from somewhere." *Which isn't false.* "But I won't say he isn't cute," I said as my cheeks flushed. So that's how I came out to Victor.

"Oh forreal?" Victor smiled at me. "I'll have to check him out the next time I'm there—platonically, I mean," he chuckled.

As much as I enjoyed the last meeting, Miles was basically the only reason I'd been looking forward to Lit Club. I lit up when he walked into the room. I wasn't too upset that Nikole wasn't able to make it, because that just gave the two of us more time to talk. He told me that he'd been going to Lit Club since last year and met his ex there. *Maybe this is how he meets his next boyfriend?* "So that book of poems you have," he finally said. "Have you ever written any of your own poems in it?"

"Oh no," I chuckled. "I suck at writing poetry. It'd be an insult to actual poets to have mine in the same book as theirs."

"I doubt that," he smiled. "Just because you don't like them doesn't mean they're bad."

"I enjoy writing stories more than writing poems," I shrugged.

Instead of asking me about my stories, he asked, "How about you write me a poem and read it to me at the next meeting?"

I stared. *Is he flirting with me?*

"I'll make it interesting too—I'll give you a few words at random that you have to use in it, okay?"

"Yeah, okay," I nodded like a simp.

Instead of opening a dictionary and pointing to 'oblivion,' or 'eloquence,' or 'celadon,' he picked them from random news headlines. "Charles de Gaulle. Price-gouging. And clinics. Okay?"

"That'll definitely be interesting," I smiled.

On the way out after the meeting ended, he made my chest leap when he asked me if I'm on Instagram. I asked him his name like I hadn't stared at it night after night before finally requesting to follow him. As soon as we wished each other a good Break and parted ways, I was back on his profile and scrolling through selfies and pics of him with his friends, his family, his dog, places he's traveled to—but no hint of a boyfriend or partner of any kind. *Perfect.*

October 5

Halloween is almost here, but the trick's on them—

72

I've already been seeing ghosts for months,
In the streets of this town, in a song I forgot to delete,
Somebody who shares your taste in cologne—
How stupid of me to think that
I could ever put you to rest when everything
Triggers a memory, a fantasy,
An endless litany of 'what ifs?'
—Do I haunt you like you haunt me?

October 6

So I guess some of the guys down the hall unscrewed AJ and Trent's peephole and put it in backwards and caught AJ slipping on a condom and going to town on his Squishmallow in 4K, so you can bet your ass I check ours every time the door's closed, multiple times just to be sure.

Kade wasn't as judgy about me wanting to get Starbucks as I thought he'd be, but then again, I can never tell if "ew Jesus Christ!" is a good or a bad thing with him. I was kind of glad he didn't come with me because I didn't want anything distracting me from Cute Barista if he was working again. I looked out for any dirty-blond hair as I stood in line, and relief washed over me like a piss I'd been holding in when he strode in and into the back with his backpack still on. He reappeared two orders ahead of mine, fumbling with his green apron behind his back until one of his coworkers tied it for him. He shouted out my name and all I could squeeze out was a "thanks," like I'd lost the ability to speak like some kind of New-Testament punishment for looking at another boy in that way. I sipped my latte at my table without tasting it, trying as hard as I could to look anywhere but at him. I couldn't concentrate on my notes for more than ten seconds. *Did I smile back? Please tell me I smiled back.*

And then to my horror, he came over and pulled out a chair at the table next to mine and unwrapped a croissant sandwich. I almost packed up and left. He laughed at something on his phone while he bit into his food. Old Trevor would've sat there and let him eat and leave without a word, but I'm not that person anymore. Cute Barista's sandwich was my timer.

"They let you take a break already?" I asked like the wires in my head weren't burning. *Way to not sound cringe, Trevor.*

He met my eyes and sent my pulse racing. Hot guys in movies always have those bright, icy-blue eyes like they're in a spearmint gum commercial, but his are this deep, cobalt-blue. "Just something quick after the rush, since I didn't get to grab anything for lunch," he shrugged.

"I gotcha." *Keep it going.* "You played at Open Mic Night a few weeks ago, didn't you?"

"I did, yeah," he nodded with a smile.

"You were really good. That song was stuck in my head for *days* afterwards," I lied.

"Thanks, I'm glad to hear you liked it!" He nodded at my bag. "Is that a *Dear Evan Hansen* button?"

I looked down at it like I forgot it was there. "It sure is."

"I fucking *love* that musical," he grinned.

"Me too," I dumbly smiled. "Do you think you'll play at the next one? Open Mic Night, I mean?"

"I guess I'll *have* to now, or else I'll disappoint my fans," he winked. He swept his crumbs into his wrapper before crumpling it up. "Well, back to the hellhole for me." I got a clear view of his name tag as he stood. *Ethan.* "I'll be seeing you at Open Mic Night then?"

"Yeah, definitely!" *You're such a fucking simp, you know that Trevor?*

October 7

I guess part of growing up is realizing that Real Friends knew what was up when they titled an album *Maybe This Place is the Same and We're Just Changing.* You'd think that the music Ryder liked would be like tequila to me, but it's so on-point that I can't not listen to it.

I'm not as stoked for Fall Break as much as I thought I would've been—yeah, two extra days of no class is nice, but I'm going to miss being away from school for four days. The trees grew more colorful and more vibrant as I made my way north—I picked up a 'My NHU Kid Is Smarter Than Your Dog' shirt from the bookstore for Dad for his birthday—until West Seneca was ablaze with them. I still don't know if it feels like I've just been home or if it's been so long since I've been home, but either way, it was like I was seeing my hometown for the first time. Yeah, the library has a new sign, but it's all the things that have always been here that seem so different to me—hence the Real Friends. Even my own room felt like somebody else's. *Why didn't I take some of my posters down with me?*

Mom—who I expected to cry and hug me like I'd just gotten back from deployment—insisted that I bring my laundry home with me, though I would've rather just spent the $3 to do it at school than lug my overloaded basket back with me. I guess she wants to try to hold on to the way things used to be, but it doesn't work that way. Dad smiled proudly, and I can't not give myself some credit—their only son was becoming a man, or so I like to think. Misha didn't give two shits that I'm back, naturally.

Dad told me at dinner—we had ribs, which, after subsisting off of Patnick food for so long, was one of the best meals I've ever had—that my mail-in ballot came the other day, and reminded me not to wait until the day before Election Day to send it in. I told them about my classes, work, and all the PG-rated things that go on around campus. "And what about your roommate?" Mom asked. "Is he messy? Weren't you worried about him not speaking English well?"

"Oh no," I shook my head as the image of Tylor's overflowing laundry basket flashed across my mind. "No, he's great. We get along really well. I'm happy I got paired with him." I told them about my other floormates, and Kade and Victor, and almost told them about Miles.

"Well it sounds like you're making friends," she said. "Is there anybody you're seeing at all?"

I just shook my head, sideswiped that she even cared or would ask me. "Nope," I shook my head. *And I get the feeling that won't be changing anytime soon.*

October 8

This town is scattered with memories—
Firsts saturate the lawn like dew,
Cluttering the alleyways—their usefulness, too, outlived—
Laughter buried beneath leaves overcome by heavy longing.
We comb these neighborhoods like saps, panning for gold—
Prospectors for the discarded exuberance of youth.
Cracked streets, those stretch marks on halcyon,
Bear witness that we haven't been the only ones aging,
The only ones shorted on sleep, on dreams.

October 9

As much as I don't care about sports, being home on a sunny Fall afternoon and eating some hearty goulash with the football game on was a vibe I didn't think I'd enjoy as much as I did. There's nothing like a warm oven on a cool day to make you feel at home.

It sucks that my Break and Madi's Break aren't at the same time, but Logan said that just means he gets to spend two weekends with his friends. I hate to admit it, but he was right when he said that I'd make new friends that would make me forget all about him and Madi. Tylor and Nikole and Theo and Kade and Victor have all made the past month-and-a-half away from my hometown friends not just bearable, but *fun*.

Logan was off yesterday, so we spent the whole day together. It was weird walking into his house and seeing his dad, even though it used to be my second home. We grabbed breakfast at Dog Ears, where I picked up a copy of *The First to Die at the End* and a curious little find the size of a greeting card titled *Einstein's Dreams*. We took our coffees and my books around the park across the street afterwards, where the breeze made me glad that I threw on a flannel.

"So," Logan said in the same way he does when he's about to tell you who he found out hooked up, "what's your roommate like? Is he weird? Cute? Gross?"

"He's pretty cool. I really like him. And *no*, not like that."

"He's not a waffle stomper, is he?" Logan chuckled.

I dry heaved. "I fucking *hope* not."

"Have you gone to any parties yet? Smooch up any cute boys yet? What's your body count up to by now?"

"Oh my god, shut *up!*" I laughed. "College parties are *eh*, Trevor Bentley Huffman. I mean, getting saucy's fun, but I don't think I'd go out every weekend. Unless I just went to a shitty party."

"Please don't tell me you do the Trevor Bentley Huffman thing down at school."

"Of course I do," I practically scoffed. "And I was told that it's *cool*, thank you very much."

"Did somebody at the shitty party say that? Because they were probably drunk off their ass."

"Eff the fuck off," I grinned.

I saw him watching me in the corner of my eye as we walked. "*And?*" he finally asked. "What about the other two?"

"My body count is *zero*, if you need to know. There are some cute guys, but no smooches yet."

We went to the mall, where there were enough Saturday shoppers to make you frown, but it was nice to be a part of civilization again after living in New Halle. I thought about stopping by work to say hi to whoever was there, but I wasn't in a small-talk mood and I didn't feel like answering the same questions I already answered twice. There weren't any records in FYE that caught my eye, but Logan of course couldn't leave without getting at least one Funko Pop figure. If I had as many as he did, I'd build a wall out of them to brick up my enemies behind. *I like my boys the way I like my enemies—bricked up.* We passed by the trampoline park on the way out, which sent my mind back to the time Dillon took me there on a surprise date. I tell myself I don't miss him, but there isn't a day that goes by when I don't think about him. *I can't believe I was so stupid to think that my first love would actually last. But what if? What if what if what if what if what if what if?*

We hung out back at Logan's before grabbing dinner at Don Juan's, and then we went over to Josh Dawkins' place for a fire. I missed good Mexican food, but I can't say the same for some of my old classmates. It's only been a few months, but some of them haven't changed at *all*, and I don't say that as a good thing. I like to think that I've changed even a little since moving to NHU, even if just my perspective—I mean, why else go away to school? Logan, Riley, and a few hard ciders were the only things keeping me from writing the night off as a waste of time. But is it better to not do something you know you won't enjoy and then be upset with yourself for not doing it, or to do it anyway and not enjoy it? Introvert problems.

October 10

You know what's high-key freaky? Stick bugs. I saw one for the first time crossing the sidewalk and I thought I was tripping. And also, can somebody tell me why there's a day celebrating Columbus but not a day celebrating whoever decided to put chocolate and peanut butter together?

I'm glad I decided to throw my longboard in my trunk before coming home, because it was a good morning for a ride down the streets where I learned the ropes over lockdown. My hoodie kept the crisp air at bay as I soaked up Fall Part One— piles of leaves, cornstalks on lampposts, dried wreaths on doors, garbage bags that look like jack-o'-lanterns. The guy on the corner's still flying his 13-star American flag, which I still don't get. Are you saying you'd like to go back to the good old days of having only the 13 original states and kick out the rest? Because if so, by all means let's fucking do it. Because you know how many of the original 13 are red states now? Like two.

I used to not really care for Fall since it was just a harbinger for Winter, but it vibes so hard. It makes me slow down and reflect on things—especially recently. Everything and everyone is changing and passing. Enjoy what you have, and enjoy it as it is. Savor what is and don't worry about what will come, because everything will come in its time. I think that's what Fall tries to tell us. It's all just transitory. Change is the only constant.

October 11

POV:

It's your last day home until Thanksgiving Break and you're on a bench in the park with your to-go mug of coffee and your book of poems, trying to find inspiration to write one for a guy you have the hots for.

October 12

So I remembered what the only thing that's worse than a song that slaps so hard that it keeps you from falling asleep is—a song that keeps you from falling asleep that also reminds you of your ex.

As nice as it was to be home, I didn't realize how much I missed it here at NHU until I saw Old Main sprouting from the tangerine and daffodil tree-speckled hills. I made sure to drop my ballot off before heading down, which was a little anticlimactic —I always thought my first time voting would feel a little more consequential than dropping an envelope in a mailbox, but it still felt good to do after having to sit by and just watch the last administration happen. God, how I wish I could've voted in 2020.

I messaged Miles to tell him that I'd written him a poem, and he made my stomach somersault when he asked if I wanted to meet up with him at Brew 22 to read it to him instead of just asking me to send it to him. *Is this my first date in college?* I wanted to flex on the others about it when we got together for dinner, but I can't stand people who do that. And unfortunately, five days of not eating at Patnick was long enough for my body to act like it's never had it before, if you sniff what I'm smelling.

"So are any of you guys gonna join Dumbledore's Army?" Victor—wearing a shirt of Kamala Harris captioned *"I'm speaking"*—asked us over his plate of some kind of mushroom casserole that looked pretty sus. I guess participation in the Harry Potter Club on campus must be low because they had a table set up in Bixby with a QR code for a Sorting Quiz to try to get new recruits. I'll be the first to admit that I can be a nerd about some things, but that seems even a little too nerdy for me—no offense to whoever's involved with it though.

"Why, are *you*?" Kade asked his roommate.

"No, but I took the quiz anyway though."

"What'd you get?" I asked.

"Gryffindor, as always," Victor said smugly.

"*Gryffindor as always!*" Kade mocked him.

The three of us took the quiz too just for poops and giggles. "I'm *telling* you, it's gonna be Slytherin," Kade muttered.

"Is this the part where you make a joke about slithering into my DMs or something?" I smirked.

He let his phone fall to the table. "Oh my god! Nobody's ever said that before! You're so fucking *witty!*"

"Fuck *off*. And speaking of witty, I got Ravenclaw, also as always."

"Boom," Kade said once he got his results. "Slytherin. Told you."

We all looked at Tylor. "Please don't say you got Hufflepuff."

"I didn't get Hufflepuff."

"Did you get Hufflepuff?"

He showed us the black and yellow badger on his phone. "I got Hufflepuff."

"Well isn't that fucking *cute?*"

"We're like...The Avengers."

"Or the Sixth Coalition," Kade said. "Oh, and I brought my bass back up with me too so Vic and I can jam together again."

"You know what?" I said as I handed him a clean napkin. "Here's a list of all the people who care."

"Go eat a shit," Kade said as he failed to bite back a laugh. He leaned back in his chair and twisted a curl of hair around his finger. "Ugh, I should've gotten my hair cut while I was home too," he said to it with crossed eyes. "I'm gonna look like goddamn Napoleon Dynamite."

"I *told* you you should have!" Victor said, with his own fresh Caesar cut.

"Where do you get yours cut?" Kade asked Tylor. "Is there somewhere in town?"

"Yeah, right on Main Street. Eleanor's my girl."

"What, do you go once a semester?" I razzed him, though I think the messy look looks good on him. He loaded a corn kernel into his spoon and pulled it back like a catapult. "Don't you fucking *dare!*" I laughed with my arms over my face. It sailed clear over my head and bounced off another table.

October 13

I woke up this morning to catch a view of the valley full of fog, rising in plumes like exhaust from some polluting machine before growing taller and rolling like actual clouds before dissipating. It was pretty cool.

Kade was under the impression that I was going to the hair salon with him and just sit there with my thumb up my ass. "You're not coming in with me?" he asked when I didn't follow him up to the door.

"Nah, I'm meeting one of my friends at Brew 22," I said, though there was more to the story.

"Oh," he muttered. I did feel low-key bad about it, especially since I let him go bowling by himself last night.

I didn't see Miles when I got to the coffee shop, so I grabbed a table for two right by the front window. I kept glancing over at the door while I waited for my chai latte and roasted red pepper panini to come out. You'd think that having two tip jars on the counter wouldn't necessarily bring in twice as many tips, but just put out ones with competing labels on them—like 'Star Wars' and 'Star Trek,' in this case—and watch them fill up with change and ones like an Old Testament miracle. I mean, that's basically what the NFL does. I let the frothy spiced milk wash my tongue and I bit away at my sandwich while I watched the sidewalk through the window for Miles. The trees just starting to lose their leaves and the on-and-off clouds made it such a Fall day. Paper skeletons in windows and fake spider webs on porch railings made it feel like a scene at the start of a horror movie when things are still peaceful with that shit's-about-to-go-down undertone.

After 20 minutes, I started to worry that Miles forgot about me. I looked back at our messages to make sure there wasn't one from him that I missed saying he couldn't make it. I wanted to message him if he was still coming but didn't want to look desperate. A nearby flier for Open Mic Night distracted me, letting my mind settle on Ethan from Starbucks and how he called me one of his fans.

"Boo!"

The voice inside my bubble almost knocked me out of my seat. "Jesus!" I said as I clutched my chest.

"I'm sorry, I *had* to," Miles laughed. "That was perfect."

I couldn't not smile at him as my breathing returned to normal. "You're looking extra preppy today," I complimented his fit, boots and all.

"I try sometimes," he grinned. "My professor wanted to go over something with me after class, that's why I'm late. Nothing bad."

He set his bag on the other chair and went to get his own drink, which was amber-colored with whipped cream and sprinkles of spices. "What'd you get?" I asked his Irish coffee mug.

"Spiced apple cider. It's to die for." He lifted it to his lips. "Oh my god. Every time I have it it's like I'm having it for the first time," he swooned. "Do you wanna try it? I don't care if you drink from the cup. Or you could try to drink it through the cinnamon stick like a straw, but I don't think that'll work." He nudged it towards me, the whipped cream already starting to dissolve in its warmth.

I gingerly took a small sip, eager to catch his cooties. "Oh my *god* is right. It's like Fall in a cup."

"Isn't it? You have some cream on your nose," he said as he took it back. "There, you got it. So did you have a good Break?"

"Yeah, it was good. It was weird going back home, but it was nice not having classes for a few days. Did you go back home?"

"I hear you. And nah, I stayed here. The drive to Urbana and back would've taken like a whole day."

"Urbana, like in Illinois?" I asked. "Why are you going to NHU instead of somewhere in Chicago or somewhere?"

He shrugged. "Why is anybody here? Aren't there schools closer to wherever you're from?"

"Yeah, that's true. My dad's a professor at the University of Buffalo and likes to remind me how I could've stayed home and gone there for *way* cheaper." *How different would things have been if I'd done that? Or if I'd decided to go to Pitt with Dillon?* "I only know about Urbana though because this one band that I like is from there."

Miles smirked. "Would that band happen to be American Football?"

We talked about music, particularly how those Midwestern emo bands know exactly where to hit you. "That's why we're drawn to it," I said. "We embrace what we can relate to, even if it hurts like hell."

He took me in for a moment before bringing up the whole point of us meeting up. "So let's hear that poem."

"Oh yeah, let me pull it up."

"It's not in your poetry book?"

"The pages are already all filled up!" I chuckled as I opened my Notes app. I cleared my throat and read, high-key worried what anybody overhearing would think of it.

"Wow, you read Yeats much?" Miles joked when I finished. "I'm kidding, I like it!"

"I'm glad you enjoyed it," I said, suddenly feeling proud of it.

I pieced together more of the mosaic that made up the person I sat with as we talked, happy that I had an excuse to take in his strong jawline and thoughtful gray eyes. He did his freshman year from home thanks to COVID. He wants to work as a film critic. He read 21 books over lockdown. He broke his arm in gym class once. He tried running away from home after he came out. He ended things with his ex after his ex ghosted him for a day, and then he found out he cheated on him.

"Oh shit, I didn't realize what time it was," I said when I checked my phone and saw that I had 15 minutes to get to Brit Lit. "I have to get to class."

"Yeah, you should probably do that," he chuckled.

"I'm glad we got to meet up though," I said as I threaded my arms through my backpack straps. "I guess I'll see you at Lit Club?"

"Didn't you see the email from Ashton? We're skipping next week because of Midterms. He just sent it this morning."

I shook my head. "Unh uh."

"Yeah. But anyway, I was gonna ask if you had any plans this weekend. We're gonna have some people over our place tomorrow night."

"Is that an invitation, or are you just showing off that you have friends?" *And can he see my chest throbbing?*

"Both," he laughed as we turned back onto Main Street. "I'll message you the address. It won't be like a full-on *party*. Just drinks and games."

"Yeah, I'd be down! Should I bring my own alcohol?" I asked like I had any.

"Nah, we'll have plenty of stuff. I'll see you tomorrow then!" he said with a wave as he split for Abernathy.

I rubbed one out after class, with Miles and possibilities on my mind.

October 14

Can you tell that I disrobe you every time
I see you, making you into whatever I want
Like a paper doll, like an unhealthy addiction?
You'd never know that I dress like every day is our first date
Just in case we run into each other and you like what you see.
Can you see the hunger for you in my eyes?
What would you say if you knew that I save your smile
For a midnight snack in my sleepless bed,
Wishing your lips were there to keep me company—
Those lips seasoned by midnight liquors,
Those lips that know a hundred boys' dorm rooms,
The night's conquest, the soup du jour,
Tasting promise, tasting triumph,
But not ever rejection—how could anyone?
And even if they never taste me
They'll never stop tantalizing me,
Keeping me craving after my favorite flavor.

October 15

I would've never guessed that Japanese math rock would be a genre of music I'd find myself getting nostalgic to, but here I am.

Miles messaged me his address along with **Come over anytime after 10 but not too late** 😊, which put me on auto-pilot all day. Even a game of *Catan* with my Axworthy friends couldn't distract me. "So I'm gonna be going out later with some of my Lit Club friends," I half-lied later on at dinner.

Kade let his fork fall to the table. "What the hell dude! I thought tonight was movie night!"

"You can still watch something without me!"

"I'm *joking* fam. You go have fun tonight. We'll just have our little sausage party without you." He gave Tylor an open-mouthed wink and nudged Victor.

"Is somebody trying to get their peen wet tonight?" Tylor laughed.

"*No*," I lied as my face got hot, although me trying to look my absolute freshest—and the condom I slipped into my pocket—said otherwise. I felt kind of bad for going out without my friends, but it was kind of nice not being the one left out for once. Trekking across campus on a Friday night alone meant I had nothing to distract me from overthinking things. *How do I know Miles even likes me? Just because he's gay doesn't mean anything will happen with us. He could be seeing somebody else for all I know. 'Trevor, I'd like you to meet my boyfriend,' he'll say with his arm around somebody infinitely more attractive than me. Maybe he's just trying to be nice to me. God, I'm so stupid. I was just seeing what I wanted to see.* I thought about just going back, but the hope of meeting somebody else carried me the rest of the way to Oakwood Apartments, whose stone-and-wood sign made me feel like I was going to Summer Camp. It was quieter than Southway, but not without its pockets of partygoers. I followed the plaques up a covered staircase to number 211, where a girl who reminded me of Harley Quinn stood smoking a cigarette. My knock went unheard under the music and voices behind the door.

"You can just go in," Harley Quinn said. "Are you one of the guys's friends?"

My fingers found my stud. "Would somebody named Miles happen to be one of the guys?"

"He would. Here, I'll go in with you." She scraped her cigarette butt on the wall and flicked it away.

The room was full of people and drinks, but it wasn't crammed like the last party and it didn't smell like weed. People stood behind the kitchen peninsula, clung to the walls, and sat around the coffee table playing *Jenga* in the light of a shadeless floor lamp with an ocean-blue bulb. One person's eyes meeting mine was all it took to make me feel like the whole room was judging me. I was contemplating leaving when one of the *Jenga* players stood up.

"Trevor! I'm glad you made it!" a tipsy Miles said over the music I didn't recognize. He gave me a one-armed hug and showed me the kitchen. What can I get you to drink? There's beer and mixers in the fridge," he said as he slapped the fridge. "This is Amelia. Here's the liquor. Help yourself to whatever. This is Brooke. And this is Adam," he said as he slapped Adam on the back. "Everyone, this is Trevor."

I was trying to decide what drink to make myself when a cute guy came over to pour himself one. He looked like somebody from a 2000s emo band with his sweeping hair and skinny jeans and oversized t-shirt. "Hey, can I have some of that?" I asked him.

"Yeah, sure thing," he smiled. He poured me some, and I winced when I sipped it. *Son of a bitch.*

"Oof, I didn't realize it was vodka," I frowned.

"It's chocolate vodka though! It's good if you mix it with orange juice." I wasn't convinced, but I tried it anyway.

"This actually isn't *horrible*," I said. The orange and chocolate flavors melded together nicely, but the vodka still burned.

"See? You're welcome," Cute Emo Band Guy smiled before returning to the game.

I tuned out Harley Quinn fake-complaining about how guys are always checking her out and tried my hand at small talk with strangers. "So how do you know Miles?" I asked the others in the kitchen. "If Miles is even the one you're friends with."

"We sat next to each other in class last year," Adam answered. "Ask him which class when you get the chance." *Nude Portraiture?*

"My boyfriend's his roommate," Brooke said. "Lincoln, the one sitting next to him. In the gray." Miles saw me looking and flashed a smile as he patted the seat beside him. I apologized to the people I stepped between on my way over to him.

"Trevor, this is my one roommate, Lincoln," he gestured to the guy on his other side who had the top of his hair dyed blond. "His name's Abe, but he gets called 'ayb' instead of 'ah-bay' so many times that we just all started calling him Lincoln as a joke, and then it just stuck."

Abe Lincoln gave me an up-nod as he held out his hand. "How's it going?"

"Linc, this is Trevor. He goes to Lit Club too."

"Nice to meet you," he said sincerely.

"What about your other roommate?" I asked Miles.

"Kollin? He's probably out getting high with his smoker friends."

I just nodded. "Adam told me to ask you about the class the two of you had last year."

Lincoln laughed as Miles smirked. *"Officially* it was U.S. History, but everybody who took the class in hopes of learning the kind of stuff you'd expect to learn in a U.S. History class was *hella* disappointed."

"Why? What'd you learn about?"

"Basically every injustice that Africans and African-Americans suffered at the hands of white people in America and all over the world," he explained. "The professor was from South Africa, so we got to hear *all* about apartheid and how European colonization totally fucked Africa over. Wham, bam, thank you ma'am."

"Didn't you say he'd say the same stuff like *every* class too?" Lincoln chuckled.

"He'd repeat himself *constantly,*" Miles rolled his eyes. "And he *hated* white people. He told all the white kids one day that he hopes we all go to hell, and like three people got up and left and never came back."

"Is he *allowed* to say stuff like that?" I laughed. Forreal though, if all of humanity can apparently be damned because of what Adam and Eve did once upon a time, then I think it's only fair that all white people pay the price for what we used to do to people who weren't white.

"I mean, he *did.* The first day he made us take a citizenship test just to rub in our faces how ignorant we Americans really are. The Black kids loved him though, and I can't blame them after only being taught the same whitewashed version of history over and over. But the class did what college classes are supposed to do—introduce you to new ideas, even if they offend you or make you uncomfortable. That's where I learned about the prison-industrial complex, and how the 13th Amendment never actually ended slavery. At first I thought he was fucking *nuts,* but now I see how on-point he was. The class was easy as shit too—I didn't even do my paper or take the Final and I still got a B in it. Apparently if you stapled a scratch-off ticket to a test you'd get extra points."

"Who'd you say it was?" I asked. "Maybe I should try taking something with him."

"Dr. Mbeki, but I think he's retired now."

"Well *shit,*" I said as I watched a girl carefully place a *Jenga* block on top of the increasingly precarious tower of blocks. "I will say, I wouldn't have thought of *Jenga* as a drinking game."

"Anything can be a drinking game," Miles said with a sip of his own poison. *Monopoly, Uno, Jenga,* you name it. Last year we put on *Django* and took a drink anytime anybody said—"

A collective groan crescendoed, drowning him out as the tower tipped over. The blocks stayed together until they didn't, exploding with a wood-on-wood *crash.* Everyone pointed at Cute Emo Band Guy and started chanting "Ass-*hole!* Ass-*hole!"* as he drained his cup. I helped gather up the blocks and saw they all had words written on them, like 'brown eyes drink.'

"You see, every block has a rule written on it in Drunk *Jenga*," Miles explained as we assembled a new tower. "Whatever the block you pull out says, you have to do."

"And if you knock it over, like poor Jimmy did," the girl on my other side chimed in, "you have to finish your drink." Jimmy shrugged with a smile.

The guy next to Jimmy pulled the first block from the new tower, damning I and all the other iPhone users to drink. The next girl arbitrarily made me and somebody named Orlando take a drink. "I'm Fiona, by the way," she said to me, which was the polite way of saying *and who the hell are you exactly?*

"I'm sorry—guys, this is Trevor," Miles introduced me to the group. "We're both in a club at school." A smattering of greetings followed, and I gave everyone a wave.

One by one, people pulled blocks and built the tower taller. *Oldest takes a drink. Pull another block. Drink three. Staring contest. Lick, slap, fondle.* Lincoln had to speak in a British accent for the rest of the game. Miles' eyes got wide when he read the loose-looking block I'd been eyeing up. "Kiss right." He turned to Lincoln, who made a face like he'd just stepped on a Lego.

"Kiss! Kiss! Kiss!" the players chanted. Some took out their phones like they'd never seen two guys kiss before. Miles and Lincoln's faces hovered inches apart before they quickly pecked each other on the lips and started giggling. Everybody cheered and whistled, turning Miles' face as red as the sun on the Japanese flag hanging on the wall. *If only I'd pulled that block...*

After some exploratory taps, I drew one on the bottom that left the Brutalist structure balancing on a single block. "Take off a piece of clothing," I read, which wouldn't have been as bad if I hadn't literally just taken off my hooded flannel. I swallowed, and squashed down my self-consciousness as I stood to pull my t-shirt off over my head. *I hope nobody's expecting a six-pack*, I thought as people hooted. I placed the block like I was defusing a bomb, only to see the tower tilt my way as soon as I sat back down. *Big yikes.* So that's how I found myself sitting shirtless in a circle of strangers with a lapful of *Jenga* blocks.

"Ass-*hole!* Ass-*hole!*"

Jimmy's chocolate-orange concoction—which we'd dubbed Tokyo Kit Kat—had gotten less harsh the more I had of it, but guzzling it all at once was like drinking gasoline. I sputtered as I reached for my shirt, disappointed that Miles' hand didn't brush against my bare skin as we gathered up blocks.

I got more comfortable with everybody at the party as the tower rose and fell two more times—once because somebody bumped the table too hard—and I was having *way* too much fun by the time I finished my third drink. It was a fun time, but it would've been even more fun if I'd been getting any vibes from Miles. *Maybe I can get a spot next to Jimmy.*

"Hey, where's your bathroom?" I tapped Miles on the shoulder.

"End of the hall on the left," he pointed.

"Don't break the seal dude!" Orlando warned me as I got up.

"If you *drink* more you're gonna *pee* more!" Brooke rolled her eyes before turning to me. "You piss as much as you need to, darling."

"Who pisses?" another guy scowled. "That's white people shit."

Purple light peeking through the door across the hall caught my eye on the way out of the bathroom. "I hope you didn't piss into my laundry basket thinking it was the toilet or anything," Miles said from behind me as I peered inside, startling me.

"I didn't," I straightened up. "I saw the lights and…I don't know. I like the way they look?"

"They *are* nice. You can get a better look if you go in, you know," he chuckled. He pushed the door open to let me step into his room. His own Christmas lights dyed everything from his bookshelf to his bed in a soft violet. I moved to try to make out the titles on his shelf when I heard the door shut. I turned to see Miles looking almost uneasy. "I feel like I should apologize, Trevor."

I blinked. "For what?"

"I feel like I haven't been a good host. I invited you over and I've barely been paying any attention to you."

"Don't be sorry! You have all these other people to pay attention to too!"

"Yeah, but…you're the one I was looking forward to seeing the most." He set his cup on his desk and took a step towards me. "I haven't been able to stop thinking about you all night."

I couldn't move.

"I can barely keep my eyes off you," he said as he closed the gap between us. *"And I've seen you looking at me too,"* he whispered into my ear, his words electrifying me. He put his hands on my arms and pierced my eyes with his own. I didn't resist, and let him put his face to mine. He tasted of booze, of desire. Our lips didn't want to pull apart, like they were glued together.

"I've been wanting to do that for weeks."

"So have I."

His lips connected with mine again, and we kissed, gently. I welcomed his tongue into my mouth, my own darting past teeth I'd fantasized about tasting. *Holy fuck is he a good kisser.* We made out as he put his hands on my waist. My hand found the back of his neck, feeling his hair. His glasses yielded to my nose. Our heads came apart again. My shirt landed on the floor. I slipped my hands underneath his and peeled it upwards and off, tossing it aside. He put his hands on my chest, sending goosebumps up my arms. *He's even hotter without his glasses.*

"I had to stop myself from doing this when you took your shirt off earlier," he breathed. We pressed our bodies together. I needed more. Our kisses became forceful, unfulfilled. I felt pressure against my groin. I grabbed him through his jeans and didn't stop, awakening something in him. He groaned and went at my neck,

sucking, gently biting as he grabbed handfuls of my butt. I threw my head back in ecstasy, dull purple seeping through my eyelids.

We kicked off our shoes. Jeans stripped themselves away. His unmade bed caught us. I pinned him to his mattress, grinding unrestrained. I moved my mouth away from his, to his neck, to his nipples, down his stomach. I pulled back his underwear. I went down and he gasped. *Please let that door be locked.* Fistfuls of hair reminded me how good I am. I gagged on him. He pushed me off, both of us swallowing air. We traded places. Our kisses were violent, lustful. He took mouthfuls of me, and I moved in tandem. *Holy shit.* I didn't know how long I would last.

"*Flip over,*" he told me.

I laid on my stomach to let him enjoy my ass. He climbed on top and I felt his dick against me, teasing me. He put a hand under my neck, bringing my face up to his. "*You have such a nice ass.*" His tongue wrestled with mine. "*I have the perfect friend for it.*"

His chest left me feeling cold without it against my back. He ran the length of his friend against my hesitant invitation. He kissed my neck and ground me into the mattress, before reaching past me towards the nightstand drawer. *Actually—*

"Hey," my voice cracked, "can we stop for a sec?"

He got off me to sit back on his feet. I flipped myself over and up to face him. "Are you not feeling that tonight?" he asked.

"I like it—I *really* like it. But yeah, I don't know if I'm feeling *that.*" My hand rubbed the back of my neck. "Sorry." *Way to kill the mood, Trevor.*

"No, don't be. Really, I understand. It's okay." He scooted towards me and threw his arms around me. "*We can still have fun.*"

Our lips locked again. Our hands felt necks, felt backs. He pushed me down and got on top, reinvigorated from making out. His tongue made me shudder before he swallowed me. I ran my fingers through his hair, pulling him in close. I felt that rush coming on deep within me. "*Oh shit, I'm getting close.*" His movements quickened. The rush intensified, more, more, until I was whimpering, begging away any dignity. I couldn't stop it if I wanted to. It spilled over me, waves surging through me. He kept his head in place as my senses returned, not missing anything. He came up with one last, slow *psluck.*

"*That was hot,*" he smiled before kissing me. I tried to pick out the taste of me.

"*Your turn,*" I grinned with a finger on his chest. "*I have an idea.*"

I laid back, my head propped on his pillow. He straddled me, slowly rocking back and forth in my mouth. I made sure to get as much as I could. I caressed his legs. He grabbed the headboard. "*Oh fuck yeah.*" His rhythm quickened. I kept up to match him. His grunts became higher, more frequent. "*Do you wanna swallow?*"

I nodded as much as I could, and ran my hands across his back. The same rush washed over him. He jolted and faltered, moans of rapture accompanying a different rush that he filled me with. I took it all. I licked it clean before he lifted himself off and laid beside me.

"Wow. *That was good.*"

We held each other, our breaths returning to normal. We kissed slowly, took each other in. His fingers raked my hair. I traced circles on his chest. "That was fun."

"I really have been wanting to do that for weeks," he broke our silence.

I raised my eyebrows. "Oh really?"

He smirked. "Let's just say that you were on my mind as I laid in bed that first night after you came to Lit Club."

"*Wow,*" I chuckled. "Well, I hope it was as good as you imagined." *It would've been if you would've let him fuck you.*

"It was," he grinned. "I'd be down to do it again, if you'd want to."

"Tonight?"

"No," he laughed. "Another time."

I smiled. "Yeah, I'd like that."

He finally got up to fish his jeans out of the mess of clothes on the floor to pull his phone from a pocket. I took in his naked body from behind. "Wow, it's already after 1:30."

I ran my hands over my face. "Ugh. I don't wanna walk back."

"You're welcome to stay here if you want," he said. *He does have a full-sized bed.*

"I mean, if you insist," I smiled.

"I insist." He tossed me my underwear and pulled on his own before climbing back into bed. We drew up the covers and spooned until he drifted off. I didn't think I would've been able to fall asleep anytime soon after being so intimate with the guy who was laying beside me, but the drowsiness that comes with sobering up eventually overtook me.

The glow from behind the curtains roused me. The Christmas lights were still on. I turned to see Miles' back gently rise and fall. I blinked away sleep as I checked my phone, low-key disappointed that I didn't have any texts. The denim sound of my jeans twisting back into shape as I pulled them on rolled Miles over.

"Hey," he said through barely-open eyes.

"Morning."

He sat up and rubbed his face. "Can I get you anything before you go? Water or something?"

"I'm good, but thanks." I slipped on my shoes. "I had fun last night, and not just in bed."

"Same," he said with a sleepy smile. He threw the covers off himself and climbed out of bed. "I'll walk you out."

"I know how to get out."

"That wouldn't make me a good host though, would it?" He got up and pulled on his shirt from last night and a pair of basketball shorts.

The other bedroom doors were shut. There was just enough natural light peeking in to make defined shapes of the scattered cups and cans and *Jenga* blocks and a crumpled pack of cigarettes. A girl whose name I can't remember sat on the couch and looked down at a glass of water she held with both hands. Miles hugged himself in the crisp morning air that met us outside. "Thanks again for coming. I really did have fun with you."

"Yeah, me too. Thanks for inviting me." We came together for one last kiss before I left. I looked back to see him give me a wave before stepping back inside.

I took the 'walk of shame' without feeling an ounce of shame—I was just some guy walking across the campus parking lots at 9 a.m. on a Saturday. *Nothing about me says dicks or mouths*, I incorrectly thought.

"*Woah*," Tylor laughed as soon as he saw me, "*somebody* had a good night."

I raised an eyebrow. "What do you mean, '*woah*?'"

"Go check yourself out the mirror," he chuckled.

Even before I turned on the light, I could see the large dark spot on the side of my neck. At least I didn't have to go to class, like the time I had to go to school with a hickey from Dillon.

"I wonder if anybody on the floor has a banana," Tylor said in an apparent non sequitur. "Holding the inside of the peel against it helps it go away a little."

"I'm *not* gonna wake people up to ask them if they happen to have a banana."

"Well wait until we go get breakfast then!"

I gave him a look. "So what, so I can sit in Patnick and rub a banana peel all over myself?" *Why don't the Health Center people tell you that fun fact while they're watching you roll a condom down the length of one?*

October 16

I believed you when you said we were endless,
But the day you chose convenience
Was the day I stopped giving myself away—
The day I stopped making promises
I couldn't promise myself to keep.

October 17

Sunita almost wrote me up for yeeting my pencil cup at the wall but how could i not when eleven children went to school today without knowing it would be the last time theyd ever do it because unfortunately for them they were black and unfortunately for everybody else they died because of the hate that we tolerate that we allow that we look away from and let blossom but thats how problems get worse and turn into bigger things but i think weve gotten there a long time ago but the america i was told to love is better than thats how things are and thats how things have been but greatness never happens with that attitude and the new apartheid and the new slavery really isnt that new when freedoms are used as an excuse for prejudice a hall pass for hate because jesus loves them anyway so what does it matter if they see wrong and dont try to right it see today as history without trying to rewrite it if america is great then please tell me why because ive waited for and looked for an answer but all ive come up with is white is right and man is right and straight is right and christian is right though were all equal but im not convinced its twenty twenty two for fucks sake do we live in dystopia a fascist state people say we dont but look it up sometime or maybe its okay if it happens in america where we get more upset over the price of eggs than we do at a bullet in the brain of an eight year old maybe if there are enough eight year old brains with enough bullets in them then itll be just another thing that just is like litter on the side of the road just dont look at it and itll go away do you want things to change then make straight people have to come out make white people get off the sidewalk for people darker then them get pushed in front of subway trains for looking suspicious tell people with six kids their choices are sin it astounds me that there arent more alcoholics but we all get drunk off something now dont we and a lack of intelligence seems to be the drink of choice but its okay because wheel of fortune will be back on and itll be like it never even happened heres a math problem and dont pop a vessel over it how many children need to get shot to death before something gets done about it oh wait i forgot its their civil liberty to get murdered senselessly lets change elections and take away womens rights and change what equality is but get the fuck away from the second for god so loved the world that he gave us the firearm made in his image so that we too can sow death on a whim what do other countries think of us are we a game show to them a comedy show because only on tv can stuff like this happen only on tv can kids be murdered and nothing changes except more get murdered only in america

October 18

Get out your telescopes so you don't miss the rare astronomical event going on —Repubes pretending to give a shit about mental health, which curiously only ever happens whenever gun rights are on the line. I wonder which one they would save if they had to choose between an unborn baby and an AR-15?

DJ Twinkle Toes made me tear up when he took a moment during his radio show to read the names of yesterday's victims. The school even had a grief counselor set up, though I feel like the atrium of Bixby might not have been the best spot for them. And then there was a girl tearfully reading a poem—"America, Reloading", which was all it took to make Andrea Gibson my new favorite poet—in the Quad that kept my feet rooted and had me crying right there along with her, fucking me up so much that I had to print it out to tape into my book. Like, why the fuck don't they make us read *that* kind of poetry for class—poetry that makes us angry and uncomfortable, poetry that makes the most horrific parts of our society stare us down? Let's talk about *that* instead of some stick-up-the-ass Edwardian sonnet with a clever meter.

If our Midterms had been a week earlier, I probably would've made a joke about how 'studying' must be a contraction of 'student' and 'dying.' I spent all weekend studying so I wouldn't feel guilty about taking an evening off to go to Open Mic Night, which Kade was already on top of. Hoping that I looked good in the flannel and beanie I threw on this morning in case I got a chance to talk to Ethan, I grabbed dinner at Taco Bell after work and watched for my Axworthy friends through the window. They stared at me like I had another hickey when I went out to meet them. "What?" I asked almost defensively.

"Nothing," Kade said. "I've just never seen you in any kind of hat before."

"It hasn't been cold enough yet for one, and regular hats make me look douchey —no offense," I added as I caught Victor's eye. "*You* look good in a hat."

"You mean hats look good on *me*," he corrected me. "And speaking of looks and fits," Victor said, "I almost ordered a shirt with an assault rifle on it that said 'the real baby killer' underneath, but I ended up not because I didn't wanna walk around wearing a picture of an assault rifle."

"Yeah, that's valid," I said as October's evening breeze stuffed my hands into my pockets. "And true."

"So how'd the rest of your night go after you abandoned us?" Kade asked, since I hadn't seen them since the night of Miles' party. As much as I wanted to, I didn't tell them that I hooked up with somebody because I hate listening to other people's sexcapades.

"It was fun. I barely knew anybody, but we played this game called Drunk *Jenga* that's fun as hell that we've gotta play sometime," I talked it up. "Only thing is we need alcohol to play it."

Kade raised an eyebrow. "Do you need a *Jenga* game to play it too?"

A cafe's-worth of people didn't let Midterms keep them from showing up to support the event. I looked around for Ethan or anyone else I knew. My eyes fell on the table where Miles and I sat not even a week ago without knowing we'd soon have our dicks in each other's mouths. I was glad when we bumped into Nikole—literally—as she and her drink scoped out the table situation. "Trevor!" she smiled. "I'm glad you're here. My friend I was supposed to meet here canceled on me after I was already here."

"I know the feeling," I empathized. "Do you remember Kade and Victor? They played *Cards* with us that one time."

"Of course I do! I'll grab a table for us before they get all snatched up."

Kade's eyes followed her. "Talk about snatched," he muttered to himself.

I couldn't not order a hot apple cider after Miles had turned me onto them. *Should I have messaged him by now?* I thought as I watched the barista concoct my drink. *But he hasn't messaged me either. Maybe he's just busy with exams.* And I guess as a treat for all of our studying, I also paid an opulent price for a half-dozen brownies for us to share.

"Are they pot brownies?" Victor asked when I set them in the middle of the table.

Kade stared at the bite he took out of his. "Who needs pot when this brownie already got me high as hell?"

I slid my phone back into my pocket after laugh reacting to Kade's Instagram story of a pic of the case of pastries captioned "*i'll eat your shitter like an apple fritter.*" "So are chai lattes like the same thing as chai tea?" I asked Victor's chai latte.

"You shouldn't have said that," Victor chuckled.

"You uncultured. Little. *Shit*," Kade spat. "The phrase 'chai tea' is redundant—'chai' is just the Hindi word for 'tea,' so by saying 'chai tea' you're just saying 'tea tea,' and you know who says 'tea tea?' Fucking peasants." I was so weak I had to set down my glass. "And also, don't you *ever* compare this"—he threw his hand towards Victor's mug in disgust—"*steamed cum*"—some shot out of Victor's nose—"to real masala chai. You're gonna have a real cup of chai the next time you come over," he pointed at me before spinning on his roommate. "And what the hell's wrong with you? I am *hella* disappointed in you."

"I just—it looked good," Victor finally coughed. "What'd you get, Trev?"

"Hot apple cider." I breathed it in deep. "It's *divine.* You wanna try it?"

Just the smell of it even made Kade's eyes go wide. "Oh my god. I wonder what spices they use?"

"I'll pay somebody to take a drink of that and tell me to my face that anything pumpkin spice is better," Victor said after he tried a sip.

"You know what they say—pumpkin spice is to apple cider as Thomas Edison is to Nikola Tesla."

"Passes blunt to the left," Victor laughed.

"Nobody says that," Kade said to me.

"I did. Just now."

"How about...pumpkin spice is to apple cider," Kade slowly said to the ceiling, "as D-Day is to Stalingrad?"

"I love it." I raised my cup. "A toast. To Stalingrad."

Kade raised his mug. "To Stalingrad."

Victor raised his mug. "To Stalingrad?"

We drank in reverence. "Hashtag never forget."

"Are you guys toasting Stalin?" Nikole asked as she returned from the bathroom. "Not that there's anything wrong with that, it's just a little—"

"Oh my god," Victor said through a mouthful of brownie. "Oh my god. Guys. These brownies. I'm fucking faded right now."

The lights eventually dimmed as the emcee welcomed us and introduced the improv group from last time—who are members of the actual Improv Club on campus—as the first act. Acoustic Guitar Guy from last time followed them. *I hope Ethan plays again tonight,* I thought as somebody in a fedora and a bowling-alley shirt did some kind of mumble rap thing. I kept worrying he wasn't going to play until a guy with blue hair, who turned out to be Ethan, took the stage. *No wonder I couldn't find him,* I smiled. Ethan plugged himself in and played a few bars of the *Halloween* theme. "Thanks for coming out," he smiled. "Hopefully this one's as fun for you as it is for me." He started playing Passion Pit—which made his dyed hair make more sense—and the rest of the instruments joined in from his phone after a few notes. His voice captivated us, the music electrified us—swarms of buzzing notes that wriggled their way into our ears and took us over. *Opening scene for a music video: thousands of people crowding to see the Pope or Mussolini or the Queen, who appears on the balcony wearing a big mouse head. EDM starts playing. Crowd gets turnt.* Ethan's hands flew away from his keyboard at the end of the song to an enthusiastic wave of applause.

The overhead lights swallowed the spots as the emcee ended the night. I stood and caught Ethan's eye with an up-nod as he moved through the room. He flashed a grin and made his way over. "I had a feeling I'd see you here," he smiled. "Trevor, right?"

"Yeah," I smiled back. *Don't flirt, don't flirt.* "You remembered my name?"

"I mean, I did serve you a coffee," he chuckled. In the corner of my eye, Victor looked like he was working out a math problem.

"I mean, yeah," I chuckled. *How many drinks does he serve though? That was a week and a half ago.* "I brought friends with me this time!"

"Um, you actually met up with *us*," Kade corrected me. I ignored him.

"I think your fan base might be growing," I said to Ethan.

Ethan chuckled. "Did you like it?" he asked us. "That was definitely one of the more...*vibrant* things I've done."

"Are you kidding? I loved it!"

"I'm about to go put some Passion Pit on my playlist."

He thanked us for our good words. "Are you in Chem Lab Tuesday and Thursday mornings?" he asked Victor.

"Yeah? With Zabinsky?"

"Yeah! We're in the same class! I sit at the table behind you."

"Oh shit, forreal? The hair must've thrown me off. But yeah, you killed it up there dude. I'm Victor, by the way. He/him."

"Ethan. Nice to formally meet you."

"How's your project going?"

"I couldn't tell you," Ethan laughed. "My partner told me she'll do it all herself."

"What? Forreal?"

"I know, right? I told her it wouldn't feel right doing less than half the work, but she insisted." He shrugged. "Whatevs. I'll take it though."

"Lucky."

"I'm Kade," Kade put an end to their exchange.

"Nikole. I'm really digging the hair."

"Do you need to get out of here right away?" I asked Ethan.

"No, but I *am* starving though. Lemme go grab something to snack on," he said as he nodded over at the counter.

"I think there might be a brownie left," I said as I tipped the lid back to reveal the last gleaming chocolate ingot. "You can have it if you want."

He hesitated. "I mean, are you sure?"

"It's all yours."

"Okay, you convinced me," he said as he grabbed a nearby chair to hang his hoodie and backpack off of. I tried not to watch him devour his brownie.

"Ethan played at the last Open Mic Night too," I told Nikole.

"Yeah, thanks for the invite," Kade said from behind crossed arms. "You *do* play really well though," he said to Ethan.

"Kade and I were in a band back home, which sounds less cool when I say that it was just a garage band," Victor said as he held his wrist behind the back of his chair.

"Garage bands are cool!" Ethan said. "I played piano in the orchestra for my school's musicals, but an actual band is hella dope."

"I guess. Piano takes a lot more talent than the drums though."

"You play the *drums?*"

"Yep," he nodded. "I have my real set back home, and an electronic one here at school with me."

"*Two* drum sets? Your parents must be loaded," Ethan said as he polished off his brownie. Victor started tapping his fingers uncomfortably.

"I'm glad to see that somebody else still likes Passion Pit," Nikole said. "I thought we all died out. Do you like Waterparks at all? And yes, I'm only asking because of the hair."

"I mean, I haven't been to one in a while, but yeah, I like them," Ethan shrugged. "What does my hair have to do with it?"

Victor and Nikole and I traded looks. "You're not gonna call *him* an uncultured shit?" I asked Kade.

"No?" Kade raised an eyebrow. "Why would I ever call somebody something so rude?"

"Oh, do you mean the band?" Ethan laughed. "I was like, *what does my hair have to do with that?* I actually forgot about them!"

Nikole pinched the air. "One does not simply 'forget' about Waterparks."

"Yeah, you fool of a Took," Victor chimed in.

"Okay, okay, you guys like Waterparks. Noted," Ethan chuckled. "This is just spray-on though," he said as he ran his fingers through his aqua hair. "I've always wanted to dye my hair for real, but my mom would flip."

"So? You're an adult. There are worse things you could do in college," I said with a wink.

"Oh, I've *definitely* done worse," he laughed.

We sat and talked classes for a while until we were ready to head out. "I'll walk back with you, but only as far as Kessler," Ethan said.

The four of us—"As much as I love a good brownie, I'm gonna go get something more substantial," Nikole said before she split—took up the whole sidewalk. I admired Ethan's hair and wished that I had the balls to do something like that as we passed the yard with The Skeletons, dressed in your standard Halloween costumes and holding plastic jack-o'-lantern buckets. "So is electropop-slash-electro rock your favorite kind of music?" Kade asked Ethan.

"It's not my *favorite*. I just like whatever sounds good," Ethan shrugged. "Pop, electronic, alternative, rap, anything really. My only rule when it comes to music is that it can't suck."

"Give us an example of music that sucks," Victor said.

Ethan laughed through his nose. "Okay, I don't like to say any kind of music *sucks*. I mean, somebody worked to create it."

"Oh no, there's definitely music that sucks," Kade rebuffed him, "and that's coming from somebody all-too familiar with the creative process."

"Let's just say you definitely won't catch me listening to country music," Ethan finally said.

"We hate country too!" I grinned.

"Did we just become best friends?" Kade asked him.

Since Kessler Hall is the dorm closest to Main Street, Ethan didn't get to stick with us for too long. "It was nice to meet you guys," he said in front of his building. "If anyone's ever in the mood for some Starbucks on a Tuesday or Thursday afternoon, you'll see me there."

"See ya!" I smiled. "Catch me in the library!"

"Catch ya later dude!"

"See you in class!"

Ethan gave us a smile before swiping himself in and vanishing into the building.

"He's pretty cool," Victor said.

"I didn't know you had class with him," I said jealously.

"Me neither," he chuckled. "I bet you wish *you* had class with your cute blond barista though."

The darkness hid the color rushing to my face. "Oh my *god.*"

"Oh my god what?" Kade said without looking up from his phone.

"Nothing," I lied. I caught Victor rolling his eyes. *For fuck's sake Trevor, stop being so afraid of what other people will think of you.* "Okay, so I kind of like Ethan."

"He seems like a likable guy," Kade said casually before stopping to look me in the face. "Unless you mean you *like* him like him?"

I swallowed. I'm still afraid that people won't want to be friends with me anymore once they find out I'm gay. *Those two words. Just five letters.* "Yes, I like guys, if that's what you're asking."

"*Nice,*" he high-fived me. "Welcome to the family."

"Um, I've *been* in the family. You like guys too then?"

"Oh yeah. Guys, girls, both, neither, everyone. I just like whoever I find myself liking."

"Okay, cool." *Pansexual then? Or I guess 'queer' would cover it. Or he can just be Kade, and that's that.*

The streetlight above us went out right as we passed beneath it. "Shit fam," Kade swore, "you know what's supposed to happen to you if that happens three times in a row?"

"No?"

"Neither do I, but if it does, you fucking *book it,*" he said like we were about to have to outrun a dinosaur. "So...do you consider yourself full-on gay, or bi, or...?"

"Nope, full-on gay. No interest in girls in the slightest."

"I'm straight, while we're at it," Victor said with his hands in his pockets. *Definitely a lowercase-s straight guy.*

"So wait, you couldn't tell?" I asked Kade. "We've known each other for like a month and a half. You *had* to have seen me checking guys out."

"I guess, but I guess I just never thought anything of it."

"Oof, and I thought *my* gaydar was shit."

"Oh, mine's *absolute* shit. But what does any of this have to do with a coupon though?"

Victor and I looked at each other. "Who said anything about a coupon?" he laughed, indifferent to the fact that the next streetlight stayed on when we walked under it.

"*You* did! You said something about a barista and a coupon!"

It took Victor another minute to get what the hell Kade was talking about. "I said *cute blond*, not *coupon!*" he laughed.

October 19

I was reading a Buzzfeed article about 'unwritten rules' that Black people need to follow and I had to stop because it had me *that* fired up. You never realize how privileged you are until you read about how people with skin darker than yours can't wear their hood up at the risk of being seen as a thug, or always have to ask for a receipt so they can't be accused of stealing. People who don't think white privilege is a thing can do us all a favor by sitting the fuck down and shutting the fuck up.

We finished de Conto's exam early today, so Kade and I hit up the vaccine clinic the Health Center had set up in Rosenberg before the Common Hour rush could swamp it. I guess the single-student study pods up on the second floor make for a good place to administer shots. I wonder if anti-vaxxers ever protest outside of pharmacies like pro-birthers do at abortion clinics? The two of us and our neon-green bandages grabbed coffee—"Oooh, let's get some Starbs!" Kade shrieked—and talked about why nobody's ever tried opening a Russian Empire-themed chain of coffee shops called Tsarbucks. The cute blond was pouring a carton of milk into a machine with his back to us when we walked in, and looked like we made his day when he saw us.

"*I think I'm starting to see what you mean now,*" Kade said in a low voice as we approached the counter.

Ethan leaned his elbows across his counter. "You guys missed me *that* much? Don't you have exams or something?"

"Oh, we did," Kade said. "*Veni, vidi, vici.*"

Ethan just chuckled. "Whatever you say."

"Did *you* have any today?" I asked him.

98

"I just had Chem Lab this morning, and then I swung by my professor's office to drop off my paper for College Writing so I could start work early. Victor was done with his in like fifteen minutes, so he either aced it or bombed it."

"I'll be able to tell from the music he puts on when he gets back," Kade laughed. "For my own sake I hope he aced it."

"Oh nice, I didn't know you were roommates," Ethan said. "You two seem like you click really well," he gestured between us.

Kade and I traded smirks. "What can I say?"

A line forming behind us forced us to actually order our drinks. "We should all hang out sometime," Ethan said as he popped lids on our cups. "Do you guys use Instagram?" *Yes, thank you god.*

"I do if you do," I said, cringing at myself.

EthanE16 is now following you.

"Hit me up if you wanna grab dinner or something!" he smiled.

"Yeah, we will!" *Oh, we will.*

True to his word, Kade made me a 'real' cup of masala chai when we went back to 239 Axworthy to hang, where angry crunchy guitars and guttural growls blasted from Victor's room. The aroma of the tea was mysterious and inviting, spiced beyond anything I could imagine. "Anytime you hear someone say they're drinking 'chai tea,'" Kade said as we set up his chessboard, "and it's not this stuff, you go ahead and you dump it on them."

I skimmed Ethan's profile after Brit Lit—I'm about to start taking a shot every time Gallagher says "to what effect"—for any hint of what team he might play for. It turns out he plays for the school baseball team, the Knights. He must've played in high school too, because there's a pic of him in an orange jersey with 'Eastwood' across the top and a big number '16' in the middle. I scoured his Instagram again after a dinner of Domino's and a completed take-home Critical Writing assignment, but didn't see a single pic, caption, hashtag, or location pin that smells even remotely gay. Even worse, there are a bunch of posts of him and the same girl with kissy faces and heart emojis in the captions, going all the way up until we moved in. Her profile, which is public and which I also stalked, is a lot of the same. *Ugh.*

October 20

You know how sometimes you'll do that thing where you're walking and then all of a sudden you'll forget how to walk? That happened to me today in the stairwell in Shaver, and like 18 people watched me trip and almost bite the staircase.

I like how I used to high-key judge people for getting Starbucks all the time and I've already gone twice this week—which is still way less than a lot of people. Kade and I asked Ethan if he wanted to meet up with us for dinner when we stopped by after class, which is how we found ourselves pushing two tables together in Patnick later on at dinner to fit all eight of us—me, Tylor, Kade, Victor, Ethan, Ethan's roommate Nate, and their friends Jada and Cassidy. The special was chicken and waffles, and everybody was rightfully flipping shit over them. And not just us—I mean *everybody*.

"You don't even know how hard I am for these right now," Kade said with syrupy lips. "Like, whoever thought to put these together is a fucking genius."

"Has anybody ever told you how loud you masticate?" I asked him with a smile.

He stopped chewing like I'd just called him the f-word. *"What* did you just say?" he asked me slowly with a full mouth.

"Masticate," I repeated. "Chewing. You're a loud chewer."

"Oh. I thought you said something else."

"That was the joke," I rolled my eyes just as Ethan came back with his own dish that only the American ethos could concoct.

"You picked a good day to get dinner," he said as he sat down, still wearing the black jeans and gray t-shirt he worked in.

"Do you not get dinner every day?" I smirked. "You should try it sometime."

"You'll have to excuse him," Kade said to Ethan.

"Moments like this make me wish that I ate meat," Victor said as he sat down with his plate of just waffles. Why is breakfast for dinner okay, but dinner for breakfast isn't?

Between the food and being done with exams, everybody was in a good mood. Cassidy and Jada are nice, but they have these loud, shrill laughs that legit make my ears hurt. If there's such a thing as a middlecase-s straight guy, that's what Nate is. "Do you like *Cards Against Humanity?"* Victor asked Ethan as we took our empty plates over to the conveyor belt to the dish room. "We're gonna play that or *What Do You Meme?* tomorrow if you're interested at all."

"We are?" I asked, earning myself a glare from Victor. "Oh wait—that's right. I got my days mixed up."

"Hell yeah! I'd be down!" Ethan smiled, making my stomach flutter.

"*You're welcome,*" Victor muttered to me.

Ethan and his friends headed for Bixby to see *Sixteen Candles,* the week's CPB movie showing. "We have movie night in our room sometimes," I told him before we parted ways without looking at either of my Axworthy friends. "We usually get wings or order pizza or something."

"Nice! Let me know the next time you have one!" he grinned. "And lemme know about tomorrow!"

"Will do!"

"They're nice," Tylor said once it was just the four of us again. "Ethan seems pretty cool."

"Some of us would say he's more than just pretty cool," Victor smirked.

October 21

This morning was one of those foggy ones that strung all the spider webs in pearls of dew. The fog even gathered around the tops of the lamp posts in the parking lots like some kind of trees from a Dr. Seuss story. The vibe was *real.* I could've just stood there and looked at it all morning.

Midterm grades are in, and they're more or less what I expected—an A in Western Civ, Bs in Computers, Physical Science, and Critical Writing, and a C in Brit Lit. I blame the professor.

My phone *pinged* with a message from Ethan saying he was almost to Swafford and I sprang from my chair to dart down to the lobby to sign him in—taking the long way to avoid the plunger jousting match going on down the hall. I was giddy at the thought of taking him back to my room, even just as a friend.

"How's it going?" he greeted the others as he slipped off his...Adidases? Adidas'? Adidii?

"*Whattup.*"

"What it do!"

"Help yourself to pizza," I offered as I grabbed him a plate from the cabinet. I tried not to stare at his smile, but didn't want to look away from him. "Are your socks supposed to not match?" I ended up asking like someone with a stick up their ass.

He looked down at them. "Huh, I guess they don't. I think the better question is why are you looking at my feet, you weirdo?"

I almost started sweating. "I wasn't—I just notice things," I stuttered, praying my face wasn't getting red.

"I'm *kidding,* dude," he hit my shoulder. "Lighten up." I was too relieved to be annoyed at being told to lighten up.

"Trevor does this thing where he judges other people's clothes," Kade explained.
"I do not!" I lied.

"Just today you said somebody looked like a slob for wearing a shirt that was too big for him!"

"It had holes in it! Nobody wanted to see his armpit hair!"

"Whatever, *mom*," Kade rolled his eyes.

"Did he just call you mom?" Ethan chuckled as he and his pizza slices found a spot on the floor.

"Yeah I did, *dad*."

"That's *enough*, kids," Nikole laughed.

We started with *What Do You Meme?* since Tylor was going out later on and he wanted to play that. Ethan was so head-over-heels for his PS5 that I wouldn't have been surprised if he'd tried to steal it. "What games do you like to play?" he asked Tylor.

Tylor shrugged. "RPGs, open world games, shooters—anything really, though I'm not a fan of playing online because people are dicks. I'm replaying *Resident Evil* since it's spooky season."

"Oh nice! I'm actually going as Leon for Halloween."

Kade perked up. "Leon Trotsky?"

We're all dressing up, but we're all keeping our costumes a secret from each other for whatever reason. I don't even know what Tylor's doing. I'm going to be a ghost-type Pokémon trainer since it's easy—I'll just get some purple clothes and some toy Poké Balls. I think I might dye my hair too, because I've low-key always wanted to do it, but was always too nervous about what people would think. But if being gay and in college isn't a valid excuse to dye your hair, then what is?

October 22

Nobody had warned us,
Not that we would have listened anyway—
How could we have possibly grasped the gravity of
The things we did, the things we swore to one another?
I willingly laid myself bare before you, in more ways than one,
Telling you things I've never before dared say aloud—
So high on chemical reactions that I didn't even
Consider that maybe you weren't doing the same.
I eagerly gave you every piece of my self, so much
That my newfound vulnerability terrified me,

But the novel delirium gave me a taste of
What it felt like to really be alive, so exhilarating that
It bowled me over like a rush of waves and
Ceaselessly crashed me down until I was nothing.
And for as much as I preach self-preservation,
We recklessly played on the edge of a precipice
With powers we didn't understand—
Half-wishing I'd fall just to give me a taste of
What it would also feel like to die,
Never thinking that I actually would,
Never thinking it would be your push that would send me reeling.

October 23

So I guess some archbishop from the Middle Ages came to the conclusion that god created the universe on October 23, 4004 B.C., although there's some uncertainty over what time of day. Maybe I should sign up for Open Mic Night as a comedy act and that'll be my only line. Actually, I'll follow that up with something about how there are people who voted for Fuckstick in 2020 and are under the impression that they're getting into heaven. I almost wish that god *did* exist just so I could watch people blabber and stutter before him when he asks, *"What bible did you fucking read?"* What's the point of praying and going to church if you let hate make a home in your heart?

Kade and Victor invited me to go out last night with them and their floormate Will, who I met last week when he tagged along with us to get dinner. The party was at Will's friend's place at Lakeview, an apartment complex down the road from the mail center just off campus. I would've asked Ethan if he wanted to come with us, but he was going to see whatever hip-hop artist CPB booked for a concert that none of the rest of us gave shit about.

In the apartment's kitchen, Kade stared at the drink selection like it was a memory game before pouring us drinks that looked like dirty toilet water and tasted like boozy apple cider. The place was garnished with chintzy dollar-store Halloween decorations, and the music rotated between pop, trap, and show tunes—I guess like half the people there were Music majors, including Will—every three songs. The only game anybody seemed to be playing was something called Tour de Franzia, which, according to Kade, is just what college students call Slap the Bag "so they don't feel so broke-ass."

"Since when have you been the authority on Slap the Bag?" Victor scoffed.

Kade raised an eyebrow. "Um, since Jeremy Duffner's graduation party after-party?"

Victor just blinked.

"Remember how I puked in their coffee pot?"

I busted out laughing. "You puked in a *coffee pot?*"

"Listen, when you know you're gonna hurl, you don't get picky about vessels."

None of us got in on Tour de Franzia, but somebody dug up a game of *Clue* with a piece of a paperclip for the lead pipe and a stale candy Bottle Cap for Mr. Green's piece, but even Kade couldn't stay focused on it for long. I abandoned it for the conversation behind me when somebody said that being "bisexual is basically the same thing as being polysexual," since I didn't even know that polysexuality was a thing.

"If you're bisexual, you're attracted to more than one gender," a girl with five piercings in her left ear explained, "but if you're polysexual, you're attracted to multiple genders."

"So if you're bisexual, are you also polysexual?" somebody asked. "Like how all rectangles are parallelograms?"

"They're not *quadrilaterals.*"

"Why have polygons when you can have polysexuals?"

"So is being polysexual the same thing as being pansexual?"

"Nuh uh, pansexual is attraction *regardless* of gender."

"This is more confusing than I thought."

Five Piercings shrugged. "And who's fault is that?"

"I love how people say that sexuality is too confusing and too mature for kids to understand until that sexuality is heterosexual," I heard myself say. "And by 'love' I mean 'it fucking pisses me off.'"

"But kids shouldn't have to worry about that kind of stuff while they're still kids," somebody said, making my nostrils flare.

"Yeah they should, because it would make their lives a lot easier. You have all these kids that aren't heterosexual or cisgender growing up hearing that those are the only ways to be. You want a sure-fire way to fuck up your kid? There you go." *Drops mic.* I squeezed past a guy telling his friend how he wants to try wearing adult diapers and into the kitchen, where I found Victor holding an Angry Orchard in each hand. "Are you double-fisting those?" I asked him. "Said the actress to the bishop."

"Wait, what?" he chuckled.

"I guess that's what they say in Britain instead of 'that's what she said.'"

He just stared. "Wait, *what* actress?"

"Never mind," I groaned. "Why *do* you have two bottles though? Are you playing Edward Scissorhands or whatever it's called?"

"Edward *Forty*hands?" he laughed. "No, this one's Kade's. Or is it this one? Either way, he had me hold his while we went to go to the bathroom."

I was about to make a masturbation joke when we heard somebody roar the f-word. Nearby conversations screeched to a halt. "I didn't know we had a couple of *faggots* here!" A guy who had to be seven feet tall had gone to use the bathroom and walked in on Kade and Will doing the kind of things two guys do in a bathroom together. I watched in shock as he grabbed Will and pushed him to the floor.

"Hey, leave them the fuck alone!" Five Piercings yelled.

"He's had a lot to drink, he doesn't know what he's talking about," Seven Foot's friend said to try to defuse the situation. "Nobody wants to start any trouble."

"Nobody except these fucking fags. Nobody wants to fucking see that!" Seven Foot said like he was ready to start throwing punches.

"Hey, that's enough buddy."

"You need to get outta here, man."

My blood ran hot. "They *had* their privacy until you walked in on them!" I yelled.

Seven Foot started towards me. "Yeah, you *would* stick up for them, wouldn't you? You fucking *fag-lover*."

Five Piercings got between us before the situation escalated further. "I swear to *fucking god* Bruce, if you don't get out right now I'm calling the police!" He just pushed her into the wall, and two other guys had him on the floor in an instant. People were apologetically telling Kade and Will not to listen to him and asked if they needed anything.

"Hey, are you okay?" I asked Kade, even though he looked like he was about to cry.

"I just need to go."

He held it together until we were in the parking lot. Victor pulled him into a hug while I stood with Will, who had tears in his own eyes. I felt like he could've used a hug too, but I didn't know if that would've been weird. "That—*fucking asshole*—" Kade cried, making me tear up. "What does he—who *cares* if two guys—"

"Fuck him," Victor said. "He's nobody. He doesn't matter."

We were the only group of people crossing campus in silence. I tried to ignore the laughter of the people who didn't have their nights ruined. "Trevor, you don't need to come back with us," Kade finally said.

"You're my friend though!" I protested. "I wanna be there for you!"

"I know that," he said like he was struggling. "And I appreciate you *so* much. You're a wonderful person and a great friend, but I am—" I caught Victor mouthing *he just needs some space* to me.

"Okay," I sighed. "I'll talk to you guys tomorrow."

I took the long way to Swafford to leave them to themselves. My anger barely subsided as I walked past the Field House and into the Quad. *I don't understand why people have to treat other people like that just because they're different. Why do people choose to be so hateful? It doesn't have to be this way. It's not fair. It's not fucking fair.* I sat on a bench near the gazebo with my thoughts until Instagram opened itself on my phone.

Hey, are you up?

I watched the sky and listened to the distant sound of running water until my thigh buzzed.

Yeah
Tipsy, but up

Is it okay if I come over?

Yeah sure thing. Something wrong?

Yeah. I'll tell you about it
I'm on my way
Coming up the steps now

Miles' face disappeared from the window just before his door opened for me. The only other person there was his other roommate Kollin, who was high as shit and watching *Rick and Morty. Was it only a week ago that I was here, playing* Jenga *without a shirt on?* I thought as Kollin and I gave each other a nod.

I followed Miles back to his room. "Thanks for letting me come over."

"Sure thing," he said a little sheepishly as he closed the door behind us. "So what's up? And can I get you anything?"

"No thanks. I'm just..." I looked around the room—homey in the light of his table lamp—to find the right words. "I just don't understand why people are so hateful."

He straightened up. "Did something happen?"

"Not to me. We were at a party, and my friend was making out with another guy, and somebody got *really* upset over it. He started dropping the f-bomb and pushed the other guy to the floor. Everyone's okay, physically anyway." Miles patted the bed beside him and I sat. "I guess I'm just surprised that there are people like that at a liberal arts college in 2022."

"There are always gonna be assholes wherever you go."

I kept my eyes on my shoes before turning to him. "Were you ever bullied or picked on for being gay? You don't have to talk about it if you don't wanna."

"I never got beat up or anything," he said after a moment. "But I got called names and had books knocked out of my hands and stuff."

"*Shit*, I'm sorry. I never had *that.*"

"That was back in high school though," he said like it doesn't matter anymore.

"Did—did you ever used to think about hurting yourself then? When people would call you names and pick on you?"

He exhaled sharply. "I mean, it made me feel weak and pathetic, even though I shouldn't have let it. Looking back, I'm actually kinda thankful for it, because I feel like those experiences just helped make me a stronger person today." He cracked his knuckles. "And besides, what other people think of me is on *them*. If someone has a problem with me, then they can go fuck right off. I'm done hiding who I am." And then after a moment, "But I never thought about like, *killing* myself, if that's what you mean."

I swallowed.

He gave me a concerned look. "You haven't, have you?"

"I used to cut myself, but I haven't in a long time." I turned my wrist up so he could see. "Look, the scars are old."

He put a hand on my back, letting a calm warmth radiate from his touch. "Listen to me," he said seriously. "If you ever need somebody to talk to and your friends aren't around, I'm here for you. You got me?"

I rested my hand on his leg. I thought about telling him everything. But instead, I looked into his thoughtful eyes before meeting his lips with mine. The thoughts weighing on my mind got lighter with each kiss until they stopped hurting.

"*Is this okay?*"

"Yeah."

I slid his glasses off. Our shirts followed. His bed held our naked bodies. Our hands pumped each other. Moans slipped into each other's mouths. On my back, his bare chest pressed against mine. My legs hugged him as we kissed hungrily.

God, do I wanna be inside you, his body told me.

I want you to, mine told him. *But...*

It's okay. Really, it is.

His mouth pulled away from mine. He climbed down me, and his warmth enveloped me. I gasped. He took me. He took it all. We flipped around. I caressed his thighs as I went. He twitched as I fulfilled him.

"I hope your roommate didn't hear us," I said between kisses afterwards.

"He probably forgot you're here," he chuckled as he put his glasses back on. "But he knows what I do with guys in my room though." He pulled up his shorts as I stepped back into my jeans. "You're welcome to stay the night again if you want."

"Thanks, but I think I'm just gonna head back though," I winced.

"Nothing like sleeping in your own bed," he smiled.

I pulled my shoes back on. "Thanks again for letting me come over and listening to me."

His arms held me. "Don't mention it. I like listening to you. And I like doing other things with you too." I smiled into his neck. We shared one last kiss. "Here, I'll let you out."

Kollin was in the exact same position he was when I got there. *Maybe he sleeps with his eyes open?* "Get back safe," Miles told me.

I couldn't stop hearing his words on the walk back. *"He knows what I do with guys in my room."* With as sweet and as hot as he is, his body count has to be higher than an 80s slasher series. Thinking about him being with a different guy every weekend, maybe even more often, makes me feel bad about myself, and I'm not really sure why.

And then go figure the *one* time nobody was around to see it, I tried to slide down The Railing and I actually fucking *did* it.

October 24

Anxiety is like trying to gather up the stars—

October 25

I saw something on Instagram that said to be thankful for Halloween even if you aren't into it because it keeps Christmas from taking over October too. I saw my first Christmas ad of the season today with a jack-o'-lantern in a Santa hat. And then people act shocked and think you're the Grinch when December rolls around and you're sick of Christmas.

Victor and I hit up the blood drive going on in Bixby, where most of the workers were in costume for Halloween. Wouldn't it be a vibe if they were actually vampires who are grossed out at the thought of sucking blood and pretending to have a blood drive is how they get it? I talked myself up to get over my fear of needles for a few minutes if it meant doing something that could help somebody, only to be told that I wasn't allowed to give blood since I've had sex with another guy in the past twelve months.

"I thought you knew," Victor said sympathetically while he sipped on instant lemonade and munched on some vanilla cookies like it was Sunday School. "I thought about that, but I didn't wanna ask about your private life."

"No, you're good," I said even though I was still butthurt about it, pun intended.

"Yeah, that's why I told you to not wait up for me," Kade said when I complained to him about it when we picked him up outside of Arrowood after his class let out. I'd asked the two of them earlier if they wanted to make a run to Wally World with me since I had to get a few things for my costume, along with the usual stuff for the room. Kade said yeah, but only if we could hit up a thrift store that's on the way. Victor put on some Satanic hard rock on the way there that I actually kind of vibed with.

"The girl who took my blood kept smiling at me the whole time," he said. "I think she thought I was cute."

Kade rolled his eyes. "She probably smiles at *everybody* so they feel relaxed."

"Well, does she tell everyone they have good veins?" Victor shot back.

"Lemme see." Kade grabbed Victor's arm and pulled it back to examine it. "Yep. Nice and veiny. Just the way I like 'em."

There were about a thousand political signs for the Repube candidates between four yards. One billboard of a yard sign had 'wake up!' painted at the top of it. "Huh, that's interesting," Kade mocked. "All this time I thought being woke was for us libtard faggots."

"I don't understand why people talk about being woke like it's a bad thing," I said. "Like, they're literally shitting on people for knowing what's up."

"And then they'll say that the rest of us need to start paying attention to what the government's *really* up to," Victor said as he squeezed his head. "I fucking *cannot* with these people."

We hit up the thrift store first, scowling at the tractor/feed store next door that had 'LET'S GO BRANDON' in bubble letters in the front window like a 2nd grade classroom. People need to start saying 'life is like a thrift store' instead of a box of chocolates because you truly never know what you're going to find. Boxes of chocolates say what's inside right on the bottom. Flip it over and read it sometime. I headed for the men's clothes section, where I found a purple-and-gray t-shirt with a jagged design and a black zip-up hoodie for my costume. I also got a navy blue button-up with yellow flowers all over it for when I want to look cute. "Can I borrow one of your hats for my costume?" I asked Victor, who was checking himself out in a plaid tweed blazer.

"Sure," he said to his reflection. "I just wanna see you in a douchebag hat."

I rolled my eyes. "Is that for your costume?"

"Oh no, I already have everything for that. I just like this."

"His costume's *bomb*," Kade said, appearing beside us in some kind of turtleneck that went down almost to his knees. "Mine's pretty dumb, but I think it's funny."

"What the hell's that?" Victor asked him. "You look like a polygamist's wife."

In Wally World, I found myself shopping for hair dye after stocking up on food and toiletries—Kade spelled out 'POOP' with mailbox stickers and wooden craft letters wherever we passed any—comparing boxes like I knew what I was doing. "Have either of you ever dyed your hair before?" I asked my friends. Victor shook his head.

"And give people another reason to call me queer, or worse? No thank you," Kade said, sending my mind back to the party this past weekend. I dropped a box of semi-permanent violet in the cart, since ain't nobody trying to have purple hair for forever.

We hit up the toy section so I could grab some Poké Balls for my costume so people won't think I'm just an angsty teenager. Victor scared the shit out of me when he squawked a rubbed chicken in my ear. "Hey Trevor, what dat mouf do?"

"They're gonna throw you out if you don't stop," I laughed. He just kept making it scream.

"That's what I sound like when I orgasm," Kade chuckled as he came around the corner to join us.

"And here I thought you just liked to play with a rubber chicken at night," Victor chuckled as he tossed it back into its bin.

"I do. That's what I call my dick. 'The Rubber Chicken.'" He held out a *Jenga* game towards me. "Do you wanna get this so you can make that Drunk *Jenga* game you won't shut up about? I crop dusted these little kids the whole way down the game aisle after I picked it up."

"I mentioned it *one* time," I laughed as I took it and laid it sideways in the child seat like a loaf of bread. Kade grabbed a giant water balloon launcher that he insisted he needed along with a package of balloons for it before we headed for the registers.

"I always use the self-checkouts so I can do my part to get the cashiers out of a job faster," Kade told me as we went to pay.

"Why?" I asked, wondering what the employee monitoring them was thinking.

"So we can get to a robot economy faster!" he said like it was obvious. "These people don't wanna do this! If we had universal basic income in place, then people could actually have the lives they *want* to live instead of doing this shit like this." He's not wrong—people have to spend their existence settling for way less than the best, and then they die. And if that's not fucked up, then I don't know what is.

We grabbed dinner at Popeye's before heading back to New Halle, since there isn't one in town and since we like to keep things somewhat fresh. I dropped the two of them off at Axworthy, parked, and dropped my stuff off before heading over to Axworthy on foot. Victor took me up to 239, where Kade had his hands wet from filling up water balloons. "I already messaged Ethan," he told me. "I told him to meet us in the parking lot by Wooster if he's not busy."

"Did you say why?"

"I just told him to meet us for a fun time," he smirked. *I wish.*

"Ooh, I should text Tylor too!" I smiled as I pulled out my phone.

Wyd rn?

Just omw back from Rosenberg
Why what's up?

Meet us in the parking lot by Wooster for a fun time 😊 😊

Kade stretched the launcher like one of those things for arm exercises as we made for the lobby, while Victor and I took turns carrying a smaller storage tote of water balloons and hitting any trash room or laundry room lights that were left on. I'm actually surprised that water balloons haven't been banned from the dorms yet, and I thought they were about to be from the way the girl at the desk eyed us up. "Do I even want to know?" she asked us with a slight smile.

"Nothing to worry about," Victor smiled back. "That's Monique, our RA," he explained once we were outside. "She's cool as long as you behave."

"I figured we can shoot the balloons down the road that runs down towards Bamberger," Kade said as we came upon the parking lot, where Tylor and his backpack were already waiting for us.

"So what kind of fun time are we talking about?" he asked me as he ran his hands up and down his sleeves to warm himself.

"I thought you might wanna sling some water balloons," I said as Kade flexed the launcher.

Tylor's mouth fell open. "Holy shit. No you did *not.*"

Victor and I held either end of the launcher and kept ourselves steady as Kade backed up and up and up and *up,* until he was almost ten feet behind us. "Three, two, one!" He let go, letting the balloon vanish in the sky.

"Where the hell—?" I started to ask when a *pop* and a splat on the pavement next to a car maybe 100 yards away gave me my answer.

"Holy *shit!*"

"*Guys.*"

"Did you *see* that?"

"No way!" Ethan said from behind us. "Where'd you get that?"

"Walmart, just a little bit ago," Kade answered.

"That's *awesome.*"

Victor went next. He pulled it as far back as humanly possible, only to have the balloon burst in the pouch and soak his crotch. "God *fucking dammit,*" he swore before he caught another that Tylor stupidly tossed to him.

"Wouldn't it have been funny if that one popped on him too?" I laughed.

"No," Victor growled as he tried again.

We had enough balloons to each go a few times. I had Ethan and Kade pivot so one of my shots could fly over the grove of trees. One of Tylor's sailed clear over Gladby. All the girls who saw us probably thought we were immature boys, and the guys probably thought we were geniuses. I don't know if Victor was *aiming* at one of the open windows on the side of Malik, but he sure hit an open window on the side of Malik. It burst on the screen and sent a shower of water into the room. And if that wasn't funny enough, the impact knocked the screen out of place and sent it falling three stories down to the ground. *"What the FUCK!"* somebody yelled from up in the room.

"Fucking *run!"* Victor laughed.

Ethan, who I discovered is the fastest of us, led the way back to Axworthy at Kade's direction, where Monique watched us from behind the desk. *Nothing sus about a group of guys out of breath running back into the building with a giant slingshot and a tub of water balloons.* "All mischief has been left at the door," Victor said as he brushed some hair back into place.

Monique could barely keep a straight face. "That's what I like to hear."

I always enjoy it when Tylor discovers something about campus that I already know about, like how the rooms in Axworthy are laid out. *"Woah. This* is different," he said as he peered through the open doors. "I don't know if I like it."

"Do you play *bass?"* Ethan asked when he saw Kade's signature instrument on its stand.

"Yeah, didn't I mention that at Open Mic Night?"

"Unh uh, you just said you were in a band. And you have games too?" Ethan lit up. "I'd be down for a game of *Monopoly* sometime!"

"You guys wanna see my drum set?" Victor asked in a competition for their attention. He gave Ethan and Tylor each the same rudimentary lesson he gave me before letting them hit away at it for a few minutes.

"Well," Kade said to Ethan as we put our shoes back on, "I'm sorry you walked all that way just for that." Water pooled at the bottom of the tote.

"No, it was fun," Ethan smiled as he tied his Adidases. "I can record a video anytime."

"What kind of videos do you make?" I asked him after Victor walked us out. Kade claimed he had to take a shit.

"Just of me playing songs. I can send you the link to my YouTube channel if you'd like." *Well now I know how I'll be spending the rest of my night.*

"Do you play any classical stuff at all?" Tylor asked him.

"Only when I *had* to," Ethan said. "I think people who listen to classical music for fun have a stick up their ass."

I found myself on Ethan's Instagram profile again after spending some time on his channel, which consists mostly of pop covers. He also posted a pic of Old Main the day before I posted mine. The one before that is his stuff packed up in his room back home—plastic crates and storage totes, a laundry basket piled with clothes, his keyboard bag, his backpack. 'The rest of your life starts today,' he captioned it. I zoomed in to see what I could of his room—posters of pop artists and horror movies, a shelf of game cases with the secondhand price stickers still on them.

Victor's Instagram story was a video of an inflated balloon floating in their toilet bowl. "How the fuck am I supposed to get this out of here?" he said. The balloon just rolled in the water whenever he'd try to pick it up. "I need to fucking PISS KADE OAKLEY!"

October 26

Loving you was like going skydiving without
Giving a shit how the parachute worked.

October 27

POV:

You're cozy in an armchair by the window in Brew 22 with the cinnamon of a spiced apple cider on your tongue and a copy of The October Country on your lap, proud of yourself for not going to Starbucks to flaunt yourself in front of the straight guy you're crushing on, though you kind of wish you had. You're wondering why everybody knows Bradbury only for Fahrenheit 451 instead of his short stories while watching the rain slide down the window and the low clouds floating by that either look like wispy Japanese or Chinese letters, but you know they're not Korean because they don't have the ovals. The girl sitting behind you is telling her friend about how she wants to start doing a Humans of New York-type thing with NHU students to show that we're all just human and we all have our own problems, and you personally love the idea although you don't turn around to tell her so. The clink of the cups and spoons and saucers makes you wish there was something a little more atmospheric playing instead of the indie folk that's on, but you still wish that you could do this every day, even though nothing's really stopping you.

October 28

I read an NPR article that said how only about five percent of plastic actually gets recycled, which is pretty annoying—and by 'annoying' I mean 'do you people not understand that we're killing the fucking planet?'

I told Kade I wanted to try a chocolate croissant from Starbucks, but he saw right through me. "He's gonna think you have a crush on him, dude."

I shrugged. "I kinda *do* though."

"But you don't want him to *know* that! You never used to get Starbucks, and then as soon as you run into him there? Boom. You wanna go all the time now."

"Not *all* the time!"

"*No*," Kade said, "but you do every Common Hour, which happens to be when he's *working*." It was a test of willpower to walk past Starbucks knowing that Ethan was in there, but messaging him to let him know about movie night if he wasn't doing anything felt almost as good. But as the hours passed without a response, I started to overthink it. *Was he not serious when he said he'd be down? Did he not think I'd actually ask him?*

Sorry, work got busy haha
I'll just be watching a movie with my friends ☺

Oh, okay
Maybe next time then?

I was talking about you guys 😆😆😆

Oh lolololol 😆

I waited in Swafford's lobby for Ethan, who was looking extra cute in a beanie and a worn-looking Mickey Mouse sweatshirt that was wet from the drizzle. "You walked across campus in the rain without an umbrella?" I greeted him like a parent.

"It's barely even misting," he said in exactly the same way I used to tell Mom '*of course Dillon's parents were there.*'

My eyes landed on the plastic bag from the bookstore he'd brought. "Don't tell me you brought snacks!"

He hid it behind his back. "Okay, I didn't bring any snacks then. You never saw any Doritos or Oreos," he chuckled. "Oh, and I made sure I had on matching socks this time."

The laminate floor squeaked his wet shoes until my carpeted wing of the building shut them up. "I watched your video you put up," I said as I led him down my hall. "I've never really listened to Gus Dapperton, but I liked it!"

"Thanks," he smiled. "I always like it when somebody gets into an artist I introduced them to."

"Same!" I grinned. "Do you wanna hang up your sweatshirt to let it dry off some? You can borrow one of my hoodies if you want."

"I think I will, actually. And nah, I'll be okay in just my shirt," he said as I took him through the door of 222 Swafford. "Hey guys!" he greeted Kade and Victor.

"*Hola.*"

"What it *dooo.*"

I grabbed an empty hanger for him and caught a glimpse of his stomach as his shirt came up with his sweatshirt. "Is that a skateboard?" he asked as he peered into my open closet.

"It's actually a *longboard,* thank you very much," I said. "It's kind of like a skateboard, but way more chill."

"I was gonna say, you don't strike me as a skateboarder. Can I try riding it sometime?" *Does the pope shit on little boys?*

"Yeah! Just let me know."

"*Sweet.* Probably not this weekend though," he said, putting a smile on my face and sending a jolt down my spine.

"*Love ussss!*" Kade whined from behind me.

We let Ethan pick the movie since it was his first movie night. "Have you ever seen *Clue?*" he smiled. "I've kind of been in the mood to watch *Clue.*"

One bag of Doritos between four guys meant they were gone before the opening credits. I'd never seen *Clue* before, and I'm not really sure why, because I loved it. Ethan and Victor kept quoting lines and Kade announced all his favorite parts. I kept wanting to reach over and pet Ethan's hair.

"What a *classic,*" he said when it was over.

Victor stretched and turned to Kade. "Did you tell them it's your birthday tomorrow?"

"No, but you just did," Kade said as he popped his fingers.

Ethan and I looked at him like he'd just won on a scratch-off. "Oh, nice!"

"Go 'head!"

"Yeah," Kade smiled as he played with one of his neon-green skull gauges.

"So he gets to wear the crown tomorrow." Victor reached over to ruffle his roommate's hair. "Whatever he says goes."

"That could be *hot,*" I smirked. "But yeah, I'm game for whatever if you wanna do something special."

Ethan nodded. "Yeah, samesies."

"We should probably get going though," Victor said. "Birthday boy has class at 8."

"Birthday boy ain't gonna do *shit*," Kade said. "Dr. Anjou won't die if I sleep in and play with myself."

I blinked. "Anjou, like the pear?"

"I always used to think that pears were some kind of bastardization of the green apple when I was younger," Victor told us.

I waited until I knew Kade was up to send him a 'happy birthday dirge' video. I must've been in an extra saucy mood, because I looked around on Redbubble for a gift for him until I found a print he'll like. Or I guess I should say one that I *hope* he likes. It only takes hearing *"What am I supposed to do with this?"* one time to make you self-conscious for the rest of your life about the gifts you get people.

October 29

I got an email today from Chase Bank telling me they froze my checking account over charges to some porn site. I knew it was a scam right away though because I don't even have a Chase account.

Kade asked me if I could give him a ride to the mail center to pick up a "pretty big package" he had waiting for him there. "How do you know how big your package is?" I asked him as he hopped in my car.

"Because I spend time with it almost every day," he laughed. "Because I know what's in it, and it'll probably be big." He was right—it was so big that he had to carry it through the mail center's door sideways.

"Shit, that *is* a big package," I said as I opened the back door for him. It was so big I could've sat in it.

"I *told* you. There's one more I have to grab too." The second one was just a care package from his parents though, so it rode back on his lap.

"Wow, I wish *my* parents loved me," I said like I didn't just pick up my own care package from Mom and Dad the other day, even if they did put candy corn in it.

I didn't have trouble finding a parking spot right up front since it was Friday, and I held open doors for him all the way up to 239 Axworthy. "You'll like this," he smiled as he slit open the tape with a pair of scissors. *Is it his Halloween costume? A Lego set? Is it—*

"Bedding?" I said to the comforter inside of it. "Why would I like that?"

"Not *that*, what's *inside* it." He unraveled a throw blankets to reveal—

"Jägermeister!" I said maybe a little too loudly.

"*Shut up!*" he hissed. He opened up the comforter to show me bottles of Fireball, apple-flavored whiskey, and spiced rum tucked in its folds. Shirts and hoodies with the tags still on them acted as packing material.

I frowned down at the contents. "I have *a lot* of questions."

"It's my birthday gift from my older sister," he laughed. "She asked me what I like to drink and hooked me up."

"And all the clothes?"

"Also part of her gift."

"*Shit,*" I said to one of the Superdry hoodies.

Victor was more impressed with all the clothes than he was with the liquor. "*Goddamn,* fam," he said when he saw them laid out on Kade's bed. "I hope she gets me a gift like this on *my* birthday."

"You think you're so fucking entitled, huh?" Kade scowled. "I *was* gonna tell you that Mom and Dad sent us care packages, but now I'm not going to."

"Forreal? Why didn't you text me? I would've picked it up on the way back from class!"

"Um, because you should be checking your email like a good student?"

Victor checked his email to see that he indeed had a package waiting for him. "*Ugh,* I don't wanna walk back over," he whined. "Can I have some of your candy if I let you have some of mine after I go get it?"

"*Fuck* no," Kade scowled.

"Asshole."

"That was nice of them to send you something though," I said. "When your own parents didn't even send you anything? *Rude.*"

The two of them were quiet for so long that it made me uncomfortable, even more uncomfortable than when you're out eating and the manager comes over and asks you how the food is. They looked from me to each other and back. "Does he not know?" Kade finally asked Victor.

I swallowed, high-key afraid I said something out of place. "Know what?"

"Kade's parents are my parents," Victor said. "They adopted me."

"So wait," I gasped, "you two are *brothers?*"

"Biologically, no. Legally, yes."

"That's *dope as hell!*" I smiled. *They make so much more sense now!*

I nudged Victor into making the journey to the mail center by offering to walk over with him. "You're gonna leave me alone on my *birthday?*" Kade complained.

"Oh, shut up," Victor shushed him. "Masturbate or something."

The day was overcast with heavy cotton clouds covering the entire sky, like we were on the inside of a comforter. *Maybe the Earth's really just a speck of dust inside a blanket?* Victor opened his care package to let me take a pumpkin-shaped Reese's cup as a thank you for going with him that I ate on the way back to 239 Axworthy, where we found Kade and Will looking obvious as hell. "So what's the move tonight?" Victor asked his brother.

"I was thinking about going to Forest Ridge Taproom for dinner, if everyone's cool with it?" Kade said like it might've been the wrong answer. I pass it on Main Street on every walk to Sheetz, but I've never been there since it's an actual sit-down restaurant. "And I was thinking about asking Ethan and Tylor if they wanted to come too?"

"Why are you asking me?" Victor frowned. "It's *your* birthday!"

"And then maybe we can go out afterwards?"

Victor rolled his eyes. "Jesus *Christ*."

I wore a button-down for the occasion, and even Tylor traded his joggers for jeans. We met the other three outside of Axworthy, and Ethan joined us at Kessler. The restaurant has a very Alpine vibe to it, with its railings and chandeliers made from polished bent tree branches. Cobwebs and strings of purple and orange lights lent it a spooky atmosphere.

"So," Kade asked as we broke bread at our round table, "how was everybody's week? Other than almost breaking a window with a water balloon and getting a misdemeanor?"

"You almost broke a window?" Will asked.

"I volunteered at the haunted maze," Ethan said, talking about the event in the Quad that SGB—the Student Government Board—and a few other groups put on.

"I've never been in any kind of haunted house before," I said to nobody in particular.

"I believe it," Tylor said.

"Forreal?" Ethan asked me. "Why?"

"I'm too much of a scaredy-cat," I said as I rubbed the back of my neck. "Plus, a haunted house would be the perfect place to murder somebody. You'd get stabbed and you'd think it's just part of it."

Kade tapped his temple. "Self-preservation," he smiled.

"It honestly wasn't that scary," Victor said. "It was more annoying than anything because people wouldn't fucking *move*."

I sat up. "You went? And didn't ask me to go with you?"

"You just said you're afraid to do stuff like that!"

"But it's the principle though!"

"Well the next time there's—*goddammit*, these fucking political calls," he fumed as he answered. "I'm already voting Democrat, and also free Palestine." He hung up. "I *swear* I get one like every day. And the amount of *texts*."

"Fucking *tell* me about it."

"I keep getting political texts for somebody named Jowanka," Kade said.

"Did you tell them you're not Jowanka?" Tylor laughed.

"Pfft. No."

Most of our weeks were pretty nondescript with Midterm grades, House Council events, and sinus infections. "Did you tell them what you said in class?" Ethan asked Victor. "About the Seven Dwarves?" The rest of us traded bewildered looks.

"No?"

"Do *tell.*"

"The professor was talking about viscosity," Victor chuckled, "and I said to the girl next to me, 'Viscosity? Is that one of the seven deadly sins or one of the Seven Dwarves?'"

"I think he was trying to get her to, you know..." Ethan pumped a fist towards his mouth as he poked the inside of his cheek with his tongue. *Well I know what image I'm getting off to later.*

"Did the professor hear you?" Will asked.

"The whole *fucking class* heard him!" Ethan laughed.

"I found five bucks on the ground at work," I segued.

Ethan raised an eyebrow at me. "I didn't know you had a job here."

"Yeah, in Rosenberg."

"Is that what you meant when you said to catch you at the library? I thought you meant you were always studying!" he chuckled. *Yeah, studying other guys.*

The topic turned to music after two large trays brought us our food. Each entree came with an entire pickle. "Yeah, I'd say I listen to pop and classical the most," Will said. "'Classical' being used loosely, of course." I caught Ethan's eye and we shared a smirk.

"Yeah, I'd have to say pop's my fave," Ethan said.

"Pop is like, *marginally* better than country," Kade said as he pinched off pieces of his bun and crushed them into cubes.

I nodded. "Yeah, pop's *ass.*"

Ethan crossed his arms. "Okay, tell me what *you* like so I can shit all over it."

"Alternative," I said simply. "It's funny—I used to pride myself on my music tastes for being different from everybody else's back home, and then I came to school and almost everybody I've met likes something that I like."

"Isn't that what college is supposed to do though?" Will posed. "Blow your world open and make you realize how wrong you are about things?"

"Damn, this pickle got me drunk as hell," Kade said after he took a bite of his gherkin.

"But I guess ultimately," I went on, "any kind of music that makes you feel anything or stirs up some kind of emotion is the best kind of music. And no, getting angry at country music doesn't count." I took a sip of my root beer. "I think anyone's favorite song is only their favorite song because of the memory they associate with it."

Instead of complimenting me on how deep and perceptive I am like I low-key hoped somebody would, Tylor instead asked me, "So you say you like alternative, but what does that *mean* exactly? Like, what's considered alternative?"

"That's easy," I crossed my arms. "Anything that the radio plays is pop. Anything it doesn't is alternative."

Kade thought for a moment. "I can get on board with that."

"But what about like...Twenty One Pilots?" Ethan asked. "Aren't they alternative?"

"Are they on the radio?"

"Yeah."

"Then they're pop."

"That's bullshit."

"What about WXNU? You listen to that a lot," Tylor pointed out as his tomato slice slid out of his chicken club.

"I mean *mainstream* radio," I said. "Doesn't the name 'alternative music' itself suggest that it's an *alternative* choice to pop? That it's an *alternative* to what the radio has to offer?"

"So then is pop punk considered pop?" Victor asked. "Like, what about Chunk! No, Captain Chunk?"

"*Gesundheit,*" Ethan said.

"Are they on the radio?" I asked.

"Not that *I've* ever heard."

"Alternative then."

"But it's not subjective," Ethan pointed out. "If I never listen to the radio, is *everything* considered alternative then just because I don't hear it on the radio?"

Before I could respond, a piece of chocolate cake appeared in front of Kade along with a group of servers singing and clapping him a happy birthday. His face flushed as he sank down in his seat. I didn't clap along because I know how much I'd *hate* it if it was me, but it was still funny. Victor must've told them it was his birthday when he went to the bathroom. "Happy birthday, you *big, beautiful bitch,*" he grinned after the staff walked off.

Kade swallowed. "I'm about a *second* away from sodomizing you with one of these pickles."

"Oh *dad.*"

"Oh, does anybody want my pickle?" I asked, making the table erupt in laughter. "I just meant I'm not gonna eat it!"

The five of us—Tylor had plans of his own—went out to a party at Will's roommate's frat brother's place at The Tenth, an apartment complex that's supposedly one of the two foremost places in town to turn up at, even if it's the farthest one from campus. We hung out in 239 Axworthy until it was time to go, where Victor and Kade jammed for us on their instruments. Kade showed the others his liquor bottles stashed in a tote under his bed before taking two for the party, passing the rum around for a "pre-game sippy-sip."

It only took two months, but I came to know another NHU tradition last night— the Drunk Bus. The wholesome university bus that runs circuits around campus and town by day turns into a shuttle of sin on Friday and Saturday nights, ferrying students to their fall from grace and back. It was standing-room only by the time we left the Kessler/Draper stop. The promise of hedonism animated the partygoers with a friskiness I haven't felt since we used to play Capture the Flag in elementary school gym class before the straight boys turned into Straight boys and ruined sports for me. It was like being on the Polar Express en route to the North Pole, and people being in costume made it that much more fun. None of us had dressed up because doing it two nights in a row would feel a little extra. A group of guys started singing "Sweet Caroline" out of nowhere and the entire bus joined in. You're technically not *allowed* to drink on the bus, but is the driver really going to stop you? Those people have to *hate* their job.

The Tenth was *crawling* with partiers. We passed groups of smokers and people being loud and people pursuing happiness as we followed Will to number 31, which had nobody watching the door. I always pictured frat parties being these crazy orgies of intoxication with endless beer bongs and people fucking right on the couch, but it really wasn't that different from the first party we went to over Homecoming weekend. Nobody was getting their bare ass spanked with a big wooden paddle, but there was a keg out back and as many Straight guys as you'd expect. It smelled of weed, but only in certain spots—kind of like how you'll be in a swimming pool and all of a sudden you'll feel a warm spot.

Kade had Will grab the whiskey from his backpack and he poured us all shots. "Gentlemen," Kade announced with his cup held aloft, "there's nobody else I'd rather spend this night with. A toast to you, my friends."

"Let's go the fuck ahead," I said before we threw them back.

Victor told anybody and everybody that it was Kade's birthday, and they all made Kade take a drink with them. I don't know how he wasn't plastered. "Kade," I told him as I threw an arm around his shoulder, "I just want you to know that you're basically my best friend. I love you fam."

"You're like one of my best friends too, fam," he said as he returned the gesture.

"You know Trevor's hammered when he starts saying 'fam,'" I heard Victor tell Ethan, who just laughed.

"I am *not* hammered!" I took a step back to show them how good my motor skills were, only to fall up against the wall and knock down a paper bat taped to it. I wanted to say something to Will about what happened at last weekend's party, but instead I found myself outside, where somebody with the same seatbelt belt as Victor was doing a keg stand while people counted and somebody pumped him full of beer like he was inflating a bicycle tire. *Oh wait, that is Victor.* The guys holding him tilted him back down to the ground, and he punched the air before going over to Ethan to take his drink back. They gave each other one-armed hugs like Heteros.

"I wanna go next!" Ethan said. Nobody knew my eyes were on his bare stomach as his shirt slipped down towards his neck.

"I didn't think you were a keg stand kind of guy," I said to Victor, but I didn't think *I* was a keg stand kind of guy either. "I kinda wanna do it too." *Did Drunk Trevor just want an excuse to give Drunk Ethan a hug? It's possible.*

"Then go fucking *do* it," Victor said as we watched Ethan chug like a champ. *What if I start choking and spit beer all over all these Straight guys? What if they realize they'd been tricked into touching a gay guy?*

Ethan stumbled as he got used to the ground again and went *"Wooh!"* without giving anybody a hug. *He better not fucking wander off,* I thought as I went up for my turn. Hands grabbed my ankles and everything inverted. I named British monarchs in reverse to make the seconds of drinking watered-down piss go faster, swallowing to keep up with the pumps. I made it to Anne before I couldn't take any more. I stumbled back to my friends and gave Victor and Ethan each a one-armed hug. *Success.* We watched a few more people try it—one guy coughed up mouthfuls of beer onto patio pavers and shoes—before we headed back inside. People vaped into their drinks so they looked like they were overflowing with fog.

"So I notice that Kade and Will aren't anywhere to be seen," I casually mentioned.

"Fam, they *leaved*," Victor said. "Will said he wasn't feeling well so Kade took him back, which means they're probably about to have a happy ending."

"Without even saying bye?" I thought about the two of them alone in his room, jealous that somebody got taken back to somebody else's room and I wasn't one of them. *But why do I even care?* There weren't any games other than pong, and by the time we'd each played our fill, we were ready to go anyway.

The Tenth hadn't slowed down at all since we'd gotten there. I wanted to experience the Drunk Bus on the return trip, but we'd just missed it and didn't want to wait for it. We hugged the side of the road on the walk back, veering in and out of the grass. "I don't know about you guys, but I had a *really* good time," Ethan grinned.

"Go 'head!" I said. I wouldn't say that I had a *blast,* but I got to spend the night with my friends. But what is having a blast if not that?

"What does that even mean?" he chuckled. "Like, hooray for BJs, or what?"

"No. I mean, yeah, obviously," I chuckled. "But no, like, if some girl kept taking shots you'd say 'she's really going ahead with that vodka.' Or if I told you I got an A on my quiz you'd say 'oh go ahead.'"

He just laughed. "Sure."

I stole glances at him, wishing it was just the two of us walking back from the party, wishing that we'd drunkenly make out behind a building or he'd take me up to his room. But Victor, who must've *really* gone ahead from the way he stumbled more than he walked, was with us. I put my arm under him to help keep him up. "Boy, you are drunk *as hell* right now."

"Nah fam," he said. "I'm just looking. I mean, I *am*, but I'm not. And also yes to the question."

Ethan and I caught each other's eyes and cracked up. "Okay, you are *literally* drunk as fuck."

"No! No, I mean I'm looking at the sky. Stop a sec." We all stopped to follow his gaze up at the night sky. "Just look at it."

"*Would ya look at that!*" Ethan said with a lisp. He put his arm under Victor's other side, resting his fingers on my arm. We all took in the sky, the alcohol and human bodies keeping the cold at bay. Even with the lights from the plaza across the street, there were more stars than I've ever seen before. "I always wanted to be an astronaut when I was little," Ethan broke the silence.

Victor nodded, his eyes wide with wonder. "Didn't we all?"

I shook my head. "Not me. It's too high up and it's too empty. Now a *pirate* though..."

"And what, the open ocean isn't empty?" Ethan laughed as we walked into another warm spot in the pool.

"Well shit," Victor sighed, "I guess I'm gonna have to cancel that *spacewalk* I booked for your birthday."

"You don't even know when my birthday *is*."

"Doesn't matter. We're not going now, you fucking *ingrate*. And I know what you're both thinking, and the answer is April 11th, so go ahead and set your reminders now." I did, just to be funny—at noon on the Friday before, my phone will *ping* with a banner that'll read '*Victor's b-day on chewsday get crunk lolololol.*'

"Done," I said. "Mine's in the Spring too. Beginning of March."

"Isn't that technically still Winter?" Ethan asked as he led us up one of the residential streets that he insisted was a shortcut.

"Shut up, mom."

Ethan pointed a finger at me. "If you ever speak to me like that again son, I'll take you up to your room and I'll spank you." *Oh dad.* "And just for the record, I didn't get a single happy birthday from either of you."

"When was yours?"

"Last month, on the 20th."

"We didn't even know you then!"

"Don't care. Still didn't get one."

"So wait, you're the oldest one out of us?"

"I guess so, unless Will's older. Why, do I win something?"

"Yeah, a reach-around!" I said.

I couldn't tell you the last time I laughed so hard. I had to hold onto a stop sign so I wouldn't fall over. Victor threw himself down into the grass, and Ethan doubled over and clutched his stomach. "Oh my god! It *hurts!*"

"I can't stop!" Victor screamed from the ground. "Is this what it feels like to die?"

I wiped my eyes on my sleeve. "I don't even know why I said that!" A front porch light flicked on, lighting up an otherwise-dark house.

"Oh shit, we gotta go!" Ethan pulled Victor to his feet and we sloppily took off down the middle of the street.

We came upon Old Main from the back, then Kessler. Ethan hugged us goodnight in front of its doors. I breathed in his cologne. "We gotta do this again sometime!" he told us.

"Fo *sho.*"

"Yeah, totes!"

We left Ethan and his building behind us. "So, bad news," Victor said in a somewhat-serious tone. "He mentioned something about his girlfriend back home."

It wasn't news to me, but my heart sank anyway. "What'd he say?"

"I don't remember exactly what. Something about how she'd think he was being a tool if she saw him doing a keg stand maybe? I can't remember. Either way though."

"You're sure they're still together? He didn't say she was his ex-girlfriend?"

"When does somebody refer to their current girlfriend as their ex?"

"I *guess,*" I sighed. "I have some worse news though," I said after the streetlight above us went out.

"What?"

"That light was the second one in a row that went out as we walked under it."

We stopped to look up at the ominously dark bulb. We turned to the next one that lay ahead, waiting for us like a trap.

"So what's supposed to happen if it happens three times?" I asked as we took cautious steps forward. "Like do we die, or what?"

"I mean, I *assume* that's what happens, but I—"

The light went out and he left me for dead. I didn't stop running until I caught up with him by Bixby. I was still panting by the time we got back to the dorms.

**I can confirm that Kade and Will are most certainly
having a happy ending** 😌
Wanna hear?

We met up for breakfast—which was basically lunch by the time we got there—and went back to 239 Axworthy for *Catan* and some tea called jeering dear darling or something that Kade said takes "a more *refined* palate to truly appreciate." It's a good day for tea too—it's like the entire sky is one single, weathered, headstone-white cloud. I picked out one of Victor's hats—a black-and-purple A Day to Remember one—before I left. Elisha's dyed her hair before, so she was able to help me with that. It reeked like a mix of paint and bleach. I low-key kind of like the way I look with it, and it's been getting me compliments from my floormates. I sent a selfie to Mom, Dad, Madi, and Logan. Mom was mildly appalled. Dad said it looks good. Madi's and Logan's responses were more or less what I expected.

TREVOR HUFFMAN WHAT DID YOU DO 🤦 🤦 😅

October 30

You know what really sucks? When you find out that a band you high-key fuck with only made one album and broke up ten years ago.

I looked myself up and down in my mirror to make sure my costume looked good—purple shirt, black hoodie that I cut the sleeves off of, black jeans, Victor's hat, belt clipped with Poké Balls—before heading over to Axworthy. Kade met me in the lobby, still wearing the half-white half-blue t-shirt he had on earlier.

"Is that your costume?" I asked him.

He raised an eyebrow. "Is *that* your costume?" *Welp, there goes my self-confidence.*

"Why? Do you think it looks dumb?"

"No, I think it looks good!" he smiled. "So what are you supposed to be, some scene kid who works at Hot Topic?"

"I'm a ghost-type Pokémon trainer!"

"Oh, okay. Oh yeah, I see your balls now! Said the—"

"Said the actress to the bishop," I chuckled.

It was weird to see Kade standing outside of 239 Axworthy's closed bathroom door, since he's almost always the one occupying it. "Trevor's here!" he called to it.

"I'll be right out!" Victor's voice called back as Kade shut himself in his bedroom.

I only had to sit and pull on my fingers for maybe a minute before Victor emerged. I didn't know where to look first—his painted face, his headpiece of leaves and antlers, his staff decked out with feathers and glowing orb, his hand-drawn runic tattoos like pine trees all drew my eyes everywhere at once. "No animals were harmed in the making of this costume," he said.

"Holy *shit*," I said to the silver amulet resting on his tunic.

"Right? I think it looks pretty badass." His red hair and Eastern-European-green eyes perfected the look.

"Are you a shaman or something?"

"Kind of—I'm a druid. They were ancient Celtic priests, but in RPGs they usually have powers over nature."

"I'm more of a necromancer kind of guy," Kade said when he reappeared. He'd traded his Kade look for matching green-and-gold short shorts and an athletic jacket that looked like they were from 1977, sweatbands, tube socks, and a plastic medal.

"What are you supposed to be, somebody who ran track 40 years ago and did porn on the side?"

"As good as one of those sounds, no." He brushed past us to one of the cabinets to grab a loaf of bread. "I'm a breadwinner," he grinned.

"I actually hate you right now," I chuckled. "So what, are you gonna carry around a loaf of bread with you all night?"

"Yeah? Otherwise I'll look like an idiot. Plus, I'll have a snack if I get hungry," Kade said as he let The Joker into their room. The look was so on-point that I almost couldn't tell who it was.

"Look at your hair!" Will exclaimed. "I like it!"

"Look at *your* hair!" I said to his slicked-back, acid-green hair.

"Did you see his *balls?*" Kade muttered to Will as he stuffed the rum and the Jägermeister and some cans of Red Bull into his backpack. He'd already posted a mirror selfie to his story captioned *"out to turn someone's son gay brb."*

I slapped my hands on my knees. "Oh my *god,* that's so *funny!* You're sure that medal isn't for being a fucking genius?"

Victor led our party like Gandalf with his hooded cloak and his staff that *clunked* on the sidewalk with every step. I thought about Ethan as we passed Kessler and his undoubtedly-empty room. He said he was going out with his friends and that maybe we'd meet up, but I've heard that enough times in my life to know it wouldn't happen. I didn't let it bother me for too long though, because a guy dressed up as a troubadour playing a ukulele told me that it was going to be a fun night either way.

Parties hit different when Sonic the Hedgehog and a bottle of mustard are passing a joint outside the door, when Mrs. Potato Head gives Indiana Jones a congratulatory kiss for flipping his cup first, when one of the pharaohs has to chug the can he cracked open in Kings, when the two halves of a peanut butter and jelly sandwich are going hard to the music together, when Yoda is playing bartender to an avocado. And what would a college Halloween party be without at least one douchebag construction worker itching to jackhammer a female referee? Marvin Bostwick from Lit Club was even there, dressed up as a 1700s Englishman with the hair and everything, showing off a pineapple.

"Pineapples were so difficult to acquire back then," I heard him telling Scooby-Doo like it was the most interesting fact ever, "that the wealthy would buy them as status symbols. People would actually rent pineapples to take to parties just to show off their wealth."

Scooby-Doo just nodded. "Did you rent *that* pineapple?"

We carved out a space for ourselves by the wall. "Gentlemen," Kade announced as he held up the Jäger. We waited for him to go on. "Eh, fuck it." He took a sip from the bottle and passed it around.

Will and I teamed up against Kade and Victor in a game of pong. Kade wouldn't stop with the Poké Ball double entendres whenever I'd go to shoot to try to mess me up. "Hey, get your balls off the table!" "I wish we could play with *those* balls!"

"Who's the breadwinner *now*, asshole?" I taunted him after Will sank their last cup. He gave me the finger.

Will and I faced off against a samurai and an *incredibly* hot incubus, whose shirtless body and red hair and bad-boy smirk and horns all made me perky down south. Kade shared bread with Jasmine from *Aladdin*—"So who'd you want to win World War II?"—and Victor was showing off his costume to the girl who hunts machines from that one game Tylor has. The more we drank, the more handsy Will and I got with each other after one of us made a cup, and the more bad thoughts I had about the incubus. I was thinking about the things I'd do to him when a hand landed on my shoulder. "Trevor?" the voice it belonged to shouted in my ear. "How's it going?"

I was too busy taking in the Charizard onesie to register who it was at first. "Hey Devon! What's up?" We bumped fists. "I haven't seen you since you quit Rosenberg!"

"I know!" he grinned as he took me in. "Dude, we both went with Pokémon! That's sick!"

We made small talk as he watched us play. "I'm gonna try to find my friend again," he said before he walked off. "I'm sure I'll see you around!"

"Are you saying you hope I get sick?" I chuckled. *I wonder if he's wearing anything under that?*

"Not at the *Health Center!*" he laughed. "I just meant here!"

I watched the incubus and the samurai—let's be real, I was watching the incubus —play their next opponents when I caught sight of Spider-Man looking right at me from across the room. I looked behind me and back at them. I pointed at myself like a dumbass, and they nodded slowly before making their way over. I couldn't move. Inside my personal bubble, they ran their hand down my arm without a word, then stroked my cheek, my chin. *Is it Miles? They're too tall to be Ethan. Maybe somebody just found me irresistible. Are we about to kiss? Whose Mary Jane am I about to be?* I ran my hand up their arm and was about to go somewhere riskier when they took off their mask.

"*Ew!* Tylor!" I yelled as I shook the gross from my hands. "What the fuck!"

"I just wanted to mess with you," he laughed.

"I was about to start rubbing your crotch!"

"Oh, *dad*," he smirked.

"When'd you get here? And are you drunk already?"

"Oh my god mom, we got here like two minutes ago. And so what if Jax and I were pregaming?" he said as he gestured between himself and Black Panther beside him. "Fucking fight me."

Kade and his bag of bread found us so we could all do Jäger Bombs. We dropped our shots into cups of Red Bull and drank together just as Victor appeared. "Are you fucking doing *Jäger* Bombs *without* me?"

"Holy *shit*," Tylor almost choked. "Victor? You look..."

"Fucking dope as hell?"

Tylor spun on Will. "Wait—are *you* somebody I know too?"

"Hi," Will said with a small wave.

Tylor put his hands on his hips and looked around the room. "*Wow.* I wonder how many people here are somebody I know?"

"I mean, isn't everybody a costume party when you think about it?" Victor said to the Jäger Bomb he poured for himself.

Kade made a face like he was orgasming. "*Bruh.*"

"Passes blunt to the left," I snickered, thinking about how much I wished that Ethan had come out with us. I slipped out my phone to message him, too drunk to care if I looked thirsty for him.

> **Hey I hope your having a good night** 😊
> **I kno we certainly are bahaha**
> **Too bad we didnt end up at the same party lol**

"Oh, there she is," Tylor said to himself before waving to somebody behind me. The Greek goddess coming our way had searing yellow eyes that made me feel like I was one wrong move away from getting a lightning bolt to the ass. "Guys, this is Amina," Tylor told us. "Amina, this is Victor, Will, Kade, and my roommate Trevor."

"I'm so happy to finally meet you Trevor!" Amina practically shrieked as she came in for a hug. "Tylor talks about you all the time!"

"Oh does he?" I asked the golden wings on her helmet.

"Amina's like one of three people I'm friends with who still goes here," Tylor explained. I can't say for sure that she was the one with Tylor and Jaxon in our room that night back at the beginning of the semester, but I've definitely seen her playing guitar in the Quad, and I feel like I've seen her longboarding around campus at least once.

Amina asked us if we wanted to get our asses kicked at Flip Cup, which is how we found ourselves gathered around a table with a pair of stereotypical nerds, a cowgirl, and a Slytherin student with a real Dark Mark tattoo. I didn't see it happen, but I guess somebody dressed up as Fuckstick showed up while we were playing and somebody else threw Marvin Bostwick's pineapple at him. Devon and some other people watched Amina school us over and over. "Read it and weep, bitches," she said triumphantly.

Devon patted my shoulder. "Good try, dude."

Victor asked us if we wanted to take a squad pic, which sent Kade running around to each of us and going "Let's fucking get a squad pic!" in our faces. I couldn't tell you how many drinks I had, but it was enough to wish that the shot I agreed to take with Devon and his angel friend wasn't anything too strong. "I like your balls, by the way," she said as she pointed to my waist just before we threw back what ended up being the only thing worse than vodka—tequila. I actually gagged. Still sputtering even after I chased it down, my chest flipped when I checked my phone and saw that Ethan messaged me back.

Sure am!
I know! Maybe well run into each other!

I started to type out a response when Devon urgently pulled me from where I stood. "Aww, this is my *shit!* Let's go dance!" *To this trap shit?*

"Okay," I reluctantly agreed. I don't know how to dance for shit, but I could certainly get on board with him grinding right up against me. *What the hell? I guess he's gay then? How does he even know I'm gay?* As much as I was into it, I couldn't stop thinking about the asshole from last weekend who walked in on Kade and Will. The two nerds we played Flip Cup with were making out up against a wall and nobody seemed to care. Their coordinating fits made the promise I'd made to Dillon last Halloween hit me like a punch to the gut, but Devon was there to put my hands on his hips and to take Dillon off my mind. *Don't be a wimp, Trevor.* I pressed myself against his back and his butt, my head on his shoulder as we moved to the rhythm of the music. I gave him a peck on his neck, my heavy breaths brushing his ear. He led me to the nearest wall once the song ended a hundred thousand *"pandas"* later and spun my hat around so our faces could snap together without it getting in the way. Our raging boners had nowhere to go but into each other. We made out in a room full of cartoons and superheroes and food with his arms around my neck and mine around his back. The rings in his nose and lip rubbed against mine.

"I bet you do have nice balls," he said into my ear. *"Wanna go back to my room so you can show them to me? My roommate isn't there."* My insides stirred. My dick practically whimpered. Who would've thought that Devon, my old co-worker who I

had a low-key crush on and hadn't seen in more than a month, would be inviting me back to his room to do gay shit with him?

"Oh yes *please*," I grinned devilishly.

His teeth bit his lip. "Lemme go tell my friend I'm gonna bounce."

"Oh yeah, I should probably do that too." I found Victor first, with two 40-ounce bottles of beer duct-taped to his hands.

"*This* is Edward Fortyhands," he chuckled before I could say anything.

"That looks fun," I lied. "I'm gonna head out."

"You gucc fam?" he asked. "Do I need to walk you back?"

"With those taped to your hands?" I laughed. "Nah, I'm fine. I'm pretty sure I'm about to get laid though," I said like I was telling him I was thinking of upgrading my iCloud.

"Oh go 'head! That makes three people now."

"Tell the others I said bye and have fun and I'll see them later."

"Kade and Will left already, hence why I said three people," he rolled his eyes. "Don't go catching monkeypox though!"

"I *won't*," I smiled as we gave each other a one-armed hug, although everybody who's ever caught monkeypox probably said the same thing.

The street wasn't any less lively than when we got to the party, even if the troubadour was gone. Devon and I walked with anticipation in our steps. I kept my arm around him and stroked his collarbone through his onesie, and he kept his hand in my back pocket. I had to keep myself from pushing him up against a tree and going to town on him. "What if your roommate walks in on us?" I asked him in a low voice as I followed him down his hall. *Could that DA tell what we're going to do?*

"He won't." Devon kissed my cheek. "He went home for the weekend."

Since Draper Hall is one of the traditional dorms, his room looks like the typical college dorm room you see in movies. In the glow of his table lamp, I watched him step out of his onesie in a tank top and running tights. My sleeveless hoodie fell to the floor. I grabbed his bare biceps and took him in. "*Mmmm*, somebody's aroused."

"Look who's talking," he smiled before meeting my kiss.

My hand did what it wanted to do to Spider-Man before Tylor unceremoniously ruined the moment. Devon responded likewise. We stopped so I could lift off his tank top before yanking off my own shirt. Naked from the waist up, we kissed mouths, necks, chests, licked circles on each other's nipples. He stripped off his tights before unbuttoning my jeans, pulling them down to the floor with him as he knelt. My underwear came down next, and he licked me like a popsicle. I gasped in pleasure as his mouth's warmth surrounded me, all of me. His hair was full of my fingers.

"*Oh my god does that feel good.*"

He finally stopped, using his spit and my ooze to pump it through his fist. He stood and let the edge of his bed catch him. I sucked him and ran my hands over his bare skin. Our kisses grew hungry, breathless. I pulled him up and spun him around so my chest was against his back. I fitted myself in his notch, grinding my hips against his as I kissed him from behind. A switch flipped in my brain and pure lust took over. He groaned through closed eyes, passion biting his lip.

We kissed like our existence depended on it. *"I want you to fuck me."*

"God fucking yes."

He passed me a condom from his drawer and got himself ready. I sheathed myself, grinning with desire at the sight of him bent over his bed. I moved into position and slapped him with it a few times. *"You ready for me?"*

He looked back over his shoulder. *"Fuck yeah."*

I guided myself in, slowly. He gasped. *"Oh my god."* I drew myself out before going back in to let him get used to me. Again. And again. And then I stayed, letting go as I slid all the way in. I rocked back and forth. He whimpered with my thrusts.

"How's that?"

"You can go faster."

I picked up the pace, spooning him upright. We kissed as I massaged his insides. The sounds escaping from his mouth almost sent me over the edge. *Holy fucking shit I forgot how good this feels.* He caressed my thighs. I put my finger in his mouth and he whined.

"You like that?" I grinned.

"I fucking love it. You feel so fucking good."

I pushed him back down, my hand holding his neck, his shoulder. He propped himself up to work himself. I grabbed his ass and his ass grabbed me back. His groans grew labored as his arm moved furiously. I purred how good he was, how good he felt. He moaned as he shot onto his comforter, and I closed my eyes as he tightened around me with every surge. I imagined that he was Kade, that it was Miles' bare back before me, that it was Dayton who was grunting profanities, that it was Ethan who was jolting from the pleasure of me inside of him. I rammed obstinately, feeling the pressure building inside of me.

"Oh shit," I breathed.

I pulled him back up to put my chin on his shoulder. My movements faltered as I released. My knees almost gave out. He moaned with me as my throbbing slowed. I panted into his neck, smiling at my conquest. We kissed while I stayed inside him.

"Oh was that hot."

"That was so fucking hot."

"You're so fucking hot."

I pulled out, tugging the warm condom off with a *snap*. Devon grabbed his tank top to clean up his own mess. "You don't know how much I needed that," he said. "I've been *craving* some good dick."

I pulled my underwear back on with a smirk. "I'm glad I could deliver."

He watched me dress as he opted to go commando. "Are you gonna head back to your place then?"

"Yeah, if that's okay."

He laughed through his nose. "It's actually *not*. You're staying until after round two. Maybe even round three."

"I wouldn't be opposed," I laughed, though I knew I'd be asleep before I could go again.

"Let me know when you get back to your place," he said after he gave me his number. "I don't want campus police knocking on my door telling me I'm the last person who saw you before you went missing."

I smirked. "Oh yeah, because I'm sure *that's* the only reason you want my number." He just shrugged with an impish smile.

We gave each other one last kiss before he let me out. "Have a good night," he smiled as he watched me show myself out. As promised, I let him know when I got back.

Good ☺

Sweet dreams to you and that sausage of yours 😜

I liked Ethan's post of him in a dark blue police uniform—complete with a bloody bandage and R.P.D. tactical vest—posing with Mario, Peach, and an order of French fries before posting our own squad pic. I'm holding up one of my infamous Poké Balls like I'm ready to throw down, Will's pointing at the camera with a maniacal cackle, Victor's standing solemnly with his staff aloft, and Kade and Tylor are crouched opposite each other, one holding up a loaf of bread and the other flashing sideways peace sign. *Finally, a squad I feel like I actually belong to.*

wallowing_tbh #squad #halloweekend
EthanE16 *high* key jelly 😩
wallowing_tbh @EthanE16 hang with us!!
EthanE16 @wallowing_tbh lmk when!
logank22 👀

October 31

Dr. Conrad, who's so proper that he barely ever smiles, knocked the whole class out of our seats today when he walked in with his sleeves rolled up for the first time, showing off forearms sleeved with tattoos. He waited until the end of the period to tell us with a smirk they were fake tattoo sleeves.

I'm still fucked up over what Victor said about everybody being a costume party. I'm sure it's not what he meant, but we're conditioned to cover up the most authentic versions of ourselves so we appear as normal as possible to try to fit society's conventions. I know all too well what that's like—and I don't just mean my sexuality, I'm even just talking about how I keep bits of trivia to myself so people won't think I'm too nerdy—but it's all of our traits and quirks and idiosyncrasies that give the human aspect of the world its dimension and its beauty. So what if you're not cishet, or aren't in a good place mentally, or are emotional, or are afraid, or if you carry trauma with you, or if you don't have a clue what you're doing? All that helps makes you the person you are, and you're all the more complex in the most beautiful way because of it. Leave the costumes for the people who've sold out to the world. Is not giving a shit about people's perceptions of you the meaning of life? Is taking off your costume the meaning of life?

Anyway.

Only a fraction of the student body went to class in costume today, and I was one of them since my costume was as easy as a change of clothes, and because I wanted people to see that I don't have a *total* stick up my ass. A few people got what I was going for and dropped me a compliment, and I felt like almost everybody was checking out my hair.

I was trying to work on an assignment at work but I couldn't concentrate because some kid nearby kept saying "verbage." I was .3 seconds away from going over and slamming my hands down on the table and yelling that "verbage" isn't a word when I noticed a crumpled-up bill laying on the floor, and my eyes widened when I picked it up and saw that it was a fifty. I was debating on whether to keep it for myself or to hold onto it in case someone came asking for it when I turned it over and saw it was blank on the back. *The hell?* I was trying to make sense of it when Kade creepily texted me **I see you found some of my prank money**. I stood up and looked around the computer lab for him like a scene in a serial killer movie but didn't see him. He didn't even come over to call me a gullible little churl or something with that shit-eating grin of his.

And then at the end of my shift, I was clearing out all the unclaimed papers that were left in the printer tray when the top one, a blog post titled *"How To Ruin Your Life,"* caught my eye. I skimmed the first few lines and accidentally read the entire thing. It pretty much said that we ruin our lives by not showing ourselves enough self-love, but the part I'm really fucked-up over said something like how the next Michelangelo could be writing invoices for a living because it's easy and pays the bills. Like, have you ever thought about how much art and how many creations never got the chance to exist because their would-be creators let the world tell them that

that's no way to make a living? Or how many people aren't able to pursue their dreams or cultivate their talents because they're too busy trying to make end's meet? I almost kept it for myself, but I figured even if the person who printed it didn't come for it, then somebody else would stumble upon it. Of course it didn't occur to me until I was back in my room that I could've just made a copy of it.

Sunita and the other Swafford RAs combined their floor socials into one big building-wide trick-or-treating event that we didn't *have* to participate in, but we didn't want to be like the uninvolved Heteros down the hall. Each floor's residents took turns visiting the other floor's open doors for a joke-sized piece of candy, which meant we had to go out and buy a bag of candy. I thought it would be a logistical mess, but it went off flawlessly. "Like shuudan koudou," Tylor said.

After we and all the other kids in town turned in for the night after trick-or-treating, the air took on that perpetual chill, right on schedule. The overbearing clouds that October prophesied rolled in and blocked out the inky, starry night. Blustery gusts broke the stillness, snatching the last of the leaves from the trees. I watched them and tried to keep myself warm as I let the resentful gray gloom of Fall Part 2 swallow me and everything else.

November 2

So I think the award for 'Most Hipster Shit I've Ever Seen' goes to the guy in Physical Science who brought a single-serve French press and a mug into class today. I'm surprised it took two months to see anything like that, given how college has been impressing me left and right since day one.

I think we should start referring to November and December 'Fallen' instead of 'Fall' to distinguish the two different seasons before and after Halloween. One day you're being all cute with your Instagram posts of leaves and pumpkins, and the next day everything's gray and bare and you're feeling depressed—at least more so than usual. That's not to say it's not atmospheric though. Just because it's not a warm and bright June day doesn't mean it's not beautiful in its own way.

I discovered my new favorite poem at Lit Club last night, "Kjære, babygulrot" by Henrik Ibsen. You'd think any poem that Marvin Bostwick recites from The Stool in its original Norwegian would be about something more profound than baby carrots, but apparently not. Nikole had us dead when she looked up the translation to read aloud for us.

So here's the thing—I really like Miles. He's smart, he's funny, he's sweet, he's a stud muffin, and we have similar tastes in music, but we aren't compatible when it comes to having sex, since we're both apparently in our seemingly-perpetual top eras. And then sex with Devon was great, but we don't really have anything in common besides a lust for each other. I guess I'll eventually meet somebody who I'm compatible with on all fronts, but why do I even want to get into another relationship anyway? Is it because we're well into cuffing season and I'm not cuffed to anybody? It's possible.

And then there's Ethan, who I'm crushing *hard* for, given the number of times I find myself on his Instagram and the time or two or four that he's been on my mind when I've been getting myself off. He came into Rosenberg today and I had to keep myself from running over to say hi. It was a struggle to keep myself from going over to talk to him again and again. I've been wanting to drop hints about me being gay, but I don't want him to think I'm hitting on him—which is what I'd absolutely be doing. I've lost friends before because of who I am, and I can't tell if he'd be chill with it or not. I'd rather just keep wearing my costume around him if it means keeping him around, even if just as a friend.

November 3

So I guess they did a study about how picking your nose can up your chances of getting Alzheimer's, and I'm *fucked* if it ends up being true.

Our discussion on the Holocaust in History today segued into a discussion about genocides in general that Dr. de Conto didn't put a stop to. Fun fact: Turkey denies that the Armenian genocide ever happened because the word 'genocide' didn't exist at the time.

"Why is it okay when the United States exterminates the Native Americans in order to let its citizens settle westwards and grow the country?" a triggered me asked the class. "Manifest destiny says it was god's will for them to be killed for the benefit of the country."

"But then when Nazi Germany does essentially the same thing," Kade took over for me, "and exterminates Jews, Slavs, and other 'undesirables' to make room for Germany to grow, it was the greatest atrocity in human history. I mean, 'lebensraum' differs from manifest destiny only in name. So why is one celebrated and the other demonized? Not that I'm sticking up for Nazi Germany or anything."

Every eye was silently on us.

"Hitler actually got inspiration for the Jewish genocide from America's genocide of the Native Americans," I added.

de Conto looked at the class expectantly. "Well? Is anybody going to answer Kaden's question?" she finally asked. The mixed responses trickled in like election results.

135

"*Wow.*"

"I guess when you put it *that* way..."

"I mean, you're not *wrong.*"

"You're nuts. The Nazis were evil."

"So what, do you hate America?"

"Of course I don't hate America," I said like it was ridiculous. "I just hate double standards." I think the fact that I get so fired up over the news shows that I don't hate America, even if half the people living in it would willingly restrict human rights if it means becoming a goddamn theocracy.

"I certainly think you two gave them all something to think about," de Conto told us after class. "I've never had a student point that out before without me bringing it up."

I caved and stopped into Starbucks to see Ethan as a treat for not going at all last week. "Hey Trevor!" he smiled like he was happy to see me as I went up to the counter. "Tall latte, right?" he asked with his hand on the POS screen. I grinned like an idiot. *He remembered my order.*

"Usually yes, but I'm not getting anything today. I just wanted to tell you that you were in my dream last night," I lied.

He raised an eyebrow. "Oh really? Was it steamy?" *God, do I wish.*

"No," I chuckled uncomfortably. "We had class together, and our professor was taking the class on a guided tour through the woods at night. There were these cardboard cutouts of monsters and fake spiders in the trees and stuff." Actually, it was the guy on campus who always has a gigantic pair of headphones clasped around his head, but that wouldn't have given me an excuse to talk to Ethan.

"Sounds creepy," Ethan smiled. "I dreamt I was trying to hide all these donuts under my bed because we were getting a room check but they wouldn't fit."

I laughed through my nose. "I like it."

"So wait, why didn't you just message me that?" Ethan asked. *Uh, so I could see you?*

I shrugged, hands clutching my backpack straps. "I had to come this way anyway."

"Was that it then?"

"Pretty much."

"Okay. I'll see you around," he said as he went back to wiping the counter. I couldn't make my feet move. I couldn't take my eyes off his butt. *He's flirting with me, right?*

"Okay, you convinced me. A tall latte, please."

He spun back to register with a smile. "That's why they hired me. Do you want me to make a flower or a heart in the foam?" *He's totes flirting with me.*

"Can you do that?"

"I mean, I doubt they'd *fire* me over it."

"I meant you're *able* to do that? Like, you possess the talent to—"

"I know what you *meant*," he laughed, letting me see his teeth. "I'm just playing with you."

I watched Ethan jiggle the pitcher as he poured the foam and tilted the cup around until a design took shape. "Was it hard to learn how to do it?"

"I mean, at first it was," he said to it. "I work at a Starbucks back home, so I have some experience."

"*Ah*," I smiled with an up-nod, "it all makes sense now." I admired his flower, driving myself wild with the thought of if he'd made me a heart instead. "I almost don't wanna drink this now. Is today latte art day, or what?"

"No," he shrugged. "I just like to do it sometimes for some of my favorite customers." *He just called me one of his favorite customers.*

"How many favorite customers do you have?" I managed to say.

"Only a few. There's this one girl who comes in almost every day who I like seeing, if you get what I mean." He bounced his eyebrows. *God. Fucking. Dammit.*

"I do," I forced a smile. I felt so defeated that I'd forgotten what feeling defeated felt like. *Maybe he likes seeing me in that way too? He could be bi.* "Have you ever played a game called Drunk *Jenga*?"

"Yeah, once," he responded. "Why?"

"We made our own copy of the game and we're gonna try to break it out this weekend, if you're into that kind of stuff."

"I am *absolutely* into that kind of stuff. I was gonna hang with one of my other friends, but I can move some things around or hit up their place afterwards," he smiled.

"Perf," I smiled back. *Stop kidding yourself, Trevor—when are they ever bi?*

On my way past Patrick I looked over to see Paul just sitting down for a smoke break on the steps of one of the side doors. She unclasped one of those purple cigarette cases and a cancer stick found its way to her wrinkled, puckered lips. She took a drag and looked up to see me watching her. *Keep walking, you fucker,* she exhaled. You couldn't pay me enough money to run up and try snatching it from her.

November 4

As much as I'm not a fan of Dr. Gallagher's class, she couldn't have picked a better time to have us read *Dracula*. Make yourself a cup of tea, put on a playlist of Romantic-era piano music, and find a seat by the window. Don't plan on getting any reading done though, because you'll be too busy getting distracted by how on-point the vibe is. Nothing like a gray, misty day to make you feel scholarly.

I was today-years-old when I grabbed a copy of *The New Halle Herald*, the school newspaper, for the first time to read over breakfast. The town of New Halle doesn't have it's own newspaper since fuck nothing happens outside of the realm of the university, so its residents get to read all about how SGB is spending their budget, how Greek life is 'giving back to the community,' how some science club made a working phone out of two paper cups and a string. An op-ed titled "Why We're Overdue for a Course on Meninism" made me double-check that I didn't accidentally grab a print copy of *The Onion* by mistake. Imagine my delight though when I stumbled across the police blotter, which columns all the incidents over the past week that either the campus police or borough police responded to. Most of them are just fire alarms getting set off from burnt food or underage intoxications or 'odors of marijuana,' but some of them are *hilarious*. *'Oct. 30—Borough police responded to a call on Spring Road about an unidentified male sitting on a porch smoking a cigar. The suspect fled the scene upon police arrival, leaving the cigar behind. A few minutes later, a nude female actor emerged from a nearby bush and also fled the scene. The cigar was collected as evidence. No further police action was taken.'* I almost spit out my food. I couldn't make that shit up if I wanted to.

I tagged along with Kade and Victor yesterday evening when they went to a handpan performance for their Music class, and then the three of us went back to 239 Axworthy to turn my *Jenga* game into a Drunk *Jenga* game since I'd told Ethan we'd be playing it this weekend.

"I can't wait for the election to be over so I don't have to listen to any more political ads," Victor said as one such ad played between songs on Kade's emo playlist. "I've heard the word 'radical' so many times that it doesn't even mean anything anymore."

"Remember the good old days when you had to try to overthrow the government or something to be called a radical?" I reminisced out loud as I scratched a pen into a block. "Now all you have to do is say that the FBI is unbiased or that the 2020 election was legitimate."

"And yet the people who call us radical are the ones who *actually* tried to overthrow the government," Victor rolled his eyes.

"I can't remember where," Kade said, "but there's a bathroom stall somewhere on campus—"

"Because you've been in so many of them that they blur together."

"—but somebody wrote 'liberals suck' on the wall, which I thought was funny. It's like, come on, we're the radical left now. Get with the times."

I recycled some of the Drunk *Jenga* blocks I liked from Miles' party—we didn't use 'chicks drink' or 'dicks drink' to keep it as gender-inclusive/neutral as possible—

and some were originals, but most of the rules were ones we found online. We added a new twist to the game too by writing a different rule on both sides of each block— if you didn't like or didn't want to do the one you pulled, you could drink to flip it to the other side, but then you *have* to do that one.

"You guys'll like this one," Victor said as he showed us one of his blocks. One side read *'Finish your drink!!!'* and the other read *'Gay chicken with left.'* I laughed because that's exactly the kind of thing I would've done as an excuse to try to kiss another guy when I was still in the closet.

"I think you made that for yourself," I told him. "If you ever wanna make out with a guy, I'm right here."

"Okay, deal," he laughed. "I'll hit you up if I'm ever in the mood."

"Rude," Kade said.

November 5

November 5, 1605 was the day a group of conspirators tried to blow up Parliament and assassinate King James, and here's to hoping that no civilian militia is ever that motivated.

I'm surprised I haven't gotten a random ass pic or a dirty text from Devon yet. Maybe he regretted taking me back to his room? Call me crazy, but for as much as I've said otherwise, I think I'd *rather* have something with strings attached than just a hookup or a friend with benefits, as hot as those benefits might be.

I was thrilled to see that the print I'd gotten Kade for his birthday was up on his wall when I went over to 239 Axworthy to chill until dinner. "Is that new?" I asked him as I nodded at it.

"Yeah! I just picked it up today," he smiled at it. "But *I* didn't order it, and everybody I asked said they didn't get it for me, so I don't know where the hell it came from."

I shrugged. "I guess you just have a secret admirer who knows you too well."

"I guess so," he shrugged, though it hit him five minutes later. *"Wait,* it's not from *you,* is it?"

I leaned over. *"Bitch it might be."*

He squinted. "Are you forreal?"

"Happy belated birthday!"

"Wow, thanks fam," he said like he didn't deserve it. "I love it. Really."

"Wow, I can't wait to see what I get for *my* birthday," Victor said from the doorway.

"Keep acting like an entitled little shit and it'll be a finger up your ass," I smirked.

"Oh *dad*," he squirmed.

We went over to Amina's room in Walcott Hall last night to inaugurate our new game, since Tylor said her room's even bigger than ours. The RA at the desk watched the eight of us all walk in all together and probably wondered what Kade and I had in our backpacks. "My friend's on her way down to sign us in," Tylor told him as we took turns writing down our names and buildings.

Amina appeared through one of the sets of doors in a sweatshirt and yoga pants. "It's so good to see you again!" she greeted those of us she met last weekend before introducing herself to those she hadn't. She gave everyone hugs except for Tylor, who got a kiss instead. The others gave me *what gives?* looks like I was supposed to know how long *that's* been a thing. She took us up to room 348, which had *four* bubble letter names on the door. Saying that her room is bigger than ours isn't incorrect—the kitchen/living room common area alone is almost as big as our entire room, complete with a full-sized fridge, a full-sized couch, two armchairs, and a handful of tables. We found one of her roommates, Ari, playing Xbox as we spilled through the door. Amina opened the door to the left to show us her two-person bedroom, which is almost exactly like ours if there was a door in the wall where my desk is. "Bathroom's around the corner if you need it," she told us.

"I'm probs gonna have to take you up on that offer," Kade said.

I admired her PS5, guitar, and longboard, but her posters were what caught my attention. They're the kind of filtered, lo-fi pictures they have at work—Pacific Coast Highway, the Santa Monica pier and the Ferris wheel, palm tree-lined streets, the Hollywood sign—and posters for bands I've never heard of, but have got to be West Coast alternative from the looks of them.

"How are we not friends?" I asked her like she did something wrong. "Are you from Cali? Going there is like my *dream*."

"I *wish* I was," Amina chuckled. "I'm just from Pittsburgh, but—"

"Oh nice, so are we," Victor interrupted her.

"Yeah, and so are half the people here," Kade said. "Let the lady speak."

"I've never gone, but I've always wanted to," Amina went on. "My roommate Kasey was in L.A. this past Summer and I'm *high-key* jelly of her. Also, *love* the shirt," she said to Victor's 'WELL BEHAVED WOMEN SELDOM MAKE HISTORY' shirt with a nod.

We set out the liquor and pop and juice we brought on the counter. Amina popped back into her room for some half-drunk bottles of vodka and premixed Long Island Iced Tea. "Okay, listen guys," she said as she took some cups down from a cupboard, "the RA on duty's one of my besties, so we'll be okay as long as we're not being super loud. So try not to be, okay?"

We made ourselves drinks and grabbed spots around the table. I practically vaulted over it to get a seat next to Ethan on the couch. I had the honor going first since I'd been the one going on about the game. I had to drink for being right-handed, and again for being the one sitting across from Elisha. I would've had to pull my next block standing on one leg if the arm-wrestling match between Kade and Nikole that Kade lost hadn't knocked the tower over.

"*Et c'est pourquoi nous ne pouvons pas avoir des belles choses!*" Victor exclaimed like a francophone Ricky Ricardo as he gestured from the blocks to the ceiling.

"You're supposed to point at the person who made it fall and call them an asshole," I said. Kade took it silently from behind crossed arms.

Will lost a staring contest to Elisha. Tylor couldn't think of another word that rhymed with 'carpet.' I was the last one to touch the floor. Ethan had to speak into an invisible microphone whenever he spoke. Victor had to call the 1-800 number on a box of Orville Redenbacher popcorn and ask if he could talk to Orville, but started laughing really hard and just hung up. Kade was in such a mood over having to take a dick pic and letting the person to his right, which would've been Amina, choose a contact of his to send it to—which he was *supposed* to do since he sipped to flip—that we finally just let him place it and take another. Ari and Victor were bound to one another in a drinking pact. We found out that like half of us have never read any *Harry Potter* books after Will had to present Tylor with two truths and a lie, which gave Will a good Never Have I Ever to hit us with later on. I felt my stomach in my throat when I pulled '*Finish your drink!!!*' because that meant the other side would tell me to play gay chicken with...*Ethan*. I eagerly sipped to flip it, though I would've happily downed the rest of the vodka if it meant having the chance to kiss Ethan. *He's totally gonna pull away though. Or maybe he won't. But what if—* "Southpaw?" I scowled down at the block. "What the fuck?"

Ethan leaned over to read it. "Doesn't that mean if you're right-handed you have to use your left hand, and the other way around?" *No shit that's what it means. What, did Victor write 'Finish your drink' on all of his blocks?*

It turns out I'm almost just as good using my left hand as my right though. "Maybe I'm ambidextrous," I said as I set the block atop the tower.

"You can't be," Tylor said seriously. "You can only be either homodextrous or heterodextrous. There's no in-between. And I hope the rest of you know that was a joke."

We got up for refills and to use the bathroom after Victor demonstrated a lack of precision bricklaying. "I didn't get to ask you," I said to Ethan as we poured ourselves more Jack and Coke, "but how was the rest of your Halloweekend?"

"It was good!" he smiled. "Nate's one friend kept going on about wanting to do a Jell-o shot up his butt, but I don't think he actually did it. And there was some preppy vampire who kept hanging around me all night. He said '*I vant to suck your dick!*' to me at least twice."

I perked up. "Did you let him?"

"Maybe if I was desperate I would," he laughed. *Can you be desperate around me sometime?*

Amina inaugurated the next game by pulling the 'waterfall' block, and god can that girl drink. She did Will dirty judging by the way he had to dance solo for a full minute. I had to be the group's butler for the rest of the game, which is how I got to be called 'Chives' for the rest of the night and some of this morning. The game ended when Elisha underestimated the reach of her T-Rex arms, and Ethan was too focused on messaging whoever he was messaging to help gather up blocks.

"This was a lot of fun," he said, "but I'm gonna go meet up with my other friend." *No, don't go!* "Thanks for having me over though," he said to Amina. "We *def* gotta play this again sometime!" I watched our hostess walk him out, wishing that he didn't have other places to be. *Is his friend just a friend, or a friend with benefits?*

"I invited him to come out with us tomorrow night," Amina told us when she returned to the room. "He said *'hell* yeah.'"

Victor looked from her to Tylor to Kade. "We're going out tomorrow?"

"Just to my friend Roland's place again," she said. "You're welcome to come along too. It's a glow stick party."

"That sounds fun," I said. *Especially if Ethan's going.*

The last game of the night was going well until I drew *'Finish your drink!!!'* and sipped to flip to see *'Gay chicken with left'* on the other side, which I'd of course get after Ethan left. Instead, my new left was Kade. I blinked. The others *oohed* at us, totally clueless that I'd low-key wanted to kiss Kade since I first started hanging out with him. And the way Kade looked back at me made me wonder if he felt the same towards me. We scooted closer together on the couch. My tongue impulsively tapped my bottom lip. Will looked at us like he was daring us to do it, but also curious to see if we'd do it. Anticipation hung silent in the air. *One of us'll chicken out. And if not, it's just one quick little peck on the lips.*

The only problem was that it *wasn't* a quick little peck on the lips. Don't ask me *what* happened, but as soon our lips touched, it was like they were stuck together. I couldn't pull away. And *neither did Kade.* We made out in front of our friends, one of whom one of us was fucking. The girls shrieked. I heard Victor go, "Oh *shit,*" dead serious. And as if the kiss wasn't bad enough, Kade and I held each other in our gazes like we almost couldn't believe it. Will sprang to his feet and grabbed his jacket.

"Will, it was just a *dare,*" Kade tried to explain, but Will wasn't having any of it. His eyes were wet as he stuffed his feet into his shoes without even tying them. "Will, wait!" Will yanked open the door and Kade jumped up to go after him. "Grab my stuff when you leave," he told Victor. "I'm gonna try talking to him."

The rest of us sat in awkward silence. I gulped as I stared at the floor. *Way to fucking go, Trevor.*

But Kade didn't—

But neither did you! You knew you shouldn't have!

Victor sighed before gathering up Kade's things. "I think I'm just gonna head back now. You want me to leave the liquor?"

"Nah," I said dejectedly. "I think I'm actually gonna go too."

It kills me to know that Kade and Will are fighting because of me. I *knew* they were seeing each other, but I went ahead and kissed him anyway. I wanted to reach out to apologize and see how things went, but I let them have their space. It was weird having weekend breakfast by myself after going with my friends for so long. The omelets didn't even taste that good. *Is that how the omelets work? Do they only taste good if you're with your friends?*

November 6

I'm not sure which I've been hearing about more: the election, or the Powerball. Imagine waking up and finding out you're $2 billion richer though. Even if you only take home 10% after all's said and done, you'd still have *$200 million*. Like, what the fuck would you even do with yourself?

"I literally wouldn't even know," Kade said at dinner. "I'd probably have a panic attack for starters."

"I'd make sure everyone I know would never have to worry about money again," Victor daydreamed. "And then I'd do so much humanitarian work that they'd name libraries and shit after me."

"I'd start some kind of shelter for kids and teenagers to go to if there's no place safe for them," I said. "And not just queer kids, but kids whose parents are abusive, or addicts, or aren't willing to take care of them." *Whatever it would take to make sure that no kid ever has the childhood that Logan had.*

They both stared at me. "Wow," Kade just said. "That's…the kind of shit we need more of."

"Remind me again why you aren't a Gryffindor?" Victor asked.

"Don't you need to be courageous to be a Gryffindor?" I shrugged.

"Courage looks different for everybody," he said like a Ravenclaw before getting up for seconds, leaving Kade and me alone at the table with the elephant in the room. I wanted to talk to him about what happened the night before, but I did that thing that white people do whenever they're uncomfortable and I just stayed quiet. Kade didn't look up from his phone as he ate, and I was hella glad when Victor returned to rescue us from the awkwardness.

Kade stuffed what birthday liquor he had left into his backpack to take to Roland's glow stick party. *Will would have been going with us too if it weren't for me,* I couldn't stop telling myself on the walk over. Ethan met us outside of Kessler with an unlit glow bracelet on his wrist and excitement in his step. "I've never been to a party like this before," he said as he warmed his hands. "It's too bad we couldn't get any molly or something."

We retraced our steps from the week before to 84 Fischer Street. We paid our way in, and stepped into what felt like glow-in-the-dark mini golf without the mini golf. Glow sticks floated around the blacklight-lit room. A box of them for the taking sat next to another bin with red and green rubber wristbands in it, with a piece of paper above it that had 'GREEN = LET'S SEE WHAT HAPPENS' and 'RED = NOT INTERESTED' scrawled in matching highlighter.

"Not interested in what?" Kade asked. "Talking about why we've never gone back to the moon?" He put his mouth to my ear. *"It's because we made a deal with the lizard people."* I was sad all over again when he didn't take either color, but hopeful when Ethan took a green one. *Hold up.*

"Don't you have a girlfriend back home?" I asked him.

Ethan shook his head. "Not anymore. The long-distance thing wouldn't have worked out." I almost glitched. *Spoken like a Dillon.*

"Who's the girl in all your Instagram pics then?"

"Oh, that's my friend Chante from back home. And yes, we're just friends," he said as he gave me a look.

"Oh okay, I gotcha," I said as I put him back on my radar, even if at the periphery.

The music was mostly the same as last week's, but less Halloween-y and heavier on the remixes. My eyes fell on the spot where Devon and I made out and I thought about messaging him, but the far-fetched hope that Ethan and I would be playing some drinking game that would lead to him confessing that he's always wanted to try stuff with a guy and asking if I'd be up for it kept my phone in my pocket. Amina and Tylor, tipsy in their red wristbands, hugged us like we were the best part of their nights. Tylor and his neon shutter shades showed us to the fridge, from which I took a tall camouflage-y red-and-green can.

"Oh *shit*," Kade said as he pulled out a hard iced tea. "You're gonna get fucking *blitzed* fam."

"Ooh, I wanna get blitzed too!" Ethan said. I passed him the one I'd grabbed and took another for myself.

I raised my can. "Here's to...getting blitzed?" Its oppressively sweet, artificially fruity, boozy taste wasn't the *worst* thing I've ever had.

This one girl started getting flirty with me and I couldn't get her to go away. *Why don't they have wristbands for your preferences too?* I thought as I tuned her out. *That would clear things up real fast.* "Dude, why didn't you tap that?" Ethan asked me like a Hetero after she finally left me alone.

I felt my face flush. "I dunno. Just not my type I guess?"

"Yeah, I feel ya." *He didn't try 'tapping that' either.*

Amina and Tylor handed Ethan and me a loss at pong, and we watched them show their next challengers to the door. My half-empty drink had me feeling bold and unconcerned. "So I see you're wearing a green bracelet," I said to Ethan's wristband. "Are you trying to leave with some snack?"

"I mean, isn't that ultimately why we're here?" he chuckled as he nodded down at my own green wristband. "I'm just tired of seeing all the same people on Tinder. I figured I might meet a new face here."

"I haven't used Tinder in *months*." I took a long gulp and chose my words. "Call me an old-school romantic, but I'd rather meet someone by just doing me instead of going out and looking for love."

"Woah, who said anything about love?" he laughed. "I'm just tryna get my dick wet." *Can he see my mouth watering?*

"I mean, yeah, that'll work in the meantime. *I* certainly haven't been saving myself or anything."

"You could always try Tinder again," he shrugged. "It'll be all new people if you haven't used it since coming to school."

"I guess. I don't know. I'd rather hook up with someone I meet authentically instead of some rando who just looks good in a pic."

"Yeah, I feel ya," Ethan nodded. "So what exactly *is* your type?" he asked as he leaned against the wall to face me. His eyes and teeth and shirt glowed under the blacklight.

I mirrored his posture. "I mean, good looks grab my attention, but good taste and intelligence are what keep it. They'd have to be sweet. Funny. Preferably have the same likes as me," I nodded. "Looks fade, but the other stuff lasts. What about you?"

"True *that*. And yeah, pretty much what you said—cute, sweet, funny, all the usual stuff," he said. *Me! Me! I'm right here!* We sipped our cans, one of us thinking we were about to have a moment there. Someone across the room must've caught his eye, because he grinned past me and threw them an up-nod. "Oh shit, I'm gonna go say hi to my friend from class real quick!" No sooner had I started to go over with him than Kade grabbed me.

"Trev," Kade said, ghost-white like he'd just seen Mothman fly across the room, "I just met a guy who said he's never eaten a piece of fruit in his *life*. In his *life!* And not even anything fruit-*flavored*."

I gave him a *you're-full-of-shit* look. "How does somebody *never* eat a piece of fruit?"

"That's what I'm saying!" he shook his hands urgently.

I tilted my can ass-up and let it drain down my throat. *Vibe check? Fried like a chicken wing.* I thought about trying to crush my can on my forehead but thought better of it. I cracked open another and floated through the party to look for Ethan. I found Victor instead, rattling off Confucius jokes to Amina, who was laughing like they were the funniest things she'd ever heard.

"Hey Trev," a plastered Tylor called to me. "You won't kiss her," he dared me out of nowhere as he nodded at Amina. *Wait, what the hell?*

At least three sets of eyes were on me and my dumbstruck face. "Just for fun?" Amina shrugged like she'd be into it. I was feeling so good that the thought of not doing it didn't even cross my mind.

"Okay," I smirked.

She set down her cup and pulled her hair back. I leaned in to meet her mouth, feeling nothing but the movements of our lips. *Yep, still gay.*

"Holy shit," either Victor or Tylor said.

"I am gay, just so you know," I told her. "Like, *zero* attraction to girls. No offense though."

"That's cool. But *Jesus Christ* can you kiss." She turned to Tylor. "Ty, you should take some lessons from him." I made a kissy face at him.

I was feeling so good, I wasn't even worried if I was feeling *too* good. I shook my head around so the glow of the glow sticks and black lights streaked across the room in cursive lines, like a long-exposure shot of a freeway. The music sounded fuzzy, even when I tried to tune into it. I remember being pissed because somebody cranked up the difficulty level on my ability to move and speak without asking me if they could. And I remember not being able to take my eyes off a guy nearby with fluorescent green hair. "Hey boy, you poop outta that ass?" I called to him with a smile. He and his friends just glared at me, which just made me want to get even more fresh with him.

"Okay, you might wanna *not* do that," Victor warned me as he led me away from them, putting too much trust in my motor skills. I fell into him and almost took us both down.

"M'okay—I'm okay," I said as I steadied myself. But even when I stopped moving, everything else *kept* moving. I staggered over to a vacant armchair and dropped down with my face in my hands so everything would stop. It didn't. *Wut the fukk wuz in that stuff?*

A hand shook my knee. "Vibe check?" Victor asked.

I just shook my head.

"I'm gonna go get you some water, okay?"

I nodded with my head still in my hands. I sat up to see the room spinning upwards *over my head* like a hamster wheel. The lights were like an amusement park ride designed to make you puke. I squeezed my eyes shut, only to watch the inside of my eyelids slide upwards like movie credits.

"Trevor." I fought with my eyes to see Victor holding a large plastic cup of water. "Here." All four of our hands lifted it to my mouth. Not only did it not help me feel any better—it accelerated things.

"I need to get to the bathroom," I mumbled as I tried getting to my feet. Victor's arm was under me before I knew it.

"Hey Ty! Help me with him."

My head rolled like it sat loose on my neck as they carried me to the bathroom. I lowered myself from the edge of the sink to the rim of the bathtub and finally to the floor. I stared into the toilet, wishing that Victor wasn't being such a good friend by staying with me to see it through. *Never wanna feel like this again.*

"Maybe if you stick your fingers down your—"

I shook my head. *"Mmh mmh."* *Not necessary.*

I know Victor's one of my best friends, because only one of your best friends would rub your back and tell you that you're going to be okay as you hurl. I'd never felt so pathetic before, and him having to see me like that only made me feel more miserable. I wiped my eyes as I watched the corn kernels from dinner get sucked down like Charybdis swallowing a fleet of ships. I gave him a weak smile. "I feel better now."

"It always does the trick," Victor patted me.

I was happy that Tylor offered to take me back, since I didn't want to inconvenience Victor any more than I already had. I was able to walk without him holding onto me, even though I felt like I was rubber. The trip passed in disjointed fragments—blue emergency lights, leaf-pasted rocks, burnt-out wayfarers, pavement-slabbed sidewalk, Tylor saying words. *Thank god Ethan missed that.* I swished some mouthwash, pulled off my clothes, and crawled into the most comfortable spot in town. The sensation of my body gently rolling without actually moving lulled me to sleep.

I woke up wondering what the hell was around my neck before I realized I still had my glow stick necklace on. I was so tired that it didn't even feel like I'd gotten an extra hour of sleep from the time change. I felt so hungover that I actually *went back to bed,* and a stream of texts from Kade waited for me when I finally got up.

What u up to fam
Wanna go get foodles?
Wanna play a game?
Dont ignore me
😿
Love meeee!!

Omg mom I was taking a nap

Uh huh sure go head
You gonna be up to grab dinner later?

Nah, ill just eat something here

Lame
We can bring you something back
But then you gotta let us hang out in your room
I know, it's awful

I asked them to bring me some McDonald's, and took a desperately-needed shower before they showed up. One bite of greasy food reminded me how hungry I was. I dug out my deck of cards and we played kindergarten games like Go Fish and Crazy Eights because those were about all that I could handle. "So," Victor said as we played War, "I think Ethan saw you last night. With Amina, I mean."

"Okay?" I said. "And?"

"And he seemed kinda out of it afterwards."

"You sure he wasn't just drunk as shit?" Kade asked.

"I *know* he was *drunk!*" Victor said. "But it was almost like his mood changed after that."

"He was probably just jealous that he wasn't the one kissing Amina," I said, though I fantasized that Ethan was jealous that he wasn't the one kissing *me*.

"I think Vic's jealous that *he* wasn't the one kissing Amina," Kade laughed before he stopped and pointed a finger gun at me. "Oh, I forgot! What are you doing this weekend?"

"I dunno. Not drinking, that's for sure. Why?"

"We're going back home for a concert on Saturday, and our friend who was gonna go with us can't now because his Robotics Club is in a competition and they keep fucking *winning*, so now he has to go to State College this weekend to see if they can make nationals, so now we have an extra ticket, and we figured you might wanna come with us and stay with us for the weekend," he said almost all in one breath. "We'd do other stuff too—we could show you the city and take you to some of our favorite places, but it's cool if you wouldn't wanna." He popped his fingers. "We figured we'd ask you since you like a lot of the same music as us."

"What band is it?" I asked like it mattered.

"Last Dinosaurs."

I bit the inside of my cheek. "So you're asking if I want to go back home with you and spend a weekend doing shit in Pittsburgh, including going to a concert? *Fuck* yeah."

Kade looked taken aback. "Wait, really?"

"Don't people from Pittsburgh speak like troglodytes?" Tylor chuckled.

"Why wouldn't I?" I asked Kade. "Are we leaving Friday after class I guess?"

"Yeah. Vic doesn't get done until 2, so—"

"I will *100%* be skipping that class," Victor interrupted him.

"Am I driving us down, or are your parents gonna pick us up?" I asked.

"Dude," Kade laughed, "I *have* my car here."

I stared at him. "How long have you had a car? Why the hell have *I* always been the one driving us around?"

"Since like two birthdays ago? And because you never asked me to?"

I frowned. "What about when you had me drive you to the mail center to get your birthday present? Why didn't you just go get it yourself?"

He just smirked. "Why lose my parking spot when you can lose yours instead?"

Tylor laughed through his nose. "You got *played*, son."

November 7

Here I am again, running on four hours of sleep,
Listening to "Mr. Brightside" on repeat,
Convincing myself it was never about 'the distance.'
And there you are, making fresh favorites
With your new forever and always—
And for their sake, I hope you mean it this time.

November 8

Early November's a weird time of year. Like, is it Christmas or not?

I was worried that less than a week wouldn't be enough time to get into a new band enough to appreciate seeing them in concert, but I've been listening to Last Dinosaurs almost non-stop for the past two days and I fuck with them *hard*.

All the 'I Voted' stickers stuck to shirts and notebooks and laptops made me think of the Star-Bellied Sneetches from the Dr. Seuss story, except the stickered students have a right to be proud of themselves. de Conto asked the class if we had plans to vote and ripped somebody a new one when he said it didn't matter since it was only a midterm election. "If everybody thought the way you did, then nothing would ever get done," she shut him down.

Ethan wasn't at Starbucks when I swung by after class, which was the whole point of me going. "Is Ethan working today?" I asked the barista after I gave her my order. *Did he walk out? Did he get kidnapped?*

"Nah, he got a new job," she shook her head. "Is 'Trevor' spelled with an 'R?'"

I raised an eyebrow at her. "...Yes?" And then when I got my drink the name on the cup said 'Clever.'

> **I was just at starbucks and the girl there said you got a new job?**

It took Ethan so long to respond that I was starting to worry if I tried hitting on him at the party and he got weirded out by me. Relief washed over me when I finally heard from him.

> **Yeah!**
> **Catch me at Bubble Up in bixby** 😊

What the hell's Bubble Up? I thought as I Googled 'bubble up nhu.' My jaw dropped. "Oh. *My god.*"

"What is it?" Tylor practically sighed without looking up from his notes. He's lived with me for long enough to know not to take me getting dramatic too seriously.

"Since *when* has there been a bubble tea shop on campus?"

He jerked his head up. "Wait, *what?*"

"Ethan apparently works there now! I guess it just opened?"

"Where?" he demanded as he went for his phone.

"I don't know!" my mouth said while my fingers relayed the news to Kade and Victor. "Somewhere in Bixby I guess!"

> **STOP WHAT YOU'RE DOING**
> **THERES A NEW BUBBLE TEA PLACE ON CAMPUS**
> **I REPEAT, BUBBLE TEA PLACE ON CAMPUS**

> **STFU**
> **HOW DID WE NOT KNOW THIS**

> **ASDFGHJKL**
> **SINCE WHEN????**

The four of us hustled to Bixby like the Patnick shits were about to do us dirty. A contemporary, minimalist tea shop full of blonde wood, vintage light bulbs, and fake succulents had replaced the blank section of boards-for-a-storefront on the second floor. The vague 'coming soon' sign didn't say what was going there, I guess to build up hype for it until it finally opened—and if so, it worked. "Holy shit," Tylor swore as he stood on his toes to see how deep the crowd went. "Are they giving shit away?" It turns out they were—a Plinko board that Ethan was helping run was set up for the grand opening, where students could win a drink coupon or a piece of swag or a straw up the ass. I tried waving over to him but he didn't see me. There's no way the place wasn't in violation of some fire code. Luckily, most of the crowd was in line for Plinko instead of getting an actual drink. I just ordered the same thing as Tylor since the menu was intimidating. We all sampled each other's drinks at a table out in the main seating area.

"Joke's on you, you all have my herpes now," Kade said as he took his tea back.

"Is it just me," I said to the deposit of boba at the bottom of my cup, "or is anybody else low-key worried you'll suck too hard and a boba pearl's gonna shoot into the back of your throat and make you choke?"

Victor shot his tea back down through his straw. "It's *definitely* just you," he laughed.

"Sounds erotic though," Kade snorted.

We hung around for a while in hopes that Ethan would get a break, but the patrons wouldn't stop coming. "Anyone up for grabbing dinner since we're already here?" Tylor suggested.

We spread a different table with wings and fries and frozen sushi. "Guys, this is a literal game changer," Kade said.

"What, mixing honey mustard and barbecue sauce?" I asked his little cup of sauce.

"No! I meant having a bubble tea place on campus!"

"Oh," I chuckled. "Yeah, for sure."

"So I guess this means you won't be getting Starbs anymore, huh Trev?" Victor razzed me.

"Not necessarily," I absolutely lied. Ethan or no Ethan though, I'll take bubble tea over poshly-priced coffee any day.

The two of them invited us over to 239 Axworthy to watch the election results and take a drink every time Steve Kornacki says "same day votes," which I obviously didn't take them up on. I'm not watching it live like they are, but I keep refreshing the election map I have pulled up on another tab. *You hear that?* Victor asked in his story with his hand cupped to his ear. *That's the sound of a red wave NOT crashing. It's fuckin lit.*

November 9

> And just as the hurting started to ease,
> I found a strip of pictures of us we took in the
> Photo booth at the mall, dated early December,
> Back when I took 'our next Christmas' for granted.

November 10

You know how sometimes you have a dream that's so eerie you wake up and you're happy that it was just a dream? Last night I dreamt that I was the only person on campus, and it was so cloudy that it was like the sky was pressing down on me. And then I found a body lying dead on the sidewalk and crows were picking at it. I had to peek through the blinds as soon as I woke up to make sure there were live people out and about.

I've heard more than a few girls talking about how they don't have to worry about transferring to a school in pro-abortion state now, thanks to the election outcome in PA. I'd like to say that I can't believe we're still debating this, but we *are* talking about America here. If people can pull the civil liberties card to justify not wearing a mask during the height of the pandemic and threaten other people's health, then I think it's fair that people can pull the civil liberties card to get an abortion. Why do people say that every child deserves the right to have a life, but then when they see a woman of color with five kids paying for her groceries with food stamps, they'll say that she should've thought about how she'd pay to feed those five kids before she had them? I can't fucking *even*. And let's take away the food stamps too while we're at it, because *that's* how you ensure someone's right to life. '*But what if Jesus was aborted?*' they'll argue. Well if god's as omniscient as he's made out to be, then I'm sure he would've had a plan B in place, pun absolutely intended.

Since we both knew it wouldn't be happening at Common Hour, Kade and I—Victor decided to give Improv Club a try—waited until later on in the evening to hit up Bubble Up. We waited with our iced brews in the lounge overlooking the atrium in Bixby for Ethan to get off work to get dinner with him.

"I wish I had the balls to do something like Improv Club," I said as I let myself slowly slide down in the smooth, ergonomically sleek chair I sat in.

"That's okay," Kade said simply. "We're each good at our own things though—supposedly."

I looked over at him. "Whaddaya mean, 'supposedly?'"

He slouched so low in his chair that his head was practically in the seat. "You've seen stuff I've made, but I've never gotten to read one of your stories."

"I just don't know if I'm ready for other people to read them," I said pathetically as I let myself slide farther down. "I'm worried people won't like them."

"That's just part of the creative process. You just gotta learn to not give a shit. You know how many times I've heard people say *my* art's shit?"

"Yeah, I guess you're right."

He went back to his phone. "Of course I am."

Maybe not giving a shit is the meaning of life, I pondered. *Mine would've been so much easier, and probably more fun, if I'd stopped giving a shit sooner. I would've been out sooner, for one. I wouldn't be so afraid to speak my mind, I wouldn't be worried about what people think of me. Kade doesn't give a shit. Victor certainly doesn't give a shit. Tylor, Logan, Ethan—they all give way less of a shit than I do, and they're all happy. How—*

Ethan's head eclipsed my view of the asininely high ceiling. "That can't be comfy," he smiled down at me in his white t-shirt with a cute kawaii bubble tea graphic on it.

"It's not," I said as I pushed myself back up.

He told us about his new job as we ate. "The pay's a little more than what I was making, and I get to keep the same hours I had," Ethan said as he poked at his boneless wings. "Let's be real though, I don't think they're gonna turn down anybody who's willing to work Common Hour."

"The place is crazy busy like all the time," Kade said as he dipped a bouquet of fries in his mixture of honey mustard and barbecue sauce that he calls 'saucy sauce.'

"Tell me about it," Ethan scoffed. "I even missed RHA last night because they asked me to come in." He squinted at something over my shoulder. "What the hell is *that?*" I spun around, but not before I caught him swiping a fry off my tray with a smirk.

"Son of a bitch," I laughed as he stuffed it in his mouth.

"You're so easy, you know that Trev?" Kade said from behind crossed arms. I gave him the finger.

"So what's RHA?" I asked Ethan after flipping through all the organizational acronyms I could think of.

"It stands for Residence Hall Association. The House Councils technically all belong to it, and we have these forums on Wednesday nights with the RHA exec board."

"So I take it you're on your House Council then?" I asked him.

"Mmhmm," he nodded.

"Are you like the President?" Kade joked.

"Mmhmm," Ethan repeated.

Kade and I traded surprised looks. "Woah, dinner with the President of Kessler Hall."

Ethan rolled his eyes. "Believe me, it's way less glamorous than it sounds."

"So hold on," I sat up, "on top of all your studently duties, you have a job, you play for the Knights, you have your House Council stuff, and you have these RHA meetings? It's no wonder you're always busy."

"It can be tough, not gonna lie. There were a couple days when I'd have literally no time for myself all day. The Knights are the official school team though—I just did club baseball," he said to me like I had any idea what that meant.

"Oh," Kade shook his finger at me, "Victor said he's gonna skip his Geography class tomorrow, so we can leave earlier. I might end up skipping Computers too if I'm feeling saucy."

"Mmkay."

"Where are you guys going?" Ethan asked curiously.

"Trevor's coming home with us for the weekend," Kade told him, ignoring my mental shouts of *shut up! shut up!* "We're going to a concert and doing some other stuff, to be determined."

"That sounds fun," Ethan said, though I've been left out of things enough times to know what pretending to be cool with it looks like.

November 12

You know how you'll be typing in all caps without realizing it and then you look back at your screen and you scare yourself? Yeah.

"I'm finna skip this one too," Victor muttered as I passed him on my way out of Computers.

"Sucks to suck," I teased him. "Catch us in Patnick if you end up bailing."

I flipped to the police blotter in *The Herald* while I waited for Kade to show. Other than somebody peeing in their roommate's shampoo bottle, it was a pretty uneventful week for mischief in New Halle. "So what else are we gonna do besides go to the concert?" I asked him as the two of us took a table.

"Not sure yet," Kade shrugged. "Fucking shit up, *that's* for sure." He rattled off some suggestions, but I got too caught up in wondering if Will would've been the one they would've brought home with them if it wasn't for what had happened. Yes, I'm still upset with myself over it.

Victor rescued at least one of us from our thoughts with the scrape of chair legs. "I would've shoved my pen in my eye if I had to sit through that for another minute," he said as he promptly started cutting into his hefty stack of pancakes.

Back in 222 Swafford, I gathered up a weekend's-worth of stuff in Tylor's duffel bag that he let me borrow before taking it out to the car Kade waved from that was parked in one of the 15-minute spots. "You know car washes *do* exist, right?" I chuckled when I got close enough to see the dirt around the rims and the streaks on the windows.

"Yeah, and you know what else exists?" he asked as he hopped out. "The possibility of the car wash doors getting stuck shut and you dying of carbon monoxide poisoning because you can't get out."

"Why not just turn your car off until somebody comes and opens it?"

"What if the world's ending and there's nobody to let you out?"

I sighed. "Well then I guess you just die."

"Exactly. You can just shove that in my trunk," he said to Tylor's bag as he popped open the trunk.

"Said the actress to the bishop," I laughed as I set it next to their laundry baskets.

Victor and I threw down the same thing five times in a row in Rock Paper Scissors before I finally won, though I'm sure he would've put on Last Dinosaurs' week-old album too if he'd been riding shotgun. I was in such a good mood that the bad drivers didn't even annoy me—the sky was cloudless, and I was on my way to spend the weekend at my best friends' house. Going over to a friend-from-school's house was always fun because I liked seeing them in their natural habitat, and especially for sleepovers, because Saturday mornings are when people are at their most candid.

"Oh *Jesus*," Victor grumbled when a large homemade sign that read 'PLEASE GOD SAVE OUR COUNTRY' bore down on us with 100,000 fun-sized American flags sticking out of the ground around it.

"I mean, that could go either way," I tried to bullshit myself.

"Nuh uh," Kade shook his head. "Nobody who votes the same way as us is stupid enough to make a sign like that."

"Or has an American flag fetish," Victor mumbled.

I knew we were getting closer to Pittsburgh when the two-lane-road-turned-highway got more and more congested with cars. It looked like your typical Rust Belt town at first—the brown river, church steeples, smokestacks, a water tower stamped with a forgettable name. But instead of fading into hills or woods, it went on and on until it turned into buildings—*tall* buildings. The city sat nestled among the swelling hills, like a secret waiting to be stumbled upon.

Kade caught me staring. "What, you've never seen a city before?"

"Yeah, but this beats the hell outta Buffalo." *Who would've thought that hills add so much character?*

He drove us through suburbs that went from nice to boujee to downright *swanky.* I was almost relieved when we found ourselves in a middle-class neighborhood again, the kind that makes up for its lack of dandelions with establishment Democrats. I didn't have to guess too hard which house was theirs, thanks to the Progress flag flying from the porch. It looks like the kind of house high school parties get thrown in in movies when the parents conveniently go out of town, though it's certainly not the biggest one on the street. "My parents are both still at work," Kade said like we were about to do unholy things as he punched in the code for the two-door garage.

"Are you saying we should take this opportunity to experiment with each other's bodies?" I asked.

"I was afraid you weren't going to get the euphemism, but yes."

"Whose car is that then?" I asked as I nodded to the kind of car that Mom would call a 'little shithead car' sitting in the garage.

"*C'est à moi,*" Victor said as we stepped across the empty garage and into the laundry room.

"Oh, that reminds me," I said, "you were in my dream last night, Kade."

He snorted. "That explains the whole exploring-each-other's-bodies thing."

"You *wish.* I went into Critical Writing and you were at the front of the room teaching the class to sing the French national anthem."

"I don't even know French!" he laughed.

Victor waved his fingers like a conductor. "*Allons enfants de la patrieeeee...*"

I don't know if I'd call their family *rich,* but the built-in speakers gave me the feeling that money's not an issue for them. The open first floor is eclectic with modern furniture, but it doesn't feel sterile or unlived-in. A jingle at the top of the stairs announced their pet, a small black-and-white dog whose ears went back at the sight of us. "Well *hello!*" Victor said in a cutesy voice. It hopped down the stairs one at a time as fast as it could and pushed itself against his legs. "*Ooh how I missed you!*" he said as he furiously petted it, its tail going a million miles an hour.

"*This* is Katie," Kade said as he scratched her butt. "She didn't know she was gonna make a *new friend today huh did you?*" She was just as excited to see me as she was to see them.

"Katie?" I asked as I gave her pets. "I would've expected Friedrich Engels or something."

"That was already her name when we adopted her," Victor explained as he slid open the back door to let her out.

"You guys have a pool?!" I said when I saw it, high-key jelly.

"*Chya.*"

"You should've invited me down in Summer instead of shitty-ass November."

"Maybe we will if you don't piss us off by then," he smirked. "We'll still be able to use the hot tub though." *Hot tub?* "We can take our stuff downstairs before we give you the tour."

Their finished game room is stocked like a bomb shelter with board games and puzzles. "Damn, you weren't kidding when you said you were serious about board games," I said to Kade with an astonished frown.

"'Serious' is an understatement," Victor laughed. "One time when he made me play *Axis & Allies*, we weren't sure what to do in a specific situation, so he called the number on the back of the rulebook to ask them."

"Well what else was I supposed to do?" Kade defensively threw his hands down. "The liberation of the East Indies was at stake!"

An armory of guitars hang on the wall beside Victor's real drum set, wooden barrels and shimmering cymbals and crooked arms and all. "I feel like there should be spotlights on that," I admired it. "Is this where you'd have band practice?"

"Sometimes, when Laura and Vince weren't home," Victor said. It took me a second to realize who he was talking about.

"They're not home *now*," I said slowly.

He laughed through his nose. "Let's put our stuff down first."

Past the game room is a sort-of den with a TV, some couches, and a recliner. "This is where we'll be crashing," Kade said like we were holing up in some safe house.

"Why would you wanna sleep on a couch when your own comfy bed that you haven't slept in in weeks is right upstairs?" I squinted.

"Why would we sleep in our own comfy bed when we can have an old-fashioned sausage party with our friend?"

I bit the inside of my cheek. "How's that different from a new-fashioned sausage party?"

He leaned in and beckoned me close. *"You'll find out later."*

I stood up, grabbing my buttocks. *"OoehOOeh!"*

Victor took his place behind his drums and passed me some earplugs from a drawer next to his throne. Even with them in, the thundering drums and crashing cymbals were *infinitely* louder than I thought they'd be. His freestyle was like a carpet bombing run. "And Katie doesn't mind that?" I asked as I popped out the earplugs after he'd finished.

He laid the sticks on his snare with a rattling *clack*. "She's used to it now. They're not too loud if you're up on the second floor."

"Says the guy who's never up there when they're being played," Kade muttered.

157

Kade's probably the only teenage guy who grows herbs that are actual herbs and not a weed plant hidden in a closet under a grow light. "So why do you have herbs?" I asked as I watched him spritz the pots in the dining room bay window.

"I cook with them. Fresh herbs and spices totally make a dish." He rubbed a rosemary needle between his fingers and took a sniff. "*Mmmm.* I'm like, *sexually* attracted to fresh rosemary."

"You *cook?*" I asked as I rubbed a leaf that left my fingers a little sticky and smelling like Christmas. "Why haven't you invited me over for dinner yet?"

"Maybe because I'm not your fucking *sub?*" he scowled. "I've used the kitchen in our building a few times. Not for anything fancy, just pasta and stuff." I took in their senior pictures hanging on a nearby wall alongside one of a girl who I guessed is their sister, Kelsey. Kade posed for his shot under a tree with a lake in the background with a smile like he's in pain. Victor either looks like a 16-year-old boy or a 46-year-old lesbian in his flannel and neatly styled hair.

I prepared myself for a Dr. Frankenstein's laboratory of half-finished art projects of genitalia when Kade opened his bedroom door on the second-floor landing, but it looked more or less like any other teenage boy's room, with his desk-turned-worktable and single bookcase with more not-books than books. A Galileo thermometer, a gyroscope, liquid motion toys, his diploma—'Kaden Nicholas Oakley'— and a soccer trophy from 2010 decorate the top of his dresser.

Victor's room looks like he went away to space camp and returned home with a newfound passion, with his rocket launcher of a telescope, 'Pale Blue Dot' poster, and bookshelf cluttered with a model solar system on wires and other space-themed trinkets. His books on politics, sociology, and astronomy couldn't have been more different than the ones Kade owns, but his diploma is identical except for the 'Victor Jacob Morozov' embossed on it. A picture on his desk of a wide-eyed kid laughing at the camera with two women behind him caught my eye on the way out, one of them ruffling his messy red hair. *I've never seen him that happy unless he's drunk.* He hadn't had to start wearing glasses yet.

Back in Kade's car, I tried to spy the city between hills as we drove closer. I drank in the skyline and tried to ignore the bouncing of the bridge we sat on while we theorized how traffic starts. Kade drove us to a busy neighborhood away from downtown, circling the block twice before finding a parking spot. Backpacked kids in kippahs—*band name idea: Kids in Kippahs*—strolled up the sidewalk with that done-with-class-on-Friday bounce in their steps. "This is my favorite part of the city," Victor said as we got out of the car, "even if I *did* get called the f-word here for wearing this shirt here before." He unzipped his hoodie to show me his 'PROTECT QUEER KIDS' shirt.

"*Forreal?*" I frowned. "What'd you do?"

"I asked the guy—"

158

"Don't lie, you yelled at him," Kade chuckled.

"—if he supports animal rights," Victor went on, "and when he said yeah, I asked him how the fuck that's possible when he's not an animal." *I'm about to get Victor a shirt that says 'ALLY IS A VERB.'*

The neighborhood quickly became my favorite part of any city too as we made our way up the street, with its tea shops and bookshops and boutiques and kosher food places and halal food places and handmade good shops and ethnic grocery stores and gluten-free bakeries and Asian restaurants. Store windows proudly displayed Progress flags and signs saying 'Stronger than Hate' and 'Stop AAPI Hate' and 'Black Lives Matter.' Other tricolor signs read "No matter where you are from, we're glad you're our neighbor" in three different languages. One store even had a big white sign that made me think of a segregation-era placard from a more-enlightened alternate universe that said 'NAZIS, KLANSMEN, AND TRUMPERS NEED NOT ENTER.' "Can I fucking *live* here?" I grinned.

"*Right?* I'd be constantly broke if we did though," Victor chuckled as he held the door to a noodle shop open for us.

A loud *THUD* scared the hell out of me before I realized it was a log of dough getting slammed onto a counter. I had trouble focusing on the menu because I kept glancing up to watch the workers slam and knead dough. There were so many options of dumplings and noodles and dim sum, but Victor made the choice easy by ordering us three servings of soup dumplings. "The first time I ever had them I actually wept," he talked them up. "It's like nirvana in your mouth." People talking things up too much usually makes me automatically not like them, but holy fucking shit were those dumplings good. No, scrumptious. No, *ambrosian.* They had my mouth watering as soon as the bamboo steamers hit the table. And I was able to eat them with chopsticks!

Kade pulled us across the street into a cramped yet cozy tea shop so he could replenish his stash, where jars and boxes and tins of tea lined the shelves, alongside tea books and tea sets and sweets and everything else you could ever need to make tea. It was like something out of Diagon Alley. "You should get some for yourself!" Kade encouraged me. "You already have a kettle in your room." I bought a few ounces each of ginger peach and another with an intoxicating almond-y scent.

A few stores fronts down from there was a board game store that had the vibe of a bookstore. You can pick up a book and get whisked away to another place and time, and board games are apparently no different. I could've spent hours reading the backs of game boxes if Kade didn't find me every two seconds to show me one of his favorites or one he wants to get.

"How adventurous are you?" Victor asked me once we were finally back on the street.

"Adventurous like going on a hike, or sticking things up my butt?"

"Oh *god* do I hope it's sticking things up our butts," Kade pined.

"I don't even know why I asked," Victor laughed as he led us into an Asian grocery store.

It was the most unusual grocery store I've ever been in, but in a good, curious way. Barely anything had labels in English. "You just gotta pick something up and go for it," Victor said as he took a long-handled shopping basket on wheels, "but I'd stay away from any kind of canned milk if I were you." There were vegetables I never even knew existed, roots as big as my forearm, an entire wall of creepy-looking mushrooms, an entire *aisle* of rice and noodles. My favorite part was all the candy and snacks that I never even knew existed.

"I can't decide if I want peach or strawberry Kit Kats," I said as my eyes went back and forth between the bags.

"Just get both," Kade said simply. "This is America, dammit. If you don't live in excess then the terrorists win." I left with both flavors of Kit Kats, a few different bottles of tea, some 'Mexican-flavored' Lay's chips, strawberry-filled cookies, and a box of Pocky—which I *have* had. We dropped all our purchases off at the car before heading down another street to another tea shop.

"But weren't we just at a tea shop?" I asked. "Not that I'm against it or anything."

"I guess tea *house* would be a more appropriate term," Kade corrected himself.

The tea house was several blocks away, which meant we saw more than a few people sitting on the sidewalks asking for change. I just followed Kade's lead, walking by without a word or a look, which felt wrong to do. "Does it make us bad people for not helping out homeless people if we're able to?" I asked them in a low voice.

"Ultimately, I'd say yes it does," Victor said with his hands in his pockets. "People can say whatever they want about them not having jobs, or that they'd just spend that money on drugs, but at the end of the day, they're people too. And if you can help somebody who's struggling, then I think you should. Kind of like how being able to do good and not doing it is the same as doing bad. And before you say it, I don't have any cash on me."

"And that's why I feel guilty," I said. "They're human, and yet we don't even want to acknowledge them because it makes us uncomfortable." And what's more entitled than *that*? Are homeless people just like litter—ugly, unavoidable by-products of a capitalist economy that'll just disappear if you just ignore it? Do you know how much money gets spent on advertising and political campaigns, and how many people that money could feed?

"I think it's a problem way bigger than anything regular people can fix," Kade said. "I mean, yeah, giving somebody money helps them, but it's just a bandage on an endlessly gushing wound. But still, that small bandage means somebody doesn't have to worry about their next meal. But then what happens when we eventually get to a cashless society?" He sighed. "*This* is why we need universal basic income—but that's socialism, and nothing makes the unintelligentsia shit their pants faster than socialism."

"But don't touch their Social Security," I rolled my eyes. People shit on socialism, but do you know how royally *fucked* we would've been during the pandemic without it?

Calling the tea house 'boho' doesn't even begin to do it justice. Between the Persian rugs, the multicolored glass lanterns, the inlaid mosaic tables, the wooden chairs worn smooth, the argentine trays, the incensed aroma, and the simple acoustic music, I was *seduced*. It isn't just a tea house—it's a meeting place, a way station in the journeys of the lives of the patrons as wide-ranging and as multicultural as the pots of serenity it offers. We took a low table with floor cushions beneath the dangling vines of a hanging planter, where a book of a menu and a little bell you had to ring to get served—which felt hella uppity doing—sat. We ordered a pot of chocolate-y black tea, brought to us in drinkware as intricate as a mosque. I savored the taste and let the ataraxy carry me off in sips. At the table behind us, a little kid and his parents were engaging each other in conversation about what they thought the sexualities and gender identities of the different *Mario* characters were. I had to look up what an oud was when I saw a nearby flier promoting which nights were live oud music nights. I thought about the kids I'd seen chaining their bikes to the squirrel-shaped bike racks on the sidewalk and how this is all just *normal* for them.

"Not gonna lie," I broke the peace, "but today showed me how much of an uncultured shit I really am. Like, I never knew places like this even *existed*. Mind equals *bpsssh*—" I let my fingers explode away from the sides of my head.

Victor smiled. "Mission accomplished." He and his brother bumped fists.

Kade leaned back on his hands. "Right? It makes you realize just how bland everything we're used to is. There's so many new and different things to experience."

"I really believe that we could eliminate hate if everybody chose to see things with open minds and open hearts," Victor said adamantly. "If people approached things that are different with curiosity instead of suspicion, we'd have way less problems in the world."

"And that's what makes you a grotesque," I said like it was a reflex. "Did I say that out loud?"

Victor fake gasped. "Are you saying I'm ugly?"

"No! It's not a bad thing!" I drained my patterned glass cup before trying to explain. "There's this book called *Winesburg, Ohio*, and in the prologue the author talks about how everybody adopts an idea as a truth that they come to live by, and in doing so they make themselves into what he calls a grotesque, which really just means 'distorted' instead of 'ugly.' I take it to mean 'unique'—that everybody has some kind of foundation for all their worldviews that they embrace and that makes them them. Ja feel?"

Victor screwed up his face. "I think ja feel."

"Ja think," Kade said to the ceiling, "therefore...ja am? J'am?"

"I try to keep that in mind when trying to figure people out, *especially* since coming to New Halle. I think it's fascinating," I said as I poured myself more tea. "And fun fact, gargoyles on buildings are only gargoyles if they spit out water. If they're just for decoration, then they're grotesques."

"This is exactly why I like hanging out with you," Victor inflated my ego. "So what would you say makes *you* a grotesque?"

I pretended to think about it. "I think that everybody's purpose is to live life without a stick up their ass. But at the same time, I think having sticks up our asses about something is what makes us grotesques. It's a dichotomy."

Kade laughed through his nose. "I was gonna say, it sounds like you have a stick up your ass about having a stick up your ass."

"I guess mine would be something along the lines of how being inconsiderate is the root of most of the world's problems," Victor said.

Kade bobbed his head. "I think that everything and everybody is art. And also what he said."

"I can get on board with both of those." I took a sip, glad that I have like-minded friends. "And just so you know," I said to Victor, "you're not ugly. You're a stud muffin."

"Wait, what?" he laughed.

"If studs were muffins, you'd be walnut," I winked.

It was midnight dark when we headed back to the car, even though midnight was still hours away. A warm glow from the host of lanterns like the ones in the tea house illuminated the store across the street. We passed by the Nazis/Klansmen/Trumpers sign, and I thought of something I was almost afraid to say out loud. "I love how unabashedly progressive this place is, but..." I took a breath. "Couldn't that make it a target for hate?"

They traded quick glances. "It does," Kade said. "We'll make one more stop before we head back."

It was only a two-minute drive. We crossed the street to what looked like a church with Hebrew letters on it. "Is this a synagogue?" I asked.

I heard Victor swallow. "Yep." I took a few steps along the fence in front, looking at the banners of handmade artwork hanging from it. "Do you know what this place is?"

"Unh uh."

"Do you remember that synagogue shooting that happened a few years ago?"

My asshole snapped shut so fast that it hurt. The goosebumps on the inside of my skin shivered me. The artwork on the fence—messages of hope, unity, strength, love, rebuilding—took on new meanings, as did the Star of David "Stronger than Hate" signs all over the neighborhood. I had to fight back the tears. I've been to Ground Zero, but this is something I *remember* happening. I *remember* it being on the news.

"It was a Saturday. I had friends over for my birthday," Kade recalled. "What does it say about our great country when kids are desensitized to mass shootings before they're even in high school?"

"It says we're a dystopia," I said. "Why is it when a person with brown skin shoots a bunch of people they're a terrorist, but when a person with white skin does the same thing they're just exercising their Second Amendment right?"

"Oh no, they're still terrorists," Kade laughed acerbically. "And anybody who says they're not can go fuck the fuck off."

"You hear about them—shootings, I mean," Victor said, "but you go about your life until you forget about them, and you don't think that it could ever happen so close to home." Kade put his arm around him. "I've *been* here before. My parents' friends invited us to come to synagogue here with them once or twice."

"Oh, I know. Remember the shooting at that grocery store in Buffalo?"

"*Shit,* that's right."

We stood, silently reflecting on the shortness and abruptness of life, and how vulnerable we all really are to ignorance and hate. "So wait," I slowly asked Victor, "are you Jewish?"

"My parents were, and I was raised Jewish." *His parents* were. "We were pretty bad Jews," he chuckled. "We rarely ever went to synagogue, and they were *very* loose and liberal."

"So, you aren't anymore? Or you are? I'm sorry, I know I'm butchering this."

"I gave it up. I always heard how god is all-loving and all-powerful, yet he lets evil exist in the world," he said bitterly. "Either he wants to stop it but he can't, or he can and he doesn't want to. Either he's weak or he's a dick, and I'm not giving him any more of my time. I don't care if I go to hell for it. And I'm sorry if that upsets you, but I really don't give a shit."

"No, trust me, I'm right there with you," I assured him. "Realizing that was what ultimately did it for me too. There are babies born terminally ill, born with cancer, born without limbs." *Babies born gay.* "Holocausts, wars, forced famines, ethnic cleansings. You know how cruel history is, Kade. And how many people get assaulted, raped, tortured, murdered *every single day?* And god doesn't do anything to *stop* it? And then Christians will stick their noses in the air and pull the original sin card? Fucking—don't even get me the fuck started." I took deep breaths to try to stop myself from getting worked up even more.

"*Woah,* triggered."

"As he *should* be."

We stood there, thinking about the unfairness of life and how that's proof enough that the god of the bible can't exist. I'm not saying there *isn't* some divine being out there, but it certainly isn't the one I was forced to read about. "I'm ready to go when you guys are," Kade finally said.

We found Mr. and Mrs. Oakley on the couch watching the end of *Jeopardy!* The final clue was something along the lines of 'the Iron Curtain stretched between these two seas.' "The Black and the Baltic," Mr. Oakley said after a moment.

"Nuh *uh*. The Baltic and the Adriatic," Kade said confidently.

"Yeah, I'm gonna say the Black and the Baltic too," I said instead of introducing myself. Their dad met my eye. Victor and Mrs. Oakley, apparently having as much knowledge of European history as a dumb jock, just waited for the answer. The 'correct' answer was the Baltic Sea and the Adriatic Sea.

"Bullshit!" their dad said.

"*Ha!* Suck an egg, losers," Kade exclaimed victoriously as he went to the kitchen to dig around in the pantry.

"There's no way that's right!" I said. *Am I really smarter than the people who come up with these questions?* "Yugoslavia wasn't a part of the Warsaw Pact!"

"*Finally*, somebody in this house who knows something!" their dad smiled at me, earning himself a smack on the thigh with the remote from his wife. He got up and hugged his sons before firmly shaking my hand. "Trevor, right? It's nice to finally meet you. Just call me Vince."

I never felt comfortable addressing my friends' parents by their first names, but I also didn't want to look like I have a stick up my ass. "Nice to meet you too, Vince."

"And I'm Laura," their mom introduced herself. "The boys told us all about you."

"Only the good things, I hope," I smiled. "Thank you so much for letting me stay, by the way."

"It's no problem at all. I was glad to let them bring you home for a weekend sleepover."

"Oh my *god* Mom, what are we, eight?" Kade whined as he spread peanut butter on some club crackers.

Victor popped some frozen pizza bites into the oven since we were hungrier for something more substantial than peanut butter crackers. Gathered around the kitchen island, the two of them told their parents how school's going—my chest sank when Kade told them there was one guy he was seeing "but things didn't work out"— and where we went that afternoon. Laura and Vince asked me all the basics—majors, hometown, family, what I thought about Pittsburgh so far. "Do you have any siblings?" Vince asked at one point.

"No, I'm an only child," I said, which isn't a lie.

Victor went up to shower, leaving Kade and me with his parents and a dirty baking sheet. "Do you want to see some of their old school pictures?" Laura asked me.

"Okay, we're going downstairs now," Kade said before I could say yes. I followed him down to the game room, where he pulled the acoustic guitar off the wall and plucked away at it from a chair.

"I didn't know you could play guitar too," I said.

"Bass guitar's still a guitar, dumbass," he said without looking up from the chords he strummed.

"You know what I—"

"Oh my *god*, I'm joking!" he stopped playing to say. "Forreal though, bass is more my cup of chai."

"Why have a fat ass when you can have a fat bass line?" I joked.

A damp-haired Victor came down in basketball shorts and a long-sleeve shirt with Katie at his heels. "Laura said to go clean up your spooge," he said to Kade.

Kade jumped up in a fury. "Tell her she can go...eat a shit!"

"She didn't actually say 'spooge,'" Victor told me as Kade stomped up the stairs.

We dug into our treats from the Asian grocery store, uncapping bottles of milk tea and tearing open bags while Kade put on *Whose Line Is It Anyway?* "Holy shit," I gasped at the peach Kit Kat like I was seeing candy for the first time. "Guys, these are fucking *phenomenal*. Why do we not sell these here?"

Kade dangled a Pocky from his lips like he was smoking a cigarette in 1920. "And yet we call ourselves the greatest country in the world."

The show had us howling so loudly that Katie gave us concerned looks before she finally just went back upstairs. "Aren't your parents gonna get mad that we're being so loud?" I asked.

"Victor has a *drum set*," Kade pointed out. "Besides, I told them we'd be having an orgy and to expect some noise."

"Please tell me you did not."

"I think 'brodeo' was the word I actually used."

After asking me if I'd like to save water by showering with him, Kade went up to the upstairs bathroom by himself. "How do you like Improv Club, by the way?" I asked Victor. "I didn't even know you started going until Kade mentioned something yesterday."

"It's actually a really fun time," he said. "You should come along sometime! You don't have to participate. You can always just watch."

"Yeah, I might give it a try," I shrugged. "Just to watch, I mean."

I emerged from the basement shower smelling of lemongrass and bamboo. "We took turns farting on your pillow, just so you know," Kade told me. "And Victor's fucking *reek* after he has those dumplings." Victor threw a throw pillow at him. "Would either of you be up for a game?" *How could I say no with all these options?*

I got up to scan their library of games and picked up the more interesting-looking ones. "What's *Votes for Women?*"

The game pulled itself into Victor's hands. "It's a historical strategy game!" he said excitedly. "You gotta pass the 19th Amendment!" Or, like he had to do, try to prevent Kade and I from passing it. He kept reminding himself that it was just a game as he struggled to halt equality for women across a map of the lower 48 States while we listened to a podcast called *Welcome to Nightvale*. In a conclusion that had us literally on our feet, Kade and I and women across the country won all thanks to a die roll in Pennsylvania.

"Do you remember the day they called the election for Biden?" Kade fondly reminisced as we packed up the pieces. "And all because of Pennsylvania, too. I was never prouder of our state. We all made stew and got drunk."

"Your parents let you *drink?*"

"Yeah?" he frowned. "It was a day of celebration!"

"That would be my Patronus memory," Victor smiled tenderly. It might legit be the happiest day of my life too—the crowds of people dancing in the streets, the 'YOU'RE FIRED!' signs outside of the White House. I couldn't stop crying.

We folded open the couch to throw a comforter and some pillows on it. "I can sleep on this one," I said, nodding to the regular, non-opening couch.

"Absolutely not," Victor objected. "You're the guest, and you'll sleep on the bed. *I'll* take the couch. Kade's too tall for it anyway."

Kade pulled back the blanket back to slide under the covers beside me. "There are *a thousand* things I could say right now," he smirked.

"*Oh dad.* Talk dirty to me."

"I'm going upstairs if I hear *anything*," Victor said as he spread open a blanket as big as an area rug. He folded his glasses with a *clack* and turned off the light.

As I lay in the basement of my best friends' house, I found myself wishing that Ethan had been able to come down with us too, and maybe it would've been him and not Kade who'd be laying less than a foot away from me in bed—which is to say that my dick made it a little hard for me to fall asleep.

November 13

POV:

You slept over at your friends' and you're the first one in the house to get up, like always.

My Mac and I sat in the cozy breakfast nook overlooking the backyard and pool until Vince came down in an old Incubus tour t-shirt, looking low-key startled to see me. "Good morning Mr.—I mean, Vince."

"Morning, Trevor. I take it the boys are still asleep?"

"Uh huh, yeah," I nodded. "I'm not sure how late they like to sleep in."

He laughed through his nose. "You might be waiting for a while." His eyes lingered on my laptop. "Are you doing homework?"

"Oh no, I'm just journaling. It's kinda dumb, but I like doing it."

"It's not dumb at all," he shook his head. "The fact that you do it says a lot about you. It's supposed to be a mark of intelligence or something. Would you like any coffee?"

I watched him scoop some ground coffee into a pair of reusable metal coffee pods. "Is Kade the only tea drinker in the family?"

"I mean, I like a cup every now and then," Vince said as he grabbed two mugs down, one of which had what looked like a bus sticking out of a sinkhole on it, "but he's on a whole other level. I don't know what got him so into it."

I shrugged. "There are worse things that he could do."

"And you've probably seen him do them," he said with a mischievous look. "I'm happy to see that he's made such a good friend though. He must really like you if he wanted you to come down and spend the weekend. I know he can be a little..."

"Inappropriate?" I offered. "Off-putting? Provocative? Eccentric?"

He chuckled as the coffee machine issued a dying *hiss*. "All of the above. Any cream or sugar?"

"Yes please, and thank you. He's my best friend though. If he wasn't the way he is, then he wouldn't be himself." I sipped my coffee, wondering how much hazelnut coffee with hazelnut creamer you'd have to drink before you turned into a hazelnut. "Aren't we all weird in our own ways?"

"I can see why you like to journal," he said. "Do you mind if I sit? The sunroom hasn't warmed up yet, and this is the next best place."

"Not at all," I shook my head.

He slid into the seat across from me. "Between you and me, we—Laura and I, I mean—were glad when the boys told us they both wanted to go to the same school, and even more so that they were going to room together, but it's nice to know that he has other people who care about him."

"What kind of a friend would I be if I didn't?"

Vince did a crossword puzzle on his phone and made frozen waffles for the two of us, breaking the silence with small talk and stories of his kids. He said that when Kade was little they'd be at the store and he'd start yelling that they weren't his parents and cause a scene. Caffeinated and fed, I typed away until Victor surfaced from the basement.

"Morning," he said to Vince before turning to me. "How long have you been up?"

I shrugged. "Like an hour or two."

"An hour or *two*?"

"Trevor, *please* feel free to help yourself to coffee and anything else tomorrow morning if you're the first one up again," Vince said to me like I'd just been rescued after being lost at sea.

Victor grabbed a banana while he let his instant oatmeal do that thing that oatmeal does. "Did you know you can use a banana peel to help get rid of a hickey?" I asked.

"I'll have to remember that if I ever get a hickey," he rolled his eyes. He dug out his DS and 3DS so we could look through his old *Pokémon* games while we waited for Kade. We got a kick out of some of his Pokémon's nicknames, from a preadolescent 'Flamer' to a masturbatory-teenager 'Penis.'

"Hey sleepyhead," Vince said to Kade when he finally came up. "Trevor and I spent all morning talking about you." He shot me a wink.

"I'm actually offended that you still aren't," Kade said as he made himself some maté.

After everyone had eaten something, taken their morning shits, and gotten dressed, we piled into Victor's shithead car to go to a museum. "Is this like an art museum, or a dinosaur-bone museum?" I asked on the way there.

"It's an art museum, but it's not your typical art museum though," Kade grinned. I knew it wasn't going to be a typical museum when we parked in front of what looked like a warehouse sandwiched between red-brick row houses instead of some stately white-marble edifice. Several-years-younger Trevor who considered classical paintings and sculptures to be 'real' art would've absolutely *hated* the place. The exhibits ranged from mannequins covered in big polka dots in a room of mirrors for walls, to a room full of dolls and pill bottles, to big gray chunks suspended from the ceiling. They were unconventional, gripping, and almost unsettling. I'd go as far as to say that I've never experienced real art before going there.

We left the museum and drove past downtown "to get some bubble tea and to get elevated," as Victor put it, which made it like the fifth day in a row that I've had bubble tea. I craned my neck to glimpse the tops of the buildings taller than any back home. And another thing I noticed that Pittsburgh has way more of than Buffalo are Ukrainian flags. "Riddle me this," I said as we passed some graffiti that said 'STAY HOME AND WASH YOUR HANDS', "why does literally *everybody* show support for Ukraine and Ukrainian refugees, but not a single person gives a shit about what's been going on in Syria? Not that I'm trying to minimize the war in Ukraine or anything, but I just don't ever see support for Syrian refugees anywhere."

"No, you're totally right," Victor said. "It's because people's great-great-grandparents are from Ukraine. They're the sweet old women who sell handmade pierogis for their church. But Syrians are brown people, so why the fuck should we care about them?" he said caustically. I was only half-listening though, because I was too busy taking in another kind of blue-and-gold that was everywhere I looked, from flags to banners to hoodies to beanies. A single skyscraper stretched over the crest of the hill ahead of us—an unmistakable, gut-wrenching skyscraper. *Oh my god— we're at Pitt.*

He's here somewhere, I thought as I looked into the throngs of people, half-expecting to see him right there on the sidewalk. *He's probably with his friends, making plans to go out later, totally oblivious that the person he'd once destroyed is so close to him.* 'This distance' that he'd used to justify breaking up with me—that mother *fucking* distance that I'd cursed and that had destroyed me—was reduced from hundreds of miles to mere blocks. On the sidewalk, I walked with my head down out of fear that I'd run into him. I was so lost in my own thoughts that I would've walked into traffic if Victor hadn't grabbed my arm. *Does anything trigger a memory of me? Does he have a new boyfriend? Where did they have their first kiss? Where did they first say 'I love you?'* Knowing that I was walking where he walks every day and that he's living his life without me in it lacerated me.

Luckily, Pitt's Cathedral that I followed my friends into put a pause on my torment. It was like being in Hogwarts Castle. The Oakley's house could've comfortably fit inside the cavernous Gothic chamber multiple times over with room to spare. Stone walls and built-in columns arched into a rib vault ceiling high above our heads. Students studied at polished wooden furniture that looked as heavy as the studded doors. *This is like an actual cathedral,* I thought as I looked from the large decorative fireplace to the stained-glass windows. *And people just go to school here like it's nothing?* I followed my friends through the corridors that ran around the perimeter—"It's too bad it's not decorated for Christmas," Victor said—like a monastery cloister, catching glimpses of rooms with different themes as tours went in and out of them. I was conscious of my footsteps in the library-quiet room as we passed through iron gates to the elevators. I tried not to think of the ever-growing void mere inches beneath our feet as we rose higher and higher up through the building's esophagus.

Once the doors opened again, we approached the windows to take in the city spilling beneath us: downtown peeking out from behind a hill, the museum where Kade's dad works, a giant greenhouse, a sprawling park. I didn't feel as on-edge as I thought I'd be about being so high up, but the pangs in my gut about Dillon persisted even as I took in the vantage beneath the dreary November clouds. I remembered how I used to feel like how the sky looked—that feeling of not being able to find happiness in anything—and I felt it start to surround me like a shroud again.

"You got to pick yesterday!" Kade was stubbornly saying to Victor once we were back in the car. "I wanna pick today!"

"*Or* we can let Trevor decide," Victor said. "What kind of food are *you* in the mood for, Trev?"

"Whatever's fine," I heard myself say.

"*I* heard him say Lebanese," Kade said.

"Yeah, sure," I shrugged.

And then as my forehead rested against the window, a thought bubbled up in the midst of all the bad ones. *Maybe I can't control all the things that happened to me, but I can control today. I get to hang and do shit with my friends all weekend, and I choose to spend it acting like* this?

"Sorry if I'm being a little poopy," I finally said. "I've just had some things on my mind."

"We couldn't tell," Kade said sarcastically. "I'm sorry, that was rude. But don't sweat it though. It's normal to be in a bad place sometimes. Or most of the time in my case," he added with a chuckle. *See? If Kade can be open about things, then so can you.*

"My ex goes to Pitt," I heard myself saying. "We were together for almost all of senior year. He was the first person I ever loved." They listened, silent as parsley. "We got accepted to different schools and told each other that we'd make it work, that we'd still try to see each other on the weekends." I wiped my eyes on my sleeve, happy that I was in the backseat. "But then he said it would be too hard to make it work. He said he'd be missing out on other things if he stayed tied up with me." He never had to spell it out, but I knew what he meant—I wasn't worth staying exclusive for. Why make the hour-and-some drive to see me sometimes when he could just break up with me and have somebody right there all the time? I wasn't good enough, and no amount of stolen liquor could tell me why.

Victor gasped. "He *actually* fucking said that?"

"Fucking *hold me back*," Kade said. "I'll fuckin' *beat* his ass."

I let out a breath. "So, yeah. I guess being here was kind of a trigger."

At the next red light, Victor turned around to look at me. "I'm so sorry dude. We would've never come here if I'd known."

"I mean, maybe some things are meant to happen for whatever reason," Kade said in a rare moment of seriousness. *No, they don't. Life's just unfair, plain and simple.* "Maybe being with him would've held *you* back from meeting someone even better." *Yeah, okay.*

The restaurant ended up being in the same neighborhood we'd spent the previous afternoon in. "I've never had Lebanese food before," I said as I pulled up the menu via a QR code. "I always thought baba ghanoush was something somebody just made up."

"Isn't everything something that somebody just made up once?" Victor asked. We split an order of falafel—which I always assumed was like some kind of taco—and if the kofte I got wasn't fragrantly spiced enough, then the cinnamon-seasoned rice it came with sure was. I couldn't tell you the last time I had something so flavorful.

Since it was too chilly to walk around outside anywhere, we hit up the tea house again—"Too bad we're not old enough to get into the hookah lounge," Kade lamented —until it was time to head to the concert venue. Victor parked on a wide, gentrified street, and a church with a queue of people lined up down the block to get inside caught my interest. "I wonder what *that's* all about," I wondered out loud. *Buy-one-get-one on indulgences?*

"That's where the concert is," Kade chuckled. Apparently there are like a thousand churches in Pittsburgh and like half of them got turned into concert venues or record stores or cigar bars or dive bars.

Like most opening bands, I'd never heard of Cafuné, but they set the vibe *real* quick with their dreamy vocals and heavy drums. After an intermission of songs that resisted genres, the lights dimmed and a buzz seized the room. Figures took their places in the dark to the sound of a spacey drone before tearing apart the room with electrifying guitar notes. Blue spotlights irradiated the members of Last Dinosaurs with a rippling azure phosphorescence that made me feel like we were at an aquarium. The songs went from high-energy to chill to upbeat to entrancing, always vibing. Not knowing most of the words made me feel like I almost didn't belong, but I was too blown away by the kind of shrill guitar notes that the universe was created to to let it bother me. I always forget how bass at a concert rattles you to your core to the point you almost feel like you're going to throw up, like a long-dormant machine inside of your body powering on for the first time. Victor broke away without warning to throw himself into a circle pit, returning a minute later with his hat askew and one of his high-top Vans in his hand.

We filed out of the sanctuary with some merch alongside the rest of the emboldened crowd, telling each other how good the concert was like the three of us hadn't just experienced it together. *Concerts hit different when you're at one with your best friends.* We listened to Last Dinosaurs—what else?—on the drive back, and I watched the river reflect the lights from the buildings and the stadiums as I thought about how the past two days felt like a coming-of-age movie. *This has been the kind of weekend I've always wanted to have with the kinds of friends I was always jealous of other people for having.*

Victor rolled down his window at a red light and poked his head out, letting cool air rush inside. "Anybody up for stargazing when we get back?" he said to the heavens. "It's a clear night."

"You can do what you want," Kade said. "*I'm* getting in the hot tub."

"I'd be up for a hot tub!" I nodded eagerly. "But I'm down to stargaze too!"

We found Vince and Laura in the dining room with delivered pizza and a '00s edition of *Trivial Pursuit* on the table. "How was the concert?" Laura asked us.

Kade walked over with his hand to his ear. "WHAT? I CAN'T HEAR YOU!"

"It was pretty lit," Victor answered them.

"Trevor wants to go in the hot tub," Kade non sequitured.

"It was your idea!" I said.

His parents just laughed. "That's why we have one—to go in it."

"Okay, yeah, it was my idea," Kade said. "But first, I gotta take a shit."

While he was doing that, I held open doors for Victor as he carried his telescope out to the driveway. I tried to warm myself as he fine-tuned the knobs and changed eyepieces. "Here, peep this shit," he finally said. "You might have to adjust it."

I twisted the knob until the view came into focus. "Is that...*Jupiter*?" Even all the way down here on Earth, however-many-hundreds-of-millions-of-miles away, I could still make out its orange stripes.

"Yep," Victor said. "Can you see the little dots beside it? Those are its moons."

I drank my fill of our largest neighborhood gas giant. "How fucking cool is that?"

"Here, I can do you one better." He rotated the telescope towards another bright dot and played with the knobs again before letting me look in.

"Oh my *god*," I gasped, but how can you not gasp when you're face-to-face with the planet Saturn, embraced by those iconic rings, tilted at the perfect angle like it was meant to be shown off?

"Right? It never gets old for me." I thought Victor was trying to take a pic of the sky until I saw he had some kind of sky map app pulled up that tells you what you're pointing it at. "Neptune's over there, but it's so far away that it just looks like a blue dot even through the telescope. Venus and Mars are below the horizon this time of year. Oh, and there's Uranus!" He aimed his phone at my butt and we giggled like 3rd graders. "Here, take a look around," he offered it to me. I saw congregations of stars, constellations, and even satellites creeping across the night sky like atoms on infinity.

"This is the kind of stuff that low-key stresses me out," I said to the endless black space beneath my feet.

"That's why Kade isn't big into space," he chuckled. "But that's why I like it though—it puts everything into perspective." I looked around at the sky, thinking about how I used to stick my nose in the air and say how the god who created all of it loves me personally. "There's an entire conversation to be had about that," Victor said, "but my ass is getting cold, and there's a hot tub waiting for us."

Their hot tub is on the back patio, which is basically a wall-less room under the sunroom. We found Kade sitting back in it with his arms hanging along the edge. "I'm not wearing anything in here, just so ya know," he bounced his eyebrows.

"You *wish* you weren't," I smirked as my borrowed pair of swimming trunks and I climbed in to escape the cold air. I let the steaming water lap my chin and the jets massage my calves, remembering how the last time I was in a hot tub was with

Dillon and how steamy it was, and not just because of the temperature of the water. *I feel like I'm in Switzerland, or the Badlands.*

"Just three bros chilling in a hot tub zero feet apart because they're mostly gay," Kade said.

We talked about concerts we've been to, how live music burrows into your head and makes the inside of your skin tingle, how all the emotions we feel are just chemical reactions, and then about our lives in general—specifically, all the things that seemed insignificant when they happened, but ended up being literally life-changing. "I like to call them 'swerves,'" I said.

"I mean, would we have ever met and became friends if we hadn't signed up for the same History class together?" Kade observed.

"Probably not," I said after a moment. "I might've made friends with somebody else, but would I have ended up in their hot tub back home?"

Victor smirked. "I bet you would've liked to though."

I rolled my eyes. "But then what life am I *not* having because I *didn't* meet that person?" *Holy fuck, I sound like Dillon.* "There's a book called *The Midnight Library* that's all about the lives you aren't living. It gets kinda wild when you really think about it."

"Oh, trust me, I think about that kind of stuff all the time," Kade said seriously. "Like how Vic and I met."

"Oh? How'd that happen?"

Kade took a breath. "Basically, our schools each took field trips to the zoo on the same day, and some kids were picking on me, and Victor stood up to them for me." *Standing up for a stranger? Such a Victor move.* "And then when we got to middle school we started eating lunch together, and the rest is history."

"Yeah, I'd say it's up there in the biggest swerves for me," Victor said, letting my mind wander to his Tower tattoo submerged under the water. "Soulmates for life."

I slid down into the water and let my eyes trace the strings of lights hanging from the ceiling. *Are we all in each other's lives for a reason? Like, out of every place and time our lives could have intersected, why did they intersect when they did, or even at all? I wonder if I've met my soulmate yet? Would I be able to tell if I had?*

"You know," I said, "whenever we first started hanging out, I low-key thought you two were boyfriends."

Victor laughed out loud. "Oh my *god.*"

"Ew, what the hell made you think *that*?" Kade asked.

"I don't know," I laughed. "I guess just how comfortable you are with each other? And the constant inappropriate comments didn't help either."

"I already *told* you dude, I'm not a fan of dicks unless it's my own," Victor smirked.

"I remember when I used to say the same thing," I chuckled.

"So when did *that* change? If you feel like sharing."

"I don't know *exactly* when—I was in middle school when I discovered that I *really* liked looking at boys. I'd think about them all the time, especially boys kissing. I never thought it was weird or anything until I heard other people saying it was."

"Teaching you to hate yourself is what the Christian right does," Kade said sourly.

"But yeah, one day I finally decided that I was done living a life that wasn't my own anymore," I said, though I didn't tell them that it was just last Spring. "And fuck anyone who doesn't like it. I'm not lying to people anymore about who I am. Nobody chooses to be born queer, but people can choose if they wanna be an asshole to other people about it."

"I think all queer people should be Gryffindors by default," Victor said. "I think coming out is one of the bravest things somebody can do. And it shouldn't fucking *have* to be."

"I'm glad my parents are atheists," Kade said. "They couldn't have been cooler with who I am. I mean, you've met them. When I told them there was a girl in school I liked they were cool with it, and when I told them there was a boy I liked they treated it no differently. But I was still nervous as shit about what they'd say."

Victor sighed. "I'm sure I won't live to see it, but I can't wait for the day when nobody has to come out anymore. Nobody who's left-handed has to come out as not being right-handed. Most people are right-handed, but some are left-handed, and that's just the way they are, period. And the two of you just being your most unapologetically authentic selves is helping us get there."

I put some pics from the concert on Instagram before getting to bed, and Ethan made me happier than he knew by being the first person to like them.

wallowing_tbh LAST DINOOOOS
EthanE16 *high* key jelly
wallowing_tbh next time!
oakley_dokey #faded

I was sadder to leave Pittsburgh than I was happy about heading back to school. I watched the hills swallow the Cathedral and then the rest of the city through Kade's car window, wondering what it would be like to go to school and live on your own somewhere so urban and cultured.

Even though their parents sent their sons off with paper shopping bags full of rations like they wouldn't be back home for Thanksgiving in two weeks, we hit up Aldi on the way back to pick up some nonperishables for the food drive one of the groups on campus is having. I got as much canned and boxed food as $20 could get me and gave Kade shit for filling his reusable tote bag with spices and cake mix and trail mix and salad dressing. "You're sure you're not shopping for yourself?" I razzed him. "Why not get cheaper stuff so you could get more?"

His eyes rested on me long enough to tell me I'd said the wrong thing. "Here's the thing about food banks," he finally said. "We just assume that the people who need to visit them live on the streets and that their lives are so in the shitter that they should be happy with whatever they get, right?" My uncomfortable silence told him he was right. "But I feel like just buying cans of vegetables and stuff like that is kinda demeaning to them. Like, just because their circumstances aren't what they pictured, that doesn't mean they don't deserve good food. I'm sure they're probably sick of all the same stuff." My eyes fell on the box I carried, heavy with canned corn and green beans and other thoughtless things. "So I like to try to get stuff that'll maybe make them forget for just one meal that their situation is less than ideal, stuff that reminds them that there's somebody out there who remembers they're still people, whether they *are* living on the streets or if they just lost their job and are trying to figure out how to feed their kids."

"Hence why we need universal basic income," Victor emphasized.

My would-be donations embarrassed me. "You're sure you're a Slytherin?" I asked Kade.

"I figured *you* of all people would know better than to assume that all Slytherins are bad," he said, shutting me right the fuck up. I put my cans back and picked up some things that *I'd* be happy to get if I ever have to visit a food bank. There are probably already enough donated cans of corn and green beans to go around anyway.

I got back to 222 Swafford with my stuff to find Tylor and Amina eating a frozen lasagna dinner that they baked in the building's kitchen. "Welcome *back*," Tylor greeted me with an up-nod. "Was your weekend everything you expected?"

I couldn't not smile. "Not at *all*."

November 14

You know how there'll be a song you'd always skip, but then you hear it live and all of a sudden it's like your new favorite song? Yeah.

And also, you know how you expect professor's offices to be these dignified chambers, and then they end up being like half the size of my room and cramped with degrees and certificates and shelves sagging with haphazard books? I found that out when I met with Dr. Averescu to sign up for my Spring classes. Freshmen get the last pick, of course. I was really hoping to get into the PoliSci class I've heard about that's all about the JFK assassination taught by a retired CIA agent, but there's only one period for it and it filled up in a fucking second, so instead I'll be taking a U.S. Military History class to satisfy my history fix. As far as English classes go, I'll actually have Dr. Averescu for Writing Creative Fiction—which I'm sure she's happy about—and I figured I'd give African-American Lit a try since Brit Lit ended up being a bust. I must've been in an exploratory mood, because I also signed up for Macroeconomics, which I'm already having second thoughts about. And I'll be rounding out my schedule with French 101, since everyone has to take a language, and I still remember a little French from school. And what are the chances that Victor signed up for the same French class too?!?!

YOOOOOOOOO
Its gonna be fucken lit 🔥 🔥

November 15

I was today-year-old when I learned that rebellious research is a thing, and I'm *high*-key pissed it's not a thing here. Like, do you know how much more I'd be paying attention in Geology if Dr. Eubanks juggled while he lectured?

"I'm glad the hype over this place died down a little," Ethan said as he slid into the seat across from me with his wrap from Percy's. "It's nice to actually take a real break for once."

I poked my straw at the boba pearls left at the bottom of my cup, sucking them up one at a time like a minigame. "I'll bet. Every time I go by the place is slammed."

His tongue licked some dressing off his fingertip. "I think you just like to come see me," he smirked. *If he can't tell I'm blushing then he needs glasses.*

"No, I just cut through the Student Center sometimes!"

He raised an eyebrow at me.

I felt my face burning. "I—I mean—well *excuse* me if I wanna stop by and say hi to my *friend* at work!" I said more defensively than I wanted to.

"I'm just playing with you!" he laughed. "Did you see the new video I put up?"

"I did!" I beamed. "I liked it!"

"I had a feeling you would," he smiled. "I know how much you like Waterparks." *If he would've said he did it just for me he might've had to resuscitate me, preferably by mouth-to-mouth.* "Did you pick out your classes yet?"

"I did, yeah. I got just about everything I wanted," I lied. "And you?"

"Yeah, samesies. Even Social Media & Society, which isn't easy to get into."

"Nice. What else are you taking?"

He thought for a moment. "Ethics in Media, Civil Discourse, an accounting class, and..." He closed one eye and bit his tongue. "Oh, Critical Writing!"

"I have that now! If you ever need help with it..." I said with an expectant look.

"Then I'll go to a tutor," he said happily.

"No! I mean, you *could*, but I meant *I* could try helping you. If you'd like."

He just smiled at me. "You really can't take a joke, can you?"

I made myself laugh with him, trying not to look at that smile for too long. "So what are you majoring in? Journalism?"

"Close. Communications."

"Do you know what you'd like to do with that?"

He sat back with folded arms. "I dunno yet. Something in the music industry."

"You don't wanna be a performer?"

Ethan just shrugged. "I've thought about it, but I don't know if I'd want that kind of life. What about you? Do you wanna be an English teacher, or a writer, or what?"

"I'm not too sure. I like reading, obviously. But I write sometimes too."

"Oh forreal? Like, stories, or...?"

I nodded/swallowed. "Yep. Short stories. Fiction."

"*That's* dope," he said, bringing a smile to my bashful face. "Are they about whatever, or is there a certain genre you prefer? If you don't mind me asking, of course."

"No, you're good." I swallowed and bit back a laugh. *He's gonna think I'm an absolute nerd.* "I like coming up with apocalypse stories. Like, different ways the world could end."

"That sounds fun!" he lit up. "As fun as the end of the world can be."

"I usually don't let people read them though," I shot down his next question.

"That's okay. Nobody said you have to. But yeah, I'm into movies and stuff about the end of the world and all that, which sounds kinda dark when I say it out loud," he laughed. "*Especially* zombies. *Love* me some zombies."

I was speaking before I could stop myself. "The one I'm working on now's actually about a parasite trapped in a glacier way up in Canada, and then as global warming melts the ice, it gets out and basically makes people into zombies, and it just fucking *wreaks* havoc," I said without trying to hide how proud of myself I was of it. "And the main character's in California, and everybody's panicking and freaking out as the infection gets closer and closer."

"I would *totes* read that," he grinned. "I mean, if you'd ever feel comfortable sharing it."

"Maybe I'll do a special release for my *fans*," I smiled like the fucking simp that I am. "I might write a prequel too about the parasite making whatever civilized species that was here before humans go extinct before getting frozen up."

He rested his head on his fist. "And you're keeping these to yourself *why?*" he asked like he was confused about it.

I felt my face flush. "I mean, it's just something I do for fun—"

"Isn't *most* of what we do just for fun? Isn't everybody's dream to make a living off of what they do for fun?"

"Yeah, I *guess*," I said as I pulled and pushed my straw through the hole in the lid with an obnoxious *squawk*. "I guess I'm just worried that people won't like them, or they'll think that they're not good and I'll lose motivation."

"So what? Fuck them," Ethan scowled. "The only reason your stories exist is because *you* created them. You should be proud of that. What if every writer thought the same thing and just never published their stuff? Or even gave up writing altogether?"

My fingers found my studs. "Then I guess...I wouldn't need as many bookshelves as I do?"

"Exactly." He balled up his wrapper and scooted his chair back. "Not that I'm telling you what to do, of course. But aren't you a writer anyway, even if you're only writing for yourself? Don't your own stories motivate and inspire you?"

November 16

One of the university's Christian outreach groups had a table set up in the atrium of Bixby today, trying to show anybody who passed by how the bible is actually a wonderful, vibrant narrative of god's divine love for us instead of the antiquated book of fairy tales that us heathens dismiss it as. I guess they forgot how the bible is used, cited, interpreted, and construed to tell people who identify as queer that their existence is an abomination, that one race is superior to the others, that people who identify as female should be subservient to those who identify as male, that people from one part of the world count as less of a person than people from another, and to repress human rights in general, among *many* other things. Like, what the fuck happened to 'do unto others as you'd have them do unto you?'

I think my crush on Ethan is getting worse. He was on my mind all afternoon until Lit Club, and even then he didn't go away. If anything, trying to listen to a recitation of a seemingly-endless Gertrude Stein poem only made me zone out and think about him even faster. Sure, I've thought about Ethan in *that* way before, but not for hours on end. I keep hoping he'll come into the library when I'm working, but I haven't seen him there since that one time. I keep wanting to drop him a hint about it, but then he might start to think I like him or something.

I was talking with Nikole and welcoming the distraction she provided from my thoughts when Miles and the friend he'd brought along walked in—and by 'a friend' I mean 'a *friend*.' "Hey Nikole, Trevor!" Miles nodded at us. "This is Branden. He wanted to come along with me to kill some time."

"Well I'm glad you came with low expectations," I said dryly, looking around to make sure Ashton wasn't right there. "I'm Trevor. It's nice to meet you."

"It's good to meet you too!" Branden said in a voice that was so high-pitched it actually startled me.

Miles took Branden over to check out the *pâtisserie du jour*—maple pecan cupcakes, and yes, they were as good as they sound. "Why do I get the feeling they're more than just friends?" Nikole asked me. We watched Branden say something to Miles, who laughed and flicked his ear.

"Why is like every Branden and Jason I know gay except for like one?" I asked instead.

Nikole mentally flipped through all the Brandens and Jasons she's ever known. "Oh my god, you're *right*. That's actually kind of bizarre."

"What's kind of bizarre?" Miles asked as he and Branden returned to their seats on the couch.

"Trevor was just telling me how his friend eats cupcakes," she said without skipping a beat. "What'd you say they do? They pull it apart in the middle and flip the top over so it's like a sandwich or something?"

"Uh...*yeah*," I nodded stupidly. "Uh huh."

"Wait, how?" Branden asked. "Like *this*?" He pulled it apart and sent crumbs all over the floor. "It's a little messy," he said with a hand in front of his mouth. Miles didn't try it.

The four of us just sat around and talked, which is when I learned that Branden can't carry a conversation about fucking *anything*—at least not about anything interesting. I'll make sure to have him on my team though for trivia night if the category's pop stars and queer internet personalities. I pretended to look sad when he had to leave to head over to Bixby for a drag show event that Proud as Halle was hosting. Nikole couldn't stay for too long either since she had to work Gladby's front desk. "So," I asked Miles once it was just the two of us and a smattering of other people, "are you and Branden like...?"

"Yeah, I think it's safe to say we are," he said with a smile like he'd just taken a drink of some spiced apple cider. "It's weird how it happened—we both went to this lecture about superheroes in world literature and made small talk before it started. We got coffee afterwards, he asked me if I had Instagram, and I couldn't wait to see him again."

I stared at his travel mug with my elbows on my knees, not even realizing that I was smiling. "Yeah, I know the feeling," I said instead of asking why he didn't want to go to the drag show with him.

He leaned forward to match my posture. "Why do you say that? Did you meet someone?"

"Yeah, but we're not seeing each other. And he's straight, so I'm pretty sure we *won't* be."

"*Oof!*" He fell back in his armchair. "That sucks. Don't you *hate* that?"

"Tell me about it," I said as I ran my hands down my face. "Why do I always crush on the straight ones? Well, *almost* always." I shot him a playful glance that made him smile.

"It's statistics," he said unhelpfully.

"I've had crushes on straight guys before, but never like *this*," I said like he was my therapist.

He shrugged. "You'll get over him eventually, especially once you start seeing other people."

"It'll be kinda hard to get over him, seeing how he's one of my *friends*."

"Ooh, big yikes," he winced. "I assume he doesn't know you like him?"

"*Pfft*. I don't even know if he knows I'm *gay*."

"What? Why not?" He lowered his voice. "Are you still in the closet?"

"No! Well, with *him* I am. I'm afraid he'll find out and not wanna be friends with me anymore. It's happened before, and I don't want it to happen with him because I really like him. Platonically, I mean."

Miles laughed out loud. "Are you sure you know what 'platonic' even means? If he's *really* your friend though then he shouldn't care about your preferences."

Hey Ethan, I just wanted to let you know that I like making out with guys and railing guys. Oh hey, you're a guy. That's funny.

"I mean, it's ultimately up to you," Miles went on, "but I think you should tell him. I'd be hurt if I found out that one of my friends had been keeping something like that a secret from me, especially if I was the only one who didn't know."

I groaned. *Why doesn't coming out get easier the more you do it?*

"For what it's worth," a voice behind us startled us, "I agree with Miles." I turned to see a forgotten Ashton sitting on his laptop.

"Oh my god! How long have you been sitting there? Have you been waiting for us to leave this whole time?"

"No," he said unconvincingly. "It's fine. I was working on something anyway." We gathered up our stuff and pulled on our coats so the three of us could go, even though Ashton insisted he wasn't in a hurry.

"Yeah, you're right," I said after thinking it over. "I should tell him."

"I think you should," Miles said simply. "And hopefully you'll meet somebody else to take your mind off him."

"Yeah, hopefully." I feel regretful and low-key jealous that Branden's the one with Miles—kind, caring, cute Miles. *It could've been you, but Branden's the one who grew a pair and made a move.*

November 17

You'd think that with as much as we're paying to come here that the university would put a box of tissues in every classroom like we're living in a first-world country. I have trouble paying attention in class as it is without people sniffling all period.

Improv Club must've made a good impression on Victor, because he was trying to recruit us to go with him. "You don't have to participate if you don't wanna," he tried to persuade us over dinner in his shirt of a Black Rosie the Riveter flexing and saying *'Don't tread on me!'* "There were a few people last time who just watched."

"Can I fondle my balls while I watch?" Kade asked.

"I'm gonna go ahead and say probably *not.*"

"You know where I *can* do that? In my bed, while I watch *Whose Line Is It Anyway?*"

"Go shit and fall back in it. How about you, Trev?"

Trying to be funny on the fly in front of people who are actually good at it is right up there with skydiving on the list of things I'd never do. But watching? "Yeah, I'll go."

Like most things here, Improv Club was way less glamorous than I pictured it to be. Instead of it being in a classroom with a stage or a platform, it's literally just in an open seating area in the old Student Union. As we got closer to what I thought was just a big study group sitting in a circle, somebody who was easily the tallest person I've ever seen came over to meet us. "Hey! Glad to see we didn't scare you off," they laughed, clapping a hand to Victor's shoulder. "It's…wait wait, let me try to remember," they said. "Vector, right?"

"I'll take Vector over Victor," he chuckled. "I brought my friend along too."

"Hi, I'm Trevor," I said, feeling small.

"Ajax. They/them." *Like the great Greek warrior?* Their grip crushed my hand as they shook it. "Happy you're here, Trevor."

Everybody said hi to us as we found spots on the floor. *This is like that first floor meeting at the beginning of the year, except everybody here looks happy to see me in a creepy sorta way.* The confidence in their voices and gestures reminded me how out of my element I was. I wished there was some kind of snack to keep me busy, but I guess unlike Lit Club, they don't need anything to entice people. Ajax stepped into the light of the overhead fluorescent and started ad libbing a performance that others cycled into on their own. I was hoping it'd be like a game or at least have a prompt or premise, but it was literally just really passionate Theatre kids monologuing and dialoguing to release all their pent-up dramaturgy.

"Typical! Selfish as always!" Ajax accused a tall, skinny girl. "But yet you'll pay ten bucks for some"—they made air quotes—"'healthy' yogurt? *You* see what I'm saying, don't you Trevor?" they said as they extended their arm towards me. *Oh fuckity fuck fuck fuck.*

The floor held me. I gaped in horror like I was staring down the barrel of a gun. "I—I—" *Is there anything I can hit myself over the head with to make myself pass out?*

Thankfully, Victor was there to save me by death from embarrassment. "Can't you ever take a hint?" he jumped in. "All she said was that she hadn't had cannoli that moist since gram stopped baking!"

I kept myself from just up and leaving, although I spent most of the rest of the time looking at the floor. Ajax thanked me for coming, and said that they hoped to see me again. *Yeah, like that'll happen.*

"Sorry they did that," Victor apologized like it was his fault. "I didn't think they'd try to pull a nonparticipant into it."

"It's okay," I lied, remembering how I used to get included in activities against my will in Sunday school. "It's not *your* fault."

"I guess you wouldn't wanna give it another chance?"

"You'd be correct." But at least I tried it—if anything, now I know what to stay the hell away from.

November 18

So I always knew that college would be a great place to people-watch, but I never thought about how good of a place it would be to people-*listen*. I overheard somebody at breakfast describe something as "Nicaraguan finger groovy" and I'm still trying to come up with what the hell they could've been talking about. And then I heard a girl on the verge of tears telling someone on the phone that she'd spent $60 on food at Sheetz last night and she didn't know what to tell her parents, and *then* I heard somebody tell their friend that they thought E.T. was cute "but not in like a sexual way."

FUCK ALL OF THIS
REMIND ME AGAIN WHY I STILL LIVE HERE????

"What's so funny?" Kade demanded. He and Ethan and I got Zukoff for lunch, where we picked at each other's General Tso's, steak quesadilla, and BBQ pork fries.

"My buddy from back home's pissed because I guess they're getting ass-fucked with snow right now," I smiled as I texted Logan back.

That's unfortunate, but that's also none of my business

"Sounds hot," he said as he took a close-up shot of his food with Ethan and me in the background. "Missing—out—loser—lol," he typed out loud. "I'm Snapping Victor."

"I didn't know you had Snap," Ethan said. "Wanna be friends?"

"Does the pope shit on little boys? What's your username?"

"'It's' with two s's, underscore, 'Ethan.'"

"The one with winking and tongue-sticking-out emoji?"

"That's me."

I raised an eyebrow. "Sounds like you have a bit of a bacchanalian side."

"Sure," Ethan just chuckled. "Do you have one?"

"A bit of a bacchanalian side?"

"*No*," he laughed. "Snapchat!"

"Oh! No, I used to, but then I got rid of it."

"He's too good for it," Kade said.

"I never said—"

"You know what? I just realized that I don't care," Kade cut me off, making my nostrils flare. "Well boys, I'm all outta booze, so we'll have to find another way to have fun tonight. And I'm doing No-Nut November, so getting frisky is out of the question."

"How about game night if you aren't going out?" I suggested. "I don't think I can stomach alcohol again just yet."

"Yeah, I'm down for game night!" Ethan said.

"Sure, why the hell not?" Kade said as his phone *ddDDakkh*'ed with Victor's reply. We looked up at him, looking bored as all hell, from beneath the edge of his desk while his Geography professor droned about the Congo River basin. Victor shifted his eyes left, then right, then gave his camera the finger.

Ethan met us at Bixby later on to see CPB's showing of *Don't Look Up* with his keyboard in tow to take over to 239 Axworthy for a jam sesh afterwards. Only in college can you see somebody take a keyboard-sized bag into a movie theater and not even think twice about it. "Is that a keyboard in your bag or are you just happy to see me?" Victor chuckled when he saw it.

Ethan smirked. "Why can't it be both?"

I'd never seen the movie before, and holy *fuck* is it on-point. I know it's supposed to be a satire, but I didn't even think it was funny because I was so shooketh by it. I almost forgot I was watching a work of fiction. "I'm actually speechless right now," I said as we filed out of the theater. "Like, that's what would happen. That's *literally* what would happen. That's how it would fucking go."

"I thought you said you were speechless," Kade scoffed.

"*Wouldn't* it though?" Victor said. "Like, there are people who would *actually* be that stupid."

"Excuse me," Ethan said like he was offended. "*Most* of my family is that stupid, thank you very much." It took us a moment to catch his sarcasm.

Kade patted his shoulder in sympathy. "Sorry to hear that, fam."

"Hence why I'm going to school on the other side of the state," Ethan said humorously.

In 239 Axworthy, Kade offered us some leftover pasta with sauce he made himself from roasted red peppers and some fresh herbs he'd brought from home— "What are noodles anyway but a vehicle for the sauce?"—before he and Ethan set up their instruments in Victor's room. It was so comically cramped, it was like they were shooting a music video. Victor and Kade played some Hippo Campus that was as mellow and hypnotic as the actual thing—Kade caressed the neck of his bass and triggered my ASMR while Victor's gentle and methodic drizzle bounced off his snare pad.

"Who's that by?" Ethan said when they were done.

"Hippo Campus."

Ethan bit his lip in thought. "I don't know if I've heard of them before."

"You *would* if you ever listened to WXNU once in your life," I muttered.

"What was that?" Ethan asked me.

"I said you'll be playing at Open Mic Night again, right?"

He slapped his forehead. "Oh *shit!* I totally forgot!" The look on my face must've been funny enough for him to laugh at. "I'm kidding, of *course* I'll be playing."

The three of them jammed with Ethan taking the lead, Kade filling in, and Victor keeping it all tied together, and then they switched it up and let Ethan round them out. *I wish I could play something other than the skin flute,* I thought as I watched. My fingers tapped along until a lightning bolt of an idea lurched me forward. "Why don't the three of you play at Open Mic Night together?" I gasped, almost upset with myself for not thinking of it earlier.

Kade clutched his chest. "Don't *scare* me like that."

"You're all *amazing*," I tried to sell them. "Even just this, right now."

Victor looked from Kade to Ethan as a small smile crawled across his face. "Why *don't* we?"

"Yeah, I think that'd be pretty fun, actually," Ethan said. All eyes were on Kade.

"I'd be down," he shrugged like they'd already discussed it.

I was eager with imagination. All I could think about was the three of them up on stage together. *Take a seat, Trevor—it's been .2 seconds and you're already stanning them.*

After they'd played to their satisfaction, Kade made tea for us before we picked out a game. "Is that a whole thing of *keef?*" Ethan nodded to a jar of green powder in the cabinet.

"Oh yeah," Kade rolled his eyes, "like I just have four ounces of keef laying around."

"I *wish* it was keef," Victor said. "Hashtag *faded.*"

"It's matcha powder, not that I'd expect peasants like you to know that." Kade picked it up and gave it a shake. "And just so you know, I was kidding earlier when I said I was doing No-Nut November, so if you *did* have something else in mind..."

Victor laughed out loud. "*You?* Doing No-Nut November? Fucking *please.*"

Since Ethan had mentioned he wanted to play it, Kade pulled *Monopoly*—which turned out to be the British version of the game—onto his bedroom floor while Victor bounced a pair of drumsticks off his rubber practice pad. The game was the same except for the different property names and a different currency, but the novelty of it made it fun, even if I was constantly short on quid. Ethan and Victor were at least somewhat courteous when I had to pay them—"*Ello guvnah! Moighty foine day for a stroll innit? But the rate's gone up I'm afraid*"—but Kade would remind me how much I worked for the hundreds I had to fork over. It was hard to keep track of all their house rules, although I *did* land directly between Victor's hat and Ethan's dog to line up all four tokens, earning us each £500. "*It's never been done!*" Victor gasped.

"Would you guys wanna do some kind of gift exchange before we leave for Winter Break?" Ethan asked after he went to Jail for the twentieth time. "Like a Secret Santa or a white elephant gift exchange?"

"*Hells* yeah!" Kade said. "We used to do that with our friends back home! And *you* owe me £18," he pointed at Victor before I could roll.

Victor looked down at the board for a moment. "I motion for a grievance, and I will now go into a filibuster." He slapped the sum down into Kade's open palm. "I also motion for Secret Santa."

I raised my hand. "I second the motion."

Ethan slapped the floor. "Motion passes. I know all about motions from our House Council and RHA meetings."

Kade felt his pockets. "You know what? I think I'm actually all outta fucks to give." Ethan failed to bite back a laugh.

"I guess we'll pick out names before we leave for Thanksgiving?" I suggested. "That way we can do our shopping while we're home."

"You know they have this thing now where you can buy things from your phone," Ethan smirked as he drew a Community Chest card. "Receive for services £25."

Kade raised an eyebrow. "What kind of services we talkin' about?"

Ethan returned the look. "I think we both know." *Only £25? I'd be paying him for those services every fucking day.*

Kade laughed at something on his phone before showing it to Ethan. "I mean, maybe if I was super drunk," Ethan laughed. Kade showed me his phone to let me see a video of me from Victor's POV that kept zooming in until my face took up the whole screen. *'Would you tap this?'* it read.

I spun on Victor. "Don't be sending Snaps of me!" *Wait, how drunk is super drunk exactly?*

"You know what's worse than people sending Snaps of you?" he grinned. "People *not* sending Snaps of you."

"You could get back at him if you used Snapchat too," Ethan said. "And think of all the ugly pics of Kade you could send. You wouldn't have to try that hard."

"Okay, you convinced me." I reinstalled the app and made a new account since I couldn't remember my old login.

"You should make your username allhorntup_tbh," Kade giggled, making us all start cracking up. "You know, since your Instagram name is wallowing_tbh?" We were laughing so hard at it that I couldn't not do it.

"Wow, all this time, and we just had to have Ethan tell him to do it," Victor smirked. I shot him a warning glance. "I wonder how many other platforms we can get him to start using," he laughed to himself as he drew a Community Chest card. "You have accrued an insurmountable amount of debt. Hang yourself."

My eyes lost focus and everything went fuzzy. *Mom's birthday—I was looking forward to his birthday dinner, too—how long would it have taken if we hadn't wanted to play Switch?—Ryder's card—'You always say how you wished that I would stop being who I am, so I got you the gift you always wanted'—*

I blinked as Victor snapped his fingers in front of my face. "Wha—?"

"You okay fam?" he asked.

"Yeah." I shook myself. "Yeah, I just zoned out for a sec," I said, though I was only half-present for the rest of the evening.

Given the number of times he landed on Free Parking, nobody was surprised that Kade won. "So what do you guys wanna do tomorrow?" he asked as we sorted the money and gathered up the deeds.

"I'll be in the library working on a group project," Victor said. "It's due on Wednesday and we haven't started it yet."

"Sheesh fam," Ethan laughed. "I don't think *I* have anything going on."

I shook my head. "Yeah, same. You wanna meet up for brunch and go from there?"

"Brunch?" Kade scoffed. "What are you, 30 years old and somewhat established?"

"Well it can't be *breakfast* since your ass is never out of bed before noon," Victor razzed him.

November 20

Sometimes I'll hear people say how they don't understand why there's a need for LGBTQ+ rights movements—that's not the term they use, of course—which is when I point to the nearest chair and tell them to do us all a favor by sitting the fuck down and shutting the fuck up. When was the last time a straight person was a victim of violence just because they were straight, like the queer patrons at that gay bar in Colorado that got shot up last night? Yeah, that's what I fucking thought. And right before Trans Day of Remembrance too? I just don't understand why people choose to be so *hateful.*

We were supposed to meet up at Patnick yesterday at 11, but I still hadn't heard anything from Kade by the time I got there. I sat by the window and took in my reflection, wondering if Ethan would think I looked as good as I hoped he would. "Morning," he greeted me in a pair of jeans instead of his usual joggers. "Is Kade on his way?"

"I don't know. I haven't heard from him yet." I bit the inside of my cheek. "My guess is he slept in."

"Do you think he'd be pissed if we didn't wait for him? I'm *starving.*"

"Nah, he'll get over it," I chuckled. "We could be here all day waiting for him."

We each took a bagel into the omelet line with us so we wouldn't pass out from hunger as we waited. "Did you just go back to your room last night after we left?" Ethan asked me as his hand caught his crumbs.

"Yeah. Did you go out anywhere?"

"Not *out,* but I hung out in my friend's room for a bit before heading back." He sucked the crumbs out of his hand. *I wonder if it was the same friend he hung out with after we played Drunk Jenga?*

We were halfway done with our pillowy omelets when Kade finally texted me.

Sorry mom but im not gonna make it this morning
I think i need to take a me day today
Sorry for being poopy 😣😣

Don't worry about it!
You just take care of yourself 🙏

Lmk if you need anything
And quit apologizing! Haha

"So Kade *won't* be joining us today," I said as I set my phone back down.

"Is everything okay with him?" Ethan asked.

"Yeah," I said, wondering if I should make something up. "He said he just needs to take some time for himself."

"Good for him for showing himself some self-care," he said as he Snapped me a pic of the blueberries on his plate he'd arranged in a smiley face that he also put on his story. "So what do you wanna do, since it's looking like it'll just be the two of us for a while?" *I mean, I know what I'd* like *to do with you.*

"Didn't you say you'd like to try longboarding?" I remembered. "Today might be the last nice day we have this semester."

"Dude! Yeah, I've been wanting to!"

I traded my jacket for a hoodie since the November sun got warmer as the day grew older. With my longboard tucked under my arm, I led the way to the level, usually-deserted stretch of road on the edge of campus near the Ski Lodge. "We'll go along the grass in case you need to jump ship," I said.

"Do you think I'll have to?" he asked, sounding low-key worried.

I shook my head. "Nah, it's flat enough that you should be fine here. Okay, watch how I stand on it." I stepped on and took my stance. "It'll probably be easier if you're facing this way, but you can see what feels better. Push with your back foot, and lean to steer. Watch how I do it." I kicked off and coasted down the street in lazy zigzags before hugging the right side and crouching to turn around. I watched him watching me until I put my foot down to brake in front of him.

"You look so steezy when you do it," he smiled. "I'm probably gonna fall right on my ass."

"I doubt it," I scoffed. "Your turn now."

He cautiously put one foot on, then the other. "Oh gosh," he said under his breath as he started to roll a little. "This is harder than it looks." The board lurched under him as he gently swung his weight back and forth.

"You're doing good for your first time!" I half-lied to encourage him. "Try pushing off now."

He gingerly pushed the ground under him to get a feel for it. "I feel like I'm gonna fall."

I held out my hand before I knew what I was doing. "What if you hold onto me while you go?"

He looked at me with a blank expression. '*What, are you fucking gay or something?*' I half-expected him to say. "Yeah, okay." So that's how I got to hold hands with Ethan.

I walked, pulling him along to let him get accustomed to the sensation of rolling with so little effort. "I'm gonna let go now, okay?" He nodded with his eyes straight ahead. I let him go without leaving his side. He unsteadily tried pushing himself along on his own, but it didn't take him long to get the hang of it. "Look at you, you got it!" I called as I watched him go ahead without me. "Remember to brake if you need to!" He brought himself to a stop a little ways down, and stepped off to turn the board around to come back to me. "Go 'head!" I said as he dismounted, even if a little inelegantly.

"I did it! I probably looked like an amateur though."

"That doesn't matter. As long as you had fun." *Take some notes, Trevor.*

"Can I go again?"

I gave him an encouraging nod. "Go for it."

He went again, a little faster and a little more confidently. He went all the way past Walcott to the parking lot where we launched water balloons from, pivoting the board with his foot in one motion, even though he almost ate shit doing it. He passed sidewalk pedestrians with the sun on his smile and thrill in his eyes, the same thrill that enthralled me when I first got my bearings. The exhilaration nearly left him breathless. "Holy crap! It's like I'm flying! And did you see me spin the board?"

"Right?" I grinned. "That's why I love longboarding. You feel unstoppable, like you're the only person alive. You feel ready to bomb a hill yet?"

"Lemme ride around for a few more hours," he chuckled uneasily.

I let him roll alongside me, teetering at times, as I thought of a good road for him to graduate up to. "Can I actually see that for a sec?" I asked as I nodded down at my board. As soon as he was back on the pavement, I was on the board and kicking the ground past me. "Catch me if you can!" I shouted impishly as I threw him a backwards glance, laughing at the look on his face before he took me up on my offer. *Holy fuck can this kid run,* I thought as he closed the gap between us.

"You ass!" he laughed. He yanked my beanie off my head and took it with him.

"Is that how it's gonna be?" I called after him. I pushed off vigorously, pursuing him at an almost dangerous speed. He looked back to see me playfully glaring at him before leaping off the road and into the grass. *"Shit."*

I circled around towards the bench near the pond, where he sat with his arms stretched across the back of it. "You were saying?" he said between breaths as I took a seat beside him.

I smiled back at him. "Okay, yeah, I deserved that."

"Yeah you did," he said as he dropped my hat in my lap.

I led him over to the road that goes from Bamberger Stadium and past the gym towards Portis Hall and the Quad, where I schooled him in some Longboarding 102. "So sometimes when you start to pick up speed you'll start to wobble. If that happens you'll wanna lower your center of gravity. Don't panic, bend your knees, and don't make any sudden movements."

"Are you teaching me how to longboard or how to escape from a wild animal?" he laughed.

"Hey, I don't know who here's a werewolf. But if those don't work, there's no shame in jumping off if it means not wiping out."

"Aw, I was really hoping to wipe out." He stayed near the curb with his arms out for balance until he felt comfortable enough to try out the middle of the road as physics did its thing. I got scared when I saw the board wobble, but he did as I said and regained his composure. He stopped where the street leveled off and jogged back up to meet me.

"I think I'm starting to get the hang of this!" he said with a glow.

"You're doing way better than Victor or Tylor did—though in all fairness, Tylor was hungover as shit. You handled those wobbles like a pro though!"

"I thought I was gonna get thrown off!" Ethan laughed.

"Oh, it can happen. I have enough torn jeans that got turned into shorts to prove it."

He hit the next one so confidently, leaning from side to side so neatly, that I'd have never guessed he'd started riding only a half hour before. "When do we have to stop?" he asked.

"Until you're sick of it," I shrugged. "I don't have any plans for the rest of the day."

"Was that sarcastic?"

"No, I really don't! But I'm happy you thought I *was* being sarcastic, because that means you've officially hung around me long enough."

"So what made you wanna start longboarding?" he asked as we made for the dorms. "Did you see people skateboarding and were like, 'I wanna do that, but actually look cool doing it?'"

"No," I laughed. "It was actually really spontaneous. We were on vacation at Ocean City the Summer before the pandemic, and—"

"Ocean City Maryland or New Jersey?"

"Maryland."

"That's where we always go! We were just there this past Summer!"

I gave him a sideways look. "*When* this past Summer?"

"Like a week before move-in. Why?"

"No *way!* That's when we were there too!"

"Shut up! We could've ran into each other without even knowing!" he beamed. *Trust me, I would've remembered if we had.*

"But anyway," I went on, "I ended up in one of those surf-shop-skate-shops without any plans to buy one, but you see how *that* story ended."

"Imagine we lived somewhere where we could *surf*," Ethan daydreamed as we started up the next hill.

"I'm happy I had it when COVID hit though, because riding around my neighborhood during lockdown was one of the few things that kept me sane. I'll wait for you here." I watched him trudge up to the top of the road, spinning one of the wheels as he went. *Miles is right—I need to tell him, today. It's not fair to him. If he's as good a guy as he seems, then he won't care who I like. But what if the other half of it slips out? 'And by the way Ethan, you're more than just a friend to me. I like you —like, I LIKE you.' And then he'll tell me all of a sudden that he forgot about something he has to do and that'll be the end of that. I hate living with secrets though, and I don't wanna have to carry around another one, even if—*

The sight of Ethan flying off the board pulled me from my itchiest of thoughts.

"Oh SHIT! Are you okay?" I called as I ran over to him.

"*Ow*," he groaned. "I *think* so. My elbow hurts like hell. At least I hit the grass and not the pavement." He stood up with a wince. "My pants aren't ripped, are they?"

I circled him. "Not that I can see."

"Well that's good," he chuckled as he started to walk it off. "Oh *fuck*." The sole of his one shoe had somehow come part way off and flapped loosely.

"Oh *shit*. Did it catch on the curb or something?"

"I think it was from the pavement when I tried to slow myself down. I knew they were on their way out, but…" He sighed. "I don't have any other shoes here other than baseball cleats."

"Do you wanna borrow a pair of mine for the rest of the week? I wear size 10."

He shook his head. "Thanks, but I wear 12s." *You know what they say about big shoes…* "Nate's wouldn't fit either."

I bit the inside of my cheek. "Well then let's go get you a new pair," I said optimistically.

"Where would we go? I don't wanna get shoes from a garage sale."

"I can drive us to the outlets. There's gotta be *tons* of places down there."

He thought it over. "I mean, we *could*. But isn't that kinda far?"

"That's okay," I shrugged. "I don't have anything else to do. Besides, I feel somewhat responsible for your shoe coming apart."

"No, I couldn't ask you to do that for me."

"I *want* to," I smiled. "Would you rather walk around flapping all over the place?"

"Why flap all over the place when I could fap all over the place?" he chuckled, making me laugh out loud.

"Okay, you've *clearly* been hanging around Kade too much too."

"Hey! Is this yours?" a guy down the road called to us from where my board had come to a stop along the curb. I hustled down to retrieve it.

"So, whaddaya say?" I asked Ethan when I returned to him. "You wanna go for a drive?"

He chewed on my offer. "If you really *want* to. I feel bad for making you do it."

"I'll take that as a yes, and it's not a problem. End of discussion. It'll be a good time."

We made a pit stop in 222 Swafford so I could trade my board for my keys. "Big yikes dude," Tylor said when Ethan showed him his predicament. He managed to fix his shoe with duct tape, which did the job, though it looked pretty butt.

"We're gonna head down to the outlets to get him some new kicks," I told him and Amina, who were playing PS5. "We probably won't be back until the evening," I winked.

In my passenger seat, Ethan connected his phone and put his entire music library on shuffle. He skipped through a lot of them, but sang along to the ones he liked. Most of them were pop songs you wouldn't catch me putting on, but some were actually kind of fire. It was a good day for a drive, even if it did take almost 40 minutes to get there. My phone kept us on the highway like we were headed for Pittsburgh, and Ethan mourned every dead animal we saw on the side of the road. The blood and chunks always make me wince, but he moaned like he was the one who'd gotten hit by a car.

"Were you a Theatre kid in school?" I asked him after a song from the *Dear Evan Hansen* soundtrack that he belted out the words to like he was on stage ended.

"I was never *in* any musicals, but I played piano in the orchestra once." He told me about his school's musicals, and I told him how I loved going and was always so envious of the kids who have the talent to sing and perform on stage. *So imagine my shock when one of them gave introverted me his phone number and said that I should text him.* "So why do you wanna go to California so bad?" he asked me out of nowhere as he watched a flock of starlings weave their signature through the air.

"Have you ever seen *pictures* of the place?" I asked like it was the dumbest question I've ever heard. "The beaches, the palm trees, the sunny skies, the mountains. It's looks so chill, so easygoing, so lo-fi, so—"

"You realize all those pictures are heavily filtered to give off that *exact* impression, right?" he tried to yuck my yum.

"Yeah, and it worked," I smirked. "Who the fuck do you think *they* voted for in 2020?" I asked as I pointed to the big 'PLEASE GOD SAVE OUR COUNTRY' sign that came into view.

Ethan scoffed. "Probably the Stupid Orange Fuck."

"That might be my new favorite name for him," I laughed. "You know what's sad though? I probably would've voted for him in 2016 if I'd been able to, even if my parents wouldn't have coerced me into it at the time." *I can't believe I just admitted that.*

"It's not sad because I probably would've done the same thing. Not that that makes it not sad. And my parents—well, at least my stepdad—would happily do it a third time."

I groaned like I'd just seen chunky roadkill. "Oh *god*, I'm sorry you have to live with that. I know what it's like to live under the same roof as a lack of moral decency."

"Which is *exactly* why I'm at NHU. I just needed to get the fuck away from there." He sighed. "So what made you change your ways? What made the scales fall from your eyes?" *Where the fuck do I even begin?*

"The short version is that I watched people who call themselves Christians and say to love everybody start full-on supporting a hate-based ideology."

Ethan cracked a smile. "I'm glad we think the same way, or else I'm not sure we could still be friends."

"Yeah, same. I'd have pushed you outta the car by now," I laughed before changing topics. "So I assume your stepdad lives with you—do you still see your dad at all?"

He swallowed. "I go to the cemetery sometimes."

"Oh shit. I'm sorry."

"Don't be. It's okay, really." He turned to me without a hint of sorrow in his eyes. "He died before I was born. He was killed in Iraq."

"Yeah, but still." *What's worse—to never know somebody who you could've loved, or to love somebody and not realize how much you loved them until it's too late?*

I tried not to let that put too much of a damper on the rest of our conversation that carried us down a series of two-lane roads after we got off the highway. I knew we were near the outlets when we found ourselves surrounded by endless strip malls and restaurants and shopping centers. Ethan wanted to hit up the Adidas store, which was busy as shit since Christmas is coming up and nothing makes middle schoolers feel like hot shit like wearing Nike and Adidas. I browsed the shoes and clothes and guys while Ethan tried on pair after pair and paid for the ones he liked the most. He dropped to the nearest bench outside and tore back tissue paper like it was Christmas morning. "What do you think?" he asked as he held up a fresh-as-fuck white-with-black-stripes mid-top.

"They wouldn't be *my* first choice, but they're gonna look so good on you," I said like the sales associate I am.

"I guess they wouldn't be, since they don't give off that preppy, *alternative-music-loving* longboarder look, now do they?" he razzed me as he changed into them.

"I've been called lots of things, but 'preppy' has never been one of them."

"There's a first for everything," he said as he dropped his old ones in the trash, though he held onto the empty box until we found a recycling station. We walked around and popped in and out of stores until we made a full lap around the place. I resisted buying anything since I'll probably get a gift card or two for Christmas, though when has that *really* stopped me before? The sun sank low enough to make it too chilly to hang around outside, so we headed over to the mall that was several tremendously busy intersections away instead of heading back just yet, which is when Ethan discovered how merciless of a driver I can really be.

"Driving is about being efficient, not nice," I defended myself.

In the parking lot, I waited for him to roll and unroll the legs of his jeans to his heart's satisfaction. "I wanna see if I like them cuffed," he said as he nodded down at my own cuffs.

"I like the look. But you might wanna step up your sock game a little." I pinched my jeans up to show him the roses on my own sock. He gave me the finger with a smile.

The mall was asininely busier than the outlets, but at least it was decorated. "*Dammit,* we missed Santa!" I said as we walked past an empty, decadent-looking throne surrounded by candy canes and iridescent presents. We stopped in Spencer's to see if they had any cool lights—"Hey Trevor," Ethan smirked as he held a large rainbow dick-shaped lollipop in front of where the real thing lay, unaware that I mentally was mentally licking my lips, "you know you want it"—and in American Eagle so one of us could step up their sock game. I'd let myself fall a few steps behind him so my eyes could travel from his new shoes up to his butt-hugging jeans to the hair I wanted to bury my nose in, only to look like I hadn't been checking him out when he'd turn to say something.

After almost getting rude with a skin care salesperson who wouldn't take no for an answer, I took us into FYE so I could file through the records, even though my tastes had long surpassed what it has to offer. "Do you have a record player?" Ethan asked the records as I flipped through them.

"Uh huh. I didn't bring it down to school though because there wouldn't be room for it between it, the speakers, and my records."

"If Victor can have a *drum set* in his room, then I think you could make your stuff fit if you tried."

"Said the bishop to the bishop," I Freudian slipped.

"What?"

"Nothing," I shook my head. "Oh go ahead!" I grinned as I slid *Yumeno Garden* out of the 'L' section. "This is the band we saw last weekend! I'm surprised they even have this here!"

We took our bags up to the second floor, where we walked alongside the swirling ribbons of light and baubles and golden snowflakes suspended from the black of the skylight ceiling, and where we found ourselves in a PacSun identical to the one back home. "Let me know if you see anything you want," I told him in a low voice. "I can buy it with my employee discount and you can just Venmo me back."

He grinned like he caught me in my underwear. "The whole California thing makes a lot more sense now," he nodded.

"I like the styles and the atmosphere and the music," I said simply. *The guys who come in are a big plus too.*

He picked up a tribal-patterned long sleeve only to put it back after seeing the price tag. "I don't think I'm gonna get anything, but thanks anyway."

"You sure? 30% off."

"I'm sure. I should save my money for Christmas gifts," he said, though he was singing a different song by the time we got to BoxLunch and its windows splayed with Jack Skellington, a Stormtrooper in a Santa hat, *Naruto*, *Harry Potter*, and all kinds of other pop culture. The clothing wasn't my style, but there were tons of accessories to choose from. I picked up a little stuffed animal Teddiursa in the *Pokémon* section, and all of a sudden it was ten years ago—playing *Pokémon* with Logan at his grandparent's house, before politics existed, and before COVID existed, and before sexualities and identities existed, and when my biggest worries were homework and if we'd be having peas with dinner. "Aww, what a cute little fella," Ethan smiled down at the stuffie.

"The first *Pokémon* game I ever played was *SoulSilver*, and this was my favorite one from it," I said to it. I gave it another wistful look before setting it back on the shelf.

Ethan held a red-and-gold collegiate-style Gryffindor sweatshirt up to his chest. "Thoughts?"

"I like it. Are you a Gryffindor?"

"Uh huh. Every Sorting quiz I've ever taken put me in Gryffindor. Which one would you get?"

I pointed to the blue one. "Ravenclaw. Sometimes Hufflepuff, but most of the time it's Ravenclaw."

"Why does that not surprise me?" He grabbed a pair of socks with lions on them to go with his sweatshirt. "You know, because I apparently need to step up my sock game," he smiled.

"Yeah, we've heard it already," I laughed. The only thing I got was a mystery box of *Lord of the Rings* enamel pins—"You really see how much of a kid's series *Harry Potter* is after reading *Lord of the Rings*"—which I had Ethan hold for me along with my record while I went to go take piss before we hit up the food court.

"I'm glad the Chinese place was giving out free samples, because I was actually almost thinking about getting some hate chicken," Ethan said as he glanced over at the place open only six days a week.

"You'll never catch me eating there," I laughed bitterly. At our table, I laid down my chopsticks to finally text Victor back after hours of ignoring him.

**Hey mom I'm all done. You wanna come over and play
a game?
We're going to go eat something, you wanna join?
Are you alive??
Goddammit mom answer me**

**Sorry, my phone was on silent lol
I'm actually out with Ethan rn, but I'll lyk when we get
back!**

(°ᵕ°)

My mind drifted to one of the alternate universes where Ethan and I were at the mall on a date instead of just as friends, buying matching sweaters or pajamas or something to throw on and take cheesy couples pics in. The forlorn wish gave me a lump in my throat, but hey—somewhere out there, Trevor and Ethan are doing just that.

"Something on your mind?" present-universe Ethan asked present-universe me.

I gulped. "Is it that obvious?"

"A little," he said with a small smile. "Wanna talk about it?"

"No," I said quickly, shaking my head. "I mean, I *do*, but...I don't know—" My eyes squeezed shut. "It's complicated."

"Well if you do, you know where to find me." He grabbed his phone to resend me the Snap he'd taken earlier at breakfast of his blueberries arranged like a smiley face.

"Why'd you send me this again?"

He shrugged. "Because something's bothering you, and I thought it might cheer you up."

I smiled back down at the blueberries. *He's so fucking sweet.* "It did."

We washed down our food with some milkshakes as we crossed the cold November evening to get back to my car. "Can you put on that album you bought?" Ethan asked me. "I wanna hear it, and you already had to listen to my stuff on the way here." He was rocking out to the first song. "This shit fucking *slaps*," he said by the fourth. "*This* is who you saw live? I wish I coulda been there." *Yeah, me too.*

The glowing clock faces of Old Main welcomed us back to campus an album-and-some later. I pulled up alongside Kessler and put on my flashers. "Thanks again for all of this," Ethan said. "Really, it means a lot to me."

"It was nothing," I waved him off. "Plus, I had a good time."

"Yeah, so did I." He swallowed before reaching his hand into his bag from BoxLunch. "I got you this while you were taking—while you were in the bathroom back at the mall," he said, almost stumbling with his words. "Just as a thank you."

Ethan? Being nervous about something? My concern gave way to the best kind of astonishment though when he pulled out the little Teddiursa stuffie from underneath his sweatshirt. "I—I figured you'd like it." My feelings went haywire.

"*Ethan,*" I finally managed to say. "I—*thank you.* I *love* it." I leaned over to hug him, the scent of his cologne still just discernible. He could've bought me a milkshake or a coffee or a dick-shaped lollipop, but instead he got me something that he knew meant something to me, something that would put a smile on my face.

"It's the least I could do for you driving me around all day," he said like it might've been the wrong thing to say.

I looked from it to him and back. *You said you'd tell him. You said you'd tell him today.* I cleared my throat. "So...remember how you asked me earlier if something was bothering me?"

He tilted his head a degree. "Yeah?"

I exhaled, low and slow. "So, I've been wanting to tell you this for a while now, but I haven't yet because I was afraid—well, I still *am* afraid—that you might think differently of me, and that you might not wanna be friends with me anymore." I monopolized his attention. "But you're like one of my best friends at school now, and I feel like I'd be lying to you if I kept on keeping it a secret from you—I mean, Tylor and Kade and Victor all know, so it's only fair to you too, but Ethan, I..." *Say it, you can say it.* "I'm gay, Ethan." I squeezed my eyes shut so hard that I saw shapes that lingered when I opened them. "You seem like the kind of person who wouldn't care, but I've lost friends in the past when I told them, and I didn't wanna lose you as a friend too." Just the thought of it made me feel like crying. Ethan's empty gaze had drifted through the windshield towards one of the blue emergency lights. "I really hope this doesn't change anything between us."

He sat without moving, with a silence that scared me more than anything else since this past June when Dillon told me that we needed to talk about something. *Please say something,* I thought. *Either tell me we're still friends, or say that I'm a freak and you never wanna see me again. Just don't leave me hanging.* After maybe an hour, he swallowed and turned to face me. "Trevor," he smiled as he brought me in for another hug, "of *course* it doesn't change anything. Being friends with you is...it would take a lot more than *that* for me to wanna stop being friends with you." The relief was so intense that it rolled a tear down my cheek. "I know it can be terrifying to tell people, but I'm *so* happy you told me. That shows me how much of a friend *I* am to you."

Friend. Each use of the word was a scalpel slice into my skin. I bit my tongue so hard I was sure I'd take it right off. "You don't know how good it feels to hear you say that," was all I said as I wiped my eyes.

"I can guess." He put his fist to his mouth. "So I have to ask—how would you rate me?"

His bluntness sideswiped me. *What the fuck?* I watched him tunnel away from me like a movie effect. He raised an eyebrow as he waited for me to answer. *Why would he tease me about this? Did Kade put him up to this?* "I—no, I mean—you're—"

I could've lied. I could've not risked throwing away my friendship with him. I could've just lived with another secret kept bottled up inside until it hurt. But the words started spilling out before my brain could knock some sense into me.

"I mean, you're a good-looking guy," I admitted, my heart beating like a frenzied metronome. "But you're straight and I respect that. Just because I'm into guys doesn't mean I wanna kiss every one I see."

He looked at me like he was about to start laughing. "So you think I'm cute?"

My face felt like I'd just downed some chili peppers. "Yes, I think you're cute," I said quickly like I was hoping he wouldn't hear, wishing that my car seat would just swallow me, or that the roof would fold open and my spring-loaded seat would shoot me into the night sky. *Victor would open up his sky map app to try to figure out what satellite I was.* "But like I said, I would never try to make a pass at you or anything."

He shook his head with a disbelieving smile. "I kinda wish you would," he said just before he took away my capacity to speak and just about everything else when he grabbed my headrest, leaned across the center, and pressed his lips to mine.

A 50-car pileup in my brain brought everything—my thoughts, the rotation of the galaxy—to a screeching halt. A space shuttle exploded somewhere mid-launch. An old film reel was snipped with scissors, spinning in a worthless circle. The first time Dillon and I kissed it was like a Fourth of July fireworks show going off in my chest. But kissing Ethan was like...the eruption of Vesuvius. Krakatoa. The inevitable Yellowstone caldera. The firebombing of Dresden. The atomic bombs. The meteor that wiped out the dinosaurs. The invention of instant noodles. And with his hand on my chest, he could feel it too. Every time I played out the fantasy in my mind it was drunken, hungry, forceful. But there in the front seat of my car—probably on display for any Kessler residents out for a smoke—it was slow, gentle, full. He still tasted like his peppermint milkshake.

When he eventually pulled away either a moment or a century later, he was heaving, his face fighting between bliss and fright. His eyes were locked onto mine, and mine onto his. *What. The. FUCK.*

"Oh, *shit*," he whispered with an anxious smile, though he sounded scared. He threw off his seatbelt and jumped out with his stuff, taking off towards the doors without a look back. I just stared at the spot he disappeared into, my chest swelling, palpitating and petrified.

"*Oh shit* is right," I murmured to Teddiursa, who smiled up blankly from the empty passenger seat.

November 21

Do you want to see a picture of the future? Then picture this: advertisements everywhere, and subscribing to everything. Whatever capitalist fuck came up with the idea of paying for things forever instead of just one time deserves the Fucking Capitalist Pig medal. Someday your fridge will have ads scrolling across it, and you won't be able to open it unless you pay your monthly fridge subscription fee. Same thing with putting on your shoes, unlocking your phone. I mean, aren't I already subscribing to sanity by taking my meds? And then after that the price of things will fluctuate in real time, like how Ubers cost more when you're going to a concert or something. Just watch.

"Hey, are you okay?" Victor grabbed me as I passed him in the hall outside of Computers. "You never got back to me. I was starting to get worried. I had to message Tylor to make sure you were alive."

I twisted my stud, feeling bad for ghosting him. "Yeah, yeah, I'm sorry, I—I just have a lot on my mind."

"What's up? Did something happen?" *Oh, you don't even know.*

"Yeah. It's nothing bad though, I'm just..." I trailed off. I wasn't feeling eye contact at the moment. "I can't really talk about it." *God how I wish I could tell* somebody. "But...yeah. It's just a lot."

"Well, you know I'm here to listen if you wanna talk about it. You think you'll be up to grab dinner later?"

"I won't have time to. I'll probably just grab something from the cafe in Rosenberg after work before I head over to Open Mic Night."

I had a million-and-one things on my mind, but the only person I could talk to about them has been ghosting me for the last day-and-a-half. Was what happened even real life? Did he regret it and is too embarrassed to face me now? Was he curious about himself, and kissing me answered his question? Has he been gay this whole time? Is he straight and just wanted to mess with me? I haven't been able to focus on any books or games, and even *music* hasn't been able to distract me. I've been auto-piloting my way through classes and work. I can't go more than two seconds without zoning out.

Yeah...I have some things to tell you
On the condition that you help me carry my stuff over
to Brew 22 ☺
Come over after you get off work?

November 22

So the Stupid Orange Fuck announced that he's going to be running for President again in 2024. I can't even *start* to fucking think about it without legit getting nauseous.

Not going to lie, but I was actually pretty bummed when I got home today and saw that Mom and Dad had already put up all the Christmas decorations. I always *loved* decorating, even if toddler Trevor just hung up one ornament. The stop-motion movies, the cookies with blurry trees or reindeer heads on them—that's when you *knew* Christmas was coming, and it always felt so surreal. I know I say that traditions have life spans, but I meant the ones I don't care about. I guess that's just another change I'm going to have to get used to.

I was too anxious to stomach a real dinner last night, but I forced myself to eat a chocolate muffin from the vending machine in the cafe in Rosenberg. I let Ethan know as I was leaving work that I'd be over in a few minutes, and was kind of surprised to see him waiting for me in his building's lobby. "I saw you walking over," he let me in with an uneasy smile. "My room looks out over the sidewalk."

You can tell right away that Kessler's one of the older buildings on campus from the herringbone wood floors and the molding along its high, ornamented ceilings. My throat felt so tight that I struggled to breathe as I followed him into the stairwell and up to the third floor, and I could tell he was nervous too from how quiet he was being. "I'm not sure how I'd like living in a traditional dorm," I finally managed to say to break the silence.

"A lot of people who live in the suites say that, but a lot of people here say they wouldn't like living in the suites," he said without turning to me. "There's a stronger sense of community here since we're all pretty much forced to interact with each other. Like, nobody feels weird going over to somebody else's room to borrow something, even clothes. Yeah, you get your own bathroom in the suites, but they feel kinda lonely."

"So does the whole floor have to share a bathroom?" I asked as he led me down the hallway. The second floor is all girls and the third is all guys. It has way more open doors than any of the suites do, giving me cutaway glimpses of the lives lived inside.

"Nah, just one between every two rooms. I know Portis has communal bathrooms though."

Nate stepped out of one of the rooms with a drawstring bag on his back. "Hey, I'm headed to the gym," he said to Ethan as he held the door to 341 Kessler Hall open for us. I gave him a nod and squeezed past the construction-paper tree and stocking with 'Ethan' and 'Nathan' taped to the door.

"He doesn't wanna go see your performance like a good supportive roommate?" I asked in a low voice.

"We're just roommates, not *friends*. Besides, he never misses gym nights."

"Really?" I frowned. "He looks like a nerd."

He laughed through his nose. "You'll change your mind if you ever see him without a shirt on." *Nothing like a good sleeper build—which means the side of the room with the protein powder probably isn't Ethan's side.* Each resident has a wardrobe instead of a built-in closet, and Ethan cluttered the side of his with Post-It notes, a smudged whiteboard, and a tiny British flag. Some of his dirty clothes hadn't made it into his laundry bag yet, which lives under his bed that's raised as high as it can go and that looks like it's never been made. "Don't judge," he said. Our eyes met for a second, which was long enough for me to see his flushed face. "I'm waiting until I go home to do laundry."

"I'm not judging," I said as I took in the details of his space, which helped me ease up a little. Pictures of pop artists and video game characters and foreign landmarks that he either printed out or tore out of magazines fill in the space between his posters on the white cinder block walls above his bed. The black wire memo board on his desk is clipped with photos of his pre-NHU life, propped up behind a desktop computer setup and a ring light. "Do you not have a laptop?" I asked, just then realizing that I've never seen him with one.

"I do, but it's just a Chromebook," he said to his desktop. "I just use this for gaming, but I don't get around to it too much. I didn't think I'd be keeping myself so busy when I moved in," he chuckled.

"That just means you're staying involved," I said as I walked over to the window to see campus from his POV. *How many times has he seen me walk past on my way to Main Street?*

Ethan opened the door to his shared bathroom after giving it a knock. The toilet and shower each have their own private rooms separate from the main one with the sinks and cabinets. "I like never see the two in the other room," he said as he nodded over to the other door. "The one's literally never here, and the other's *super* shy. He always waits until he hears us shut our door before he comes in." He let out an exhale. "It's kinda disappointing, because I imagined the four of us being best friends and everything."

"Are either of them waffle stompers?" I asked.

He stopped tapping his finger on the doorframe to turn and squint at me. "Waffle *what?*"

"Waffle stompers," I repeated with a stupid grin. "You know, somebody who shits in the shower and stomps it down the—"

"*Oh my god,* I'm gonna throw up!" He paced circles around the room to calm himself down. "I *hope* to god they're not! I'm never gonna be able to—oh my *god.*" He made a sound like a mix between a laugh and a gag. "Are you hungry? Do you want any chips or anything?" He slid a plastic tote out from under his bed to reveal a cache of junk food and PopTarts and ramen.

"No thanks."

He took a snack cake and hopped up on his bed. He motioned to his shirt-draped chair. "You can sit," he invited me. I did, running my hands back and forth along the armrests as the seconds stretched on. *Here it comes, here it comes, here it comes.* He bounced his leg as he wolfed down a bite of the cake. "So first of all, I shouldn't have just up and kissed you like that," he said. "I'm sorry I—"

"Why, was it that bad?" I joked to stifle my anxiety.

"No," he chuckled. "No, it was...better than I ever imagined."

I frowned. "Wait, better than you ever—*what?*" *Is he saying what I think he's saying?*

"I'm *saying* that kissing you in real life was better than all the times I thought about it," he spelled it out for me as a smile broke across his face. "And I've thought about it *a lot.*"

"But wait," I screwed up my face, "aren't you straight?"

He laughed as he fell back onto his mattress. "I'm gay too, Trevor," he said, sitting up as he ran his hands down his face. I glitched, his words flashing across my mind so rapidly that they almost gave me an epileptic episode. "I'm gay as *shit.*"

I swallowed. *This can't be real life.* "You—you *can't* be gay."

"Can't I?" he raised an eyebrow.

"You don't act gay," I said stupidly.

"Oh *please.* Do *you* act gay?"

"Since when though?" *He must be seeing somebody—that's why he apologized for kissing me.*

He chuckled. "I guess since always?"

I blinked. *I still can't believe this.* "Why haven't you ever told me?"

He shrugged. "Probably the same reason you never told me. Because we've both been through shit because of it, or we've been accused of being gay before we even knew it ourselves, and it's just easier for us if we let people think we're what they expect us to be." *Yeah, no straight guy could say that.* "Plus, I was afraid you'd be weirded out by me if you found out."

"That's why I didn't want *you* to know that *I* was!" I exclaimed. "But why not tell Kade or Victor though? You were afraid that *they* of all people wouldn't be okay with you being gay?"

"I was worried they'd tell you," he shrugged.

"But you used to have a girlfriend though, didn't you? And what about the girl who you said would come in for coffee all the time who you thought was hot?"

"I just said all that so people would think I was straight."

"People being me," I said more than asked.

"Not *just* you, but yeah."

"Well, it worked," I said, still in disbelief about everything.

He let his legs swing off the side, his bare ankles visible. "I had a feeling *you* were gay until I saw you and Amina kiss at that party."

My face flushed. "I was wondering if you saw that."

He nodded. "I did, and I felt so...*crestfallen*. Like, you'd been charming me for a month, and in that moment I thought I'd never get to have you. I wanted so *badly* to be in her place. I was so upset that I left after that. I just came back here and cried in bed."

I got up to sit on his bed beside him, sad that I'd made him feel so bad that he spent a Saturday night crying in bed. "I'm sorry I made you feel that way," I said. "It was probably a good thing you left though, because I went from 100 to 0 *real* fast," I chuckled. "But even if kissing her *did* get me hard, I could've still been bi—which I'm *not*." I put my hand down in the space between us, hoping he'd do the same. "But *wait*, what about when Kade and I kissed?"

He looked at me like I'd just called him the f-word. "You and *Kade* kissed?! *When?*"

"When we played Drunk *Jenga* in Amina's room. *That* was on a dare too! You didn't see that and think I was gay?"

"I do *not* remember that."

"Maybe it was after you left. But yeah, that was why he and Will stopped seeing each other."

"Kade's gay too?"

"He's either bi or pan or poly. But all the times you saw the two of them together, you never thought anything of it?"

"I just thought they were buddy-buddy," he shrugged.

I laughed. "And I thought *my* gaydar was shit."

"*Okay,*" Ethan drawled out, "but even if I *was* there to see that, you kissing him was still on a *dare* though. It sure would've made me even more jealous though."

"Jealous of me or of Kade?"

"Oh my god, are you even here for this conversation?" he laughed as he buried his face in his hands. "Trevor, the first time you and Victor came into Starbucks, I couldn't stop checking you out. I had to get away from the frontline when your drink was ready because I wasn't sure I'd be able to speak to you." *Ethan? Afraid to talk to me?* "But then the next time you came in I talked myself up to try to go talk to you. You have no idea how nervous I was," he grinned sheepishly.

"*You?* You don't know how nervous *I* was!"

"I'd always check out guys who came in, but you were the person I was the most excited to see stop in." His hand millimetered closer to mine. "And I didn't stop to see you at work—as much as I wanted to—because I didn't wanna weird you out if you weren't gay, or look like I was trying too hard."

"So just to confirm," I blinked, "you've liked me this whole time?"

"*Yeah.* You've been living in my head rent-free," he laughed as his hand found the top of mine. His fingers laced between my own, and I swear little cartoon hearts and leaves blew past like in *Heartstopper*.

And then I started to laugh, because there was no way that our conversation could actually be happening. "I just—this can't—*how* is this real? *How* can the guy I've been crushing *so hard* on be telling me he's been crushing on *me* too?"

"I don't know!" he grinned. "It's crazy, isn't it?"

"So just to be clear, we've both been keeping *the same secret* from each other because we were too afraid that we'd scare the other away? And we somehow thought *that* would get us together?"

He nodded. "Sounds about right."

I slapped my hand over my eyes. "Why are we like this?"

"Didn't we just go over that?" he laughed.

"So...are you seeing anybody?" I asked slowly, wild over what his answer would be.

He bumped his foot against mine and squeezed my hand in his. "Nope. Are you?"

"Nope," I said. My heart was beating so hard I thought it would explode. We shifted ourselves so we could look into each other's eyes and we kissed, a kiss without any confusion or alarm—the volcanoes were still going off in my chest though—just a mutual, unearthed wanting that felt so, so, right. *Still not convinced this is real life though.* He laid a hand on my collarbone and I rested mine on his leg as we showed our true feelings for each other.

"Is it just me," I stopped to say, "or are you hard too?"

I felt him smile. "I might be."

My insides somersaulted. "Wanna take advantage of Nate being at the gym?"

"I'd *love* to. But I have a song to perform, remember?"

"Oh *shit!*" I pulled back and looked for the time. "I totally forgot! Do we have to go like right now?"

"We have a few minutes," he said. He leaned back on his bed, smiling, inviting me to join. *Okay, maybe it is real life,* I thought as we just laid there together. *Still not sure how, but I'm not gonna argue with it.* "And also," he said when it was time to go, "I'm not out to anybody other than a couple of people. I never even told Nate, but he'd have to be pretty dumb to come back to the room to find me and another guy in here with the door shut and not think anything of it." *How many other guys has he had in here?*

"Say no more," I promised him.

We couldn't even make it out of the building without me wanting to feel his hand in mine again. Brew 22 was filling up fast, which made me wonder how many people *actually* went home for Break a day early. I got myself a slice of warm apple strudel with a scoop of vanilla ice cream while Ethan took his keyboard from its bag and set it up next to some exotic-looking instruments that were already there. I physically couldn't go more than five seconds without looking over at him. *So what's gonna happen now? Are we gonna become friends with benefits? What if it turns into something else? Am I ready for that again?*

Nikole showed up first, followed by Victor and Kade, and then Tylor and Amina, who all got in line for coffees or desserts. "How're you doing?" Victor checked in on me once it was just the two of us and his white peppermint mocha. "You seem like you're in a better mood now."

I nodded, grinning like an idiot. "Yeah, I'm good now." *So, so good.*

After an Improv Club skit, a folk song by Acoustic Guitar Guy that hit like a canticle, a Tiny Tim song with uncanny vocals, and a few forgettable acts later, Ethan was finally up. "Thank you," he said as a few people clapped for him. "I hope everyone's okay with me toning it down a little from last time." Somebody whooped from their table. "This is a Chainsmokers song, but it might not be one you know." He brushed his hair away from his forehead. "Can you dim the lights a bit?" he asked someone at the back of the room. "Thanks. This is 'Bloodstream.'"

And he began to play—slow piano notes rose from his dancing fingers, and he sang his words whole and undecorated. The slow, definite drums joined in from his phone before the piano notes turned into rising synth notes that squeezed us with their piping voices. I'd heard the song before, but it hit different in light of the conversation we'd just had in his room. The song may have been toned down, but the applause certainly wasn't. "Thank you all so much," he told the patrons. "You make this so fun for me. Have a good Break, good luck with Finals, and I'll see you all next semester!"

As good as he was though, Sunita and a few of her friends performing traditional Indian music blew him out of the water. I thought I knew what evocative music was, but *holy shit*. It sounded like how a cup of masala chai tastes. *"Gurl!"* Kade fake-called to the stage through a cupped hand. "Fuck the caste system! Holla at ya boy!"

We drew our Secret Santa names after the show ended, since it was the last time we'd all be together before heading back home. We wrote our names on torn-up pieces of notebook paper and dropped them into Victor's hat, redrawing names until we each had somebody else's. I looked down at Victor's name looped in his own cursive handwriting and scanned the table for any clues of who ended up with mine.

We were deciding on a dollar limit when somebody walking past our table did a double take and 180'ed back towards us.

"Holy *shit*," they said. "Kaden *Oakley*?"

Kade's head snapped up and his mouth fell open. "No *fucking* way. *Alex*?" He jumped to his feet and they embraced like long-lost siblings. "What are you doing here?"

"I *go* here," Alex laughed.

"I thought you went to Penn State!"

"I did for a year, and then I transferred. But look at you!" He reached up to ruffle Kade's hair. "Little Kadey's in college now!"

"Shouldn't you have graduated already though? You and Kelsey were in the same grade."

"I picked up a double-major, so I'm in my super-senior year now." His smile only widened when he noticed Victor sitting there. "No way! You go here too?"

"*Somebody's* gotta keep an eye on this kid," he smiled as the two of them slapped hands. "What it do! I don't think I've seen you since Kelsey's grad party!"

"I've just been living it up as much as I can, while I can," Alex smiled. "That's *awesome* that you two are still sticking together. Props to your friends for being able to put up with both of you," he chuckled as he looked around the table at us.

"Oh yeah," Kade said like he forgot we were there. "Everyone, this is Alex. He and our sister Kelsey were friends in high school." He went around with our names and Alex gave us all a wave.

"You can play *really* fucking well," Alex said to Ethan just as Acoustic Guitar Guy appeared at his side. "This is my housemate Matt," Alex told us. "Real name Matthias, which he *hates*, so please call him that as much as you can. Matt, these are Kelsey's little brothers and their friends."

"I don't hate it nearly as much as Alex hates being called Alejandro," Matt grinned.

Alex winced. "He's not wrong."

We introduced ourselves to Matt, and Alex caught up with Kade and Victor for a few moments as the place emptied out. "Here, lemme give you my number," he told the two of them before he and Matt left. "Our place is always open if you ever need somewhere to turn up."

Kade's eyes lingered on the door after they'd left. "What are the fucking chances?" he chuckled.

I offered to help Ethan carry his things back to his room as the rest of us got up to leave. "*You're just hoping to get a kiss*," he whispered with a grin.

"*It's possible*," I smirked back.

I grabbed some McDonald's to take back to Ethan's room since I hadn't had any real food since breakfast, while the others just headed back to the dorms. "Have a good Break if I don't see you again," I bid them farewell before Ethan and I split for the Golden Arches. The Skeletons were already having their own Thanksgiving dinner in their yard, seated around a folding table set with plates and a candelabra and all. *I'd literally rather eat dinner with skeletons than with my own family.*

I was disappointed to see that Nate was back in 341 Kessler, gaming with some friends on his Xbox. Ethan and I talked like we didn't wanna make out with each other as I ate. I wanted to stay as long as I could, but the longer I stayed, the longer I'd have to fight keeping my hands off him. "I guess I'll get going," I finally resigned with a weak smile. "I probably won't see you tomorrow, so I hope you have a good Thanksgiving."

"Here, I'll walk you out," he smiled like it was the last time we'd see each other. I followed him down the empty hallway to the cold stairwell, where he turned and hugged me on a landing. "I hope you have a good Break too," he smiled, his eyes looking deep into mine. "I'll be thinking about you the whole time."

"So will I," I said as I leaned in to kiss him. It would be less than a week before I saw him again, but he felt as essential to me as water all of a sudden, as essential as air. And that scares the hell out of me, because I know the risks of giving too much of myself too quickly to another person, and I told myself I'd never let it happen again.

November 24

Thanksgiving's pretty mid when you think about it. You just sit around and eat and it's supposed to be this great thing. I think everybody goes hard for Thanksgiving to distract themselves from how white people exterminated the Native Americans, but you can't talk about that or else your conservative relatives will say you're just trying to erase our great American history. I don't know why we can't make it through *one* family gathering without somebody getting political. Forreal though, what is it with cishet, white, conservative men not being able to just shut the hell up? Like what, do you think repeating some bullshit you heard on the 'real' news channel is all of a sudden going to convince me that I'm wrong about all the conclusions I've drawn on my own? Imagine all the shit *I'd* get if *I* said out loud whatever was on *my* mind. I guess your thoughts aren't valid if you're younger than everybody else at the table. And this is all on top of hearing that an English degree isn't good for anything unless I either want to be an unemployed editor or make $20,000 a year. So yeah, it was a fucking blast. At least my hair isn't purple anymore. Also, isn't gluttony supposed to be a sin?

I try not to do the whole '*I'm grateful for*' thing on Thanksgiving because I've learned that being grateful should just be part of your mentality instead of one single day of reflecting on it. But I think the other half of being thankful that people forget about is to be mindful that nothing's a promise, and anything can be taken away from you without even a moment's notice.

November 25

I wish I'd gotten the stick out of my ass sooner and downloaded Snapchat a while ago, because I could've been seeing pics of Ethan and what he's up to this whole time. I can't put anything on my story without wondering if he'll like it or think it's stupid, but my chest still jolts every time I see that he's viewed it. We've been Snapping each other on top of texting each other, but I can't wait until we're back at school so I can see him in person again.

It's weird to think how inseparable Logan and Madi and I used to be, and how I've been going months without seeing them, a week without texting them, or a day without them crossing my mind. I guess that's just the way life works, but that doesn't mean I wasn't thrilled to see them both again. The three of us gave Black Friday a big middle finger by having Friendsgiving at Madi's place, getting all fat and sassy off of leftovers.

"Promise me you won't *ever* take home-cooked food for granted," I said to Logan as we committed gluttony.

"Like, I'd probably slit someone's throat to get my hands on a walnut tart like this on campus," Madi said as she helped herself to another eighth of her mom's specialty.

"That's what you get for leaving me here all by my lonesome," Logan said as he folded his hands over his stomach.

"Transfer somewhere!" Madi said.

"Not all of us can just afford to up and go to a real school, *Madison*. Though I *have* been thinking about it."

"Where've you been looking?"

"Nowhere yet," he shrugged. "I just said I've been thinking about it."

I tried to steer the conversation to school stuff that we could all relate to. Madi said she's already pulled two all-nighters, which is asinine to think about—though that's coming from somebody who's content with just being a B-student, which probably isn't the best attitude to have if it's costing me five figures. Logan's community college classes are all over the place: he claims that his Psychology instructor makes you write a 14-page paper if you miss a test, but then the Midterm

208

for his American Government class was a crossword puzzle in Comic Sans font. "So tell me about all the boys you two've been seeing," he asked us.

"Well, there's this one guy who's been staying in my room almost every night," I said.

Madi's jaw dropped. "Shut up!"

Logan just gave me a look. "Other than your *roommate*, asshole." Madi backhanded my arm.

"Okay, *okay*," I said once I stopped giggling. "Forreal though, it turns out my one friend who I've had a crush on is gay. *And* he's been crushing on me too."

Madi grinned like Christmas had come early. "Give us the *deets!* So are you dating, or hooking up, or what?"

"All we did was kiss a couple of times! And I mean *literally* a couple. Well, three times, actually."

"Do you think you two'll start going out?"

"I dunno. I don't know if I'm ready for another relationship yet, but I also literally can't stop thinking about him."

"Are they on Instagram?" Logan asked.

"Yeah, here." I pulled up Ethan's profile and let him scroll.

"Okay, yeah, he's good-looking," my lowercase-s straight friend admitted as he passed Madi my phone.

"Oh, *Trevor*," she said from behind her hand. "Oh *damn*."

I couldn't not smile. "I know, right?"

"I'm actually *jealous*. I think I need to send him a follow."

I took my phone back. "What about you? Have you found yourself a man yet?"

She looked like she didn't know how to answer. "I mean, there was one guy I was seeing for a hot second, but it wasn't anything serious. I just don't wanna be tied to someone while I'm in college." *Just like what Dillon told me.*

"What about you?" I gave Logan an up-nod. "Any guys you're seeing?"

"Ha ha, *no*. And I'm not seeing any girls either. *Although*," he said after a moment, "there *is* this one girl I sit next to in Sociology. We're not *together* or anything, but we grabbed something to eat after class once. That's about it."

The rest of the afternoon and evening saw us sprawled across couches and recliners in agony, watching Christmas movie after Christmas movie. *"Gauges?"* Kade captioned his story of four colorful pairs of new gauges. *"More like GAY-ges! *sob*"*

209

November 27

The weather here in New Halle feels like a warm Spring day compared to the shit back home. It snowed *all day* yesterday—the perfect kind of day for stove-top s'mores and a nine-hour game of *Axis & Allies* with Logan.

Madi and I went to the mall this morning before I left since I still hadn't gotten a Secret Santa gift for Victor. Between the place being a fucking anthill, not knowing what to get him, my coat making me too warm, and my coat also being bulky enough to be too inconvenient to carry, you could say I was kind of testy.

"Well, what kind of stuff does he like?" Madi asked me.

I stopped in my tracks. "Oh my god, you're a genius! And here I was trying to think of all the stuff he *doesn't* like!" She waited until some asshole kids ran between us to smack me. "I dunno. He's into music—he actually plays the drums—he likes outer space, board games, video games, women's rights, gay rights, human rights in general." I told her about how he tells people his pronouns, all his shirts, and how he shouted down that asshole's asshole with the bible in the Quad. "He legit might be the most progressive person I know."

"I like this Victor guy already," Madi smiled.

"Go send him a follow! But just as long as you all don't start hanging out without me." So that's how Madi came to be Instagram moots with Victor, and Kade after I told her about him.

"Yeah, he seems like a good egg," she said as she scrolled through Victor's posts.

"Speak of the devil and he shall appear," I said as a Snap from Victor came through of him wearing an artificial wreath on his head. *'This is what jesus wore when they crucified him,'* he captioned it.

We found ourselves in that store that sells calendars and games, a few of which I recognized thanks to Kade and Victor's game room. "This one looks like it could be fun," I said as I read the back of one called *Machi Koro*, which was all it took for the overzealous employee who overheard me to fly into a commercial about the game. His description of it as *"Monopoly* meets *Sim City* but in a card game" sold me out of curiosity more than anything. I found Victor's gift there too—a jigsaw puzzle celebrating trailblazing Black women in American history. I'm not sure how much he enjoys puzzles, but he'll love it for the content.

"Peep my new game," I captioned the Snap I sent Kade of *Machi Koro*.

"👀👀 my dick *hard* rn," he Snapped back.

November 28

I wonder if anyone's ever tried to make a perpetual motion machine out of a motion-activated water fountain, like a gigantic one with a water wheel under it? I can't be the first person who's ever had this idea.

I figured Dr. Padar just wanted an extra-long Break when she sent an email to the whole class saying that Computers was canceled for the day, but then Dr. Eubanks emailed us all saying that Physical Science was canceled too, and *then* Dr. Conrad emailed us the same thing about Critical Writing. *What the eff?* "So...all of my classes are canceled today?" I called to Tylor through the bathroom door.

"Yeah, samesies," he called back. "It's the first weekend of deer hunting season, and I guess enough people skip class to take a long weekend to go hunting that the profs just don't have class sometimes." I felt myself scowl. *What kind of redneck fuck part of the country do we live in?*

"So what I'm hearing," Victor said a little while later as he sat backwards in my chair, "is that we could've stayed home another day before coming back?"

"What you *meant* to say," I said as I brewed some mugs of ginger peach tea, "is that you're glad to have a free day to hang out with us, right?"

"I don't know how people can shoot deer for fun," Ethan said. "Do you know how desperate I'd have to be to kill another animal? I don't even like the idea of fishing."

"I'll throw a tantrum right now if we don't start playing," Kade threatened from the floor in front of an unboxed *Machi Koro*.

We played a couple games, passing dice and plastic coins like we couldn't hold onto them. It was a struggle to sit next to Ethan and keep my hands and mouth off him, but I 'accidentally' bumped his foot with mine a few times. "Did you know that 'machi koro' means 'dice town' in Japanese?" I asked Tylor like a know-it-all.

"I actually did *not*," my bemused roommate said.

Kade grabbed his phone to fact-check me. "No it *doesn't*," he frowned.

"That's what the guy in the store told me!" I said, though I knew I was fucked.

"Well the guy in the store's full of shit. It says right here it means '*around* town,'" he said as he shoved his phone in my face for me to see.

Unfortunately, not having to go to class didn't mean not having to go to work. It was extra hard to pull myself up off the floor to go knowing that the others—Ethan in particular—would stay and keep playing or doing whatever without me. "You guys don't have to wait for me to get done to go get dinner," I said glumly.

"Oh, we weren't going to," Kade said matter-of-factly. My phone buzzed a moment later, and a text from Ethan saying **I'll wait to eat with you** ☺ warmed my chest.

Rosenberg was packed with students. I don't know if people used their surprise free day to catch up on everything they slacked on over Break or what, but I was so busy loading printer paper and putting away books that I was barely able to get any of my own studying done. My heart leapt when I saw Ethan coming over to the desk before the end of my shift. "I figured I'd just wait here for you so we could go eat from here," he smiled. Those last minutes *dragged*, especially when I'd glance over at the periodicals and catch him looking over at me.

"Did you hang out with the others that whole time?" I asked as we headed for Subway.

"Pretty much. We played some more *Machi Koro* and then chilled in their room."

"I wish I had a room like theirs that you could chill in," I said with a smile that he returned.

"I wish you did too."

We ate our subs in a booth by the window. The wreaths on the Main Street lamp posts made it feel like a town out of a Hallmark movie. "Did you have a good Break?" I asked him.

"Yeah, it wasn't bad. My mom and stepdad were surprisingly pretty good. But the rest of my family couldn't keep their mouths shut at dinner and kept pissing me off."

I rolled my eyes. "Say no more."

He looked up at me with a smile. "I couldn't wait to get back and see you," he said in a low voice.

"Yeah, me neither," I smiled back as I bumped his foot under the table. "Remind me why we ate here instead of taking these back to your room?"

"Because Nate will be—*wait*, hold on." He screwed up his face. "It's *Monday*, not *Sunday!* It feels like a Sunday because we didn't have class. He should be at the gym!" He turned back at me. "So to answer your question, I don't know."

We carried our wrapped-up sandwiches to Kessler like we were being followed. Nate was already back from the gym, so we had to sit and finish our food like bros. I was about to say how I wish I had my Switch with me when Ethan asked me if I wanted to go play pinball in the rec room. "Your rec room has a *pinball machine?*" I asked.

"Don't do it, man," Nate warned me. "He's too good at it. You'll just be standing there watching."

I eagerly followed Ethan down to the ground floor, but he strode right past the rec room. "What—?"

"Follow me," he said quietly. *Hella* confused, I trailed him past the front doors, past the DA watching something on their phone, down the hallway on the opposite side of the lobby, to a door with a plastic plaque beside it that read 'House Council.' He looked left and then right as he swiped his ID to get us in, holding onto the door handle as it shut to keep it from making noise. "Don't turn the light on," he told me, which was when I figured out what was up. Between the narrow window in the door and the large windows on the far wall, there was enough secondhand light for me to make out the rectangular table and the half-dozen-or-so chairs around it, but dark enough that no spying eyes could discern anything inside. He pulled me into the corner and held me close. We looked into faces we could barely see. His hand found the back of my neck, and mine found his chest. We moved our heads together and kissed like we weren't sure how to do it.

"Can't the other House Council members get in here too?" I breathed.

His whisper warmed my cheek. "Let's hope they have better things to do." He made a space between my jeans and my underwear and filled it with his fingers. His joggers let me feel everything. The fear of being caught vanished as we grew. *Walking in on two guys making out in the dark is understandable, right?* I put my hands in his pants and pushed them down. I got to my knees, my fingers grasping the band of his underwear.

"Is this okay?"

"It's more than okay."

They caught on him as I pulled them down. I laid my hands on his groin to guide my mouth. "Ohhh," I heard from above. I went slowly, rhythmically, my tongue leaving him wanting nothing. He stroked, clawed at, my hair. "Wait." He withdrew. "Are you okay with swallowing?"

The mere thought of him shooting in my mouth made me ooze. "Fuck yeah." I went back to it, my head pumping like it was on a piston. My hands felt his stomach, ran up and down his thighs, grabbed his butt. My fist intensified the sensation for him. He started to sway, pushing to meet my mouth. His stifled noises made me relentless.

"Oh shit," he whimpered. He stopped swaying. He started pulsing. He shot the back of my throat. He grabbed my shoulders for support as I milked him.

"How was that?" I asked between kisses.

"Hot as fuck," he said into my teeth. *Can he taste himself on me?*

"I almost came just from doing that."

"Now that wouldn't have been fair." He pivoted our positions, pinning me to the wall with his hands and his body and his face. He knelt down and undid my belt, exposing me. He ran his fist up and down my length.

"Mmm. Yeah." His sudden warmth made me gasp. Breathless, I fell against the wall. My fingers raked his hair. *He's definitely done this before.* I gently rocked back and forth, forward and back. *And he knows what to do with his hands too.* "Do you want mine too?"

He sucked, panting as he pulled off. "You don't even know." He engulfed me again. I met him over and over. I felt like I was floating. Ethan making my fantasies real brought me to my boiling point, and I had to keep myself from collapsing. I tasted something on his tongue that wasn't there before. We pressed our foreheads together and I felt his face smile. *"Oh shit,"* he breathed breathlessly.

"I know, right?" I chuckled. *"God, you're so good at that."*

"You don't know how many times I've thought about that."

"Probably no less than I have."

We stood in the corner of the office and held each other in the uncharted territory we were discovering together. *What if it happens again? And then again after that?* Behind his head, I saw a shadow pass across the window in the door as somebody went past. "We should probably get out of here before another hornt-up couple has the same idea," I murmured.

"So what, we're a couple now?" he joked, making me glitch. *Yes.*

Wait, no I don't want that.

I'd love to be a couple with him.

I'm afraid to do it again though.

I so wish we were a couple.

But you could get hurt again.

Ethan wouldn't hurt me.

That's what you said about Dillon.

He peeped the hallway before opening the door. He led us to the lobby, stopping at the front doors. "Oh wait, I forgot your stuff's still up in my room," he laughed to himself.

I raised an eyebrow at him. "Wait, so we're not gonna pinball?"

He raised an eyebrow back. "Do you really want to?"

"Yeah? Why do you think I was so eager to get down here?"

Nate wasn't kidding about Ethan being good at pinball. I spent less time playing than I did watching him play, but I enjoyed watching *him* more—the way he sticks out the tip of his tongue when he concentrates, his wicked smile when he saves himself from losing. His eyes would flit over to me for just long enough for him to mess up.

After I'd satisfied my pinball fix—most of my plays ended with my ball going right down the middle between the fluttering flippers—we went back up to get my stuff and made out in the privacy of the stairwell for as long as we dared. I looked back through Kessler's front doors as I walked off to see him watching me from inside, and I couldn't not grin at him. He smiled back, so hard that he looked like he was laughing. I gave him a wave. He waved back. I blew him a kissy face. He blew one back, making my chest fizzle as a whirlwind of cartoon leaves and hearts swirled at my feet.

November 29

Remember when I said how college lets you do you, and how professors don't care what you do? Today the girl who sits next to me in Brit Lit brought a box of fake hands into class with her. I couldn't stop looking at it.

I was today-years-old when I let somebody from NHU read one of my stories for the first time, and that somebody was Ethan. I emailed him the one I just finished about the parasite in the glacier and all I can think about is if he'll like it or if he'll think it's dumb.

Since it was the last one before the holidays, Ashton brought Christmas, Hanukkah, and Kwanzaa cookies to Lit Club, which I thought was pretty cool, even though I doubt any of us WASPs celebrate Kwanzaa. We debated what the best pangram is before deeming 'sphinx of black quartz, judge my vow' the winner, and 'waltz, bad nymph, for quick jigs vex' as runner-up.

"So did we bore Branden away?" I joked with Miles.

"Oh, no," he said seriously. "We're not seeing each other anymore."

My hand found my mouth. "Oh shit, I'm sorry."

"It's alright," Miles said glumly. "Really, it is. Our personalities clashed, and we don't share the same interests."

"Well, I hope you end up finding somebody with interests and a personality that don't clash with yours, if you're after something serious."

"Thanks, but I'm not sure if I am."

Not wanting to make him dwell on it, I said, "So I told my friend what we talked about last time. Everything's good." *Better than good.*

He smiled. "I'm glad to hear it!"

Nikole gave me a curious look, and I couldn't hold it in. "Ethan didn't know I'm gay," I explained. "I was nervous how he'd react, but he's cool with it."

"How did he not know you're gay?" she asked. "Has he ever *met* you?"

I defensively closed my Mac. "What's *that* supposed to mean?"

"You kind of stare at guys all the time is what I mean," she chuckled.

My face must've been as red as the icing on the cookies. "I do not!"

"Oh yes you do," Miles chuckled as he got up for another cookie.

"I actually feel like Ethan's the one I see you checking out the most," Nikole said before laughing to herself. "Wouldn't it be a vibe if he was gay too and secretly liked you back?"

215

December 1

So I think I was abducted by aliens this morning. My alarm went off, and then my second alarm went off right after it—I mean like *immediately* after it—and people who've said they were abducted by aliens always cite an unexplainable lapse in time, so yeah.

All I could think about all day yesterday and today was what Ethan thought of my story. I had to keep talking myself out of asking him if he'd read it yet, and thankfully he didn't keep me waiting when I stopped for bubble tea.

"So I finished your story last night," he said flatly as he started on my drink.

My chest quaked. "And?" I asked as casually as possible.

His face broke into a smile. "I *loved* it."

I lit up. "You did?"

"Yep," he grinned. "Read the whole thing in one sitting."

I narrowed my eyes. "Are you just saying that because..?" *Because we had our dicks in each other's mouths?*

"No, I liked it because you're a good storyteller."

My unconvinced arms folded themselves across my chest. "What'd you like about it?"

"My favorite part was the premise. I feel like there's never a focus on things as they're falling apart, and your story has that. It's a perspective that I feel a lot of zombie movies miss." *Catch me, for I'm swooning.*

"Well, thanks," was all I could say. "I'm happy to hear you liked it."

"No, thank *you* for letting me read it. I know it was an exercise in vulnerability for you." And then after a moment, "I really think other people would enjoy it."

I broke our eye contact. "I've thought about maybe submitting them to *Crane*, the student-run magazine that—"

"You should! Like in parts? You could always even do it anonymously if you'd—"

"No," I shook my head. "I'd want people to know who wrote it. But I've read some of the stuff in it, and I feel like I'm not good enough for it though. It seems too cool and artsy for me."

"I mean, you could always still *try*. The worst they'll do is say they won't publish it."

"Maybe," I said vaguely.

"Well, I won't keep bugging you about it," he said as he sealed my drink shut. "What are you up to later on?"

"Nothing, I don't think. But I know Victor has Improv Club, and—"

"I didn't ask what *Victor's* doing," he smiled. "I asked what *you're* doing."

"Oh," my eyebrows jumped up. "Nothing then. Why?"

"I was gonna ask if you wanted to come over and play *Mario* or something," he said as he shook my drink, swirling the ice and boba into a cyclone. "You'll have to bring your Switch though."

"It sucks that Nate will be there."

He smiled, his tongue sitting behind his teeth like it was ready to pounce. "He won't. Thursday's gym day too."

"Mmkay," I bobbed my head with a face-splitting grin. *Well* then."

I bounced across campus with Nintendo's most popular home console and a handful of condoms—you never know!—stuffed into my backpack without even noticing the cold. *I'm gonna be alone with the guy I like who likes me back.* My mind explored all the ways the night could go until I found myself in the inviting glow of Kessler's front windows.

"Hey," he grinned as he let me in. He looked extra huggable in the red Gryffindor sweatshirt he bought the day the line between dreams and reality blurred. "Nate hasn't left yet, so we'll have to play for a bit," he said as the stairwell echoed our footsteps.

"What else would we do?" I asked like I didn't know.

His smile tempted me. "There's this other thing I had in mind."

I stole a kiss while I could before Nate came back with his clean laundry. It felt like it took him forever to throw on some running tights and some outerwear before he finally left. We played for a bit in case he came back for anything, until Ethan paused the game, closed the door, and even checked that the bathroom door was locked. I pulled the curtains closed and turned to see him beaming at me with those eyes. "Well *hello*," he smiled as he took my arms.

"How's it going?" I smirked.

We took our time, savoring each other like we were the most expensive thing on the menu. I caressed his shoulder, his arm, his cheek, his leg, his dick. *"Mmmm,"* he purred into my mouth, feeling me all over. He pulled away to take me onto his bed. On top of him, I slid a hand up his sweatshirt, over the knob in his joggers. It was a good thing we didn't get around to taking anything off yet, because we had about two seconds between hearing Nate punching himself in at the door and being walked in on. I flew off of Ethan, who forcefully shoved a pillow into my useless hands.

"I hope I'm not interrupting anything," Nate laughed uneasily. "Why's the door shut?"

"Oh," Ethan replied as he caught his breath, "we had an impromptu pillow fight because *somebody* was upset that I keep winning," he said as he met my eyes. "And I shut the door because I didn't want Conor to see us playing and invite himself in."

Nate just nodded. "That's fair."

"Is the gym closed or something? You weren't gone for too long."

He dropped his bag at the foot of his bed. "Yeah, there was actually a gas leak."

Ethan and I kept on playing like our parents were in the room with us. I didn't let myself stay disappointed though, because I still got to spend time with the boy I like. Nate didn't prop the door back open out of consideration for us. "Do you wanna go get a drink from the vending machine?" I asked Ethan, who smirked a little when he saw me wink.

"Yeah, I could go for a drink," he said as he grabbed his slides. We breezed right past the rec room and shut ourselves in the House Council office again.

"Where'd you go for a drink, Sheetz?" Nate chuckled when we got back to 341 Kessler.

"I was showing Trevor the House Council room," Ethan answered truthfully.

I was on autopilot when we resumed playing. *This feels like more than just hooking up. I have something with him that I didn't have with Miles and certainly not with Devon, though I did have it with Dillon—and where that could lead to scares me. It can't just be hooking up.* I finally packed up my stuff and Ethan walked me out. "What are you doing this weekend?" he asked in the stairwell between kisses.

I smirked. "Just me, or the others?"

"Either," he shrugged. "We can still hang with them, but we don't have to stay with them all night."

"True. I dunno. I *might* be able to tolerate the smell of alcohol again by now."

"Well either way, we can always just hang with them and then sneak off," he said with a sly grin.

I nodded like a simp. "I'd be okay with that." We kissed again before he let go of my hands that I don't remember him grabbing.

I tried not to groan out loud when Tylor came back to 222 Swafford and said he'd been working on a group project in Rosenberg all evening.

December 3

The what: time travel. The how: going to the North or South Pole and walking in circles around it. Would you *actually* go back in time? Probably not. But would you *technically* though? I don't *know*. That's why we need to be funding this stuff.

I met Ethan and Kade for a Patnick lunch and scanned the police blotter in *The Herald* while I waited for them. The highlight of the week was somebody's parent calling the police for a wellness check because their kid wasn't answering their texts or calls and they ended up just being asleep. Ethan and I managed to wear the friends-who-haven't-been-making-out-in-private look until he had to head to his last class of the day, though Kade was too busy complaining about his own Computers class that he probably wouldn't have even noticed. "Nothing makes me wanna gouge out my eyes more than that *travesty* of a class," he grumbled. "Like, I fucking *know* how to make a pivot table!"

Amina invited us over for drinks and games in 348 Walcott last night but told us we had to supply our own mixers, which I was fine with because I was planning on making a run to the store anyway to get some stuff for the room even though I'll be back home in two week's time—which, how the hell is it the end of the semester already? We got to meet Amina's roommate Kasey—the one who was in Cali over the Summer—and I eagerly listened to her stories about how the traffic is worse than you could ever imagine, the June Gloom, how tourists are the only ones who wear shorts, how the grass is all dead, how every meal comes with avocados on the side, how it smells like weed everywhere. "L.A.'s okay, but San Diego's the most gorgeous place I've ever been to," she told me.

I ran my hands down my face. "*Ugh*, I wanna go so *bad*."

"Tell me about it," Amina pined alongside me. "Let's take a trip there. Just the three of us. We'll post pics of us being fabulous."

I hadn't had anything to drink since that glow stick party almost a month ago, but just because I haven't had any alcohol doesn't mean I haven't been under the influence or something or someone else. "Has anybody ever played a game called Mao before?" Amina asked as she shuffled a deck of cards.

Ethan and Tylor both laughed out loud. "*Yes*."

"No, but he deserves to get played after the way he played China," Kade said with a glance my way.

Amina dealt out the cards. "So it plays kinda like Crazy Eights, but with a twist."

"What's the twist?" I asked.

"You'll see," she smirked as she flipped over the top card. "I'll start. Everyone ready? Begin." She laid down a card. Tylor laid down a card. Kasey laid down a card. Nikole laid down a card.

"What do I do if—" Victor started to say before Amina cut him off.

"Talking," she said as she slid him a card from the deck.

He stared at her. "What?"

"Talking," she said as she slid him another card.

"Hold on—" Kade started to say.

"Talking," she said as she slid him a card.

"Wait a second," Victor said, getting annoyed.

"Talking," she said as she slid him a third card.

"So we're not—" Kade managed to get out.

"Talking," she said as she slid him another card.

"You're slow learners," I laughed, earning myself a card.

"Why're *you* allowed to talk?" Victor said to Amina.

"Talking," she said as she gave him yet another card.

Victor looked through his cards with puffed-out cheeks. *"Icantputanythingdown!"* he said all at once. Amina pointed to the deck. He drew one and looked at her with a forceful shrug. They pointed fingers and shook heads at each other.

"Point of order," Amina finally said, setting down her cards and letting Victor's and Kade's grievances break against her. "You just draw one card, and if you can't play it, then the next person goes," she explained. "You get a card if you talk, and since you're trying to get rid of all your cards, you won't talk. Or *shouldn't* talk."

"So it's like Crazy Eights meets the quiet game?" Nikole asked.

"There's gotta be more to it," I said as I took a tolerable sip of rum and Coke. "Or else you two wouldn't have been so stoked to play it," I nodded at Ethan and Tylor.

"There are a few more rules to it, but you'll learn them as we go," Amina said casually. "Everyone ready again?"

"No," Victor grumbled.

She picked up her cards. "Point taken."

Amina's suitemate Ari laid down a card. I laid down a card. "Going out of turn," Amina said as she slid me a card. *Whatever.*

Ethan laid down a card. Kade laid down a card. "Failure to say 'have a nice day,'" Amina said as she slid him a card.

He threw his cards at the floor. *"Fuck* this shit," he swore as he got up to pace around.

We started over and she explained the base rules to us: you have to say 'have a nice day' if you play a 7, Jacks are a free pass if you don't have anything to put down, Aces skip the next player, and you have to say 'Mao' when you play your last card. "And whoever wins the round gets to make a rule for the next game, and all the rules stack."

"Fuck me in the *ass*," Kade muttered.

It was a struggle to remember all the things you had to say as the game went on. "The emperor does not approve—I'm a bloody bugger—big dicks and *Criminal Minds*—'oh my glob'—'quoth the raven nevermore,'" I said to the 3 of Clubs an hour later. And then it really got chaotic once Tylor made the rule that you had to take a drink whenever you had to take a card. People were forgetting shit left and right and making all kinds of illegal plays. Victor, who had yet to win a single round, laid down his last card and carefully recited the litany required of him.

"Fucking *finally*," he breathed.

Nikole slid him a card. "Failure to say 'Mao.'"

He and Kade bounced first, since all the cards Kade had to take meant he wasn't feeling too hot. I'd hoped that Tylor would stay over in Amina's room so Ethan could come back with me to 222 Swafford, but in a big middle finger from the universe,

Kasey slept in her own room since she and her boyfriend had broken up, which meant that Tylor slept in our room. So that's how Ethan and I ended up in the backseat of my cold-as-shit car, drunkenly making out and blowing each other.

What are we? I thought as we cuddled afterwards to keep warm. *We're not boyfriends, but he's definitely more than just a friend to me now. Are we friends with benefits? Do we even need a label for us? I don't know what's scarier—him thinking of me as just a friend, or me falling for somebody again. But it's happening whether I want it to or not. I'm falling for him. I'm falling for Ethan.*

December 4

Sometimes I'll have days when I'll start to feel overwhelmed by all my papers and upcoming Finals, but then I remember that there's probably someone somewhere in the English countryside who's the servant to a crotchety old man with zero chill whose last name is Bates and has to call him 'Master Bates' without laughing, and then I don't feel like I have it so bad.

Promising ourselves to start crunching for Finals tomorrow, Ethan and Kade and Victor and I spent most of today playing *Catan* and *Machi Koro* and explaining to Kade why he would be the first of us to die in a zombie apocalypse until Victor finally stood to go. "I'll feel bad if I don't get *something* productive done today," he said with a stretch.

"Well *that* definitely makes one of us," Ethan said.

"Yeah, you *nerd*," Kade laughed. Victor sleeved his arm through his coat and gave him the finger.

"Well, that's about it," I said to Kade to try to get him to leave so Ethan and I could have some alone time. "I'd say we could play *Mario Kart*, but we only have two controllers here."

"That's okay. I'm fine with taking turns," he said as he took a seat on the couch. *Goddamn you Trevor for just having to say something.* I made sure Ethan saw me roll my eyes. I thought Kade would've been satisfied after a few races, so imagine how much he'd overstayed his welcome by the time we finished *four* Grand Prix cups.

"You're gonna let me go get wings all by my lonesome?" he asked us as he pulled on his shoes. "What if I get kidnapped or killed?"

"I think you'll be fine. I'm honestly not that hungry though," I lied. *Maybe for a different kind of meat.* "Are you?" I asked Ethan.

He shook his head. "Not really, no," he said unconvincingly.

No sooner had my door shut behind Kade than I was on the couch beside Ethan, who sat waiting for me with his temple on his fist. "I was starting to think he'd never leave," I said as I sat sideways to face him.

He mirrored my pose. "Tell me about it," he said as we leaned in to kiss. Our tongues danced together, and my hands were in his hair, on his thigh. We'd just started to move down onto the couch when a *swthit* and some *beeps* blasted us apart.

"Hey Ethan," Tylor said as he slid off his backpack. *Goddammit to hell.* "I'm not interrupting anything, am I?" he laughed. *Goddamn these fucking goddamn roommates.*

"Nope. We were just having a staring contest," I said bitterly.

"*Sure* you were," he rolled his eyes. "Remember to keep three bible lengths of space between the two of you," he chuckled as he went into the bathroom.

I traced circles on Ethan's knee with a sigh. "*Do* you just wanna go grab something to eat? I actually *am* pretty hungry."

"Yeah," he resigned. "Maybe this is the universe telling us we *should* be studying instead of trying to do unholy things with each other."

"To hell with the universe then," I smiled as I gave him another kiss before Tylor could keep me from doing *that* too.

December 5

> what we started on the couch
> we finished in the shower
> only you were in my thoughts
> and I was all over

December 6

Today I heard somebody in Patnick saying how they don't understand why food options have to be so 'political' in reference to there being vegan and gluten-free options. So being considerate and inclusive of other people's diets is being political? Like, worry about your own shit.

We got our first real snow of the season today. This afternoon saw me wistfully looking out over the winter wonderland through the windows in Rosenberg, wishing I could be building a snowman or going sled riding instead of spending the afternoon working on my History paper. I say that like I just build snowmen all the time. My paper's on the ethnic cleansing of the Germans from the parts of Germany that were suddenly parts of Poland and Czechoslovakia and the Soviet Union after World War II ended, because it's one of those things I'd never heard about before. I'm still not sure if I feel bad for them or not.

Hey
Can I ask you to do me a favor?
I've been feeling kind funny ever since the weekend
and i'm lowkey worried its an sti. Would you be able
to please go to the health center to get tested? I just
wanna be sure its nothing serious
I'm gonna try to get a test too

Great, as if I wasn't stressed out already. I must've been wearing my thoughts, because Kade asked, "Something on your mind, fam?" when he returned to our table with another armful of books. After you have to re-shelve all the books people take, you become more conscious of how many you take—like how working retail makes you more polite towards employees in stores.

I looked up from Ethan's text. "Can I lie?"

Kade dropped the stack next to the others. "No."

I avoided his eyes. "I've been hooking up with someone and now they're worried they might have an STI. They want me to go get tested."

"Oh go 'head!" he lit up. "For hooking up I mean, not STIs. Anybody I know?"

"Um...yeah."

His hands slapped the table. "Shut up! Who?"

"I can't tell you." *But how I wish I could.* "They're not really out yet, so—"

"Say no more. You feel fine though, right?"

"Yeah. Physically, anyway."

"Good looks, sis," he said before laughing out loud a moment later. "God, I hope it's Ethan. No, I hope it's Victor! Oh my god, I'd *die!*"

I'd never been to the Health Center before, but I'd heard it's a joke. You can go in for anything from strep throat to food poisoning and they'll just give you some ibuprofen. I put on a disposable mask offered at the reception desk and thought about how the only other time I'd been inside of Draper Hall was when I hooked up with Devon over Halloweekend. I only had to sit and stare at the condom vending machines for a few minutes before I got called back. Take a fucking guess which student worker ended up seeing me.

"Trevor?" Devon greeted me from behind his own mask. "How've ya been?" *Well this won't be awkward.*

Sitting alone with him in an examination room was as uncomfortable as Styrofoam rubbing against Styrofoam, but he didn't make any jokes about why I was there, or bring up the last time we were in a room together—which is to say that Kade could never do the job. *'Maybe you should just wanky-wanky instead of hanky-panky,'* he'd say in the same voice he talks to his dog in. I'm glad I only had to get my cheek swabbed, because I don't think I could pee into a cup if somebody's waiting for me to do it. "This must be a convenient job for you," I said to make the minutes pass faster. "All you have to do is go downstairs."

"It's pretty nice," Devon nodded. "Most of the people who come in just have a cough or are worried they might be pregnant. Any emergencies go right to the hospital." *Is he also thinking about me being balls-deep inside him?*

I had a feeling that my test would be negative, but I was still relieved to hear it. "Alright, everything looks fine, so you're good to go. Oh, and here." He handed me a small paper packet of ibuprofen. "Take these with you just in case you end up feeling anything."

December 9

I was today-years-old when I learned that there are internet cables *running across the bottoms of the oceans*, and now I have *infinitely* more questions. Like, do you know how *wide* the oceans are? And how *deep*? How fucking long are these cables? What if some bottom feeder decides to bite into one? Does the internet go dark?

I can't wait for Secret Santa, if just to have a break from studying for one evening. Tylor hasn't touched his PS5 since last week, and I haven't seen Kade or Victor outside of a library or a classroom building or a dining hall since Sunday—but I did see Ethan though when I went over to 341 Kessler for *Mario* and making out as a reward for finishing my last-ever essay for Brit Lit. I know I shouldn't let somebody occupy as much space in me as I let him do, but I don't care. What can I say? I'm young, dumb, and hormonal.

"What are we?" I softly asked him afterwards as we laid together on his couch. "Are we just two friends who like to kiss and hook up, or...?"

I expected him to chuckle and say, *'Yeah? What did you think we were?'* But he surprised me when he rolled to face me and responded with, "What do you want us to be?"

I swallowed, deliberately and anxiously choosing my words. "Well, seeing as I really, *really*, like you, is it...?" *It's so ridiculous I almost can't even say it.* "Would it be crazy to say boyfriends?" His eyebrows shot up. "I mean, not yet obviously, but I...I think about you *all* the time. I've liked you ever since I first met you. And the fact that you like me back is still *crazy* to me."

"Well, it's—"

"Wait, I'm not done yet." And then before I could stop myself, I was spilling the one desire that had been furiously gnawing away at me, making myself more vulnerable than I've ever been since my last relationship. *Stop it, you and Ethan aren't in a relationship.*

But that's what you want, isn't it?

"I wanna be more than just friends-with-benefits, more than people who only show affection for each other when nobody's looking. I wanna run with you and see how far we can make it." *I know what I'm asking of you though, so believe me when I say I understand if you're not ready for that yet.* "But I need to know if that's what *you* want too. I'd rather swallow a hard truth than keep chasing something I can never have."

Ethan was silent for so long that I started to think I broke him. "I've never been in a real relationship before," he finally said into the room. "Only ever hookups. Honestly though, I've been with *you* more than anybody else. But the whole 'openly gay' thing scares the *shit* out of me. I'm so jealous of people who aren't afraid to be themselves. It's so *constricting* not being able to just be me. Like, there are times when I feel like I'm actually suffocating," he said in a shaky voice.

I rubbed circles on his back. "Trust me, I know what it feels like. Nobody deserves to feel like that, especially somebody as kind and as sweet as you."

His hand rested on my leg as his eyes pierced mine. "Trevor, being your boyfriend would be a dream come true, *god* you don't even know."

I braced myself for the impending 'but.'

"But I owe it to you to get comfortable with myself first. I don't wanna keep you a secret, and you don't deserve to be kept a secret. *Neither* of us do, not from our friends or anybody else. I wanna show you off, I wanna skip through the Quad holding hands like we're in some romantic comedy." And from the way he smiled, I knew he wasn't just saying things. "I just don't know if I'm ready to be open about myself just yet," he said like he was apologizing to me. Waiting for his next words twisted corkscrews into my skin. "But I'm gonna work on it," he said with determination in his voice as he squeezed my hand. "For both of us. If that's what I have to do to get us there, then I'll do it."

I squeezed him back, smiling the kind of smile you can't hold back. "And I'll be there for you along the way. I'll wait for you, because you're worth waiting for."

But is he worth the risk? Because once upon a time, somebody else told me everything I wanted to hear, and I didn't realize until it was too late that those were the words that ended up hurting the most when he decided to destroy me.

December 12

Physical Science—done. Computers—done. All that's left is to turn in my papers and take my Critical Writing Final on Wednesday, which is to say that in a few days' time I'll be back home for Break with my first semester of college under my belt. I'm almost out of the tunnel, but being out of it will definitely be more bittersweet than I thought it'd be.

I swung by Kessler to pick up Ethan on my way to the store after he'd texted me to ask what I was up to for the rest of the day. "We're going home in like three days, what could you possibly need from the store?" Ethan asked as he hopped in my car in a blue-and-white NHU puff ball beanie. "Did you run out of toilet paper?"

"No," I laughed. "I wanna get some hot chocolate and cookies for Secret Santa later on."

"Well aren't you just a good host?" He grabbed my hand, and it sank in that I'm going to have to go five weeks without seeing him, or any of my friends for that matter. One of The Skeletons dressed in a Santa suit handing out presents to the others from an upholstered armchair made me think of being forced to watch *The Nightmare Before Christmas* back at the beginning of the semester. I pulled into the parking lot and got hit by the sudden fantasy of Ethan and I buying groceries for our apartment.

"I figured you were just gonna get premade cookies," he said as I picked out some logs of dough. "Are you gonna make those in the kitchen in your building?"

"I was actually just gonna lay them out on my desk and hope that they'd bake by themselves," I said, dodging his slap. "I thought it'd be cute if we made them together."

"Sounds perfect," he grinned, but his mood wasn't as bright by the time I was grabbing some dollar decorations by the registers.

"What's up?" I checked in on him. "Are you worried about Finals?"

He shook his head. "I'm just not looking forward to going home for Break. I mean, I'm looking forward to not having assignments, but I'm not looking forward to going back home."

"Oh." I didn't press the subject until we were back in the car. "Is it your family?"

"Uh huh. They don't know I'm gay."

I grabbed his hand, thinking how he said how constricting it is not being able to be himself. "Say no more."

"They're really religious and conservative too, so I don't expect them to be very accepting of me when they find out," his voice cracked. "I wouldn't be surprised if they throw me out."

My heart hurt in empathy. "They wouldn't do that," I said, though I know full-well that it isn't a guarantee. "*Trust me*, I know how scary it is. My parents were the same way, but they're okay with me now."

"That doesn't mean mine will be."

"No, but..." *I don't know what.* I gave his hand a little squeeze. "All I know is that you aren't home yet, so why let your parents ruin today for you?"

He squeezed mine back. "Yeah, you're right," he smiled. "Thanks for the TED Talk."

Nikole was on DA duty when we got back, typing away on her laptop. "Don't tell me you two are hanging out!" she exclaimed like it was illegal.

"We are," I said as I signed him in. "We hustled all weekend so we could relax today. We're doing our Secret Santa gift exchange later on."

"Oh yeah, that's right! Can I come over just for fun and watch? I'm here until 6."

"Go for it, girlfriend."

She handed Ethan his ID back. "Perf. Enjoy your afternoon. And keep the door open!"

"She always says that when I'm signing someone in," I explained. "Which is mostly just Kade or Victor."

"Oh okay," Ethan nodded. "So how many times have you slept with them?"

"I've lost count. I actually just finished up with Kade before you texted me."

Ethan helped me tape and string up the paper decorations, which I wish I would've thought about getting sooner so I could've enjoyed them for more than a couple days. I made tea and we played *Mario Party* on the couch under a blanket. Tylor and Amina and Jaxon and another friend of theirs were down at the outlets, so we didn't have to worry about looking too gay with each other. "This is actually really cozy," he said as he sipped his tea. "What flavor is this again?"

"Almond-flavored rooibos. I think it fits the vibe," I said as I looked from the room to the flurries beyond the window.

"Roy-bose? I think you just made that word up," Ethan chuckled. "But yeah, this is the vibe."

I nodded. "Much hygge."

"Okay, now *that* you just made up."

"Unh uh! It's a Danish word for a feeling of comfort and coziness!"

He raised an eyebrow. "Use it in a sentence."

"I don't know. 'The vibe is hygge?' You got me curious now," I said as I paused the game to look it up. "Okay, it's a noun. So, I guess like, 'having tea and sitting under a blanket with you on a cold day is hygge?' No wait, that'd be an adjective."

"You can be so cringe sometimes, you know?" he chuckled.

"Don't lie, you like it."

He slipped the controller off his wrist so he could stroke my cheek without it smacking me in the face. "You're right, I do." I slipped my own off and shifted so we could take in the details of each other's features. *I still can't get over those eyes.* My fingers ran through his perfectly tousled dirty blond hair that still hasn't decided whether it wants to be blond or light brown. "What?" he smiled.

I shook my head and smiled back. "Nothing."

"What?" he giggled, making me giggle with him.

"Nothing! Just...*you*."

He poked my cheeks. "Has anyone ever told you how adorbs your dimples are?"

I rolled my eyes. "Yeah, my grandma."

"And all the hot guys you've had sex with."

"*No,*" I said before going in for the kiss. The softness of our hoodies mashing together took the hygge level through the roof as we held each other. My hand eventually found its way to where his legs branch off. "*Speaking of sex with hot guys,*" I purred.

He moved my hand away. "I've actually been thinking about those cookies," he smirked. "They've been calling my name." He cupped a hand to his ear. "Do you hear them? *Ethan! Ethan!*"

"And *I'm* the one who's cringe?" I laughed. "You forreal wanna make cookies right now?"

He flung the blanket off. "There are few things I'm more forreal about than cookies. Our dicks will still be there later."

I traded Nikole my ID for the key to the kitchen. Ethan was content staying there with the cookies as they baked instead of playing pool or not-pinball, running his hands up my sides and playing with my hair. "What if somebody comes in?" I asked as I flicked my eyes over at the door.

"Let them," he shrugged. "I don't give a shit."

"Really?"

"Okay, maybe just a little." Our mouths met, our heads rested together. We let go of each other only to pop in the second batch.

"Warm cookies right out of the oven are my *fave*," he said as he scooped up one in gooey pieces. I cleared my throat. "Okay, *second* fave, I guess." He had another as he hopped up onto the counter with his legs spread so I could stand between them and taste the sugar cookie on his tongue. He made us stop when the timer went off, though I would've been okay with letting them burn. I gave the largest container I found a quick wash before filling it up with our baked goods.

"You made cookies?" Nikole said when she took back the key. "I'm *totes* coming over later now."

"You can have one now if you want," Ethan offered. "You just have to message us if you see Tylor coming back."

"Heck yes," she said as he popped off the lid. "I startle myself when I think about the things I'd do for a cookie." Ethan and I traded a knowing glance while she wasn't looking.

I caved and munched on a cookie while we finished our game, which just made my cold tea taste that much more bitter. Ethan somehow won despite losing almost every minigame. "Loser makes us more tea," he said with a shit-eating grin.

"Why do that when I can do this instead?" I asked right before I started to tickle him. He yelped and curled into a ball.

"Stop!" he laughed/screamed. "I'll kick you!"

I let up since I didn't want him to kick the table and send our mugs flying. He jumped up, but I bear-hugged him and pushed him onto my bed, where I started tickling him again. Not going to lie, hearing him squeal was really turning me on. He managed to flip us around, and he pinned my wrists to the bed.

"Well well," he said breathlessly. "How the turns have tabled." He leaned down to kiss me, and the tents we were pitching told me we both knew what was next. He sat up to take me in.

"What?" I smiled.

"If you'd have told me that day we first met that someday I'd be in your bed, about to have sex with you—"

"Who said anything about having sex?"

He wiggled his butt around on my crotch. "Um, if the bulge in your pants was Braille, it would say, 'I wanna be inside you.'"

"You're so fucking cringe," I laughed as I pulled him back down. *This is way nicer than doing it in the House Council room.* My fantasies of what we were doing were always of us stumbling back from some party like Devon and I had, and we'd end up in one of our rooms and he'd say how he'd always wanted to experiment with a guy. But there we were, totally sober at 3:30 in the afternoon, stripping off our sweatshirts and shirts and pants, and there's nobody else I'd have rather stripped down with than Ethan, looking *hella* adorable in his Superman underwear.

"I have some condoms in my bag," he smiled.

"Oh no, please, I have *tons.*" I rolled over and opened my dresser drawer. He took the opportunity to clap my butt.

"Why do you have so many condoms?" he laughed.

"They're from Condom Bingo! You didn't have Condon Bingo in your building?" I asked as I took one out along with my bottle of probably-stale lube.

"They probably saw you and were like *this guy's gonna get so much ass, we'd better give him a few handfuls,*" Ethan chuckled. I went to tear open the wrapper, but he snatched it and flung it onto the floor. *"We don't have to rush,"* he breathed into my ear, making my hairs and something else tingle as "Feelings" by Lauv started to play from his phone.

We explored all of us, orbiting one another like binary stars. He was a painting behind glass I finally got to appreciate up close, the book that turned out to be spellbinding, the map that colored itself in as I explored it. I'd forgotten what it was like to make love to somebody, as Victorian as that sounds. We savored each other before hungering for each other in the most wicked, the most excellent, of ways. I looked up at him, his eyes inches from mine as we teased each other. The gentle rocking of our bodies became eager. Our breaths burned with fire.

"You ready to give it to me?"

"Oh am I."

I pushed the bottle into his hand and sheathed myself with another condom. *Maybe there is a god after all, and maybe he's cool with this kind of stuff?* Our eyes were locked together as he reached a hand behind him to ease it in. *And if he's not, then the devil can fucking have me.* He let me enter him a few times to get used to me. I adjusted my legs once he was comfortable to bring him close. He swept my face with his hair, gasped into my neck, locked his teeth with mine. We spoke the primeval lingua franca, crying out to each other, to god, to the upstairs neighbors. We whimpered curses and passion-splintered praises into each other's mouths. It was more than just sex with the cutest guy I know—his looks were what caught my attention, but it's his personality that keeps me wanting him, his sense of humor, his kindness, his talent, his optimism, how he isn't obnoxious or arrogant or full of himself, even when he has every reason to be. And I don't feel like I have to try to make it work like I did with Dillon. It's almost like whatever we have was already there and was just waiting to be unearthed, as much as we tried to ignore it or dismiss it. *Maybe we were meant to happen,* I told him through the swells of my body, through the affection in my eyes. His own eyes, his tender lips, his enraptured motions told me—at least I like to think—*yeah, I felt it too.*

I'm surprised that I lasted as long as I did. I told him I was close and he kissed it out of me, clasping me with every part of him, inundating me in a frenzied euphoria. I fell onto him, trying not to lay in his own calligraphy on his chest.

I pressed my forehead to his. "Holy *fuck*," I panted.

"*Holy fuck* is right," he breathed. "I can't believe we just did that."

"Yeah, samesies." I flicked my eyes towards the wall beyond my head. "I'm pretty sure Lekan next door knows what we just did though."

"Do you care?"

I shook my head with a grin. "Nope. Do you?"

"*Hell* no."

"What if Patnick Paul was watching us?"

"Oh Jesus Christ," he slapped me.

I put on my best old-smoker-lady-with-a-gravelly-voice voice. "*You boys are making me moist.*"

"Oh my god, *stop!*" he stuffed his face into his hands. "You're gonna make me throw up!"

Arms and hands let go of bodies so I could grab him a shirt to clean himself with. I pulled off my condom and buried it under some trash. Our clothes crawled off in reverse, and we held each other on the couch. Sex is great and all, but cuddling with the person you shared it with afterwards is *hella* underrated. I'd forgotten what it feels like for home to be another person instead of a place.

"I've always heard people say that sex is better when it's with somebody you care about," Ethan said. "Now I know what they meant."

I gave him a squeeze. "I'm happy you feel the same way." Footage of our relationship played in my head, how we went from strangers at Open Mic Night, to acquaintances at Starbucks, to friends at a party or in my room, to whatever wave we're riding now. "What do you wanna do until they come over? Play some more Switch, watch something, or...?"

He nestled his head into my shoulder. "I vote we put something on and stay just like this."

We reluctantly reverted to bro mode once Kade and Victor came over with a paper shopping bag. "Have you two been watching *Bob's Burgers* and jerking each other off all day?" Kade asked in an uncanny Linda Belcher voice.

"We were playing *Mario* earlier. And we made cookies too."

Victor's eyebrows shot up. "*Woah.* Cookies."

"Is that what you kids call it these days?" Kade joked as he headed into the bathroom. "BRB, I gotta shit."

"Dude!" Victor said like he was angry. "We *literally* just came from our room!"

I forced a laugh, suddenly high-key nervous about the jokes and innuendos they've been making all semester. *What are they gonna do when they find out that two of their friends have been getting each other off? I wanna tell them that Ethan and I are more than just friends, but that's not my call to make.*

With Tylor and Amina back, and Nikole fresh off of desk duty, I don't think there's ever been so many people in our room. Ethan helped me make hot chocolate for everybody, standing close enough to me that nobody would see us stealing pinches and pokes and pecks.

"Is that a new shirt?" I asked Victor when I sat back down, nodding at his shirt of two skeletons kissing in an ornate frame with the words 'The Lovers' underneath the image. "It looks like it'd be a tarot card."

"Yes, and it is," he smiled. "Number six in the Major Arcana."

"I have a pair of gauges with the same thing on them," Kade said, drawing my eyes to the Progress flag ones he had in. "Somebody asked me if I was from Portland once because they said they look like the kind of gauges somebody from Portland would wear."

"I don't mess around with tarot cards," Nikole said seriously. "Tarot cards or Ouija boards."

"Some people on my floor tried to make a Ouija board out of the top of a pizza box once," Ethan said. "They did a salt ring and everything."

"How'd that go?" Amina asked.

"It didn't," he chuckled.

"Did something happen with tarot cards or Ouija boards that made you stay away from them?" Victor asked Nikole.

"Nope. There's just things out there that we don't understand, and I'd rather just keep to myself and vibe. Ain't nobody need all that extra stress."

Tylor licked up his tiny marshmallows with his tongue like an anesthetized frog trying to catch flies. "*Preach.*"

"I mean, when the Spanish came here searching for gold, the Native Americans thought they were gods because their armor was shiny and they'd never seen shiny armor before," I said. "Humans have been around for like five seconds in the scope of everything, but yet we act like we know everything."

Kade slurped his cocoa. "And that has fuck to do with *what?*"

"I'm just saying there's a lot that we don't understand that we chalk up to being ghosts or god or whatever."

"Passes blunt to the left," he said. Ethan took said blunt from him. "Can we do presents now?" Kade asked me like I was in charge.

"Isn't just enjoying each other's company with some cookies and cocoa enough of a gift?"

"If so, then I got ripped off."

Amina and Nikole sent us out into the hall so they could put the gifts on the floor without anybody knowing who brought what. "I think Kade should go first, since he clearly has ants in his pants over it," Ethan said once they let us back in.

"Says the one who was grinning like a dorky bobblehead when I brought it up," Kade zinged as he slid onto the floor to check the gifts for the one with his name on it. "This feels like a book, so I'm gonna guess it's from Trevor," he said as his gift bowed in his hands. I just shrugged. He ripped off the glossy silver paper to indeed reveal a book. "*A journal for the times you need to smooth out those restless thoughts*," he read off the cover. "Yeah, this is totes from you."

"Nope," I smugly shook my head.

"Really? Who else would give such a lame-ass—I mean, *thoughtful*, gift?"

"*I* would," Tylor said. "It's full of fun prompts and stuff. I actually thought about keeping it for myself and giving you something else, but that wouldn't be in the spirit."

Kade flipped through the pages. "Well I always have restless thoughts, so I'll *for sure* be using this. Thanks fam."

Tylor's gift was a skull that looked like it belonged to a steampunk Frankenstein's monster, complete with silver and copper bolts and gears and staples in it, with a small clock for an eye. "This is dope as *hell*," he said as he turned it over in his hands.

"And here I was worried you weren't gonna like it," Ethan chuckled. His gift was a Bluetooth speaker with lights that changed colors with the music.

"It's waterproof too," Victor explained, "so you can use it in the shower or whatever."

"Shower time just got steamier," Ethan smirked. "I'm gonna play the shit out of this thing though!"

I nervously watched Victor tear open my diligently-wrapped gift. *Quit worrying, of course he's gonna like it.* "Woah," he said to it. "Now *this* is clutch."

Ethan leaned over to peep it. "What is it?"

"A puzzle celebrating notable African American women," he said as he took it in. "And I don't even know who half of these people *are*, which is pretty sad." I think what's *really* sad is how everybody only ever gets a glorified, whitewashed version of American history in school—the Founding Fathers, the goddamn pioneers, the Civil War. I can't wait for elementary schoolchildren to be taught how American history is both more unhallowed and more colorful than it's made out to be—and then they'll learn about how gender isn't binary and that trans people do in fact exist. "You know me too well," Victor smiled.

I reached for the last present. "Since this is from Kade, I'm expecting something penis."

"I hope you like riding horse cock, you homo," he laughed before throwing his hand over his mouth. Victor smacked him on the leg.

"It's okay," Ethan smiled. "He told me."

Kade was still shooketh with himself. "I am *so* sorry dude," he apologized to me.

"It's fine," I said, *beyond* grateful that that wasn't how Ethan found out about my preferences. Kade's gift to me was a Shakespearean insult generator in book form. "*You pribbling, tardy-gaited bum-bailey!*" I said gleefully. "I love it!"

Once we'd opened, played with, and tried out our gifts to our contentment, we played a few games of *Machi Koro* and reminisced about Christmases and Haunukkahs past. I must've been in an extra-good mood, because I heard myself asking the room, "Would anyone wanna hear one of the short stories I wrote?" All eyes were on me. *Wait, can I actually rescind that offer?*

"Does the pope shit on little boys?"

"*Bet.*"

"I didn't know you wrote stories!"

"Me neither, and I *live* with him!"

"I am *high-key* curious."

"Yeah, let's hear that shit!"

"Are you gonna read them the parasite one?"

"*You* got to read one?!"

My Mac found itself in my hands and everybody eagerly watched me as I navigated through Google Docs. "How many have you *written*?" Kade asked as he peeped over from his seat on the couch.

"A handful," I said as I instinctively turned the screen away from him. I took a breath, stoked and nervous at the same time. *Ethan liked it, so why wouldn't the rest of them?* I just read the first few paragraphs, making the effort to speak slower and clearer than I typically do. All attention was on me, which I didn't even mind. I stopped and waited with bated breath.

"Is that the whole thing?" Nikole asked.

I shook my head. "It's just the first part. But I can send it to you so you can read the rest of it on your own, if you want to."

"*Dude*," Victor's open mouth said, "are you *forreal*? Of *course* I wanna read it!"

"And that wasn't for a class or anything? You did that just for fun?"

"Send me that shit so I can finish it right here."

"When's the Netflix movie coming out?"

"I like listening to you read," Nikole said. "You actually have a *really* good reading voice."

"Yeah, your cadence *totally* changes," Kade said. *Maybe 'Kade' is actually short for 'Kadence,' like some old Puritan name?*

"And Ethan knew about it first *why*?"

Ethan's eyes met mine. "I don't know. I guess we were talking about majors and stuff, and it just came up somehow?" I answered, which isn't false.

"Okay, but next time you write a story you're gonna let us read that shit, 'kay?" Victor said so forcefully that it sounded like a threat.

I nodded with a grin. "Yeah, of course." *See how bad that was?*

I could tell Ethan was in an off mood after Kade not-outed me to him, and especially after I made myself vulnerable to the others. He drummed his fingers and was uncharacteristically quiet except for a few forced laughs, and I didn't have to try to guess too hard why.

"So I have something to tell you guys too," he said out of nowhere. My head snapped up—I didn't think he was going to tell them like that, and not so soon after he promised me that he would. "You're all pretty much my best friends at this point, and I feel like I'm not being fair to you if I keep on keeping it from you." *That* got everyone's attention. "I don't think this'll change anything between us, but..." He swallowed, taking deep breaths. I would've held his hand through it if he wasn't sitting so far away. "I don't—I don't like girls. I'm...not straight." He shut his eyes and tilted his head back, bracing himself for whatever response he was expecting.

Victor pulled him into an eye-bulging hug while Tylor patted him on the back. "Why would that change anything?" Victor asked softly. "If anything, that just makes me respect you more."

Kade slid off the couch to put a hand on his shoulder. "I know it's way easier said than done, but don't be afraid to be who you are. And don't ever apologize for it."

Nikole gave him a hug too, and Amina patted him on the knee. "You couldn't be anything that would make you not a part of this family."

Ethan sniffled as tears ran down his nose and cheeks. "You don't know how good it is to hear that. I can be myself around you all now. It feels like an actual weight's been lifted off me." He caught my eye, and I just smiled back, my heart stirring with pride for him.

"Don't you have anything to say, Trev?" Victor asked me expectantly.

I looked around at each of them before my eyes landed back on Ethan's. "I know how scary coming out is, but that just makes it all the more freeing when you do it." Straight people can be ally all they want, but they'll *never* know what it's like. "I'm glad you told them. I'm *proud* you told them."

"Wait, you *knew* already?"

"Yeah. You told me, what?" I asked Ethan. *A lifetime ago?* "A couple weeks ago?"

"What the eff? What makes *you* so special?"

Ethan answered him for me. "I told Trevor first because, well…" He looked to me either for permission or encouragement with a wild smile. I gave him a nod. "Trevor and I are…kind of seeing each other," he said, making us both blush and sending my heart fluttering.

Victor brought his hands together in a flabbergasted clap. "Shut the front door! Forreal?"

"That's awesome!"

"No cap?"

"You two'll make a *hella* cute couple."

Nikole looked between the two of us, putting two and two together. "So wait, when you told me earlier to text you if Tylor was coming back to the room, were you…?" Our expressions said it all. There was a used condom in the trash to prove it.

"So *that's* what you meant when you said you were playing *Mario?*" Kade smirked.

"*No,*" I said, though there *has* been a trend.

"How long have you two been seeing each other?" Tylor asked like we'd won the lottery.

Ethan and I looked at each other. *When we hooked up last and I asked him what he wanted us to be?* "I don't know," Ethan finally said. "The first time we kissed was when we went to the mall a few weekends ago. So sometime between then and now?"

"That's so cool!"

"I'm happy for both of you. I really am."

"I'm almost jelly."

"So if two gay guys who are bros and who aren't in a relationship yet give each other head," Kade said like he was reading a math problem, "is it just a brojob, or is it considered gay? We need to stop sending people to space and start answering these questions."

Since we'll all be leaving on different days, we said bye to each other like it'd be the last time we'd see each other until next semester, though I know I won't be leaving without seeing Ethan again. "I'll see you tomorrow maybe?" I said into his ear as I gave him a non-platonic hug.

"Yes," he smiled. And then we kissed right in front of our friends, not even caring that they were hooting and whistling at us. Because when we kiss, we're the only two people on Earth.

December 14

On the plus side, the guy at the bookstore at the beginning of the semester who told me they wouldn't buy my books back was wrong, even if I did get an abysmal amount back for them.

Tylor left yesterday afternoon, so Ethan and I had the room to ourselves for the evening. We made the foreplay last as long as possible and the sex as passionate as possible. We spooned afterwards, our chests rising in tandem. I was so at peace that I could've drifted off to sleep. *It's been such a long time since I've fallen asleep next to someone I...next to someone who makes me feel the way he does.*

"This might sound crazy," he said, breaking an eternity of silence, "but it almost feels like this is *our* room. Like, we're roommates and we live here together." *Are his eyes looking around the room, imagining the life we could have together?*

I smiled into the back of his neck. "It doesn't sound crazy at all." Two gay roommates who have secret crushes on each other but who are too afraid to make a move sounds like the premise for a series. How long would it have taken for one of us to open up to the other? How much sooner would we have kissed for the first time? And as small and unassuming as it would be, the room would be *ours*, from arranging and decorating it together, to greeting each other with a kiss when the last of us would come back at the end of the day, to asking how each other's day went as we worked on our assignments, to making dinner together in the building's kitchen, to falling asleep next to each other every night in our two-beds-pushed-together bed. I'd be at every House Council meeting to support him. I'd get to hear him practicing for his Open Mic Night performances. I'd get to be there with him and for him at his most candid, his most genuine, Ethan self. *Maybe not right now. But someday, I hope.*

We put on *Resident Evil: Welcome to Raccoon City* on my Mac in my bed, still naked under the covers. "I wish I didn't have to go home for Break," he said with his head on my shoulder.

"I mean, you don't *have* to. You'll just be here alone for five weeks."

"Being alone might not be as bad as somewhere you don't belong."

I squeezed him close to me. "My parents *probably* wouldn't be up for letting you stay with me if I asked them, especially if they knew what kinds of stuff we'd be up to almost every day."

"*Almost* every day?" he chuckled. "Why not *every* day?"

My eyebrows shot up. "Really? You'd wanna do that every day for five weeks?"

"You wouldn't? Okay, maybe every *other* day then."

"Wow, it's too bad we *aren't* roommates then," I smirked. "I'm already looking forward to round two."

"Oh?" He traced a finger down my chest. "That makes two of us then." He pecked at my lips before moving to my cheek and then my neck.

We kept watching while we waited for me to refuel. It's definitely a creepy movie, but the scariest part was when a message from Devon popped up in the corner of my screen.

Heyyy ☺
Did you go home yet?

Oh shit fuck.

"Who's Devon?" Ethan asked curiously.

"One of my old coworkers from the library," I said, both scared and confused.

"Why's he asking you if you went home?"

"I don't know. He quit like months ago, so—"

I'm slightly drunk rn and really h-word and wishing
that dick of yours was rearranging my guts again 😬

Fucking goddammit to motherfucking hell. I paused the movie like it would stop any more texts from coming through. Ethan sternly watched me from behind arms.

"Okay, so we might've hooked up," I said as my chest pounded in the worst way. "But it was *one time*, and it was back at Halloween! That was the last time I saw him!"

"And he just decided to text you out of nowhere to see if you wanted to sleep with him again?"

"Apparently!" I just about yelled, shocked that Ethan would think that about me. "What, you think I'd *lie* to you about something like that? Do you think I just go around sleeping with people behind your back?"

"I don't want to, but that's kinda what this looks like right now."

"I'm *telling* you, that was the only time I was with him! It was a one-time thing!" *Why won't he believe me?* "He didn't even try coming onto me at the Health Center, so I don't—"

"Hold on," he said, sitting up straight. "You saw him at the Health Center?"

"Yeah, when I went to go get my test! The test that *you* made me get!"

"You just told me you never saw him after Halloween, and then in the next breath you're gonna tell me you wouldn't *lie* to me?" He swung himself off the bed and started reaching for his clothes. *God fucking damn shit fuck.*

"No, I wouldn't—that doesn't—Ethan, *please*—"

"You know, after that first kiss," he said after he popped his head through his shirt, "I blew off *anybody* who tried talking to me, even old hookups who showed me a *really* good time, because the boy of my dreams told me that he liked me, and I pushed *everything* out to make room for him. But I guess I was just being stupid."

"No! It's *not* stupid! I did the same thing for *you!*" I pleaded through my tears. *How is seeing me crying not enough to convince him?* "Please just listen!" *We can't leave this way! You can't tell me this is how it ends!*

He laced up his shoes—shoes as old as our relationship—and zipped up his coat. "You and *Devon* can go and have at it now, not that my permission matters." He opened the door, and I only then remembered I was butt-naked. "Bye Trevor. Have a good Break," he said without looking back. And then he was gone—gone not with a hug and a kiss, but with resentment and a slamming door. I struggled into my jeans and hoodie, stuffing my ID into my back pocket before taking off down the hall after him. I threw open doors without caring how loudly they slammed against the walls, tore past the alarmed-looking DA without an explanation, and ran out into the night-sized freezer. I looked around wildly, seeing him nowhere, calling his name everywhere. The biting sidewalk stinging me through my socks was nothing compared to the chilly, merciless evisceration he left me with.

I forcefully blocked Devon's number and cried into my pillow, damning everything—how Ethan felt betrayed because of me, how it wasn't even my fault, how it could very well be the end of us, how we didn't even get a real chance. He didn't answer any of my calls. I drafted and edited a novella-length text in my Notes before sending it, checking every 40 seconds for a response while Midwestern emo pounded into my ears at an unhealthy volume. Is this really how it ends for us? The brevity of us, and all the things we could have been and all the things we'll never be weighed down my car along with my clothes and other things as I drove away from

New Halle. Yes, I know that everything comes to end eventually, but I didn't stop to think that that could apply to us—and certainly not so fucking soon.

December 15

With the decorations up and the Christmas movies on and Mom's candle spicing up the house, I should've felt warm and at home instead of cold and empty. I tried to distract myself by brainstorming Christmas gift ideas—since it's 10 days away and I've done *zero* shopping—but I couldn't go more than eight seconds without seeing Ethan walking out and my door slamming shut. I tried telling myself that he wasn't texting me back because he was busy, but every hour that passed without hearing from him made me think more and more that I wouldn't be hearing from him at all. And when my phone finally did light up with a message from him, it didn't make me feel any better.

Hey
I'm really sorry for ghosting you
I need to talk to you
Can I call you later when I get home?

It was the longest 'later' of my life. I spent all afternoon mentally preparing myself for what he'd say and rehearsing what I'd say. Nothing could keep my attention. My phone launched itself into my hand as soon as it rang.

"Hello?" I answered.

"Hey," Ethan said, looking like he hadn't slept either. Just hearing the sound of his voice put me more at ease than I'd been since we'd last held each other, even though he seemed reluctant to meet my eyes. "I've been wanting to talk to you but I've been so nervous. Forreal, you should feel how sweaty my hands are right now," he said without laughing. "I can't stop thinking about what happened."

"Yeah, me neither," I said with a chest full of ice.

"I can't believe I acted like that. My emotions were running high, and I just—" He sighed and blinked like there was something in his eye. "It's just that I've been with guys before who sweet-talked me just so they could sleep with me, and the thought of you being no different than them, it just..." He sniffled. "It *really* fucking hurt."

"I'm sorry you felt that way because of me," I said, sad at seeing him sad.

"No, don't be sorry. It was all me. It's my fault that we didn't get to say goodbye to each other. I'm so fucking *mad* at myself." And from the way he shook his head, I could tell he meant it.

"It wasn't your fault," I shook my head back. "It was just a misunderstanding."

"Either way," he said. "Can we please just kiss through our screens and pretend like that whole thing never happened? There's nothing I want more than that right now—well, other than doing it in person." His smile, however small, warmed me for the first time in over 24 hours, like creamy hot chocolate was pumping through my veins. *He still trusts me. He wants to keep trying.*

"Absolutely," I grinned before we shot each other a kiss. "Oh, and I blocked Devon's number too, so you don't have to worry about him anymore."

"You didn't have to do that," he said to his lap.

"Really, it's okay. I'll block whoever-I-need-to's number if it means keeping yours."

Instead of telling me I was stupid for pushing people out of my life for him, he instead asked, "So are you in your room? Can I see it?"

"Nope," I said before switching to my rear camera and swiveling in my chair to give him a sweeping view of my bedroom.

"Holy *books* Batman," he said. "You weren't kidding when you said you read a lot."

"When do I ever kid about anything?" He just gave me a look. "To be fair though, I have a lot that I haven't read. My buddy Logan gives me shit for it all the time. He says that I 'accumulate' books."

"He's not wrong," Ethan chuckled. "Most of the books I have are graphic novels and ones I've had since middle school that I just never got rid of."

"Do you have the *Heartstopper* books?" I asked.

"I didn't know those were books," he frowned.

I showed him them lined up on my own shelf. "The first rule about movies and series is they're *always* based on books."

"I've never even watched the show," he said like he'd just realized it.

"Isn't it still on Netflix?"

"Yeah," he said in a defeated tone. "But then my mom or stepdad would see that I'd been watching it, and then they'd start asking me why I'm watching 'some gay show,' or if I think I'm gay."

"*Do you think you're gay?*" I asked seriously, making him snort.

"But that's why I went away to school though. I'm not gonna spend the last years of my youth not being allowed to be myself and doing what I want."

"And then someday you'll move out of your house, and nobody will be able to make you be anything you don't wanna be," I encouraged him. *God, I hope I get to be there with him for it.* "And in the meantime, you have New Halle to figure out exactly what that is."

"I think I just want to be happy," he said after a moment. I was about to tell him that that's all I want too when Dad called me down for dinner. "Be down in a minute!" I yelled back. "I gotta go. He probably already thinks I'm masturbating since I have the door shut."

240

"It'd be hotter if you were," Ethan said slyly.

I gave him a mischievous smile. "I'm glad we talked that out though."

"Yeah, so am I," he beamed. "Like, so glad."

"You'll have to show me your room next time!"

"For sure! Go eat dinner, you cutie pie." He blew me a kiss and I blew one back.

"See you later, you studmuffin."

I checked my phone after dinner to see that he'd sent me a Troye Sivan song that he said makes him think of me, and I sent him back one by Waterparks that makes me think of him, which is how we ended up sending each other songs back and forth all night, enough to make a playlist out of.

December 17

POV:

You're listening to Troye Sivan and wondering who the hell you are anymore.

I was today-years-old when I paid that spice and tea store in the plaza a visit so I could pick up some loose tea. You'd think that Mom and Dad had never seen a hot beverage before from the way they watched me make a cup of it. I like to defy expectations, but I hate it when people always make a big deal out of it when I do.

I spent most of the day with Logan in his basement, talking about school and life while playing *Gran Turismo* before switching to his *Lord of the Rings* edition of *Risk*. "Anything new with that girl from your one class?" I asked him.

"You mean Sara?"

"I dunno. You never told me her name."

"Well pay attention," he pointed at me. "It's Sara. But no, not a whole lot. I know what coffee shop she works at though, so I've stopped to see her a few times."

"That's how I met my man!" I tapped my temple. "Great minds."

"Oh yeah, Emilio or whatever. So are you two like, official?"

I couldn't not smile. "Yeah, I guess we are."

"Are you gonna go Instagram official? Did you fart in front of him yet?"

I laughed as I looked down at the glyphs scratched into the tabletop from when I used to go over to his house after school and we'd struggle with math homework together. Ethan and I have been texting and Snapping each other almost nonstop, all the way up until when my phone's glow is the only light in my room, and the fizzing champagne bubbles in my chest keep me from falling asleep. I've been feeling something more for him that I'm almost afraid to admit, but if something scares the hell out of you and excites you at the same time, then you should go for it. So you heard it here first—I'm in love with Ethan. I'm in love with Ethan Eastwood.

241

December 19

Another thing I didn't think I'd miss about being away from NHU are the strings of Christmas lights Tylor and I put up. I went and dug some extras out from the attic and arranged them on the top and sides of my bookcases, but it's not the same. God, it hasn't even been a week and I'm already missing school.

It's not too often that Mom and Dad and I all get thrilled about the same thing, but me making the Dean's List is one of them. My Brit Lit essay must've not been that awful since I ended up with a B in the class. I searched the list for Ethan's name after he'd told me he made the List too. *Ethan Eastwood, Majoring in Communications, from Rosemont, Pennsylvania.* The drive there would be just under six hours.

"I didn't know you collect calendars," Ethan smiled when I called him later on to congratulate him.

"They're not *calendars*, they're *records*," I laughed, though I knew he was joking. I rolled off my bed to show them to him and the Starburst-orange vinyl spinning on my turntable. "Do you know who this is?"

He rolled his eyes. *"Duh.* Wallows." He listened for a few seconds. "It doesn't sound that different from what I stream."

"You have to hear it in person," I said. "Not to get all purist or anything, but I think music on vinyl just sounds better. Like, it has a fuller sound to it."

"Let me guess," he smiled, "I wouldn't have a refined enough palate to appreciate it?"

"Correct," I nodded. "I'm happy to know I got you into Wallows though."

He laughed out loud. "Oh, you're so cute. *Dylan Minnette* is why I got into Wallows."

"That's fair."

"For some reason I always pictured you having like, *crates* and *crates* of records," Ethan went on. "Like how cool kids in movies have tons of records."

"Records are like friends to me—it's the quality, not the quantity," I answered like the introvert I am. "Besides, I feel like people who just accumulate records just for the sake of having them are posers".

"You mean like people who accumulate books?" he smirked.

I realized as I was replacing the record in its calendar-sized sleeve that I hadn't gotten Ethan a Christmas gift. It took an evening of browsing, but I found him the *perfect* one.

"Days since I sharted myself: 0," Kade felt the need to Snap me from his bathroom.

December 22

So it's gotten to the point now where I literally cannot go more than a half hour without texting or Snapping Ethan. I was afraid that I'd look like a simp at first, but I don't even care anymore.

We usually can't call when his parents are around, but I got to see his room since they were out burning heretics or something. "So you saying how you're just 'pretty good' at baseball is clearly a lie," I said when he showed me the skyline of trophies on his dresser.

"Would you rather me brag about it like some dumb jock?"

"Maybe an emotionally intelligent jock," I joked.

"I'd actually be offended if you considered me a jock," he chuckled. "So Trevor likes jocks, huh?"

My face flushed. "*No. Maybe.* Not overly masc ones, anyway."

"I think jocks *have* to be overly masc by definition," he laughed as he fell back onto his bed. "Don't be ashamed of it. I like cute longboarders."

"Well then you're in luck," I smiled. "Forreal though, your humility is why—well, is *one* of the things I love about you."

He flipped over onto his stomach. "Does Trevor approve—*woah*, I didn't know you had a cat," he said as Misha walked across the top of the couch behind me.

"Yeah, we do," I chuckled as I reached to pet her. "I think cats are overrated, Trevor Bentley Huffman. It was my mom's idea to get her."

"I'm more of a dog person myself, Ethan Lucas Eastwood," Ethan smiled.

I raised an eyebrow. "Why'd you call yourself by your full name?"

"Because you did?" he frowned. "I just thought that's what we were doing."

"I say my name instead of 'to be honest' since it's the same as my initials. You know, TBH. It's a long story."

"Oh. Well, this is embarrassing," he chuckled. *Ethan Lucas Eastwood though.* Just saying it in my head makes my insides feel warm. "What was I saying? Oh yeah— what does Trevor think of my sock game today?" He wiggled his feet sticking up behind him.

"Oh my *god.*" I laughed. "Yeah, sure, they're great." And for whatever reason, him being cute like that was all it took for me to start spilling my true feelings for him out of nowhere. "So I need to tell you something that I've been thinking about for a while now, and I don't care what you think, but I love you Ethan." That one sentence left me breathless. He stared at me like he was watching me strip. "I love you."

He blinked. "*Woah.*" Woah what? *Good woah or bad woah?* "Nobody's ever said that to me before, other than family."

243

"You can call me crazy or say whatever you want, but it's the truth." The longer his silence went on, the stupider I felt for thinking that he could ever feel the same way about me. *Did you really think somebody could actually love you back, Trevor?*

His room rolled around him as he sat up. "What if I said…I love you too?" he smiled. *There go the Heartstopper leaves and hearts again.* "I can't believe I finally get to say that to another guy," he said like he really couldn't believe it. "I love you too, Trevor." My stomach somersaulted faster and faster. *Ethan said he loves me back. Ethan loves me back.*

"You don't know how good it feels to hear that," I said like I was euphoric.

"I do, because I just heard it too," he grinned like he was high. "You know, when I would dream about what it would be like to finally have a boyfriend, I always thought about the sex part of it, but *nothing* could've prepared me for what it would be like to fall in *love*. I've always been single though, so I wasn't sure if what I'd been feeling this whole time was love or something else. I mean, I've seen enough people fall in love with the idea of being in love rather than the person themself, so I kinda already knew what love *isn't*, if that makes any sense. I know it's more than somebody just liking you back, as easy as it is to think so."

"Yeah, it does," I nodded. "I was with somebody once who was more in love with being in love than they were with me." I laughed through my nose. "So what was it about me that made you wanna give up the single life?"

"How did I know I was in love with you?" He looked off-screen, the sun shining on his face even though it had set hours ago. "Trevor—for months, the best part of my day was seeing you, or even just getting an Instagram message from you. But I had the feeling something was up once I literally started *dreaming* about you, and I'd wake up and be so upset that it wasn't real. And now the boy I used to get so excited to see come in for coffee—the boy of my dreams—is here telling me that he loves me."

I felt myself welling up.

"You're nerdy, but in a cute, cool kinda way. You're smart and you're funny, but also laid-back. Your obscure taste in music, the fact that you longboard, and your sense of style all make you so one-of-a-kind. You're just so…*you* without caring what anybody has to say about it, and I love that about you. And you're so sweet and kind and loving—I can tell that you genuinely care about me, which is something I'm not used to from other guys. And this is all on top of you being *incredibly* good-looking. I fucking love you Trevor," he said, detonating bombs in my stomach.

"And I fucking love you too, Ethan," I said through happy tears. "I wish we were together right now, because I wanna hug you so bad."

"I wish we were too. I don't deserve you, and I don't just mean because of how I made us say goodbye to each other."

"I thought we weren't gonna talk about that anymore?"

"It'll be quick, I promise," he assured me. "I cried so fucking hard after I stormed out of your room that day. I've had guys treat me like I was nothing, or like I was just an afterthought, or like I wasn't boyfriend material, or like I was just a body for them to use."

I sniffled. "I hope you know I'd never do anything on purpose to try to make you feel that way, right?"

"I know," he said as a tear rolled down his cheek. "Like I said, I just overreacted and let my thoughts get the best of me."

"No, that was fair of you," I said. "And letting your thoughts get the best of you is *my* job, mister," I laughed.

He chuckled after a moment. "We really need to stop making each other cry."

"That's just how it works. We're gonna make each other laugh, and we're gonna make each other cry, but there's nobody else I'd rather laugh and cry with."

"Yeah, same here," he smiled. "Remember that glow stick party, and how we were talking about what things we wanted in a person?"

"Uh huh," I nodded.

"I wanted so badly to just straight-up ask you if you thought I was all of those things," he said as he twirled his hoodie string around his finger.

"You probably would've had to catch me, because I would've fallen over," I laughed. "I would've said you're all of those things and more. You think *I'm* sweet? Only the sweetest guy ever could have gotten me *this*." I showed him the Teddiursa stuffie he'd bought for me at the mall.

He lit up. "You took it home with you!"

"How couldn't I? It's cute and makes me think of you." I tried balancing it on my head for him but it kept tumbling off. "And your talent at singing and playing music is *way* more attractive than me supposedly being smart. And if you think *I'm* good-looking—"

"Which you *are*."

"—then you should see yourself. I'm hideous compared to you."

"Stop it!" he laughed. "No you're not!"

"You make me wanna just, *ugh*, kiss you slow and gentle one moment, and then just plow you the next."

He stroked his chin with a smirk. "I'm listening."

So that's how we ended up stripping off our pants and underwear and talking dirty as we jerked off to each other. Thank god Mom and Dad weren't home, though I'm sure it wouldn't have been the first time they would've heard their son getting off with another boy. "Welp, this shirt's getting washed now," I said once we were finished.

"And I'm due for a shower now too," Ethan said as he looked down at the mess he'd made on himself.

"Well, I'm gonna let you do that before the KGB gets home," I said as I carefully pulled my shirt off. "I'm looking forward to us doing that together in person," I said with a wink.

"Yes *please*." His bed shrunk away behind him as he got up off of it. "Alrighty, have a good night. I'll talk to you later."

"Yeah, you too. Goodnight." And then I hesitated, like I was about to ride my bike without training wheels for the first time. "I love you."

He beamed at me with a face-splitting grin. "I love you too." We blew each other kisses, and he was gone. It was a 47-minute call.

My mattress caught me, and I stared at the ceiling as I pictured the movie scene for what had just happened. We'd be in the Quad on a cloudless day. Some upbeat song would play from all over. We'd say 'I love you' for the first time and kiss just as the chorus came in, right there, stadium-rock loud. Students and professors would come together in a flash mob as champagne and confetti rockets into the air with absolutely no ejaculatory undertones. I texted him the song for that scene— "Lovesick" by Peace—and he sent me back song after song after song.

December 24

A.S.—"Post Humorous" by Gus Dapperton

Dear Dillon,

In another life, Trevor and Dillon are giving each other the Christmas gifts they'd put so much thought into right now. In a past life, Trevor and Dillon are fantastically unaware that they'll only get one Christmas to spend together.

Do you have Christmas lights hanging up in your dorm room? I've lost track of how many nights I'd lay in my bed under the gentle glow of those melancholy lights, imagining they were all galaxies, all different universes where Trevor and Dillon are still together. I'd get lost in them, wishing that you were there cuddling with me, pointing up at all the different possibilities of our future together. *In that one we just got our first apartment together, we're on vacation at the beach there.* I don't know if you had as much hope for those dreams as I did, or even any at all, but thanks for going along with them anyway, even if it all would just make the eventual heartbreak hurt that much worse.

I can't believe how stupid I was. It's nothing against you—I just can't get over how quickly I gave myself away to the first person who liked me back. But I guess that's just how first loves go, right? One person shows you some attention, and you shove everything else out of the way for them. Looking back, all the tension I felt that I figured was just part of a relationship was really the cracks starting to show. If you have to make it look genuine, then it probably isn't genuine. You were just the first one to realize that we'd never actually work out, the first of us to admit that a love that's convenient couldn't last if we wanted what was best for ourselves. We were just in love with the idea of being in love. We were convenient for each other. Our lives intersected at the wrong time for the wrong reasons, even if it felt nothing but right.

I never thought I'd say this, but thank you for bringing us to an end, because I sure as hell know it would never have happened if it was left up to me. What you did caused me unimaginable pain, but it was really the best thing for me. Because now I'm looking up at those lights and I'm making the same wishes again, but they're not with you anymore.

When you made us strangers again, you told me it was because you didn't want to miss out on the things that being with me would've kept you from, but I never stopped to think that maybe the same thing could've been true for me too. I wasn't looking for love when I first met Ethan, because having your heart torn to shreds can do that to you. But the more he hung around me and the more I got to know him, I found myself falling for him whether I wanted to or not. He's considerate, he's sweet, he's caring. He has these deep blue whirlpool eyes that suck you in, and the most adorable smile. And he doesn't have to do anything over-the-top for me either to make me feel like I'm his main character. Sure, we annoy each other and we've had our disagreements, but I wouldn't trade him for anybody, not even you.

I hope you find your own Ethan if you haven't met him already. I hope you find the person who makes your legs bounce and your stomach flutter from just thinking about him, the person who you want to know everything about, the person who keeps you up at night in the best way under the glow of your own Christmas lights.

Merry Christmas Dillon. I hope you find your happiness. I really do.

Sincerely,

Trevor

December 25

Remember when I told Logan how getting hit with a blizzard was none of my business? Now it's my business. I've never seen so much fucking snow in my life. Mom and Dad have never seen so much fucking snow in *their* lives. We gave up on trying to shovel it until it stops, though it's not like we're going to be going anywhere anyway thanks to the driving ban. It made me happy in a mean way to see that it's like -25° down in Pittsburgh though. "Take that you turds," I Snapped Kade and

Victor. Victor responded with a selfie of him grinning and flashing a peace sign with the rest of the family covered in flour in the background, rolling and folding dough on their kitchen island. *"Pyrohy,"* he captioned it.

I really don't think I could've asked for a better Christmas Eve though. We baked cookies and watched Christmas movies in our comfiest clothes with the fireplace on, and if *that's* not hygge then I don't know what is. I legit can't remember the last time Mom and Dad and I spent time together like that. Maybe Ryder being gone just makes us that much more appreciative of one other.

I had all day to do it, but I waited until before bed last night to call Ethan. "I was wondering if I'd get to talk to you today," he answered, wearing a plain black t-shirt and—

"Oh my god," I gasped.

He spun around like there was a bat in the room. "What?"

I gawked at him. "How long have you worn glasses?" They're clear-framed, like the kind of glasses I could see Kade wearing if he had bad eyes.

"Since like, 3rd grade?" he laughed. "I wear contacts most of the time though, obviously."

"You should wear your glasses more often. And here I thought you couldn't get any cuter," I smiled, making him giggle. "So did you have a good Christmas Eve?"

"Yeah, it wasn't bad," he shrugged. "My family actually behaved themselves—but then again, I hung around my little cousins for most of the night. How about yours? That blizzard is on national news."

"Yeah, we physically can't go anywhere. It was the most low-key Christmas Eve ever. I loved it."

We talked about how magical Christmas used to feel when we were little, the *one* toy we were so stoked to get, the terror of having to leave our rooms to go to the bathroom out of fear of being seen by Santa, how the magic died when we found out that Santa isn't real, how much more fun it was to open actual presents instead of an envelope or taking stuff out of a stocking—'stuff' being *Pokémon Violet*, a pair of AirPod Pros, a gift card, candy, and deodorant. "I knew something was up when I realized that all my gifts had *bar*"—he yawned mid-word—*"codes* on them."

"Somebody's sleepy," I chuckled.

"I *am*. I'm gonna have to get to bed or else Santa won't come."

I yawned too, because of the thing where you yawn after you see somebody else yawn. "You think you're gonna get any presents with how naughty you've been?" I smirked.

"That's true," he said, putting a finger to his bottom lip. "I *have* been a bad boy."

"I'm about to get to bed too though, so you'll have to seduce me later," I winked at him. "I'll talk to ya later, you sexy little elf." After we said our *goodnights* and *I love yous*, I hugged Teddiursa close in bed, wishing that it would turn into Ethan like a Christmas movie miracle.

Ethan Snapped me a dick pic this morning captioned *"merry christmas!!* 😌*"* followed by an ass pic captioned *"wish you were here to stuff my stocking* 😺*."* I screenshotted them before returning the favor. What I expected to be more Christmas nudes ended up being pics of him holding a brand-new Switch over the bottom half of his face, and a top-down view of an immaculate, still-boxed pair of Air Force 1s.

Kade's Snap story was a pic of him, Victor, and their sister Kelsey all throwing different poses in presumably-new sweaters. *"Why we look like we about to drop the hottest album of 2022??"*

December 26

> Expectations are like the itchy sweater I was
> Forced into wearing at the holidays—
> Sit, smile, and behave,
> So "everybody" can enjoy themselves.

> -another decoration

December 29

Ethan talked me into grilling a peanut butter and jelly sandwich—like how you make grilled cheese—and I've been living my life wrong this whole time. It was like big, warm gobs of cum in my mouth. It was like eating a pastry.

I knew that going out the day they lifted the driving ban would be a nightmare, but I was so tired of being stuck inside that I didn't care—at least not until we were actually out driving. The books and clothes and board game I got made it worth it though. Logan and Madi and I finished off the last of the Christmas cookies, exchanged our gifts, and were inaugurating my new game when my phone's screen lit up from the floor with an incoming call from Ethan.

"*The* Ethan?" Madi asked as I reached for it.

"Yeah! I'm just gonna say hi real quick and tell him I'll call him back later."

"Why don't you have a pic of him as your background?"

I shushed her with my hand. *Please don't be naked,* I thought as I answered. "Hey babe. And before you say anything dirty, Madi and Logan are here with me."

"Babe? That's a new one," he grinned in his glasses. "And I wasn't *going* to, but now I'm thinking about it. Hi Trevor's friends!"

I held out my phone so they could see each other. "Hi!" Madi waved enthusiastically.

"What's *happening*," Logan casually asked from the floor.

"What game are you playing?" Ethan asked me once he was face-to-face with me again.

"*Ticket to Ride.* I just got it today. I'll have to bring it down with me."

"Go 'head! I don't wanna keep you from your friends though. Call me later?"

I wasn't about to be that guy again who ignores their friends as soon as they're seeing somebody. "Of course," I smiled. "Love you."

"Talk to you later! Love you too!"

"You two are so cute," Madi said after we hung up. "You should've seen the way your face lit up when you saw it was him. Have I mentioned how attractive he is?"

"Several times."

"You said he plays baseball, right?" Logan asked. "Does he pitch or catch?"

I snorted while Madi swatted him with the rulebook. "You can't just *ask* someone that!"

"I think first base, actually," I said.

"What, is that as far as you've gotten?" he said without skipping a beat.

I got the green light from Ethan later before calling him. "You don't really talk about your friends that much," he said.

"I dunno. I figured you wouldn't be interested in hearing about people you don't know. You don't talk about *yours*," I pointed out.

"That's fair. Though I'd just make you jealous if I did," he smirked.

We got on the subject of high school politics, high school drama, and girls who'd flirted with us. "I was content with having just a few friends over a lot of acquaintances in high school," I told him. "I wasn't socially awkward or anything, but I was a nerdy introvert who barely got involved in anything. I wish I'd done more though." The pangs of regret stung like paintballs on my skin. "I feel like I just let it all pass me by."

"Well, I'm sure COVID didn't help," Ethan offered. "And it's easy to feel bad about yourself when you look at all of your own experiences and compare them to the ones other people seem like they're having."

"That's why I stopped using Facebook and Twitter."

"But to be hon—*I mean,* Trevor Bentley Huffman," he said, making me smile, "I think you were smart to stay true to yourself."

"Doesn't mean I didn't miss out on things," I muttered.

"Yeah, but now you have the chance to not let that happen again. We're already an eighth of the way through our time at college, so how will you spend the next seven-eighths of it?"

"Shit, you know I'm not good at math," I chuckled to try to downplay the truth of it. "I feel like I've been doing a pretty good job though. 16-year-old me would've probably stayed in my room with the door shut."

"I'm glad to hear it," he smiled. "So what else did you buy besides that game?"

"Some books, some clothes. I got a sweatshirt like the Gryffindor one you have, except mine's Ravenclaw."

"Copycat! But now we can take cute couples pics together!"

"Yeah, in a *month*," I rolled my eyes. "Send me a pic of you in your sweatshirt and I'll send you one of me in mine. We can be cute and have each other as our background pics."

"I get to be a background pic?" he gasped. *"Noice."*

He sent me a selfie of him cheesing it up in his Gryffindor sweatshirt after we hung up, and I sent him back one of the trying to look goofy yet scholarly in my Ravenclaw-blue. And speaking of shirts, the one I got for him came today and I love it. I'm absolutely keeping it for myself if he's not ready to wear it yet.

December 30

I was today-years-old when I tried shawarma for the first time from that place in the food court, which would've never happened if not for a semester of trying new things and having friends who are more cultured than me.

Our kitchen was alive with Mom making her Linzertorte and Dad and I assembling checkerboard cookies for our postponed Christmas gathering with the family, which ended early for me after Uncle Richard fondly reminisced, "Remember when Jake from State Farm used to be white?" and then everybody started going on about how things are going to shit because of "the Blacks" and "the Mexicans." I didn't even try to argue with them—I just drove my ass home. And that was on top of Brayden and Mason saying shit just to get me worked up. It's funny how when they say something repulsive they're just playing around, but when I tell them to shut the fuck up then *I'm* being disrespectful. Is it because they're older than me? Does being older give you a pass to say whatever the hell you want, even if it's downright offensive?

Family was always just a given when I was younger, especially at Christmas, but then I learned the hard way that it's as transitory as anything else in life. I'm always mindful that every time I see Grandma could very well be the last. I hadn't seen her since graduation, so she was all ears when I told her about school—not in any great detail of course. And then we had a moment that hit me pretty hard.

"I'm so proud of you, Trevor," she said in a quivery voice like her Parkinson's had spread there too.

I never bring up my sexuality around her since I mentally assume she's still living in 1958, so I surprised myself when I asked in a louder-than-normal-so-she-could-hear-me-clearly tone, "Even though I like boys instead of girls?" Because you know, that tends to be the dealbreaker. I'm not even really sure why I said it.

She studied me from her houndstooth wing chair like I was a puzzle. "Nobody in our family was ever raised to sit in the backseat, Trevor." I wordlessly hugged her, putting all my love and appreciation and thanks into that hug.

January 1, 2023

TFW the new year starts on a Sunday.

I brought Drunk *Jenga* home solely to take to whatever New Year's party we'd find ourselves at, which was at Ian Umoh's place. His parents were celebrating their anniversary in New York City and had to be as dumb as a bag of hammers to think their son wouldn't have a party while they were away. 17-year-old Trevor would've been freaked to know that he would someday be one of those guys back home on Break from college who brought a drinking game that none of the high schoolers had heard of. The seniors hounded me about college parties and what it's like being able to sleep with people whenever I wanted, like that's all you do in college. I actually don't mind the kids a year below me though because they're not as full of themselves like a lot of my class was/is. And speaking of classmates, I guess Chris Burkhart is bi?!?! Like what the hell? He told us how he finally got the courage to come out after a few weeks into the semester "after some experimenting." Why couldn't he have wanted to experiment when we were still in school together?

I learned that Madi knows her way around a pong table from the way her and I schooled everybody who challenged us. It felt kind of violating to play pong on an actual dining room table instead of some beat-up thing that looked like it was ready to collapse. I Snapped Victor a video of the party when A Day to Remember started playing because I knew he'd appreciate it. He and Kade were at a party in somebody else's basement, where nauseating patterns of light spun on everything. 'YOOOOOOOOO!' he responded in a button-down shirt and tie like he was somebody with a desk job getting drunk on a Friday night.

The alarm I had set for 11:50 went off, sending me to search for a quiet spot upstairs. After walking in on some bored-looking guys sitting around a bong on a bedroom floor, and *almost* walking into something much more sensual by the sound of it, I shut myself in Mrs. Umoh's office, where the muffled bass was all I could hear of the music below me. I looked around at the certificates on the wall until background music that wasn't from my own party snapped my head back to my phone. "Babe! I was just about to call you!" Ethan smiled in a glittery plastic bowler hat.

"*Sure* you were," I grinned. *Even tipsy in a cheap bowler hat, he's adorable.* "On a scale of 1 to cheeseburger, how much are you feeling it?"

"Uh...like 7 and a packet of ketchup? You?"

"Just enough to be giggly and feel good. I'm not tryna get fucked-up or anything." He raised his eyebrows at me. "What? I'm not!"

"Uh huh sure, go ahead. Are you okay to drive?"

"*Pffft.* Absolutely not. But I walked, so it's okay—it's like only a few streets away from my house. What about you?" I looked at the pastel-pink curtains he sat against. "Where are you?"

He waved me off. "I'll get a ride with somebody who's not drinking. And I'm in a former classmate's sister's bedroom. Where are *you?*"

I put my hand on my chest. "*I* am in the home office of a high school chemistry teacher."

"Well excuse *us.*"

We stared at each other for a moment and both started to speak at the same time. "You go first," he laughed.

"I was just gonna say that I really wish you were here. Or that I was there. I don't care which."

"That's what *I* was gonna say! It'd probably better if I was there though."

"Can you make it here in the next five minutes?" I asked.

"If I could have *one* New Year's wish come true, it would be that I could be there with you tonight."

"Well that's my wish now too, so it *has* to happen," I said longingly. "I miss you so much."

"I miss me too," he laughed. "Forreal though, I'd give anything to be with you. I guess I'll just have to wait until next year to have my first New Year's kiss." The pit of my stomach dropped out. *'Next year,' just like how Dillon and I talked about 'next Halloween' and 'next Christmas' like they were givens.*

We talked about how the parties we were at were going until a few minutes to midnight, when Ethan told me to get back down to my own. "Nuh uh, no way I'm letting you go into the new year alone!" I protested.

"You can take your phone *with* you, you know," he grinned. "And I'm supposed to believe you're a Ravenclaw?"

"Aren't you gonna go back to your own party?"

He just grinned. "I'm already with everyone I need."

Back in the great room, Madi grabbed my arm like I'd been gone for years. "Where *were* you? Get over here, it's almost time!" She stumbled as she led me by my sleeve over to Logan.

"Say hi to Ethan!" I said as I showed them my phone. Ethan smiled and waved.

"Hi Ethan," Logan said.

"Ethan! Oh my *god*, where *are* you?" Madi asked like she'd been trying to contact him for days. Logan and I caught each other's glance and stifled a laugh.

"A friend's house in Rosemont," he answered.

"Where's Rosemont?" she asked like lives were at stake.

"Outside of Philly."

"Why are you there?"

"I live here."

"That *sucks*. That really sucks." She cupped her hand around the back of my phone, looking at him like he was in exile. "Oh my god, he's so cute. How is he so cute, Trevor?"

"I dunno," I laughed as I flicked my eyes to the TV. *30 seconds to go.* "He just is," I beamed at Ethan.

"Look Maura," Madi said as she tugged on Maura Massey's arm. "Say hi to Trevor's cute boyfriend."

Maura smiled and waved. "Hi Trevor's cute boyfriend."

"Why is it always the girls who think I'm cute?" Ethan asked once we were face-to-face again.

I raised an eyebrow. "*Only* girls?"

"You know what I mean."

New Year's always feels like I'm about to go on vacation or something. 20 seconds. Like it's exciting because the whole world's celebrating, but at the same time it's kind of scary because nothing can stop it. 15 seconds. It's inevitable. 13. Is that what it will feel like to die? Knowing that you're about to cross an irreversible boundary, and no amount of pleading or bargaining or fear or anything will make it stop? 7. Isn't going from non-existence to existence a sort of death too? 4. It won't stop. 3. I can't make it stop. 2. Somebody make it stop! 1.

The room erupted in cheers all at once, like we were really into sports and our team just won. The couples kissed long and slow while the rest of us hugged. "New York, New York" blasted from the speakers. Ethan and I blew each other kisses, and I broke away to have a moment just with him.

"I like that song," Ethan smiled. "I'd love to see New York City."

"I'd love to take you there," I said as I brushed confetti out of my hair, thinking of us kissing on a hotel balcony overlooking the biggest party on Earth. *Maybe next year*, I almost said.

A door opened on his end, and he dropped me into his lap. *"There* you are!" somebody who sounded *way* drunker than Ethan said. "I was looking for you! Why are you in here by yourself? You missed the ball drop!"

"I needed somewhere quiet to talk to my friend," he said. *His friend.*

"We're gonna play Kings. You in?" The guy sounded like he was right there.

"Yeah, I'll be down. Please get off me."

"What's *with* you all of a sudden?"

"Go. I'll be right out."

I heard movement and the sound of the door not shutting. "Alright, but come on."

"You still there?" Ethan's face reappeared. "Sorry, he's been annoying as fuck all night," he apologized. "But I guess I should get back to the party. I'm glad I got to bring in the New Year with you," he smiled.

"Yeah, me too," I answered with an empty feeling inside me.

"I'll talk to you tomorrow, okay? Be safe getting home." He blew me a kiss. "I love you babe."

"Love you too."

And then he was gone. A balloon came down from the ceiling and bounced off my head. *What would he have said to Mystery Intruder if I wasn't there? Is he really playing Kings? "Sorry about that, it was just this one annoying guy from school. Come on back in."* I couldn't stop thinking about it. I felt nauseous. The thought lingered on the walk home, hung beside me while I put on my *of-course-I-wasn't-drinking* face in case Mom and Dad were still up, and kept me awake, spreading like black tar in my skull. *Is he fooling around with somebody else? Am I just being paranoid?* My bed tossed me until I heard my phone vibrate. It was a link to Ella Fitzgerald's "What Are You Doing New Year's Eve?" from Ethan, who must've remembered how I said it's one of my favorite Christmas songs.

Hey babe 😊
Just wanted to let you know i love you and miss you
and i wish we were with each other tonight and i
cant wait to bring in the next year with you so mark
it on your calendar 😊
Sleep tight 😴 😴 😴 😴

I held my phone close and listened to the song with an uncontrollable smile. My chest glowed with warmth. I've never been so happy to be my stupid, overthinking, Trevor self. *I can't believe you think he'd go ahead and* cheat *on you, you turd.*

Kade's Snapchat story this morning was a sideways view of his room from the POV of his bed. *"PSA.....if a bottle of rum has 151 on it.....that DOESNT mean it has 151 flavors."*

January 3

I'm sure the Oakley/Morozov household is having a party at their house tonight because of this whole the-majority-party-can't-even-elect-a-Speaker-of-the-House bedlam. I fucking love it.

Trying out shawarma gave me the nudge I needed to place an order from an Indian place down the road in Orchard Park. I got butter chicken on Tylor's recommendation as well as a few starters, because when in New Delhi, amirite? It smelled more intriguing than pungent, unlike anything I'd ever smelled before. I could almost hear Sunita playing her sitar as I breathed it in.

"I didn't know you liked Indian food," Dad said with a wrinkled nose when he leaned over to see what I'd gotten.

"I don't. This'll be my first time trying it."

He gave me a bemused look. "See what happens when you go away to college?" It was so good that I literally couldn't stop eating it, to the point that my stomach hurt. I even broke my vow to never make a food post on Instagram.

wallowing_tbh Why have doses and mimosas when you can have dosas and samosas?

hayashi_photography 😎

oakley_dokey YES MY BROTHER क्या यह सर्वोत्तम नहीं है ?

EthanE16 😉

logank22 right there with ya @EthanE16

January 4

When does wishing other people a happy new year become weird? Do you still tell people Merry Christmas on December 28th? Yeah, I didn't think so.

"I've never read *Treasure Island*," Ethan said when I set my phone down on my bookshelf to change shirts after our virtual rope-blasting session. "Is it any good?"

"Yeah, I liked it," I said as I stepped back into my underwear. "It's been years since I read it though."

"What would you say your favorite book is?"

I didn't even pretend to have to think about it. "*The Perks of Being a Wallflower*, followed by *The Catcher in the Rye*."

"Never read 'em."

"Hashtag *shooketh*, but also not surprised."

He raised an eyebrow. "What's *that* supposed to mean?"

"You just don't really seem like a reader."

"I mean, not like *you*. There were a few books we had to read that weren't bad. I really liked *Simon vs. the Homo Sapiens Agenda*."

"I wonder why *that* would be," I chuckled as my finger ran up the spine of my own copy. "*Wait*, they had you read *that* in school?"

"Oh my god no, I read that on my own," he laughed. "Can you imagine?"

"That's why I was surprised," I said, though it *should* be allowed so gay kids can see that it's okay to be gay, which I guess is what the fascist Repube media means by 'sexualizing kids.' If you care so much about kids then maybe get them vaccinated or get a gun buyback program going instead of forcing them to go to church.

"I watched the movie over my friend Chante's house," Ethan told me, "and I remember thinking, *that's me. That's who I am.* I couldn't deny I was gay after that, as much as I wanted to. I remember being so upset knowing that my mom and stepdad would never be as accepting as Simon's parents were if I ever came out to them. But yeah, once I found out it was a book, I borrowed it from the library and read it under the cover of the night." I couldn't tell if he was joking or not. "Did you ever have a moment like that? When you knew you couldn't bullshit yourself anymore?"

"Yeah," I nodded. "It was junior year. Madi and Logan and I went to the movies and then got food afterwards, and there were these two other guys sitting on the same side of their booth, holding hands under the table and pecking each other on the lips. And I couldn't stop glancing over at them. I felt so *envious* of them."

"That was pretty recent then," Ethan said. "That makes me feel not so bad about myself for being late to the party."

"Don't feel bad at all. Nobody's journey's are the same." I bit the inside of my cheek. "I came out to the two of them that night."

"What'd you do, slide in beside them and ask if they were looking for a third?" he laughed.

"Not the two *guys*," I groaned. "Madi and Logan!"

"I know, I'm just being a pain," he smiled. "How'd that go though? I guess it must've gone well if they're still friends with you."

"Yeah. I thought Madi might try to make me her trophy gay best friend, but I was more worried about how Logan would take it."

"So what'd you say?"

"We were at his place later on and I kinda just asked them out of nowhere if they'd think any differently of me if I said I liked boys. I was so scared that I was shaking. They hugged me, and I cried my eyes out."

"I wish I had the balls to come out to my friends," he said forlornly.

"But you did though," I reminded him.

"I mean my friends here at *home*."

"You'll get there," I encouraged him. "Like I said, you go at your own pace. Do you wanna borrow some other gay books in the meantime?" I asked to try to put him in a better mood. "I can bring them down to school with me."

I've never seen him get so stoked about reading before. *No, not just reading—finding validation.* "Really?"

"Of course. We need to make up for your deficiency of vitamin gay. And every banned gay book you read takes a year off the life of a homophobe." It's funny how the Repubes want to ban books because they think they'll make kids gay, but then they'll say that guns aren't what kill people—and by 'funny' I mean 'shut the fuck up.'

Ethan sent me that meme later on of the two guys texting each other "*goodnight bro*" and "*goodnight buddy*" in their own beds and smiling at the thought of fucking each other.

Us AF 😄😌😉

January 6

I've lived through a lot of forgettable days, but January 6, 2021 isn't one of them.

It was the first week of class after Break, and I was playing *Minecraft* when the notifications started coming in. I *never* watched the news thanks to the shitshow that was 2020, but I was glued to the TV. Is that what it was like to watch the news on 9/11? To know that you're watching a line in American history get crossed, that things aren't ever going to be the same again? I think that was the moment where Mom and Dad went, *you know, maybe this guy's not as righteous as he says he is.* Ryder was fucking livid. "*Are you gonna give the asshole a fucking pass on this too?*" he bellowed at them, pointing at the TV. For all the bible verses that Repubes construe and interpret for their own benefit, you'd think something as plain as "*Thou shall not have any other gods before me*" would be pretty unequivocal. How fucking dumb were we to think that all the fascist bullshit nonsense would die with 2020, and that everything would just go back to normal once the election was over?

January 8

So I think it's safe to say that out-of-control tipping culture is what's most wrong with our society, no contest. Not the hate and the ignorance, not the putting party over country, not the people who whip out their freedom card as an excuse to shit on other people's rights. Like, we're already paying jacked-up prices and now *we're* supposed to bear the cost of people's wages instead of the billion-dollar companies they work for? That's the kind of shit the people of France executed the monarchy over.

Kade sideswiped me when he texted me to tell me I should read a book called *Everyone in This Room Will Someday Be Dead*, because I've never seen him even pick up a book. I returned the gesture with *It's Kind of a Funny Story* now that I know he reads, since that seems like the most Kade book I have.

As enamored as I am with Ethan, I'd be lying if I said I wasn't a little nervous about being his first relationship. Dillon and I were each other's firsts, and we had no idea what the hell we were doing. We were so thrilled to be out and to be ourselves that we wanted to show ourselves off, but it was like everything we did was just to check a box on the High School Relationship Checklist just to feel validated. *Kiss in the hallways every chance we get—check! Make out at the movies—check! Flood our social media pages with each other—check! Hold hands everywhere we go—check! Convince everyone, including ourselves, that we're the perfect couple—check!*

"You know, like how they say not to cut down the first Christmas tree you see?" I said when I opened up about it to Ethan. "You can't tell me I'm the perfect person for you when I'm the only one you've been with."

"I don't think there's such a thing as 'the perfect person' for anybody," he said. "I think overlooking someone's imperfections and putting in the work to build a relationship with them is what makes them perfect."

"I mean, yeah," I admitted. "But even so, why would you wanna be with *me* out of all the other guys out there?"

"Look, I don't care if the reasons why I love you make sense to you or not," he said so seriously that I almost got defensive. "Just because you're my first boyfriend doesn't mean that my heart doesn't know what it wants. Maybe I *don't* have anybody to compare you to, and honestly, I hope that I never do. If I didn't wanna see what we could become, then you would've just been another guy I knew once. Don't you wanna see what we can be?"

"Of course I do," I nodded, terrified, but in a zooming-through-the-cosmos-in-wonder kind of way.

And then he said something that's been high-key haunting me ever since. "Believe me, if I didn't have forever in mind, then I wouldn't be wasting my time."

January 10

POV:

You're browsing Switch games to see if there's anything worth picking up when you overhear a woman looking for a game to get for her kid for his birthday but she's looking at old Sega games and she says the ones that cost $2 are too expensive for her and you leave without buying anything because you feel so privileged in the worst way and you tear up in your car because some people's lives are that hard and it doesn't have to be that way.

January 13

You know what pisses me the fuck off? A Black man—Tyre Nichols, because say their names—getting beaten by the cops just for being Black, and the cops getting away with it because they're white and white people can get away with anything. *Literally* fucking anything. Can you fucking imagine if Obama had tried to stage a coup to keep himself in power? Or if a crowd of Black Lives Matters protesters tried storming the Capitol to facilitate said coup? Why are all Muslims terrorists but a murderous cop is 'just a bad apple?'

Madi goes back to school tomorrow already, which sucks because I feel like the three of us barely got to hang out. And our Spring Breaks don't line up, so I probably won't see her again until Summer. The three of us spent our last day together just hanging out and driving around without a destination. As I watched the sun set fire to the horizon, I couldn't help but think about the person I was when we hung out for the last time over the Summer, and how nervous I was about going to New Halle only to discover how fun it would be, so anxious about living with a stranger only to end up with the chillest roommate, so worried about not making any friends only to meet people I'd share blood with. And of course, I sure as shit didn't think I'd be falling in love again anytime soon.

We ended up at Applebee's and split five different appetizers like it was senior year again. "Can we promise not to be strangers this semester?" I asked as I tried to catch a strand of cheese from a loaded nacho.

"Can we please?" Madi said as she wiped sauce off her face. "I keep telling myself I'm gonna make time, but then I keep getting caught up with stuff."

"Yeah, I'd like that," Logan said, making my asshole clench. I hate to think what it feels like to have your two best friends move away and forget about you.

I made room on the table to lay my hand down. "No being strangers this year."

They put their hands on mine. "No more being strangers."

Kade's Snapchat story was a pic of a meat tenderizer on the counter next to a chicken breast. *"Beating my meat brb."*

January 16

I don't know why the people who made calendars put Christmas at the beginning of Winter instead of at the end of it. That way there'd be lights and decorations up all Winter to make the snow and the gray not feel so depressing.

I could tell Ethan was pissed about something when I answered his call and he was muttering "I can't fucking *stand* them" to himself. Flurries fell around his hooded head.

"Hi," I said cautiously. "Is something wrong? Why are you outside?"

"Yes, and I'm taking a walk because I needed to get away from my family," he said in an annoyed tone.

"Why? Did you come out to them?"

He scoffed. *"No.* Jesus fucking Christ, I can only imagine how *that* would've gone over," he laughed bitterly. He stopped walking to take a few breaths. "Gimme a sec," he said with closed eyes. *"Okay.* Hi babe. How are you?"

"Good? Cozier than you from the looks of it." Hearing the wind on his end made my velvety faux-fur bedspread and my mug of tea that much warmer. "I think I already know the answer, but how are *you?"*

"I'm *great,"* he said sarcastically. "The family came over for my mom's birthday and basically everybody ganged up on me."

My jaw dropped. *"What?* What for?"

"Pffft. Anything. Every fucking thing turns into an argument, and I'm getting *really* fucking sick of it."

"What happened today?"

"So almost my entire family's beliefs are the *complete* opposite of mine. Politics, religion, you name it."

"That's not a good start."

"It's not. But I guess they think the only reason I'm starting to speak my mind now is because I'm going to some liberal arts school and I think I know everything now. But I've *always* thought the way I think. I've just stopped giving a shit about keeping my opinions to myself, because if everybody else is allowed to speak their mind, then why can't I?"

"I think we might have the same family," I said. "But good for you. You shouldn't be expected to just sit there and shut up. You're entitled to a voice." *Maybe try taking your own advice sometime, Trevor.*

"You'd think," he rolled his eyes. "My family says they aren't racist, but then they'll say shit like, 'I was at the store the other day, and nothing against Black people, *but...*' and then they'll say something prejudiced about Black people. Or like, 'this car was blasting music and *of course* they were Black.' And then if I ask them what the point of them mentioning that they were Black was, they'll tell me I'm just being dense or that it was just an observation."

I nodded. "Yep, sounds accurate."

"But anyway, I'm *high-key* surprised that nobody said anything about how Tyre Nichols would still be alive if he'd just 'listened to the police.'"

I swallowed, choosing my words deliberately. "I mean, I'll mention somebody's race or ethnicity, but only if I need to make some kind of distinction. When my family says the stuff they say, they're only doing it to validate their bigotry. You know what I mean?"

"Yeah, I do. I don't think anybody's *totally* unbiased, but I would never think of myself as being inherently *better* than somebody else just because I'm white and they're not."

"I know you don't. If you did, then we wouldn't be talking. Like at *all*."

"But anyway, my aunt was saying how 'Arabs'"—he made air quotes—"shouldn't be allowed to own guns because 'you just don't know what they're up to,'" he spat.

"Oh my god, you're joking. *Forreal?*" I don't understand why people get so upset about foreigners coming here and living among us. Like, if we're constantly telling the rest of the world that we're the greatest country on Earth, don't you think people are going to want to come check it out? And don't even start with that *'they need to come into the country legally'* bullshit. The concept of a person being illegal makes as much sense to me as internet cables on the bottom of the ocean floor.

"Believe me, my chest was *pounding*," Ethan went on. "I factually pointed out that white conservative men are the ones who shouldn't be allowed near guns since most mass shooters—or should I say terrorists—fall into that demographic, and the shit. Hit. The fan. You have to remember, these are the same people who ask me when I'm going to buy an assault rifle."

"When *are* you going to buy an assault rifle?" I joked to try to lighten the mood a little.

"Well, seeing as I don't have any plans to kill a lot of people in a short amount of time, never." He sighed. "I'd be fine if I never had to see them again. I wish I could just move away."

"Can you pull off an accent?" I asked. "We can tell my parents you're an exchange student friend and need somewhere to stay over Break."

"Have you been listening to anything I've been telling you?" he asked forcefully. "Sorry, but I'm just tired of not being able to be myself. It doesn't help that I'm in a mood right now. That, and it's fucking freezing out."

"I can tell," I said.

"I just need the rest of this week to go by so I can get back to school."

"Maybe we can get an apartment in New Halle together and just live there until we graduate," I said, sending my own mind racing.

He smiled for the first time the whole call. "That'd be nice." *God, wouldn't it?* "Well, I'm gonna try to collect my thoughts and prepare myself for when I go back inside."

"Okay, good luck." I blew him a kiss. "I love you."

"Love you too babe."

I feel awful that he has to put up with that. At least *my* parents eventually came to their senses, but to not even have *them* on your side? *Sheesh.*

January 18

POV:

You're listening to "Ceremony" by New Order in the dark and the years you didn't get to live and the people you weren't allowed to love and the things you didn't get to experience are torturing you and the salty taste of your tears reminds you that as much as it hurts this is what it means to be human.

January 19

I really hope Zukoff has some Indian options, because I don't think I can go months without having it in my life.

Ethan and I have been calling each other every day, even if just to prop each other up against a stack of books or a baseball trophy while we play Switch or whatever and talk about our day at work or a new artist we started listening to. "So remember how I told you I wanna work on being more comfortable with myself and not caring about what people think of me?" he asked as he cleaned his glasses with his shirt.

"Yeah?"

"I think I wanna start going to the Proud as Halle meetings at school," he said. "I feel like that'd be a supportive environment for me."

I nodded. "Yeah, that's a good idea."

"Would you wanna go with me?"

I swallowed. If the people who were at the table for it at the Club and Organization Fair are an accurate representation of it, then all I can picture is it being celebrity gossip and reality shows and 'yas bitch' and 'slay queen' and people being dramatic and people thinking they're fabulous—not that there's anything wrong with that, but it's just not the vibe I'm going for. I guess Dillon's gay friends left that bad of a taste in my mouth—and *no*, not like *that*. But college isn't high school, and I'd be doing it with Ethan. "Yeah, I'll give it a try."

He raised an eyebrow. "You sound like you don't want to."

"I mean," I shrugged, "you know me. I try not to follow the crowd."

"That's kind of the point though," he said with a furrowed brow. "I *want* to fit in."

"You're right," I shook my head. "I'm just being dumb. Ignore me."

"You can say no if you don't want to, I'm not gonna *make* you."

"No, I'll try it," I smiled. "It's important to you."

He smiled back. "Thanks babe. I won't make you go again if you don't like it. At least you'll be able to say you tried something new." Which, isn't that the point of all of this?

January 21

I think the extra fee they charge you to have the cost of getting your taxes done taken out of your return is just another way they try to fuck over people who can't afford to just throw around $40. Same with late fees, overdraft fees—basically any fee. Like, what fucking capitalist shit swine came up with that? *Oh, you don't have enough money? We're going to charge you even more money as punishment.*

Everything I need to last me until March is all packed: my Switch and games, the two board games I have to my name, the heaviest clothes I own, random stuff from the pantry Mom's trying to get rid of, and a plastic crate heavy with books for Ethan and me. I'm starting him off with the lighter stuff—*Red, White & Royal Blue*, the *Heartstopper* series, *What If It's Us* and *Here's to Us*, the *Dante & Aristotle* books, *The Gravity of Us*. "You think these'll last you six weeks?" I captioned the Snap of them I sent him.

Forreal though, I'm so ready to get back to New Halle, and not just because I'll get to see Ethan again. I miss my friends, I miss being back in Swafford, I miss walking to class, I miss the NPCs—I miss *everything* about campus. I even miss Patnick a little. Going away to college terrified me at first because I didn't know what could happen, but now it's that same promise of possibility that excites me, that makes me feel like NHU is where I *belong*. Is this what it feels like to bleed blue and white?

Look out NHU, here comes ya boy.

RESOURCES

As someone who struggles with/has struggled with anxiety, depression, self-love, and just being happy in general, it was important to me to give some of the characters in this story the same struggles, because readers whose minds aren't always kind to them need to see that they're not alone. It's okay to not be okay.

The Trevor Project: Call 1-866-488-7386, text 'START' to 678678, or visit thetrevorproject.org

988 Suicide & Crisis Lifeline: Call or text 988, or visit 988lifeline.org

Crisis Text Line: Text 'HOME' to 741741, or visit crisistextline.org

ACKNOWLEDGEMENTS

In the acknowledgements section of a book called *Dojo Dilemmas* by Joseph Cucci, the author says that he was worried what people might think of him after publishing his book. I was also worried at first what people would think of me after reading my story, but then I remembered that life's too short to always live for the comfort of other people. Besides, anybody who has a real problem with it probably voted for Trump multiple times and doesn't have any room to talk about what is and isn't moral.

Reading paragraphs of names in the acknowledgement sections of books made me think that I may have done the writing process 'wrong' somehow. Self-publishing this book means that I had no editor, agent, etc., nor was I part of any kind of book club that gave me encouragement—but that's not to say I didn't have my own fan club. Endless thanks to Dalton Dornish, Ricki Rumbaugh, Courtney Becker, Destiny Chamoun, and Jeffrey Brandle, whose enthusiasm, support, and suggestions for this story—even in its unrefined versions—helped make it possible.

The proper thing to do here would be to name every person I met at Slippery Rock University, because every person who made an impression on me during my time there made it into this story in one way or another. (So yes, if you were at SRU between the Fall of 2012 and the Spring of 2015, you could very well have been the inspiration for a character or line in this story!) But, that would be a lot of names, so here are the ones who deserve it the most: DJ Wolfarth, Collin Burke, Jim Kovacs, Aaron Kollar, Tyler Malorni, Sarah Hammond, Tanner Lewis, Danielle Wolfe, Tommy Wolfe, Kelly Williams (Jelly Fladden), Tom Williams, John Riggio, Tyler Hahn, Bob Calabrese, Nate Smith, Kyle Perza, Jess Horgos, Jackie Metcalfe, Mike Capo, Ashley DeWitt, Mindy Hood, Becca M., Paula Mims, Cole Vecchio, Walker Martz, Matt Eichler, Casey Carreiro, Darryl Andrews, Zach Rapp, Jamie Peace, Carl Izzo, Bronte Soul, EJ Christopher, Ray Scalise, Patrick Beswick, Dr. John Golden, Dr. Aaron Cowan, Dr. Joseph Alessi, Dr. Thomas Daddessio, Dr. Jesus Valencia, Dr. Rhonda Clark, and of course, Boozel Jake.

And even though they weren't part of my SRU story, it'd be wrong to not give a shout out to Tyler Wagner, Josh Butler, Jon Sammel, Connor Rudge, Nicole Bell, Nick Quinn, Brandon Cannon, and Dr. Julian Gallegos from CCAC.

Thank you to all the bands and artists who helped bring this story to life and who have always been there for me. This story would not be what it is, nor would I be who I am as a person, if not for the music you've made. You change lives in more ways than you know.

Thank you to the WSRU and WNHU college radio DJs (New Halle University's college radio station was originally named WNHU until I discovered it was already a real college radio station), and to the people who compiled all the YouTube playlists of relaxing Nintendo music, for giving me my favorite music to write to.

Thank you to all the authors who've inspired me with their stories and who've given me books to get lost in—Stephen Chbosky in particular for writing *The Perks of Being a Wallflower*, without which this story would not exist.

And because I love him and can't pass up the chance to embarrass him, thank you Dalton. Even though you were so unimpressed with the first draft that you didn't read the entire thing in a single day (just kidding), I literally would not have been able to dedicate myself to writing this if not for you tackling chores and giving me space and time to work on it. The people you love are the people you do dishes for. I love you more than you know ♡

And I'd like to give a shout out to myself, which I feel is something authors should do more often. Writing a book takes *a lot* of work, time, and dedication. The fact that I managed to write this whole thing without losing motivation is almost miraculous. So, Ryan: go 'head! I'm so fucking proud of you.

And of course I'd like to thank you too, because what's a story without an audience? Out of all the books out there, you chose to spend time with *this* one, the one that *I* created. I hope you enjoyed reading this as much as I enjoyed writing it. I hope you discovered something new, whether it be an artist or a different way of looking at the world. But if you take only one thing away from this story, let it be this: the world will never get better unless we start choosing love over fear.

Ryan Wagner didn't major in English or Creative Writing, nor was he any kind of Fellow at his school. The last piece of fiction he wrote before this story was a one-page assignment in 10th grade. He's just a guy who had an idea pop into his head one day and who never gave up on it. He enjoys music that slaps, dumplings of all sorts, fish tacos, books written by people who don't have a stick up their ass, video games, and tabletop games, among many other things. His dislikes include people who don't know how to drive, entitled white people, and perforations in cardboard that don't perforate, also among many other things. He lives in Pittsburgh with his fiancé and their dog.

Ryan in 2025
(Photo credit: Dalton Dornish)